D1193359

Some of Skippy's Blues

Canadian Cataloguing in Publication Data

Taylor, Margie

   Some of Skippy's blues

   ISBN 1-55207-004-2

   I.   Title.

PS8589.A907S65 1997   C813'.54   C97-941057-6
PS9589.A907S65 1997
PR9199.3.T39S65 1997

Interested readers are invited to consult
our evolving catalogue on the Internet at
http://rdppub.com

Margie Taylor

Some of Skippy's Blues
a novel

Robert Davies Multimedia Publishing
MONTREAL–TORONTO–PARIS

Copyright © 1997, Margie Taylor
ISBN 1-55207-004-2

All rights, including moral rights, reserved
This is a work of fiction. Any resemblance, real or imagined, to
any real persons is entirely coincidental.

Edited by Elaine Shatenstein

Ordering information

General Distribution Services
1-800-387-0141/387-0172 (Canada)
1-800-805-1083 (USA)

or from the publisher

Robert Davies Multimedia Publishing Inc.
330-4999 St. Catherine St. West
Westmount, Québec, Canada H3Z 1T3
☎ 514-481-2440 ▤ 514-481-9973
e-mail: rdppub@vir.com

The publisher wishes to thank the
Canada Council for the Arts,
the Department of Canadian Heritage
and the Sodec (Québec)
for their generous cultural programs
which supported this work.

For Ken

Introduction

St. Anthony of Padua was one of several saints called Anthony (Anthony of Kiev, Anthony of Novgorod), and not, of course, to be confused with Anthony of Egypt, religious hermit and ascetic circa the year 300 and probably the very first monk. That particular Anthony fought with none other than the devil himself, who appeared to him variously as wild beasts, seductive women or as other monks bringing him bread while he was fasting. Such visions, real or hallucinatory, were not accorded to Anthony of Padua, who had to settle for fame as a Franciscan preacher and death at the age of thirty-six after an attack of dropsy. Patron of the poor, it is fitting that a church in this neighbourhood should bear his name.

Since the early years of this century the old church has kept watch over its shabby, working-class flock like a great hovering bird. Once it was the largest building for several miles around, the heart of a community of immigrant Italians. Ten years ago it was abandoned for a newer building in the suburbs as the children and grandchildren of the original parishioners laboured and grew rich. Well, richer. They moved out of the old neighbourhood and left it to transients and newcomers from Poland and the Ukraine, and the poorer countries of middle Europe who'd been swallowed up by the Soviet bloc after the war and existed now only in the memories of their former residents.

Construction workers and their families live here, carpenters, millworkers; they inhabit two- and three-storey frame houses dating back to the Great War, and small brick bungalows scattered here and there with doors and window frames painted bright colours and each with a carefully tended vegetable garden out back. In these homes, bouquets of plastic flowers, regularly dusted, take pride of place in the front windows, hand crocheted doilies occupy every available surface and antimacassars still cover the backs of chairs and sofa cushions. A homesick ghost from Estonia, Latvia or Lithuania might enter any one of these houses and be comforted by the smells of plum dumplings, pyrogies stuffed with cheese and potatoes, borscht served hot with sour cream and pumpernickel bread. While the rest of Cambrian Bay, perched on the very tip of the Great Lakes in

Northwestern Ontario, discovers the delights of the TV dinner and the fast-food restaurant, the women in this part of town still feed their families traditional, nourishing meals of cabbage, pickled onions and sauerkraut soup.

St. Anthony's of Padua stood empty for years, its windows boarded up, its doors locked, the wrought-iron fence rusted and in need of repair. But it has been re-discovered and resurrected not as a church but as a community centre. Upstairs, the pews and altar have been removed and temporary walls erected to shelter a walk-in clinic, a small library, a drop-in centre. And next to the side door there is a sign that used to tell the hours of the morning and evening mass, that now reads, "Dharma Cafe and Coffee House: Open Nights Thurs Thru Monday". Underneath, in careful lettering, someone has painted the words: Skippy Jacques, Prop.

I.

Skippy Jacques got sick in the summer of 1953, after two days of playing baseball in the field behind his house. Standing in the outfield under searing blue skies in one of the hottest Augusts on record, he and the neighbourhood kids played till their faces were purple with the heat and their hair stood up in stiff, sticky cowlicks at the back of their heads. Ignoring the calls of their mothers to come in for lunch and then dinner and, finally, bed, the boys played on, cracking the ball time after time against the bat and stretching their skinny legs as they raced around the bases, pretending not to notice the cluster of neighbourhood girls gathered near home base who were, of course, pretending not to notice them.

Finally, the long day stretched out into evening and it grew too dark to see the ball.

"Tomorrow," the boys called out to each other. "Meet you here tomorrow morning, first thing. Don't forget."

The following morning Skippy awoke from a dream of being chased by a malignant dwarf brandishing a huge battle-axe and called out to his mother that he felt sick. She came into his bedroom and sat on the bed next to him, and felt his forehead.

"My throat hurts," he said. "It hurts when I swallow."

"You have a touch of the flu," she told him, and told him to stay in bed and brought the radio in from the kitchen so he could listen to the Happy Gang and made rice pudding, his favourite, the kind with raisins.

She had to leave him to go into work, but she came home at lunchtime and checked on him and he had turned off the radio and lay on his back with his eyes closed — it hurt to keep them open. "William?" she said. "Are you all right?" There was something in her voice that was never there when she thought he was faking it, like he did sometimes when he wanted to stay home from school. And calling him 'William', she only did that when she was worried. Or angry, and he didn't think she was angry this time.

He wanted to reassure her, and so he tried to sit up, and found that it was a huge effort and made him dizzy, so he fell back against the pillow. She left the room and he stared up at the ceiling and noticed for the first time the pattern made by old stains and leaks and cracks in the paint. Before, they had been harmless lines and spots; now he saw they formed a face, the face of a grinning clown, eyes askew, leering down at him. He turned away and squeezed his eyes shut, the imprint of the clown's face fixed upon his eyelids. Out in the hallway, his mother picked up the telephone and asked to speak to the doctor.

"Yes, but his neck is stiff, and he says his legs feel heavy."

There was a pause, then: "Are you sure? I mean, [something he couldn't make out, and another pause]. All right. Yes. Thank you."

He had to pee. His mother had told him to stay in bed but he had to go now. Sitting up again, slowly, he swung his legs over the bed, and stood up. It was like looking into the wrong end of a telescope; his feet stretched down into the distance and his head and shoulders brushed against the ceiling. I must be ten feet tall, he thought, just as the room filled with a gray cloud and the floor came up to hit him, smack, right in the face.

INFORMATION FOR RELATIVES OF PATIENTS
(from the Isolation Hospital's Polio Epidemic Record, 1953-1954)

1. ARE VISITORS ALLOWED IN THE ISOLATION WARD?
Because the patients on our ward have diseases which are contagious, visiting is not allowed, except in special instances.

2. WHAT CAN YOU DO TO HELP OUR PATIENTS?
Although the patient cannot phone or write to his relatives or friends, he can and will enjoy receiving mail every day, as assurance that those at home are remembering him. Toys, magazines, letters, cards, flowers or small comforts will be greatly appreciated. Send small, light-weight inexpensive things. Remember, the patient cannot take them out of the isolation ward.

3. WHAT SHOULD YOU DO WITH THE PATIENTS (sic) CLOTHING?
We would like you to take all the patients clothes home with you. When you get home, wash all the bedding, and clothing that is washable and dry it in the sunshine. Materials which are not washable should be aired for eight hours and then ironed. The patients room should be aired for twenty-four hours.

Faces that were as strange as the ones in his dreams, wearing masks, pulling and poking at him with fingers in rubber gloves, and heavy hot towels placed on top of him, everywhere, on his legs and his back and his chest, every fifteen minutes, all day long. He was put in a pillowless bed with something called a fracture board underneath the mattress and a footboard to keep his feet upright. And his mother was nowhere around. He was abandoned, left in this strange place with other motherless boys, some who cried all the time, some who lay still and never moved. Polio, the doctors told him, what they used to call infantile paralysis, and his mother could catch it, and she might give it to his sister who was only five, and so she couldn't come to see him for two weeks. But what was two weeks? Who could know how long fourteen days might be when you were sick and hurting everywhere and couldn't do anything, nothing for yourself, not sit up and eat or comb your hair or even pick up the comic books the kids in his class had sent?

Flowers were everywhere, boring old flowers with cards, and the nurses (who were nice, really, but he wanted his mother), the nurses sat beside him on his bed and read the messages in the cards: Get Better Soon, with hugs and kisses from Mrs. Stanley's Grade Five class and the kids had all signed their names, even Kenny Evans and Lou Frigeri who never liked him and there was a Mickey Mouse balloon and a box of chocolates. But they couldn't come to see him because he had polio and he was in isolation, and after a few days when it didn't hurt so much he began to feel a little superior to all those kids who'd never been in isolation, maybe never even been in a hospital, except for something like getting their tonsils out and that was nothing, nothing to getting polio.

His mother sent notes addressed to him, dropped off at the reception desk and brought up to him by the nurses. There was a card with a puppy on the front, and inside she had written: "Dear Skippy, This puppy wants you to get better soon so he can come and play with you!" Another time she sent him a bag of chocolate coins covered in gold paper, with "For Luck" printed on the tag. And a big book with a red cover, "The Reader's Digest Complete Omnibus", with stories about pirates and "The Sinking of the Bismarck". He couldn't sit up in bed and hold the book but it stayed on the night table where he could see it and in the afternoons the nice young nurse with the curly hair sat by his bed and read to him from it.

At the end of the isolation period, he was moved into the regular children's ward, and his mother came to see him, hurrying along the polished floor with her quick steps, wearing a light blue jacket he remembered and a yellow dress he didn't. She hugged him until he had to push away and he was glad to see her, but shy after all this time.

"When can I go home?"

"Oh, Skippy," and her eyes filled with tears and she smoothed his hair away from his forehead although it didn't need smoothing and wouldn't answer his question.

She sat on the bed next to him and took his hand and told him that he had been very sick (well, of course he knew that!) and she had prayed very hard for him the whole time and they must thank God that he was going to get better, because many children didn't, and the thing about God was that He always answered prayers but He didn't always give you the answer you hoped for. And this time He had helped Skippy get better, but the polio had damaged a nerve in his left leg, had killed it, actually, and this nerve could not be repaired. So Skippy would always walk with a limp but the wonderful thing was that he would walk, he would not have to live in a wheelchair like poor Mrs. Sanders who couldn't go to the movies or anything, she had to be in that chair all the time. Skippy wasn't going to be like that. And that was such a small thing when you thought about it, when you thought about what might have happened, and they should be very grateful that he was all right and was going to be able to come home and everything was going to be almost exactly the way it used to be.

Then she told him that his sister had been sick, too, for a couple of days, and her throat had hurt and she had dragged her right foot. But then she recovered and was absolutely fine, so there you had two miracles in two weeks, it really was wonderful. They had so much to be thankful for.

In his dreams, he always ran. His legs were strong and healthy and he soared over haystacks and leaped into the air to grab at branches of trees, which he always caught. Sometimes he ran along endless, sandy beaches which curved out into the sea and disappeared into the horizon; more often, he raced through tropical forests, feeling the moist green undergrowth beneath his naked feet. He hunted, or was hunted, but loved the chase and woke up laughing, his chest heaving with excitement.

These dreams were so vivid that as he grew older Skippy began to think they were real, that he really had run along beaches and through forests that way, before he'd got sick. Everything good, it seemed, had happened before he had polio. The years before his illness formed a kind of golden age in his mind where he had always been happy and everything had been perfect. Afterwards, in spite of

God's answering his mother's prayers, his life was very different. For one thing, he missed the first month of school that year, and when he went back in October the kids had all formed their friendships and got used to the new teacher and they were shy from not seeing him for so long and a little afraid of him, with his stiff, lurching walk. He was different, now: he had gone into hospital as one of them, and had come out a cripple.

Cripple. He could think that word but he wasn't allowed to say it. It was worse than swearing, worse than anything. He had said it to his mother, once, the first day back at school in the fall, a day spent sitting at the very front of the class, where Mrs. Stanley made a fuss of him and paid lots of attention to him, trying to be nice, her kindness embarrassing him, making him stand out more than ever. At recess he stood outside in the playground and a group of kids gathered around him, curious, hanging back a little, until finally one of them, Eddy Pasternak, a big, fat kid who was always playing the clown, spoke up: "What happened to your foot?"

"I had polio."

"Oooh, germs," said Eddy, pretending to shrink in fear, and a couple of the boys laughed.

"What's polio?" a girl wanted to know.

"It's something that makes your throat hurt and your arms and legs sore, and it can kill you."

"It didn't kill you, though."

"No, it just killed the nerves in my leg."

One of Eddy's friends called out: "Are you contagious?"

Skippy shook his head. "No. Not any more."

He waited, prepared to answer all their questions, if this is what he had to do, if this was what was required before they would accept him once again. But there were no more questions; in twos and threes they turned and ran off and he stood there alone, next to the monkey bars, until the bell rang. In the afternoon, he spent the recess period at his desk, his head bent over a history text book, reading the same passage over and over: "Samuel de Champlain spent three winters in Acadia, the first on an island in the St. Croix River, where scurvy killed nearly half the party, and the second and third, which claimed the lives of fewer men, at Annapolis Basin."

After school he limped home and fell on the couch where he lay in misery until his mother came home from work. "How was school?"

"Awful. I hated it. I hate being a cripple."

She slapped him across the face and he cried out in pain, it was so sudden and unexpected.

"Don't say that. Don't you ever use that word again."

And she was sorry right away for it and hugged him and stroked his hair. "That's a state of mind, Skippy. If someone calls you that, then he doesn't know anything. Your mind is healthy, your body is strong, you just have a leg that doesn't work. That's all. You are not a cripple. Do you hear me?"

So he never used the word again but he knew that although his mother might choose to believe differently, his mother did not matter very much in the larger scheme of things. His world was dominated by the cruelty of children and they were always going to see his bad leg before they saw any other part of him. He would have done the same.

2.

When Skippy was twelve he went to Sunday school for a time, dragged there as a victim of one of his mother's spurts of religiosity. The temple of choice this time was an unprepossessing one-story brick building in the industrial section of town, with the misleading title of "The Chapel of Brotherly Love". The chapel's parishioners were a straight-laced, humourless bunch, and their minister was given to diatribes on the wickedness of the Pope and the need for constant vigilance against impure thoughts and behaviour.

"I believe," he thundered from the makeshift pulpit, looking directly into Skippy's soul, "I believe that if you die with one sin unforgiven, one evil thought unconfessed, you are going straight to Hell!"

Skippy was left with two relics of that ordeal: a lifetime phobia of walking over sidewalk gratings for fear of collapsing through them and falling into Hell, and the picture on the cover of a Sunday school paper thrust into his hands as he made his way out of the building when the sermon was finally over. It was a painting of two young men, in old-fashioned clothing with swords at their sides, their arms clasped around each other's necks. The caption on the bottom read, "The soul of Jonathan was knit with the soul of David, and Jonathan loved him as his own soul." Skippy kept that picture in a drawer in his room and long after his mother had lost her enthusiasm for the

Chapel of Brotherly Love, Skippy took the picture out and looked at it. *Loved him as his own soul,* he would think; that's what it's like to have a friend.

By the time he reached the perilous, bittersweet years known as his "teens", Skippy had forgotten how to relate to anybody outside his family. The other kids took it for granted that he was a loner; he sat by himself on the bus to school, never went to parties or dances, never got asked anywhere and never asked anybody. It was really the safest way. Even his friends from his former life — "former" meaning his life before polio — had long stopped calling or coming around. There was no point: he wouldn't go anywhere, wouldn't do anything, and even his mother finally gave up pushing him to get out of the house, go make friends, have a little fun, for goodness' sakes. He never actually said it was because of his leg; instead he let it be known that he preferred to read and listen to music. His mother got him a crystal radio set and late at night he lay in bed and picked up WLS in Chicago. The songs coming out of the darkness, filling his head with music, soothed him, helped him to sleep, while the voices of the announcers caressed his ears. Who needed the friendship of a bunch of stupid kids when there was this display of intimacy between him and the radio each night?

Labour Day weekend, 1958. It was hot and sticky and the town was deserted. The sky hung like a lid over the bungalows and the flat squares of lawn, compressing them with the weight of its heat, so that even the cats and dogs that usually prowled the neighbourhood took refuge in the coolness of garage corners and the mossy darkness under backyard water tanks and tool sheds. No one who had a choice was moving around on this particular Saturday; those with the means to do so had escaped to "camp", the one- and two-room cabins with makeshift furniture and fly-clogged screen doors, two or three hours out of town. These fortunate few, relishing the prospect of three days of fishing and canoeing, away from the rat-race that was Cambrian Bay (pop. 46,500), had driven out the night before just ahead of the traffic and were even now, at this moment, dangling their feet off the end of rickety wooden docks, sucking back beers and congratulating themselves for having had the foresight to grab these places right after the war when everybody wanted to live in town and lakefront property was being practically given away.

Those who didn't own such rustic hideaways — or didn't know someone who did — made do with Memory Beach in the north end of town, where girls in their middle teens paraded in twos and threes up and down the sand, aware of the furtive glances of middle-aged men and the outright stares of skinny young boys nursing the faint beginnings of moustaches on their sweaty upper lips. Heavy-set women anchored themselves on thick woolen blankets, distributing egg salad sandwiches and bottles of Royal Crown cola to, hyperactive children with sandy legs and throats hoarse from shrieking. It was a reflection in miniature of the town itself, this beach, democratic and working-class, its citizens practically rubbing thighs together, their conversations overlapping, their smells commingling.

Skippy's mother was there that afternoon; she'd gone with her friend from work, the one named Irene whose husband had left her and so, as she put it, "We're in the same boat now, Jean." Although it wasn't the same, not really; Skippy's father hadn't walked out on his family — he'd died, fallen into some machinery at the plant — but the accident had left her without a husband and with two small children to raise and she'd had to go out to work just like Irene. So it amounted to the same thing.

Irene had a car, a big old '49 Chevy she'd bought second-hand with her first paycheque, and there was room for her and Jean and Irene's youngest in the front, and Skippy's sister Mandy and Irene's son Norman in the back. There would have been room for Skippy, too, but he loathed Norman, who was only two years younger than him but liked to play "royalty" with Mandy, and parade around in his mother's bedspread, pretending to be Catherine the Great. Skippy was unsure as to just who Catherine the Great was, but he was properly revolted that a thirteen-year-old boy should indulge in this kind of play-acting, and speak with a lisp when there was no need for it. Irene was always trying to throw the two of them together, it seemed; she would show up to take his mother to bingo and Norman would be there at the front door, ready to spend the evening with Skippy.

"He's a sensitive boy," Irene confided to Jean. "He doesn't have a lot of friends. It would be nice if Skippy would, you know, take him under his wing, you know?"

Skippy, who had observed Norman squeezing his zits into their bathroom mirror when he wasn't flouncing around the back yard in a pair of disused lace curtains, thought there might be other reasons for her son's lack of popularity, and he didn't think sensitivity had a whole lot to do with it. Thankfully, his mother didn't force the issue. Oblivious, for the most part, to the code of conduct among teenage boys, she had to admit that there was something just a little odd about Irene's son Norman. She colluded with Skippy, inventing school outings and homework projects for him which tied up his evenings or forced him to stay, studying, in his bedroom when Norman was over.

On this particular Saturday he begged off with a sore throat and his mother, after suggesting that the warm sun and fresh air of the beach would make him feel better, let him off the hook. Instead, she made up a batch of peanut butter sandwiches (Irene was bringing hard-boiled eggs, and some bottles of cola) and told Mandy to hurry, Irene would be there any minute. Skippy curled up on the couch to watch television with the living-room drapes pulled shut and when the Chevy pulled into the driveway and Irene honked the horn, his mother stopped in the doorway and asked him one last time: "You're sure you don't want to come? It's beautiful weather and it won't last. This'll probably be our last day at the beach."

Skippy shook his head. He was looking forward to having the house to himself. "Be sure to say 'hi' to Norman for me," he called out, keeping his eyes glued to *Howdy Doody*. His mother ignored that remark and tugged down on the legs of her Bermudas, taking one last look at her hair in the mirror.

"Be good," she said as she left. "We'll be back before supper."

It was pleasant, at first, with the house so quiet except for the TV and nobody to tell him to turn it down or change the channel. By lunchtime, however, the kids' programmes were finished and a boring show about fishing began on one channel and a learn-to-cook show was underway on the other. He turned the set off and went to his room and read for a while, but nothing grabbed him. He flipped through his comics — *Have Gun Will Travel* and *Wyatt Earp* were his favourites, along with *Strange Tales* and *Journey into Mystery*, but he'd read them already. He wished he had a good book to read. Earlier in the week, he'd gone down to the library and persuaded them to put *Mandingo* on hold for him, on the pretext it was for his father. It was in the adult section and they were strict about those things. Twice since then he'd called to see if it was in but it wasn't, and he figured it would probably take a while; books with sex in them tended to get renewed. Look how hard it had been to lay his hands on that one about the guy with the three sexy daughters, *God's Little Acre*. Just thinking about that book made him hot — he'd read it every night in bed for a week, hiding it under his mattress and then whacking off before going to sleep.

Skippy felt the beginnings of a familiar warmth in his groin and thought he might whack off right now, it being one of the few times neither his mother nor his sister were around to barge in at an inappropriate moment. Dropping his comics on the floor, he pulled off his pants and climbed into his unmade bed, pulling the covers over him. Closing his eyes and cupping his right hand over his penis, he conjured up Miss Kitty, owner of the Long Branch Saloon, an older, experienced woman who knew the ways and needs of men, after a long day of riding herd on the dusty plain. Week after week he'd seen her "girls", one after another, lead cowboys up the wooden stairs at one end of the bar and disappear just out of range of the camera. What went on in those rooms, Skippy wondered? What unspoken acts were carried out, too sexy to be shown on TV but obviously considered, at least back then, a necessary and rightful reward for a hard-working cowpoke? Skippy could imagine; Miss Kitty herself, of course, never went "upstairs", but, this being Skippy's own fantasy, he allowed her to lead him up that rickety staircase and into one of the unseen rooms.

"Come here, sweetheart," she would drawl, taking his hand and placing it gently on her voluptuous breasts. While he stood there, taking in her full, womanly figure clad only in a corset and black fishnet stockings (he'd seen a drawing, once, on a cocktail napkin and this was what he believed all women had worn under their clothes at least until the nineteen-thirties — the bras and girdles of today were a huge disappointment and a definite backward step for mankind), Miss Kitty expertly took hold of his belt buckle and within seconds had his pants down to his ankles and his penis in her soft, white hand.

This was generally as far as he got before coming, although he always told himself he was going to delay the moment at least until she'd done something erotic, like place his member between her breasts or even — ecstasy of ecstasies — given him a blow job. But the explosion always came long before her mouth got anywhere near that part of his body, which was probably just as well: this was Miss Kitty, after all, friend of James Arness, in her own way as respectable as the next person. There was something a little bit degrading about picturing her with some guy's dick in her mouth, even if it was his own.

Afterwards, Skippy lay on his back and stared at the ceiling. It was hot outside, he could feel it even in this darkened room. A few cars went by and some kids were playing "kick the can" a couple of houses away. He should have gone to the beach and he would've, too, if it hadn't been for Norman. God, that guy was a pill. A homo, he figured, and a sudden, unwanted image arose of two guys "doing it". It made him feel weird, almost sick, and he quickly pulled his pants up and sat up. He'd take the bus downtown, he decided, to Billy Dee's record store. That was something he hadn't done in a while and it would take his mind off — well, off stuff. And maybe, if he got back in time, he could whack off again before his mother got home.

Billy Dee was a local radio announcer, or DJ, as they were

beginning to be known, and he had the afternoon slot, three to seven weekdays on CKLB. He played the best music. All the usual stuff, for sure, so you couldn't escape "Volare" and Sheb Woolley's "Purple People Eater", but Billy played coloured music out of Chicago as well. Skippy had listened to him all summer, lay in his room with the window open to catch the odd breeze and heard him talk to callers in between records:

"Hey, Billy, I think you're the most."

"Well, hey, I think you're the double most. Who's this going out to?"

"I'd like to dedicate this to my boyfriend Rick who's tree planting in the bush this summer."

"I bet you miss him."

"I sure do."

And so on. Skippy wanted to call up, too, and he would have if he could have somehow disguised his voice. Not that he had anybody to dedicate a song to; he just liked the idea of touching base with Billy Dee.

Anyway, the next best thing was hanging out at Billy's record store, The Dee-Vine Record Emporium, and thumbing through the piles of LP records and forty-fives. The store had signs up everywhere, saying, "Browse all you like — we're in no hurry", and "Take your time/To rush is a crime". This being the kind of town it was, the country and western section was the largest, taking up one whole wall, but there was lots of Sinatra and Elvis and modern jazz. Skippy always headed straight to the back, past the pop stacks of The Everly Brothers, Frankie Avalon, Paul Anka and Jerry Lee Lewis, back to where the black music was: Fats Domino's "Blueberry Hill" (although Pat Boone's cover version had sold more copies), Chuck Berry and Little Richard and old stuff like T-Bone Walker and Muddy Waters who sang like they'd invented the music. There were current hits, of course, but they were interspersed with old 78s, some of them going right back to the thirties. It was in this section that he often found records he'd never heard played on any radio station, anywhere, and was a part of the store he usually had all to himself.

He was counting on that being especially true on this particular afternoon, the last hot weekend to get out of town before school started. It was always better when he could take his time going through the stacks and not have to feel self-conscious if someone else was watching him, or waiting for him to be through with a pile so they could get their grubby hands on it. He hoped the store would be empty; he didn't want to be rushed.

A tall, skinny kid was hunkered down in front of a stack of Little

Richard albums and Skippy, who didn't see him at first, almost tripped over him.

"Sorry," he said and the kid looked up and smiled. He had straight black hair and sideburns and was wearing the kind of clothes Skippy had only seen in magazines. A pink shirt with winged collar standing up at the back, blue jeans too long and folded a couple of times to make a cuff and white buck shoes. And no socks. He was like a character out of a comic book, but a good-looking one, with brilliant white teeth and high cheekbones that reminded Skippy a little of the singer, Richie Valens, only thinner. Skippy smiled back and turned his attention to a box of forty-fives labeled "M": The Midnighters, the Mills Brothers and one he hadn't seen before by a guy called Clyde McPhatter. Skippy picked the record out of the box and as he turned it over to examine it, it slipped right out of his hands. The kid next to him caught it before it hit the floor.

"Good choice," he said, taking a look at the forty-five. "You a fan of Clyde?"

His voice was soft and heavily tinged with an American accent, something out of the deep south, and it took Skippy a moment to decipher.

"Oh, yeah. Actually, I'm not sure. I've never heard of him before."

"He sang with the Drifters on Atlantic. Then he got drafted, and now he goes solo."

Skippy was confused. "He sang on the Atlantic?"

The kid laughed and stood up. "The label Atlantic. The labels are what it's all about. I always look for the labels. I mean, Decca, you're gonna get Louis Armstrong, but if you want to go back further, get really old stuff by him, you gotta look for Bluebird. And Bessie Smith, she's mostly on Columbia. Or if you're lucky, you might find the old Black Swan label. Those are real old, back when they called them race records. You like that old stuff? I been collecting it for years, since I was seven or eight. I got a really old 'Memphis Blues' by Armstrong. Now that's my all-time favourite, because that's where I'm from."

"Memphis?" Skippy had no idea where Memphis was, or even what it was, exactly, but it sounded exotic. Like this kid — as different from your average born-and-bred Cambrian Bay kid as it was possible to be.

"You bet. Me and Elvis Aaron Presley, the Memphis Flash." He put his hand out and introduced himself: "Benny Carter, fresh from Memphis, Tennessee."

Skippy took his hand and shook it. "My name's Skippy Jacques."

"Pleased to meet you, Skippy. You from here?"

Skippy grimaced. "All my life."

"Well, that's all right. This seems like an all right town to me. It ain't Memphis, but I guess it'll do. Here, look what I found." Benny bent down to pick up a 78 he'd set beside him on the floor and held it out to Skippy: "Time Out", by Count Basie and his Orchestra. "This is a real find. I can't believe nobody's come in here and grabbed it. There's a great Lester Young solo on this. You know him? He plays tenor sax. Lots of guys, they prefer the Bird, but I like tenor. It's so sweet. You look in some of those old record stores in the south and if you're real lucky, you might find a Vocalion label, with stuff by Lester Young."

It seemed to Skippy that this Benny Carter was quite a talker. Skippy, who lived such a quiet life, sometimes going all day without saying two words to anyone except his mother and sister, had never met anybody who had so much to say and said it all in such a great stream of words. It would have been too much coming from anybody else and some of it made no sense (the Bird? Who or what was that?). But Benny had such a soft voice you didn't mind listening to him all night, if that's what it took. At least, Skippy didn't.

It turned out Benny and his parents had moved up to Canada so his father could take a job teaching at the college ("Mod Am Lit," he told Skippy and then explained: "Modern American Literature — Faulkner, Hemingway, Steinbeck. You know, the usual," he said and Skippy nodded but the names meant nothing to him). Mrs. Carter taught piano and Benny had learned to play when he was just a kid, but what he really wanted was to play the saxophone. His parents were against it — they felt it wasn't a really proper sort of instrument, in the classical sense — but they had promised to buy him one for his birthday next year if he would settle down and do well in school. School, Benny explained, was not really the main area of his life. What he wanted was to be a musician:

"Can't you just see yourself, man, sittin' around with a bunch of guys in the middle of the week while all the stiffs are doing their joe jobs as accountants, and here you are having a drink in a gin mill, crossing the country all the time playing in dance halls and honky-tonks, jamming with a bunch of guys till four in the morning, you and Count Basie and Lester Young and Buster Smith, just sitting there making music and having some laughs? And wearing those cool threads and those porkpie hats? It would *make* me, something like that. If I could live that life, and know what it's like, man, I could do just about anything."

Skippy nodded, bemused. He'd never really thought about what he wanted to do. But this picture Benny painted, well, it was pretty attractive. With people like that, you could be anybody you wanted to be, he thought. No one would think twice about your leg.

"Yeah," he said, "it would be pretty neat, I guess." And then, because that seemed such an understatement, he added, "It would be wild."

"Wild. You got it. It would be the best."

They stood at the back of the record store and talked till it was practically closing time, about music. Benny explained about Charlie Parker — the Bird — and race records and how Willa Mae Thornton had been the first to sing "Hound Dog", 'way back, and Elvis had copied her, which was cool because he made it okay to sing coloured. Benny had even seen Elvis, once, when an uncle of his sneaked him into a club where he was performing:

"It wasn't much use, though," Benny said. "There were girls there screaming so loud you could hardly hear a thing. But I saw the man. I got that to tell to my grandchildren."

Benny's record collection took up seven cardboard boxes and dated back almost three decades. "I could listen to a different record every day for the next year and a half, and still be only about half through it." He wasn't boasting, just stating a fact. He explained that his uncle, the one who'd taken him to see Elvis, had given him a head start. He'd been a musician before the war, and still played some Saturday nights, and he'd given Benny his own record collection when he decided to "go straight", as he put it. Since then, Benny'd been adding to it every chance he got.

All of the above, and more, Skippy learned that first Saturday in September. But what was most amazing, to both of them, was that Benny was going to be attending the same high school as Skippy and would be in the same grade. He was almost a year older but he was having to repeat a year, owing to the higher educational standards set in Ontario, so they'd most likely have some classes together, a fact which they both agreed was truly cool.

By the time they'd decided on their purchases (an album, "Here's Little Richard", for Skippy and the Clyde McPhatter forty-five, and a couple of forty-fives for Benny — "Good Golly Miss Molly" and "Johnny B. Goode" — besides the Count Basie 78), it was almost five-thirty, and as they made their way to the cash register at the front, Skippy was suddenly conscious of his leg. Surely his new friend would notice. It would make a difference. It always did. But Benny said nothing until the two of them were outside, standing on the sidewalk, a hint of the coming cool weather making them shiver in their shirt sleeves.

"What happened to your leg?"

Skippy braced himself, and looked away. "Polio," he said, trying to be casual. Like it was no big thing. "Got it when I was ten. Killed the nerve." He concentrated his attention on some far-off point down the street. His bus would be coming in a few minutes. In half an hour he would be home, his mother would be back from the beach and have supper on the table, his room would be waiting for him. Fine. Good. That's the way he wanted it. He was concentrating so hard on that imaginary spot in the distance that it took him a moment to realize Benny was asking him something.

"What did you say?"

"I said do you want to come over to my place and listen to some stuff?"

"Sure, okay. Tomorrow?"

"Tomorrow, man."

Skippy got on the bus, clutching his record to his chest, and found a window seat near the back. As the bus pulled away from the sidewalk, he turned to watch his new friend Benny Carter loping down the street, resplendent in his pink shirt and genuine alligator leather belt. Cool, he thought, that guy is really, really cool.

His mother was pleased he'd made a friend, although at first she wasn't sure just what to make of Benny. His good looks were rather unsettling and he was polite in a courtly, old-fashioned way that made her suspicious the first time she met him, as if he was pulling her leg and she wanted to let him know she wasn't fooled. After all these years, too, she was over-protective when it came to her son, afraid he might be hurt, afraid that, after having nobody close in his life for so long, he might give his heart away and have it broken. She told herself it was silly to feel like this and she should just be grateful that Skippy finally had let someone pierce that armour he wore and had made a friend, like everybody else. Still, when Benny came by that first time and the two of them left to go downtown and "hang out", she stood at the front window and watched them leave, and told the living room walls that if that boy ever let Skippy down, she'd kill him. Then she laughed at herself and thought how Maurice, Skippy's father, would have laughed if he'd been around to hear her say it.

"Jeannie Bean," he would have told her, in that slow, sexy way he had when he was thinking about how good her behind looked in that particular dress, "you are one silly little woman." And he would pull her towards him and she, after looking around to make sure the kids were out of the room, would respond with passion, because she'd never met anyone she loved the way she loved Maurice

Jacques. And she never would. Not now. Not ever.

The Carters had arrived at the end of July and bought a house out by the golf course, a large, rambling place which had been owned by a retired colonel, and Benny had the entire third floor to himself. That Labour Day Sunday, in the first of what became many sessions in Benny's cluttered bedroom, listening to Lester Young deliver the intense one-two punch of the tenor sax, Skippy learned that Benny'd had a younger brother. His name was David and he'd come down with meningitis the year before and had died in the hospital, and Benny's mother was changed now, more nervous and careful about things. She worried all the time that something would happen to her older son, as well, some nameless *something* would creep up and strike him down in his prime, and his father had finally decided the only solution was to leave Memphis and move somewhere safe. They picked Canada, because it was cold and peaceful and she might learn to relax again and stop grieving for the loss of one son and the potential loss of another.

"I don't know, though," Benny said, stretched out on his bed with his eyes closed, the music wailing in the background, "I don't think she'll ever get over Davey. I know I won't."

Skippy wasn't sure what to say. He asked Benny what he was like, his brother, and Benny opened his eyes and gave a little shrug.

"I don't know," he said again, as if he'd thought about this before and hadn't been able to come up with an answer. "He was just a kid, you know? Sort of annoying, like kids are, you know the way they can be? I liked him all right, I just never thought of him too much. And then he was gone and I wished I'd been better to him, you know? Done stuff with him, helped him out more. That's all."

"You probably did lots of stuff with him, you just don't remember." Skippy sensed his new friend was feeling badly and he wanted to say something to make him feel better.

"I showed him how to tie a reef-knot, once, and a sheepshank. He was a Cub Scout and he was doing it for his badge, and I showed him how. He was pretty happy about that."

"Sure. I bet he was."

There didn't seem to be much more to say about that and the boys were quiet for a time. The record ended and Benny got up to put on another. There was a knock on the door and Benny's mother entered, holding a plate of sandwiches.

"I thought you boys might be hungry, shut away in here all afternoon." She smiled at Skippy and when she did you saw where Benny got his looks — the same wide, white smile, the same lustrous brown eyes. She held the plate out towards him. "Do you like music, too, Skippy?"

He took a sandwich and thanked her and said that, yes, he liked music a lot.

"I don't know as much about it as Benny does, though."

"Oh, Benny." She said it as though a person couldn't be expected to know music the way Benny did, and smiled at her son fondly. "Now Benny, he's just crazy about music, aren't you, son? He's what you'd call an *aficionado.*"

It was the kind of proud, affectionate teasing mothers did and she accompanied it with a ruffle of her son's hair that would have embarrassed Skippy to death if his own mother had done something like that in front of another guy. But Benny didn't seem to mind at all; he just grinned and took the plate from her and set it down on the bed.

"You bet, Mama. I know my stuff."

After asking if the boys wanted anything else, Mrs. Carter prepared to leave the room but stopped in the doorway and turned to where Skippy sat on the bed, holding his sandwich in one hand and an album cover in the other.

"You seem like a nice boy, Skippy," she said, in a voice that was almost formal, but kind. "I hope you and my son will become very good friends." There was a hint of benediction in what she said — it called for a response of some kind. But before Skippy could say anything, Benny laughed and said yes, they were going to be great friends, blood brothers, even, and Mrs. Carter said well, she hoped they wouldn't go that far. But you could see she was pleased and when she went out and shut the door, Benny grinned over at Skippy.

"She likes you," he said and held up a sandwich as proof. "Cut off the crusts. She doesn't do that for just anyone."

"I like her," Skippy said. He said it because he felt he should say it but also because it was true.

His friendship with Benny protected him like a warm blanket all through high school and gave him, for the first time, an identity outside of that of "cripple". It rested lightly on his shoulders and kept away the barbed remarks, the shaded humour of other guys, the casual, slighting dismissal of the girls who looked upon him, if they considered him at all, with pity and just a hint of contempt — not bad looking, too bad about the leg. Benny, they would have been willing to make allowances for, with his dark brooding eyes and his high Indian cheekbones. Taken on his own, Benny was handsome, in an exotic way, although there were rumours that he was a half-breed, in spite of his middle-class parents and their fancy old house that said "money". He made friends with kids on the reserve, and he didn't care who knew it. If the mood grabbed him, he'd head out to the old mountain road, stick out his thumb and hitch a ride all the way out to the collection of ramshackle houses where the Indians lived. Girls shared stories of wild summer nights where Benny had been seen partying up on the first ledge, dancing by the campfire or wandering off to sit out on the furthest rocks, drinking wine and staring up at the stars. Pretty girls noticed him, and the more daring ones even flirted with him now and then, but there were few who were willing to go out with him, not that he usually bothered to ask. And anyway, he was always with that gimp, so there must be something strange about him. Skippy knew him better than anybody and even Skippy felt he only knew his friend so far and no further. What he did know of Benny was that he was a dreamer, he lived in a world of heroes, and musicians, and men of great deeds. He ached to be grown up and out of the house, he longed to start living.

"You know what I want to do, man?" he confided one rainy afternoon, as they lay in Benny's room, surrounded by 45s and old 78s and copies of Billboard magazine. "I want to start travelling, and never stop. I want to get up each morning and leave wherever I'm staying, and walk down a brand new road every single day. And never repeat myself." And as if the very thought of all that moving about was too much to contain, he jumped up from the bed and started pacing around the room.

"Would you ever come back here?" Skippy wanted to know.

"Here?" Benny stopped walking around and stood for a moment, thinking about it. "I don't know. I don't think so. Why would you want to do something you already did? No, I don't guess I'd come back."

Then they were both quiet for a long time and finally Skippy changed the subject.

For as long as Skippy knew him, Benny would regularly disappear for three or four days at a time, throw a few things into a knapsack and head off into the bush, telling nobody, or hitch a ride down Highway 61 to Duluth or as far as Minneapolis-St. Paul. He never told Skippy when he was planning one of these trips (maybe they weren't even planned, maybe they were just something he woke up in the morning having to do) and of course there was never any suggestion that Skippy might come along, he'd never manage a trek into the bush, he'd just hold his friend up. So he'd stay behind and the first he'd know his pal was missing was when he got a call from

Mrs. Carter, her voice high and tense with worry but trying not to show it.

"He'll be back soon," she'd say in that soft drawl that was so much like Benny's. "I'm sure he hasn't gone far."

"No," Skippy would reassure her, "I'm sure he hasn't."

It was useless asking Benny where he'd been when he returned from these jaunts, as he called them ("I had a little jaunt," he'd say, smiling at the sound of the old-fashioned word, conjuring up images of snappy young men in old-fashioned Model T Fords). If he'd been in the bush, he'd bring back a fish or a piece of birch bark with a poem written on it, something he'd composed while sitting by a lake watching the deer come down to drink. The time he made it to Minneapolis he brought back some cloudy water in a jam jar ("The Mississippi, Skippy," and then they both started laughing at the way the names went together and that's as far as Skippy got finding out what Benny had discovered on that particular trip).

And once he was gone a very long time, almost three weeks, and Skippy was desperate with worrying about him and Mrs. Carter finally broke down and called the police and they were useless once they learned how many times he'd disappeared in the past. Forget it, they told her, the kid likes to take off, he'll be back, we don't have the manpower to go chasing all over the country every time some dumb kid goes missing. That was the year Skippy was eighteen, when they were in their final year, and Benny took off just before the Easter break, hitchhiked all the way to New York City and stayed with some people he met in the Village and came back raving about the Beats: Jack Kerouac and Alan Ginsberg and William Burroughs. He brought back a stack of paperback books and dumped them on the coffee table in Skippy's front room: "On the Road," "The Dharma Bums", "Naked Lunch" and one that was simply called "Howl".

Skippy picked up one of the books — "The Subterraneans" — and flipped it open: "...no girl had ever moved me with a story of spiritual suffering and so beautifully her soul showing out radiant as an angel wandering in hell the selfsame streets I'd roamed in watching, watching for someone just like her—-"

"What is this stuff?" he asked and Benny told him it was about beatniks in San Francisco and that Kerouac had written the whole thing in three days.

"It's intensely cool, man. Kerouac hangs out with this coloured chick who's half Indian, and they smoke pot — tea, they call it —"

"Drugs?"

"Yeah, man, they do drugs, marijuana, you know, and some of them are junkies, they take heroin and don't do much except sit around all day but it's just so cool. I tried it, in the Village, the marijuana, I mean, not the heroin, and it makes you feel so great, so relaxed, I brought some back for you, man, let's do it."

"Are you crazy? You can go to jail for that. They can put you away for seven years, I read it in a magazine."

"Relax, man, nobody's going to jail for smoking a couple of sticks of pot. Come on, Skippy, it'll make you feel good. Don't you want to feel good?"

"What I want is to stay out of jail," Skippy said but he took one of the marijuana cigarettes and stuck it between his lips, just to show that he, too, could be cool. Benny lit a match and they got it going and passed it back and forth between them, Skippy taking short, hurried puffs, quickly handing it back to Benny each time as if he was afraid it was going to explode. Benny took deep drags and held the smoke in his lungs for a long time before releasing it. When it was finished, Skippy waited for something to happen.

"I don't feel anything," he said.

"That's okay, sometimes it takes a while. Here," and Benny pulled two more out of his shirt pocket, "let's do another."

Sprawled on the orange shag rug in Skippy's living room, leaning against the couch for support, they passed the marijuana back and forth and in between drags, Benny talked about the quality of the pot, that this was good stuff from Mexico, not home-grown American shit, and Skippy was amazed at the knowledge his friend had picked up in the three weeks he'd been away, and he smiled and agreed with him, waiting for something to happen. But nothing did until he stood up to change the record on his mom's hi-fi and then it was like the time he'd been sick and had tried to get out of bed: he shot up into the air, his head so far away from his feet it might be pressing against the ceiling and he felt very dizzy but in an agreeable way, with a lightness between his ears. He stood there, swaying slightly, looking down at his friend who was miles away, a warm, fuzzy little spot at his feet and he knew this was how it must feel to land on the moon. Benny was looking up at him and laughing and Skippy started to laugh, too, but he couldn't laugh and hang on to his place on the ceiling, so he floated back down to the couch and lay back on the cushions and laughed for a very long time. And each time the laughing subsided he would sit up part way and catch his friend looking at him, so happy, such a pleasant, open face and that would set him off again. So they spent the afternoon smoking the rest of the dope and laughing and after a while they were very hungry so they headed into the kitchen to raid the refrigerator, and ate up all his mother's Neapolitan ice cream but did it very deliberately, first the chocolate, then the vanilla and finally the strawberry, a colour at a time, being careful not to let one flavour run into the other. When the ice cream was gone, they found half a bag of Oreo cookies on a top shelf behind a sack of All-Purpose flour and they shared the cookies and ate them very carefully, prying the top wafer off and eating it first, then licking the vanilla centre until the second wafer was completely smooth and dark and then eating that as well. It took a long time to finish the cookies, eating them this way, but it was important to do it right.

By the time the cookies were gone, Skippy was feeling tired and things had calmed down, so he curled up on the couch and watched Benny put another record on the hi-fi. The marijuana had a different effect on Benny, it energized him, speeded him up so that he wanted to keep going, find more food to eat, do more stuff. He sat cross-legged on the floor, beating out a rhythm to the music by slapping his hands on the coffee table and then suddenly he stood up and said, "Come on, man, let's go to the park, let's go hang out with the kids on the swings and the teeter-totter, what do you say?" But Skippy was too tired to make a move and he shook his head and closed his eyes for just a minute and when he opened them, Benny was gone and the light coming in through the Venetian blinds had changed, it was cooler now and the sounds of the street told him it must be late in the afternoon and his mother would be home from work soon. His head hurt, just a little, and he lay on the couch and watched the sun shift slowly across the room, from the television, upon which rested his parents' wedding picture, taken right at the beginning of the war, his mom in a short-sleeved dress of cornflower blue (the colour of her eyes) and a strip of midnight blue velvet for a hat with a feather set right on top, no earrings or necklace, just a corsage of pink roses pinned to her shoulder and the little missing piece of her front tooth where she'd been hit by a baseball when she was twelve painted in by the photographer's assistant. His father, too, solemn and impossibly young with his hair dark and curly, unwilling to be slicked back even for a wedding, and the two of them looking like brother and sister with the same blue eyes, the same clear, honest smiles, belonging without question to the same class, if there were classes in Canada at the tail end of the Depression. A trick of the light, but he could swear their faces were moving, the eyes blinking, the mouths forming silent words: a little advice, perhaps, from the old man, who'd disappeared so suddenly, so unexpectedly, leaving as a legacy the nickname given his son because of the way he'd sort of skipped when he first was learning to walk.

He got up and made his way over to the television and picked up the photograph, studying the face of his father, struggling to remember the things he knew about him, the things he had been told. Maurice Jacques, younger son of Gaston, left school at sixteen to go to sea with the merchant marines and just naturally found himself in the navy five years later when the war broke out. He came home on leave and married Skippy's mom and was shipped out two days later, before the photographer even had time to print the wedding photo. For two glorious years, Maurice made the only real friends he would ever have, lived as intensely as he had ever dreamed he would, enjoyed the war every single, solitary minute. And then he was wounded and sent home and spent the rest of the war working at the munitions plant, making tools to fight the enemy, weapons to be used by able bodied men who were out there being men, not stuck in this one-horse town surrounded by women and kids and old fogies. His life was over before he turned twenty-four.

It was better when the war ended; then his friends were back, too, most of them, and they got together Friday nights at the Legion Hall and drank and told stories to each other about the fighting, and no one minded that the same stories were told each week, or that each man coloured them the way he saw it, sketched in the details from his position behind the gun, down in the trenches, kneeling on the floor of a sub. From time to time Maurice ran into men he'd fought with who didn't take part in these weekly gatherings, who didn't want to re-live old times. These men smiled and slapped him on the back, asked him how he was doing, what he was up to, but then went on their way, anxious to put the whole nightmare behind them. Maurice couldn't understand these men; for him, the war had been everything, it had made him and he had no desire to forget a moment of it, not ever.

As Skippy held on to the photograph, trying to focus, the light shifted, moving down the front of the television and along the living room rug, and the picture gradually slipped into the general dimness of the room. It was too dark now, the faces had gone still, the mouths had stopped moving. Whatever the old man had been trying to say, it was no use now trying to figure it out.

That night when his mother came home from work she saw an empty cookie bag on the coffee table, the cleaned-out ice cream carton lying in a sticky heap on the kitchen counter, crumbs all over the living room rug. She was about to raise hell when she saw her son curled up on the couch, fast asleep, clutching her wedding picture to his chest. Carefully, she pried the photo from his grip and placed it back on the television set. Then she took a quilt from the upstairs closet and covered him with it, before starting supper.

Benny left him the Kerouac book and Skippy read it in three days — well, three nights, really, picking it up when he got home from school and lying in bed with a bologna sandwich and a bottle of Royal Crown cola, lost in the story of this guy Percepied and his weird relationship with a Negress named Mardou. Benny had explained that the hero was really Kerouac himself and the characters in the story were all poets and writers he hung out with in New York, except that he'd set it in San Francisco. And there really was a Mardou Fox and she sounded like the sexiest, most exotic woman in the world. Overnight Skippy's fantasy woman was transformed; he left Gunsmoke's Miss Kitty leaning against the bar of the Long Branch Saloon and embraced the slim, silky body of Mardou Fox. What must it be like to go to bed with a Negro woman, he wondered? For that matter, what must it be like to go to bed with any woman? Skippy was almost nineteen years old and he'd never even necked with a girl. He knew it was mostly lies, the stuff the other guys bragged about (nobody, not even Delores Farrell, would get down on her hands and knees and beg Fatso Felicante to put it in, no matter what he said) but he figured those guys had at least done it once, at least had a taste of it, not like Skippy who had never kissed a girl, never felt a breast, never seen any girl naked except his sister who was just a kid and didn't count.

He was afraid of dying young, in a car accident or off fighting a war in some foreign country, without ever having had sex. And even if he did by some miracle meet someone who liked him back, how could anything happen? What kind of guy was such a sex fiend he was going to throw himself on top of some girl at the movies, or in her living room with her mother and father upstairs in bed? Skippy was a romantic and in his mind the setting had to be perfect: a private room somewhere, with a fireplace and candles and the Platters on the hi-fi singing "Smoke Gets in Your Eyes". Not the back seat of a car where every teenager he'd ever heard of got laid, and definitely not within a mile of his own house, with his pushy younger sister always butting her nose in and his mom who seemed to read his mind if there was even the smallest thing wrong and couldn't let anything go, but always wanted to know what he was doing and how he was feeling and all. She'd know in a minute if he had some girl over at the house and did it right there on the couch. And none of the girls he knew had places of their own, they were all just kids, like him. Actually, when Skippy really thought about it, it amazed him that anybody his age had sex, ever. But they did and there were enough pregnant girls dropping out of school to get married or take a "hairdressing course" in Winnipeg to prove it. All around him people were having sex and he was just one big dumb virgin who couldn't figure it out.

Benny knew the truth, that Skippy was a virgin, and Skippy knew that Benny wasn't, hadn't been since he was fourteen, a fact that just blew Skippy away, thinking about his friend whom the gods perpetually smiled on even to the point of giving him sex with an older woman when he was just a kid. ("She was my baby-sitter when I was a little kid," Benny told him, "five years older than me. I was crazy about her." What happened to her, Skippy wanted to know, and Benny told him he heard she'd got banged up by some guy who worked for her father and she had three kids in three years and now she was fat as a house. "But she sure was sweet to me and that's a fact," Benny said in that dreamy Tennessee voice.)

In spite of this very favourable first experience, Benny still held to the view that sex was a good thing, but not anywhere near the be-all end-all that the guys in school liked to make out.

"It's amazing when it's happening," he said. "It's all you can think about, like looking through a microscope and the whole world is in this one thing, everything's squished into this one moment, but when it's over, you feel kind of empty and you wish you'd stayed kissing or maybe even holding hands. You know what's better? Dancing. Dancing with the right girl is ten times better than sex and you better believe it."

Skippy wasn't in much of a position to compare, since he'd never done either. The fact was, except for what he read in books, he knew nothing about girls. And most books assumed you knew something and left out the critical information that actually told you what to do. No way he was even going to ask Benny that kind of stuff, like exactly where it went in and all that. No book he'd ever read had said, "You put it in exactly eight inches south of the belly button" — that's the kind of information he needed. And what did you do with the stuff afterwards? If it was anything like jerking off, it must get pretty messy. Did it all go up into the girl and you came out clean as a whistle, or was it all sticky and you had to mop it up, and who was supposed to do that, the guy or the girl? Were you supposed to plan ahead and bring a box of Kleenex with you? And what did you say when it was all over? Did the girl say, Thank you for a lovely time, like when he'd worked up his nerve to ask Ramona Stitch to see John Wayne in *Rio Bravo*? He'd wanted to ask her out for ages and it surprised the life out of him when she said yes, probably because she felt sorry for him more than anything, and he'd sat next to her all night wanting to put his arm around her but afraid she'd hate it, and then they took the bus back to her house and all the way he pictured how he'd kiss her goodnight, right on the lips, because it would be okay then, being the end of the evening, and at the front door he leaned forward and she turned her cheek away just at the crucial moment and slipped inside. If anyone said thank you, it'd be the guy, wouldn't it? It was the girl doing him a favour, not the other way around, but he'd never heard of a guy saying thank you after doing it. The problem with books was that they were written by people who'd done it and had been doing it for years, most of them, and they'd generally forgotten there'd ever been a time when they hadn't known all about it, so they were pretty useless when it came to the details.

The only person who could have helped him would have been Benny, but Benny would have laughed, not in a mean way, just the way he laughed at most things, because it was a pretty funny world, when you thought about it.

3.

The road trip was Benny's idea, in the first place, although once he'd brought it up, it seemed to Skippy as if the plan had been there, just waiting to come to life, for ever. Like Kerouac and Cassady. Carter and Jacques had the same kind of ring to it, a couple of modern-day explorers, riding the wide open road, following the blacktop.

They took the giant Atlas from Mrs. Carter's desk and sealed themselves away in the upstairs bedroom, making plans: east to New York, of course, and straight into Manhattan, steering clear of suburbia and the creeps and squares, out of respect for the Beats that had once ruled the city. They'd stop at all the subterranean haunts of their idols — the apartment on East Seventh that had once housed Ginsberg and Burroughs, the Eighth Street Bookshop and the White Horse Tavern, tourist traps now, Benny said, but harbouring the ghosts of what once had been. Then down the eastern seaboard and across Georgia to New Orleans and the Gulf, wintering on the

Mexican beaches until late March or April. Then they'd make their way up the California coast to Malibu where the chicks were and settle on the beach and learn to surf. At least, Benny would. Skippy's leg would keep him out of the hunky beach boy category but that was okay — he was going to be a writer anyway, a poet, and you didn't need to look like Mr. Universe to scale the peaks of heroic verse.

And finally, up to San Francisco, to the City Lights Bookstore and the bar with the world's most romantic name: The Lost & Found Saloon. And there, like birds of the desert who've reached their oasis, he and Benny would stay and write and become part of the whole San Francisco scene.

They'd been talking about it since Benny's trip to New York and for Skippy, at least, it became an obsession. Everything, he thought, was changed by the fact that he and Benny were going on the road. He sat in the cafeteria where he was supposed to be studying while the other guys were in gym, staring out the window as his classmates struggled around the muddy running track that circled the football field, and thought, It doesn't matter. What did they know about life? It was all mouth and muscle with those guys: whose dick was the biggest, who was already shaving every day. They flicked towels at each other in the locker room and called each other nicknames like Sudsy and Meatball and Wally (which, by the way, was short for "Walrus", not "Walter", and was because the guy in question had huge upper teeth and an abundance of body hair). If you were one of "the guys", you had a nickname; he and Benny were just Jacques and Carter, respectively.

Next winter, after graduation, these high school heroes would be sweating their butts off at the mill, while he and Benny lay on a beach somewhere on the Gulf of Mexico, drinking tequila and soaking up the rays. It was almost more than Skippy could bear to concentrate on finishing his year, passing his exams, getting through the next few months until they were finally out on the highway. Until they were free.

They'd have to do their time at the mill, too, of course. They'd need to work for at least two months, saving every penny in order to be able to leave in September. But two months, it was nothing, it'd go by like *that*. And then one day early in the fall, Benny would pull up in front of Skippy's house in his '59 Pontiac, a present from his father the college professor, and Skippy would climb in beside him and close the door.

"Where to, man?" Benny would ask.

"New York, man," Skippy would reply. "Put the pedal to the

metal and don't stop till you hit Greenwich Village."

The shock came towards the end of August. It was a Friday afternoon and they were taking their lunch break — four more hours until the end of their shift. The lunch room was just a small, closed-off space at the far end of the building, where it was almost as noisy as the main room but not quite. Usually, during the summer, he and Benny took their sandwiches and their bottles of cola and went to sit outside on a grassy hill a couple of hundred yards south of the main building. The spot had the advantage of being quiet and gave them a view of the city, to the northeast, and the cemetery to the west. But, depending on which way the wind was blowing, the effluent from the towering mill chimneys could end up wafting towards you, and the sickening, sulfurous fumes took away your appetite and made you want to puke.

You weren't supposed to criticize the stench, no matter how bad it was. "Smell of progress," everybody said. Or, "Smell of money." The economy of the town depended on that mill. It and three others and the shipyard and the railway paid the salaries of every third person who lived there. And the others, the ones like Benny's dad who didn't directly work for the mill or the CNR, they wouldn't have jobs either if it hadn't been for all these sons and daughters of millworkers and grain inspectors and railwaymen, who needed to be fed and clothed and sheltered and educated. If you lived in the Bay, you didn't badmouth the mill.

But it had been raining all morning and the grass would be wet and so they'd eaten their lunch inside, where it was noisy, smoky and overheated and the naked fluorescent lights buzzed overhead. Benny had been very quiet but there was nothing so unusual in this; lots of times he sat with his head buried in a book while the others razzed him and called him "Mister Studious." Benny never minded being teased — he just looked up and smiled now and then, took a bite of his sandwich and went back to whatever it was he was reading. This week it was something called *The Tin Drum*, by a guy with a German-sounding name. It was a thick, hard-cover book from the library and it looked like a kids' book except there were so many pages and no illustrations. Benny said it was about a guy in a mental hospital, writing about his family; Skippy, who often borrowed books after Benny had read them, thought he'd give this one a miss.

But on this particular day, Benny wasn't reading his book. He sat at a corner of one of the four long trestle tables and ate his lunch, slowly, methodically, his eyes on the bread and the pinkish-brown slices of ham peeking out from the iceberg lettuce and mayonnaise.

He ate as if it was requiring his whole being to get through this meal, paying no attention to any of the conversations going on around him. Twice, Skippy asked him if he was okay. Each time Benny looked up, briefly, and nodded.

"Yeah, I'm fine."

And went back to eating his sandwich. When it was all gone, he drained the rest of his cola and stood up, leaning against the table as if it took an effort, just to stand. Skippy thought he must be sick; there was something wrong, that was for sure. With fifteen minutes left in the lunch break, they could have hung out for a while, chewed the fat, but Benny said he had to get back to work and that was it — he picked up his hard hat and left and Skippy stayed where he was, watching the back of him retreat down the wide aisle next to the paper machine, and disappear around a corner.

One of the guys at the table spoke up, a fat jerk named Leon who was always horsing around, sticking his nose in everybody else's business.

"Your buddy's pretty quiet today."

Skippy nodded. "Yeah. I guess he's not feeling too good."

"Maybe he's in lo-o-ove," the fat guy said and added, leaning forward to command Skippy's attention, "maybe he got himself laid." He drew the word out, with relish: "Lay-ed," like he could picture Benny right there and then, spread out with some girl, going at it like crazy.

"Yeah, maybe." It was usually best, Skippy had found, just to agree with these types. You didn't want to get into a fight if you didn't have to.

"Of course," Leon continued, and now he flicked his wrist at Skippy, in what was supposed to be a coy, effeminate gesture, "you wouldn't know about that, would you? I mean, you don't like girls, now, do you?"

The tone was openly hostile, the guy was sneering at him, daring him to strike back, and a few of the others around them had turned to watch, to see what Skippy would do. He swallowed and tried to sound casual, friendly, like it was all in fun, even though it obviously wasn't.

"Sure I do. I like girls a lot."

"You do?" Leon opened his eyes wide in mock surprise. "Well, fuck me. And here I thought you were just a little pansy. Hear that, boys?" Leon turned to the others, his audience, and appealed to them. "Little Jacques here says he likes girls after all."

The other guys shrugged; they hardly knew Skippy, he was just a kid, one of the high school crowd hired on in the summer to work clean-up — they had nothing against him.

Turning back to Skippy, Leon said, in a fake-sincere voice, "Honest, Jacques, I really didn't know you liked girls. I thought Apache there was your boyfriend."

"His name's not Apache." Skippy felt the blood rushing to his head and he began to tremble, although he tried to keep his voice steady, not wanting the guy to know he was getting to him.

"Well, whatever his name is, he sure as hell looks like an Indian. And I hear he likes those little squaws on the reserve, eh? I hear he has a hell of a good time out there."

It wasn't the first time he'd heard it; Benny'd been called an Indian lover before — at least once, to Skippy's knowledge, to his face. Skippy had been there and had wanted to defend his friend, but Benny didn't seem to realize he even needed defending. He didn't think it was such a bad thing, to have a reputation like that. He did have some Indian friends, he went to parties with them sometimes, he hung out on the mountain with them. He might even have done it with an Indian girl or he might not have. He never said, but not because she was an Indian; apart from relating the story of his first sexual encounter, Benny just didn't talk about stuff the way other guys did.

So when some creep had come up to him in the park one night and stood there with his buddies, taunting Benny about liking "cripples and Indians", he just looked off into the distance like he didn't hear the guy. Skippy was the one who got mad, he was the one who wanted to fight back, but Benny never saw the point.

"It's just dumb," he said afterwards, when they were walking back home. (The guys had left, eventually — nobody ever came so far as to actually throw the first punch at Benny. There was something about him that warned them off.)

"I mean, first of all," he continued, "there's nothing wrong with liking Indians, it's nothing to be ashamed of. And second, they're just showing how stupid they are, saying something like that. Just making themselves look bad."

It was the kind of thing Skippy's mom might have said, sensible, level-headed. Yet Skippy wished his friend would've got mad and punched the guy's lights out — he could have, he was big enough and strong, in spite of being skinny. He could've made mince meat of that guy, although there were his buddies to consider. Three of them, two of him and Benny; it was probably better that Benny had taken the peaceable route. Still. It would have been satisfying to see that guy flat on his back with his nose bleeding and two black eyes. He'd called his best friend an Indian lover and called Skippy a cripple. He really would have liked to have seen the guy in some serious pain.

Now, taking his cue from Benny, Skippy concentrated his attention on his sandwich. "You don't know anything," he said, sounding braver than he felt.

"Oh, don't I?" Leon turned to the other for support. "This kid thinks I don't know anything, you hear that, guys? Should I tell him what I know? Should I let him in on a little secret?"

"Aw, forget it." This from a guy down the table. "Leave the kid alone, Leon." A couple of the others agreed. They were looking to eat their lunch, relax for a while before going back to work. They weren't in the mood for a fight. And anyway, it was obvious Leon wasn't going to get anything going with this scrawny little high-school kid. He had a bad leg, for Chrissake, he wasn't going to get physical.

But Skippy had responded and that was all Leon wanted. He liked to "needle" people like this; it amused him to push and see how far he could go before they pushed back. He would goad and prod and tease a person just to the point of violence and then, when they threatened to haul off and punch his face in, he'd draw back and grin and say, "What's the matter, can't you take a joke?" It was a fat boy's sort of bullying and Leon had never grown out of it.

Now he leaned over the table towards Skippy, as if he had some great secret to confide, and grinned. "There's this buddy of mine, he's a cop, eh, and last weekend he gets a call to go break up a party on the reserve. Some of the young bucks had a little too much firewater, things got out of hand. And who do you think was there, making out with some squaw in the back room? Who d'you think it was, eh?"

Skippy said nothing and the others had gone quiet, too, wanting to hear the punch line.

"Skinny white guy named Benny Carter." Leon drew it out, with relish, announcing it to the entire table. "The Indians, six or seven of them, they get hauled off to the clink to cool off for the night, but not your little friend. No, sirree. They dump him in the back of the cop car, eh? Take him out to the dump and give him a little lesson in race relations. And then they take him home to his mommy."

It was a lie. Benny would have told him if something like that had happened. Then again, Benny didn't always tell him everything and something like that he might have wanted to keep to himself.

"I don't believe you." Skippy stood up and gathered up the remains of his lunch.

Leon looked up at him and the grin on his fat face didn't waver.

"Go ahead, Jacques, go ask your boyfriend what happened. He'll tell you. Maybe he'll even give you her name, so you can go get a little tail yourself. But I don't think he'll be going out there any more. Not for a while, anyways."

Before Skippy reached the door the hum of conversation had picked up again; the scene would be forgotten in minutes. Just Leon, being his usual asshole self. The guys were used to it; he went too far, sometimes, but mostly it was in good fun and it made the lunch break more interesting. Besides, he never picked on anyone important, he never picked on anyone who could fight back.

Skippy made his way to the dry end of the paper machine where Benny, with some time still left in the lunch break, was sitting on the floor, propped up against the calender stack, staring off into the distance. He looked around and saw Skippy and nodded, patting the floor beside him.

"Have a seat, *compadre*."

They'd been teaching themselves Spanish, in preparation for the trip, and had taken to greeting each other with "*compadre*" and "*amigo*" and "*paysan*".

Skippy lowered himself on to the floor next to his friend and before he could say a single word, Benny told him the trip was off.

"I'm sorry, *amigo. Lo siento mucho.*"

Skippy didn't absorb it at first; he'd been expecting to hear something about the party on the reserve, Benny's version of what had happened with the police, and this announcement about the trip, it made no sense.

"What do you mean? What are you talking about?"

"The road trip, man. I'm sorry, but I can't go."

He was kidding, of course. Pulling his leg. They'd been planning it for months, they had two weeks left to work before leaving, everything was all set up. But his friend wasn't joking. There was no smile, no hint of a tease. He was serious.

"Is this, is it because of the weekend? Because of the party?"

He was thinking that maybe the stuff Leon had told him and what Benny was saying now were connected, somehow. Maybe Benny'd had to pay a fine or something, maybe he was going to have to go to court. But that was okay; Skippy would help him out with the money and if there was a court case, well, they could wait. They could still go.

Now it was Benny's turn to look confused. "Party? What party?"

"The party on the reserve. Leon — he told me what happened. About the cops coming and all. Is that why you can't go?"

Understanding dawned and Benny gave a brief laugh. "Aw, shit, man, that was nothing. Just a couple of police throwing their weight around. I don't care about that." (He said it "po-lice", with the accent on the first syllable, in that southern way he still had. He'd probably always sound a little bit different, no matter how long he lived in the north.)

"Well, then, what? Why are you saying it's off?"

Benny looked at his friend for a minute and his smile faded. "I'm sorry, *amigo*. I wish it wasn't so. But I got responsibilities now, I can't just take off."

And then, in the five minutes that were left before the whistle blew, Benny told him about the girl he'd met on his trip to New York in the spring. Her name was Margaret and she worked as a waitress at this bagel place he'd gone to, in Greenwich Village, and she'd taken a liking to him and given him free bagels with extra cream cheese and he'd asked her out, and seen her a half dozen times and even written her once when he got back to Cambrian Bay. And he hadn't heard anything and had almost forgotten about her — almost, but not quite, because there was something about her that was so sweet, you know? Not what you'd expect to find in a girl from a big city like New York. And then yesterday he'd got home from work and there was a letter waiting for him, and it was from her. She'd written to say she was having a baby — his baby, and it was due some time in January (just when they were supposed to be lying on the beach in Mexico, right in the middle of the road trip) and she was so sweet, she wasn't going to say anything to him, just let him take off and deal with it herself, can you believe it? But she had decided to write him after all because he might want to know he was going to be a father and she said he wasn't to worry about it, it was her responsibility, and of course he'd phoned her right away and told her he wasn't the kind of guy to abandon a girl in this situation and she wasn't to worry, he'd take care of everything. He was sending her bus fare and she was coming up to Canada, because she had no family in New York, nobody to care for her but him. So Skippy could see how it was and how Benny couldn't go on the trip now, not now when he was going to be a father.

Skippy listened to all this and said nothing and then, just as the whistle blew and the machines started up again all around them, he said the one thing he wished he hadn't said; if he could have bitten off his tongue and not said it he would have, but he was just in such a state of shock, he said the first thing that came into his head, which was, Was Benny sure it was his? And right away he wished like anything not to have said it, because Benny looked like he'd been hit in the face, and then he just looked very sad and said he never thought to hear something like that come out of the mouth of a friend. And it stayed there between them, what Skippy had said, although they never referred to it again, either of them, but there was no taking it back.

So the trip was off. Skippy told his mother he'd changed his mind, had decided to stay in town after all, and she was glad to hear it, although she wished he seemed happier about it and wondered what he would do. He told her Benny was getting married and she was grateful it wasn't *her* son who'd got himself into this situation, although she liked Benny and was sorry for his parents, since it was obviously a shotgun wedding.

On a clear Sunday afternoon in September Margaret arrived by Greyhound bus all the way from New York and she and Benny got married the following day in the city clerk's office, with Benny's mother crying away like it was some kind of funeral and his father sitting there stony-faced and hurt. Skippy was best man, and Margaret's best friend, Linette Olson, who had come up on the bus with her just for the wedding, she was the maid of honour. Linette was a complete fool and ugly into the bargain, but they all went out to Chan's Paradise Gardens afterwards and had Chinese food and Chan supplied a case of beer, just for the occasion. They were all underage, except for the parents, but Benny was a favourite of the restaurant-owner and he made an exception in this case. People were always making exceptions for Benny Carter. Benny's father stood up at one point and made a toast to the bride, welcoming Margaret into the family, and you could see he was trying to make the best of a bad situation. Benny's mother didn't even try. She just sat there looking like she'd lost her best friend, and every now and then she glanced in the direction of Margaret's stomach as if she expected the baby to pop out right then and there.

The only ones who acted as if they were really at a wedding and not a wake were Benny and Margaret, who actually did seem to be in love, in spite of hardly knowing each other, and Skippy's mother, who always liked weddings and had more to drink than she was used to and kept saying that Margaret was "cute as a button".

"Isn't she cute?" she kept asking Benny's mother, who tried to smile and be a good sport about it, but you could see in her eyes that this was a sad day for her. "Honest, Kate" — Benny's mother's name was Katherine, Kate for short — "Honest, Kate, they are the cutest couple those two. That baby's going to be some kind of movie star, I tell you."

At this, the mention of the baby, the reason for the whole dreadful ceremony, Benny's mother burst into tears and her husband had to take her home. He gave Skippy's mom a lift, too, and with the older ones out of the way, the party finally got off the ground, and Benny ordered more beers and the four of them stayed until closing time. When it was time to leave, Linette stood up and tripped over Skippy, falling into his lap, where she sprawled and looked up at him in a way that was meant to be coy and flirtatious.

"I think I'm a little bit drunk," she said. She was completely sloshed, in fact, and Skippy, who was a little unsteady himself, had to hold on to her and steer her to the door. They got into the back seat of Benny's Pontiac and Linette immediately turned to Skippy and said, "I hope you're not gonna try anything."

Then she put her arms around his neck and pulled him towards her and they necked a little until she had to get out and puke. When she got back in the car she was very subdued and there was a sour smell of vomit emanating from her. She sat right over against the door and didn't look at Skippy once and when Benny dropped her off at the YW, where she was staying, she got out of the car and headed straight for the front entrance, without a word. Margaret leaned across Benny and called out to her, "Linny, are you okay? You want me to come in with you?"

The girl stopped and turned around and managed a smile. "Don't be silly," she said, sounding thick and still a little drunk. "Go have fun with your hubby. You're a married lady now." Then she turned and made her way to the door, wobbling on her high heels, and Skippy noticed that, from the back, she was actually pretty good-looking. The next morning she got the bus back to New York and Skippy never saw her again.

He stayed in town that winter, waiting for Margaret's baby to be born, since there didn't seem to be any point in taking off for the States on his own and anyway, he couldn't drive and it wouldn't be the same, doing the trip by Greyhound. He was laid off from the mill, then got a job at the Canada Car plant, part time, two or three days a week, so he took to hanging out at the Carter household, if you could call it that.

Benny and his new wife had rented one of the little, war-time bungalows down in the old Ukrainian part of town and immediately got themselves a living room suite and a dining table and four chairs and a washer/dryer unit on credit. It was cramped, there was hardly room to move, but it was kind of cozy, and Margaret adopted a stray cat and they named him Cassady. Skippy liked to come over at the end of the day and sit on the couch with his feet up on the coffee table and stroke Cassady, who saw him as a kindred spirit right away and would only sit in his lap when he was around. Benny managed to be kept on full time at the mill and they apprenticed him to one of the millwrights, so he could learn a trade, but he'd been switched to the graveyard shift at the end of September. He'd sleep until just before suppertime, so that when Skippy got there he was still a little rumpled and sleepy-eyed, but in a good mood and glad to see his good friend Skippy. The three of them had supper together — spaghetti with Chianti wine, holopshe, pork chops with applesauce, and chicken fried the southern way, the way Benny liked it. Margaret was a good cook and for the first time in the years that Skippy had known him, Benny was starting to lose that beanpole look and put on a little weight. After supper the three of them would play a little cards, maybe go down the street to the Royal Alex and watch the strippers, just for a laugh. Nobody ever asked for I.D. at the Alex and if you didn't draw attention to yourself you could sit there all evening, drinking draft beer and playing shuffleboard.

Around eleven Benny'd get ready for work — his car was parked on the street out front but it cost too much to keep it running and so he took the bus to the mill. Skippy watched while Margaret packed her husband a lunch and stowed it in the Roy Rogers lunch bucket Benny'd had since grade five and used all through school because he liked it so much, and then Benny would come out of the bedroom in his overalls and plaid shirt, slip on his work jacket and say, "*Adios, muchachos.*" That was Skippy's cue to stand up and stretch and say he'd better be on his way but Benny would talk him out of it.

"No, *amigo*, don't go yet. My bride gets lonely on her own. Stay and read poetry to her and talk to the baby." Then Benny would laugh and kiss Margaret good-bye and put his mouth down near her tummy and say good-bye to the baby, as well. And then he'd leave. And that was how Skippy and Margaret got to know each other that winter, sitting there talking about stuff each night after Benny had left for work.

It surprised him how easy it was to talk to Margaret. She didn't say much, but she had a comfortableness about her that made you feel you could tell her just about anything. As a rule, Skippy would have felt uneasy, alone in his friend's house with an attractive woman; he would have spoken carefully, thought out his words beforehand so he didn't give the wrong impression. But with Margaret it was different. For one thing, she was pregnant, so he didn't think of her the way he thought of other girls. She was a mother — well, almost, and that put her into a whole other category. And she didn't find his ideas weird or even particularly funny. Take his thoughts on good and evil, for instance. Skippy would never have confided this to anybody else, not even Benny, but with Margaret it just came out naturally:

"Here's how I figure it," he told her one night, settled on his side of the couch, Cassady curled up in his lap. "Hitler was evil, there's no denying it. He did terrible things, a normal person couldn't even come up with some of that stuff. So evil exists, it's out there. But most people never come across it. And goodness is like that, too. It's there, it's real, but it doesn't *mean* anything. Most of the time, you're not really one way or the other, you're somewhere in the middle, just going along doing your job, taking care of your kids, maybe going out for a beer now and then, fooling around. And then, one day, a kid runs out in front of a car and you're right there and you dive out in front of the car and save the kid, and you're a hero, right? And the papers write you up and say what a great guy you are, and they pin a medal on you, maybe. But it's just that you had the opportunity, you know what I mean? You could turn around tomorrow, maybe, and rob a bank. You'd still be the same person, nothing would've changed. Just a different opportunity."

Taking care not to disturb the cat, Skippy reached for his bottle of beer and took another sip. He was warmed up now, and Margaret was nodding and listening attentively, and he was sure that he was onto something, if he could only decide what it was.

"The thing is, without evil, without the Hitlers of the world, you wouldn't have the heroes either, you can't have the good without the bad. They're part of the whole, right? Yin and yang and all that. Positive and negative. Black and white. So when you look at it like that, it takes away the responsibility of the individual. You know? I mean, if we can all be good and we can all be evil and the only thing that changes is the circumstance, then how do we ever know what we are? I mean, if I was a kid living in Germany in the thirties, wouldn't I want Hitler to win? Wouldn't I go to war and fight for my country and maybe kill a few Allies? Would that make me evil? Would that make me a horrible person? No, I'd just be some poor sap of a Kraut who was born on the wrong side, that's all."

Margaret nodded, and said, "And if Hitler had won, if the Germans had won the war, that kid would be a hero."

"Yeah. And by now the history books would all be telling us how the evil Americans and the Canucks and the English had tried to destroy the great Aryan nation. And who'd be around to argue?"

"Skippy," she said, all of a sudden, "feel this. The baby's moving."

Gently, he placed a hand on her firm, round belly and waited for the sharp, sudden thrust of a tiny foot, or an elbow, or a fist. In the face of that small, amazing affirmation of life, that demand to be noticed, it came to him that his great, lofty concepts were just a lot of words, taking up space, meaning absolutely nothing. This was what counted — this was *real* goodness — and if he could have sat there on that couch with his hand on the stomach of his best friend's wife for the rest of his life, he would have. He absolutely would have, and he didn't care what anybody thought.

4.

The thing about Margaret, Skippy decided, was that she grew on you. The first time he saw her, getting off the bus at the Inter-city depot, worn out from two and a half days of travel and clutching her handbag against her chest like a newborn child, he thought she looked ordinary. It was windy and she'd tied a scarf around her head, babushka-style, and the coat she was wearing hung open in front. Surely his friend Benny Carter deserved better. A Mardou Fox, at the very least.

But then he'd come to notice how soft and wavy her hair was, how her eyes were fringed with heavy, dark lashes and they weren't really brown at all but green, almost, or gray, depending on the light. And she had a trick of tilting her head when she was looking at you and keeping her eyes on your face as if you were the most important person in the room — in the world, even. It was flattering; it made you want to keep talking so she would keep looking at you in that way, keep those warm, dark eyes focused on yours.

He put it into words, once, when he and Benny were sitting together at a table in the Alex, between strippers. It was after midnight on a Saturday, which meant Benny didn't have to leave to go to work and they could all sleep in the next morning. Margaret had gone to the ladies' room and the two of them watched her get up, slowly, from the table and make her way across the room, holding herself carefully so as not to bump into anything and hurt the baby.

"She has an inner beauty," is what Skippy said and it came out more formal, more pompous than he'd intended. "She's pretty inside," he amended. "You feel it, when you're with her."

Benny nodded. "She's an old soul. I think maybe in another life she was my mother."

"Yeah?" Skippy considered this for a moment. "I'm not sure I could, you know, *do* it with a girl if I thought that. I mean, if I thought she used to be my mother."

His friend laughed and raised his beer glass in a toast. "Here's to incest," he said, "it's all relative."

And when Skippy looked shocked he laughed again and said, "I'm *joking*, man. *El chiste, si?*"

Margaret came back to the table and stopped behind her chair, looking from Benny to Skippy and back.

"What?" she asked. "What is it? Why are you looking at me like that?"

"We've been discussing your inner beauty," Benny said, taking hold of her hand and pulling her gently down into her seat. "We think you should package it."

"Put it in a bottle and sell it," Skippy said. "Inner Beauty, no preservatives added."

Margaret laughed and reached for her glass. "You're drunk," she said, fondly. "The two of you are completely bombed."

They were, of course, but they still thought she was beautiful.

Over the course of the winter Margaret told Benny the story of her life — what there was to tell, as she was only nineteen, a few months older than Skippy. She'd been born illegitimate, her mother being an unmarried girl still living at home, and was given up for adoption right away. Skippy thought this was a sad thing and said so, but Margaret said no, the girl had done the right thing by giving her up even though she, Margaret, could never had done the same.

"If Benny hadn't wanted to get married," she told him, speaking softly and looking down at where her hands rested against the fullness of her stomach, "I was all prepared to have this baby on my own. But I knew I was stronger than she'd been. I've been through more and living through things makes you strong."

Margaret had lived through a tough childhood; the people who'd adopted her appeared to change their minds after a while, especially after they had their own little son and daughter. From the time she was five or six it was made clear to her that there was one set of rules for their natural children and another for her. This might have made another sort of person bitter and resentful and Margaret admitted she'd been unhappy a lot when she was young. But things had turned around when she was fifteen — her mother, her real mother, the one who'd given her up when she was just a girl herself, had come looking for her, had come right up the steps to the house in New Jersey where Margaret's family lived and introduced herself.

"She never got married and she never had any other children, just me, the one she'd given up, and she was determined to find me." Telling Skippy this, Margaret's eyes lit up like a child's and he saw that to her it was like a fairytale — she, the modern-day Cinderella, her mother the good fairy godmother. "She had to go through so much, trying to find me. They don't like to let you know anything, when you give up a child. But her brother was a lawyer and he knew some people who could help and, well, she found me."

"And you went to live with her?"

Margaret nodded. "She was a secretary in the city, right downtown. And she had an apartment and at first I just went to see her on Saturday afternoons, and then I started going Friday right after school and didn't come back till Sunday after supper. And then, around Christmas — this was about six months after I met her — I told my mom and dad, my adopted mom and dad, that I wanted to live with my mother. My real mother. She wanted me, too, but of course she wouldn't ask something like that, she wouldn't feel she had the right. So I did, I asked. Well, not asked exactly. I told them, I said, I want to go live with her. And they said I was ungrateful and I always had been and what else could you expect and a lot of other stuff but it ended up that I packed my stuff and went to live with her."

She spoke about this time like it was a dream, a miracle, sort of, which it was, in a way. "I went to a new school and every night we ate supper together and on weekends we went to museums and art galleries and she took me to the movies. We went everywhere. We saw everything."

The good times lasted for two years, until Margaret's mother had got sick. "She had cancer and it was a bad kind, it just ate her up in a couple of months. She got to see me graduate, which she wanted so much, but she didn't last very long after that. She left me her pictures and her clothes and what money she had, but there wasn't much and most of it went to pay for the hospital and the doctors and all that. Her brother, my uncle, he wanted me to come live with him and his wife but I didn't want to leave the apartment. It made me feel near her, you know?" She paused, and Skippy looked for something to say.

"Gee," he said finally, "that's tough."

"Yeah." She looked up and smiled at him. "Anyhow, I thought about it for a long time and finally I decided to find a job and go to work. She wouldn't have liked that, she wanted me to go to college.

But when she died, I don't know. I felt like everything that happened, it had all made me older, and I couldn't go off to school in the fall and be one of the kids. You know? And there wasn't enough money for it, anyway. So I got a job at a department store, and then I got laid off, and then I landed the job at the bagel place and that's where I met Benny."

When she saw Benny the first time she just knew, she said, that he was the one. "You might think it's bad," she told Skippy, not looking at him, looking down at her hands, at the plain gold ring she wore now, "to make love with a person when you've only just met him. I mean, you might think a girl who would do something like that is sort of a tramp, you know?" Skippy opened his mouth to protest, but Margaret continued. "But with Benny I just liked him so much the minute I saw him and he was so sweet and everything, I just wanted to be with him right there. I didn't care about waiting or what he thought about me or if he was going to respect me afterwards. I just wanted to be with him. You know?"

Skippy did know. He could imagine a girl coming face to face with that skinny, good-looking friend of his, who smiled in such an open, direct sort of way and whose voice still held a promise of the South. It didn't seem strange to him that she would trust him immediately and invite him back to the apartment she'd shared with her mother and spend the night making love with him in a big double bed with the window open to the heat of the New York night. (These were details she didn't have to share with him; he just knew the way it had happened.)

"He was the first," Margaret said, in a voice so low Skippy was not entirely sure he'd caught it. "You might not believe that, seeing as how I went with him so quickly and all, but he was. The first one. The only one." And because he was the first, she'd made no preparations, taken no precautions, and when he'd left to go back to Canada she was not unhappy to find she was pregnant.

"I wanted there to be something of him inside me," was the way she put it. And it was so simple a thought, and so pure, that he took hold of her hand and held it, because he thought then that he'd never met a girl so strong or so deserving of his respect. They sat like that, together, on the couch, until she suddenly stood up and said she'd make him some coffee.

"I bet I'm just boring you to death," she said and when he said no, she wasn't boring him at all, she smiled and told him he was a good listener. "I'm glad we're friends, Skippy. We are friends, aren't we? By now?"

Skippy said yes, they were friends, and she seemed happy to

hear it. "I'm glad," she said again. "I felt bad about the trip when Benny told me. I never wanted to, you know — spoil things for you."

"You didn't spoil anything," Skippy told her and was surprised to realize that when he said it, he meant it.

Benny seemed to think that this was a great thing, his best friend and his wife getting along so well. "I think it's cool that you two dig each other so much," he told Skippy one evening after supper when the two of them were sitting out on the front porch while Margaret cleared away the dishes. Skippy had offered to help and usually she let him, but tonight she'd seemed a little tense, and she said, "Never mind, go on will you? Just let me get it done." So Skippy waited a moment by the kitchen door, wondering if he should press the point, then decided to leave well enough alone and joined Benny outside in the cool night air. It was November and unseasonably warm for the time of year, but still too cool to be out there for long. Benny was perched on an old wicker sofa that the last tenants had left behind, all sad and caved-in looking but better than trying to sit on the steps which were wet from the rain that had fallen earlier in the day and a few dead leaves left over from the fall.

Benny had bought himself a Bowie knife and he was whittling away industriously on a piece of eastern pine — he'd taken up carving recently (he told Skippy he liked the image of a man on his front porch with the outdoor light on and a pregnant wife making herself busy inside) and he was making a real mess of it. Benny didn't show much talent for wood carving, none at all, in fact, but he didn't seem too worried about that. It was the picture it conjured up in his mind that he liked, and the nice, monotonous motion of scraping the blade back and forth over the wood.

Skippy found it irritating. It didn't fit his image of his friend; the old Benny had never needed to find things to keep his hands busy. He'd been content to sit and cradle a bottle of beer for hours or, lacking the bottle, just let them rest by his side. It was his mouth that did the moving and his mind that couldn't sit still, not his hands. He was a person comfortable in himself, Skippy had always thought, and had admired him for it. Now, when he wasn't whittling, he was drumming his fingers on the kitchen table, tapping out a tune, or fiddling with a pencil, anything to keep his fingers moving, take his mind off things. Off what, Skippy couldn't imagine. Wasn't he married to the best, most understanding girl in the world? Didn't they have a nice little home, a warm, cozy place to come back to at the end of the day (or at the beginning, in Benny's case) and wasn't he going to become a father very soon? When Skippy considered all of this that was there for his good friend, all thoughts of wanderlust and living a beat life in Mexico and California and seeing the world flew out of his head and he was convinced that to live the life of Benny Carter was the only thing that made sense in this world.

Skippy sat down on the beat-up old sofa next to his friend and watched him whittle. After a moment Benny looked up and said, "You ever wish we'd gone on the road?"

This was the first time since the wedding that Benny had mentioned the trip. Skippy had to think before he answered.

"Oh, I don't know. Maybe. It would've been fun."

Benny stared at the piece of wood he was holding. "Does this look like anything at all to you?"

Skippy considered it and replied that, to be honest, it did not.

Benny tossed it into the bush at the side of the porch and set his knife down beside him. "Useless," he said.

"What was it supposed to be?"

Benny shrugged. "Who knows? I just picked it up and started carving. I figured after a while it'd start to look like something. They say sculptors do that, they take a piece of rock and start chipping away at it and pretty soon the shape that's inside it starts showing. I read that somewhere, anyway."

"Maybe it doesn't work with wood, only rock."

"Maybe."

Benny was restless; he started tapping on his knees, some tune inside his head, then gave up on that as well. Shoving his hands in the pockets of his pants, as if that were the only way to keep them from fidgeting, he leaned back and gazed up at the house, to where the sagging roof drooped over the doorway.

"This place is a mess," he said and Skippy, who'd never given the house a second look and had assumed Benny hadn't, either, studied it now and had to agree: it was not in very good shape. The outside walls needed painting and the wood around the windows was rotting and falling away in places. Still, it was where Benny and Margaret had settled, where they were "nesting", as Benny had said in the beginning. It was their very own place, even if it was rented, and no one could tell them to turn down the music or go to bed — they could stay up all night if they wanted, like a couple of kids playing house.

"I've been thinking about Lester," Benny volunteered.

He meant Lester Young, the tenor saxophonist. Skippy knew that; he and Benny still listened to old recordings of Count Basie and his band, although they liked newer stuff, too — Ray Charles, the Miracles, Roy Orbison.

"He was pretty young when he died."

"Forty-nine," Skippy said, proud of himself for knowing. March the fifteenth, nineteen fifty-nine. There'd been a small piece in the local paper, in the entertainment section. Skippy'd found it and shown it to Benny. They'd played "Time Out" and some other old '78's and toasted the man with Royal Crown colas — Skippy remembered it well.

"That's not so old," Benny said. "I used to think if you got to forty, that was all you needed. But now, I don't know."

"The good die young." It was a goofy thing to say but something needed to be said.

Benny nodded, slowly. "Yeah. I guess they do." After a moment he asked Skippy if he thought Lester'd had any kids and Skippy shook his head. He didn't know.

"I think maybe he didn't," Benny decided. "If you're going to live the Life, you can't get tied down. You gotta keep moving."

It disturbed Skippy, although he couldn't say why, to hear his friend talking like this. He'd never known Benny to regret anything — he'd always seemed so sure of what he was doing and which way he was headed.

"You know what Gregory Corso said about marriage?"

Skippy shook his head; he knew the poem but didn't remember the lines.

"He said it's what you do so you won't be sixty living alone in a furnished room with pee stains on your underwear."

There was a moment's silence which neither felt inclined to fill, and then Benny sat up and reached under the cushion of the sofa.

"Hey," he said, "look what I found today." He retrieved something shiny, that glittered in the dark, and held it out to Skippy. It was a sort of two-pronged frame with a thin strip of metal fixed at one end and it fit just neatly into his hand.

"It's a Jew's harp," Benny explained. "I found it this morning out on the sidewalk there, coming back from the bus stop. It'd been stepped on so I cleaned it up and it's as good as new."

He leaned back, stretched out his legs, put one end of the harp between his lips and began to pluck the strip in the middle. It produced a flat, reverberating twang that was not unpleasant; it reminded Skippy of sounds from his childhood, from the schoolyard. He couldn't put his finger on why he liked it but he liked it.

Benny took the harp out of his mouth and grinned. "I'm going to play this for my little girl, when she's born. I'm going to show her you can make music out of anything, any way you want."

Skippy was relieved. Benny seemed more cheerful now, talking about the baby.

"So it's going to be a girl. You're sure about that?"

"Oh, I'm sure. She'll be one perfect little girl, that baby, with ten fingers and ten toes and when she grows up she'll have a voice like Billie Holliday."

"More like Ethel Merman, if she takes after me." Margaret had appeared at the screen door and Skippy could just make her out, a dark, soft outline against the light in the hallway.

Benny looked up at her and laughed. Whatever had been bugging him, it seemed to be forgotten. Margaret, too, seemed happier now. She looked at Benny, his long legs taking up half the porch, and said, "Come in, you sillies. It's freezing out here. You'll catch pneumonia."

Benny stood up and slapped his hands against his thighs. He was revitalized, energetic, his moodiness of a few moments ago tossed aside. "Let's go to the Alex," he suggested, an invitation that included both Skippy and Margaret, as usual. "I want to hear some music, I wanna make the scene, man."

Margaret came out and joined them on the porch. "You just want to see some girls' bodies that don't have stomachs out to here," she said but she sounded happy. She knew Benny didn't care how big her stomach got.

He put his arms around her from behind and stroked the front of her belly. "What could be more beautiful than this? You should be up there on that stage with the rest of the women, showing off your beautiful body."

So they put on their coats and went down to the hotel and watched the strippers and the three of them clapped when the girls finished their act and called out encouragement, although most of the patrons watched in a silence that was almost sullen, as if they resented the women on the stage for showing them exactly what they'd come to see. Benny always said it took a brave woman to do something like that, especially when most of them were not exactly young anymore, and they needed to know that someone still thought they were sexy. Margaret pointed out that one of the women, in particular, was old enough to be his mother, and Benny gave her a hug and said, yes, that was right, she was somebody's mother and that was all the more reason to make her feel good about what she was doing.

"So you just come here to watch and clap because you want to help people out?" She smiled over at Skippy, as if the two of them were the adults here, indulging Benny, the child. *Their* child.

"That's right. Saint Benedict, that's me. Patron saint of strippers and pregnant ladies." And he gave her a kiss right there in the hotel and Skippy looked away, not because he was embarrassed but because he wanted to give them some privacy, even if it was a Tuesday night and the place was practically empty.

Skippy was laid off two weeks before Christmas. He wasn't surprised, he'd been told mid-winter was always a slow time at the plant and he, being only part-time and low man on the totem pole, would probably be the first to be let go. The supervisor gave him his paycheque and promised he'd be top of the call-back list in the spring when they started hiring again.

Skippy didn't mind; it wasn't like he'd planned to make the plant a career or anything. It was just not great timing, was all, with Christmas being so close. He had enough to buy his mother a present and something for his younger sister, Mandy, but he'd wanted to get something for Margaret as well, since she'd been so nice to him. However, once he'd handed his mother money for his room and board and set aside a little to keep him going until he found another job, there was really nothing left for a present for Margaret.

And then he thought about the poems. For the past three years, Skippy had kept a coil-ring notebook in which he wrote down the poems he'd made up at night, lying in bed, listening to the radio. He'd never shown them to anyone, not even Benny, although his friend knew he wrote them and had extracted a promise that Skippy would let him read them before they were published. In the back of his mind, Skippy had this thought that one day he'd get them typed out, like a manuscript, and send them to some New York publisher. They needed work, though; it would be a long time before he'd be ready to hand them over to anybody.

Except Margaret. She knew he wrote poetry; she'd even confided, once, that she used to write little poems herself, back when she was living with her family, just to amuse herself.

"Did you save any of them?" Skippy asked and she shook her head.

"Oh, no, they were silly, just kid stuff. I'd be embarrassed to look at them now. And they all had that rhyme, you know — duh-da-da-da-*dah*, duh-da-da-da-*dah*. The way kids make things up. I used to write them at night and tear them up the next day, before I went to school. Just in case my mom or dad got hold of them and teased me, you know?"

Skippy kept his poems under his mattress, not that his mother would come snooping around in his bedroom. Not any more. He was a man now, old enough to vote, almost, and she respected his privacy. His sister might come into his room, if she wanted to borrow a magazine or was looking for a comb or something, but she was fourteen and absorbed in her own life and not very curious about her brother. To her friends, if they asked, she'd say her brother was a little weird, he liked old-fashioned music and he was hardly ever at home any more.

"His friend Benny's pretty cute," she allowed, "but he's married now and Skippy practically lives over there. Honestly, I hardly ever see him."

Still, there'd been that one time, a couple of years ago, when he'd come home early on a Saturday afternoon, to find his sister sitting cross-legged on his bed, surrounded by three of her obnoxious, adolescent girlfriends, reading aloud from his notebook in stentorian tones of fake *gravitas*:

"…and still I seek/And seeking find/My fingers hold to nothing/My legs are weak/My eyes are blind/The prom queen's disappeared."

It wasn't all as bad as that but it was enough to have the girls in fits of giggles, and Skippy stood in the doorway for just long enough to feel his cheeks burn with anger and humiliation. Wordlessly, he marched towards the bed and grabbed the notebook out of his sister's hand, glaring down at her as if he would hit her if she sat there a moment longer. She wasn't about to wait around for it; immediately she and her friends scrambled down from the bed and stumbled out of the room, and in a moment he heard them, from the safety of her bedroom, burst into the kind of hysterical laughter only young girls or the seriously deranged can manage.

Deliberately, Skippy tore that page from the notebook and ripped it into small pieces. The Prom Queen wasn't a terrible poem — there were others that were worse — but he would never have been able to read it again without hearing it in the mouth of his sister. Most likely they'd read the others, as well, but at least he hadn't been there. He'd been spared the mortification of hearing some of the other, more intimate verses, being recited and parodied in that fashion.

His sister apologized later that evening and his mother, overhearing, took her to task on the importance of respecting another person's privacy and the seriousness of what she had done. Mandy was quite tearful in the end and went to bed early and full of remorse, but it made no difference to Skippy. He was cold and indifferent towards her for the better part of a week and he made sure the notebook was never again left out where it could fall into the wrong hands.

A lesser person might have given up writing poetry altogether but Skippy, after a week or two of resisting the urge, went back to it finally, because there were things he couldn't express any other way. Maybe a lot of what he wrote wasn't very good but it was like anything else, wasn't it? You only got better by doing it, by sticking to it. Surely, if he kept at it, he'd one day write something important, something moving. He even, after a while, relented towards his sister and allowed that she might have done him a sort of favour, in a way. After all, didn't all writers have to deal with criticism? You couldn't be too thin-skinned if you were going to put your most personal thoughts on paper. Somebody, somewhere, was going to make fun of you. It came with the territory.

And so on the afternoon of the twenty-fourth, Skippy dropped by the house on McQuaker Street and handed Margaret a flat, square package wrapped in gold foil and tied with a ribbon. He was suddenly shy, when he gave it to her, and planned to just leave it and go, but Margaret told him to come in, she had something for him, too.

"You didn't have to get me anything," he said, which sounded ungrateful. It was only because he was embarrassed.

She said she knew that: "I wanted to get you something." She handed him his present and said, "It's a book," which he could tell by its shape, and added, "It's by Lawrence Ferlinghetti. I asked Benny and he said this would be good. I hope you like it."

"Thanks," said Skippy. "I won't open it till tomorrow."

"Right. Me neither."

It was ridiculous how awkward the moment was, as they stood in the small dark hallway of the little house, with the radio playing Christmas carols in the background. The exchange of gifts had opened up a space between them where before there had been a solid, unspoken connection. Not sure what to do next, Skippy said he should go, and Margaret asked if he couldn't stay a while longer, Benny was out but he'd be back before supper.

"No, I'd better go. I promised my mom I'd go to my aunt's with her. Family stuff, you know."

Margaret nodded. She and Benny were going to his parents' place the next morning, and were staying there until Boxing Day. "They'll have a tree and turkey and everything," she said, wrapping her arms around her because of the cold air from the doorway. "That's why I haven't bothered. Next year, though, with the baby here, we'll put up our own tree."

She looked down at her stomach and smiled, although when she looked back up at Skippy, he thought she looked tired and a little pale.

"Is it all right?" he asked. "Are you feeling okay?"

"Oh, sure. I guess I'm just looking forward to having it over and done with, if you know what I mean."

He didn't, but he could imagine. She didn't have long now — less than four weeks. It would be strange, he suddenly thought, to see what she looked like when she wasn't carrying a baby inside her. The whole time he'd known her, the whole three months, she'd been pregnant.

"Well," he said, again, "I'd better go."

On an impulse, Margaret leaned forward and kissed him, lightly, on the cheek. "Merry Christmas," she said and gave a quick little laugh. "I hope you like your present."

"Merry Christmas," he responded. "I hope you like yours."

It was a week later, New Year's Eve, when he saw her again. Benny had called the day before and said he had the night off and Skippy should come and spend the evening with them.

"We'll ring in the new year together," he said. "Champagne, paper hats, the whole juliana." That was one of Benny's words for a really great time. He used it like some people used "shebang" or "shindig."

"Come for supper," he added. "Margaret's making something special."

Skippy wanted to ask him if Margaret had liked her present. He wanted to know what she thought of his poems, yet he hesitated to find out. If she thought they were bad, or even mediocre, he wondered how he'd face her afterwards. He was regretting having given them to her in the first place; he should have waited, he should have worked on them some more, made some revisions.

Instead, he asked if Margaret had had a good Christmas, and Benny said, sure, it was great, she'd got lots of stuff for the baby, of course, and even a pretty silk blouse from his mother to wear once she got her figure back. It sounded as though Mrs. Carter had come around, eventually. Like most women, the nearer it got to the birth of the baby, the easier she found it to concentrate on the prospect of a grandchild and forget the circumstances surrounding the conception.

Skippy arrived at the house the following evening around six and found it dark, uninviting. The porch light was out and the curtains were closed and he wondered if somehow he'd made a mistake. Benny had meant tonight, hadn't he? This was New Year's Eve, they were supposed to celebrate together.

He climbed the stairs and knocked on the outside screen door, waited, and knocked again. Finally, a light was turned on and Margaret appeared in the hallway. She opened the inside door and stood there, looking out at him through the screen, as if she was confused: he could swear that she didn't recognize him. Then she said, "Oh. It's you." And let him in.

It was very quiet in the house, although there was a smell of food coming from the kitchen — either they had just eaten, or were getting ready to sit down to dinner.

"Where's Benny?" Skippy asked, taking his boots off and placing them next to each other on the small rubber mat by the door.

"He's not here."

She took his jacket from him and placed it carefully on a hanger and hung it in the closet, slowly and with a certain amount of ceremony, as if the act of hanging up a jacket was unfamiliar and she was not quite sure how to go about it. He followed her into the tiny living room and sat down on the edge of the couch. Was he to stay? Should he apologize for intruding, make excuses and leave? The room was in darkness; Margaret seemed oblivious to it and sat down carefully on the large chair across from him, easing herself into it until her back was supported by the cushions. She moved very slowly these days, she was so big with child, and yet, from behind, you wouldn't have known she was pregnant. Except for that huge tummy billowing out in front, the rest of her was slim and girlish. She had taken to sitting so her hands rested on top of her belly, which was high and full ("It's a boy," she'd told him. "Benny thinks it's a girl but I think he's wrong. His mother told me you always carry high with a boy,") so the effect was almost comical, but serene. Now she said, "I don't think he's coming back."

"Pardon?"

Skippy figured he must have heard wrong and he looked over at her with a smile on his face, as if he knew she was making a joke. She was sitting very still, not looking at him, and he noticed that her hair, which was thick and wavy and usually pinned back off her face, had come out of the white plastic barrettes and was in danger of falling into her eyes. He waited for her to say something, to explain the situation, and when she didn't, Skippy suddenly became aware of his stockinged feet, resting on the oval mat under the coffee table. There was a hole in one of his socks, the right one, where his big toe pushed against it, and now, for some reason, it was all he could think about. Surreptitiously, he began to wiggle his toe, trying to slip it back down through that hole. He felt he should say something but then he thought it was more important to wait, to let her explain what was going on. He didn't want to say the wrong thing.

Eventually, after what seemed like a very long time, Margaret reached her hand up to her hair and carefully placed a stray lock back behind her ear. That seemed to set things in motion again and she turned to Skippy and smiled at him. "Funny, isn't it?" she said, but as soon as she said it, she stopped smiling, as if she heard her words hang in the air and realized how unfunny they sounded.

There did seem to be a difference of some kind in the claustrophobic little house, although Skippy couldn't quite put his finger on it. The TV trays stacked in the corner, the Blue Mountain pottery on the coffee table, they looked now what they were: attempts to achieve a "homey" air carried out by somebody who was too young to really have the knack. How old was she now? Nineteen, almost twenty, younger than Benny although she always seemed older, being female and having that quiet acceptance of things men never got. But she was a kid, really, even the big belly couldn't hide that, too young to be put in charge of another human being, too young to deal with someone as complicated as Benny Carter.

As for Benny, when he thought about it, Skippy discovered he wasn't really surprised that Benny would leave. He'd accepted it all too easily, he'd been too willing to sacrifice his plans and ambitions on the altar of family duty. Skippy wasn't half as wild as Benny but even he would've balked a little, displayed the odd rebellious streak before falling into line and walking the straight and narrow.

As if she'd only just remembered it, Margaret told him she'd made him some dinner. "Wait here," she said. "It's all ready."

With some effort, she pushed herself out of the chair and made her way slowly into the doll-size kitchen, no more than a few feet from where they were sitting. As soon as she left, Skippy reached down and yanked the wool of his sock over his big toe, willing it to stay that way until he got his boots on again. Margaret was opening and closing cupboards, gathering up silverware, getting something out of the oven.

What now? he wondered. If Benny was gone, what did this mean for him? Should he even be there if Benny wasn't? Would she be puzzled to come out of the kitchen and find him still sitting there, on the couch, as if nothing had happened? Maybe he should leave now, while she was out of the room, before he had to offer advice or take control in some way. The thought occurred to him that she might expect him to do something and just thinking that made his heart beat faster and his mouth go dry. Maybe she'd want him to go after Benny, to find him and bring him back. Like the time his younger sister wandered off and his mom was frantic, although she tried not to show it and kept saying, "It's all right, she's somewhere in the neighbourhood, she'll be back," and finally she took hold of him and said, "Skippy, you know where she goes, you know her hiding places, you go find her now. Go on" (her fear making her voice harsher than she intended) and Skippy headed out the back yard and down the lane towards the gray brick school building, not knowing where he was headed but with this awful cold lump of responsibility in his chest. He never did find her; late in the afternoon a police car arrived in front of the house with his sister in the back, eating a Fudgsicle and full of herself for being the centre of attention of the whole neighbourhood. And now here was his best friend's wife about to issue the same command and he'd have to put on his boots and his jacket and head off into the cold on New Year's Eve with no real idea where to look but hoping that Benny, too, would just turn up, if they waited long enough.

Margaret came back into the room and set a plate and a knife and fork down on the table in front of him. "You must be starving," she said, and then, almost formally, "Will you excuse me?"

With that, she turned and left the room. He heard her heavy footsteps on the old wooden staircase — after a moment, there was the sound of her bedroom door shutting. Skippy waited and then, because he couldn't decide what else to do, picked up his knife and fork and began to eat. She had placed two pork chops — grilled, not fried — on his plate, next to a baked potato, sliced open and slathered with butter and sour cream. And a serving of creamed corn, his favourite. She must have made this just for him. Benny hated creamed corn, she never served it when he was around. So she had planned this meal for him, knowing Benny wasn't going to be there and he had to eat it now, all of it, although his mouth was so dry he could hardly swallow and everything tasted like sawdust. When he was done, he took his plate, knife and fork into the kitchen and rinsed them in the sink, setting them in the rack to dry. Then he wiped his hands on the tea towel — "Home Sweet Home" was printed along the top and the bottom, in colourful letters — and hung it, folded in half, over the handle of the refrigerator. He came out of the kitchen and stood at the bottom of the stairs.

"Margaret?" he called.

There was no answer. After a moment, he climbed the stairs, moving noiselessly, as if he were in a house where some great sorrow had taken place. When he reached the landing, he hesitated for just a moment, then knocked on the door of her bedroom.

There was no answer so Skippy called her name again and waited a moment before trying the handle of the door. It turned and the door swung open and he stood there for a moment, his eyes adjusting to the darkness of the room.

"Margaret? Are you sleeping?"

After a minute he saw that she was curled up on the bed, her back to the door, a blanket pulled over her so only the back of her head was showing. She didn't move, didn't answer him, but some-how he knew she was awake. He approached the bed, his feet making no noise on the carpet, and wondered if she'd even heard him enter. When he got to the bed, he stood at the far side and whispered, "Margaret, are you okay? Can I do something?"

With an effort she turned over and faced him; the room was too dark to see much, but the light from the hallway reflected in her eyes. He felt, looking down on her, much as he had years ago when an uncle, wanting to make a man of the poor, fatherless kid, had taken him out hunting one fall. Skippy had brought down a young deer and standing over the fallen animal he felt a terrible regretful sadness. Right now he had that same sorrowful feeling and it made him kneel down beside the bed and take hold of her hand. It was cold, the room was cold and as he got used to the dark he saw what a small, sad room it was, with only a bed and small brown chair by the window, where she'd thrown her dress and her nylon stockings.

Skippy stroked her hand. "Can I do something, Margaret? Tell me, what can I do, how can I help?"

After a moment she said it again, "He's not coming back, Skippy," and then she started to cry and he realized by the way she said it and the way her eyes were puffy and sore looking, she'd been crying up here for a long time, probably the whole time he was downstairs in the living room eating the meal she'd made. This made him feel awful, to think of how he ate it all up like some kind of greedy pig while she lay here in bed crying her eyes out. And he wanted to make it up to her but most of all he wanted to find a way to get her not to cry.

"Don't cry, Margaret," and he stroked her poor cold hand, "it's okay, he'll be back," and as he said it he believed it, for some reason, and that belief must have communicated itself to her because she did stop crying and when she said, "Do you really think so?" she sounded more hopeful than before.

Skippy leaned towards her and suddenly he was convinced he was right and he was eager to make her see that Benny, his buddy, his very best friend, would be back, he'd do the right thing, he wouldn't just abandon the two of them like this, he was a good guy, honest he was. And she reached out with her other hand and patted his face. Then, in a voice that sounded shy, she told him she had liked his poems. "I thought they were wonderful, Skippy. Especially the one about — the one at the end of the book. I liked that so much."

Madonna-in-Waiting, he'd called it, writing about Margaret, the way she moved with a heavy grace, the soft roundness of her face, her hands. The way everything about her, every inch of her, was pure, unspoiled, untainted. He had even (and it embarrassed him, a little, to remember this) speculated on what her body must look like under the folds of her maternity dresses, those great unwieldy costumes designed to hide the perfection of her pregnant form.

In a soft, almost teasing voice, she said, "You've immortalized me, Skippy. You've made me famous."

Then, suddenly, he heard her gasp, and she turned her head away from him, her shoulders heaving, and he realized she was crying, harsh, painful sobs as if she was unwilling to be seen like this, to be laid bare before him in this way.

So it was partly just to comfort her but also because she had run her fingers along his cheek and said she'd liked his poems, that Skippy just naturally slipped into bed beside her and put his arms around her and began stroking her back and her big round tummy and her breasts. And she let him; she stopped crying and pushed her body close to him and they fit together in spite of her being so pregnant and Skippy found that he knew exactly what to do without even thinking about it. If he had stopped to think about it, it wouldn't have happened: she was Benny's wife and she loved him and wanted him back and he was Benny's best friend and he wouldn't for the world do anything to hurt him. But there was no stopping and no thinking, only this huge desire to come together and when she took hold of him and showed him how to enter her from behind, it was all so smooth and so perfectly encompassing that there was no room for any small, still voice to say, "Now, look, Skippy, maybe this isn't such a good idea."

Afterwards, they lay there for some time, not moving, his head resting on the smooth, warm skin of her back. He was sweating, they both were, although after a while he began to feel the chill of the room once more. Slowly he pulled himself away from her and reached for the blanket which had been shoved to the bottom of the bed. He drew it over the two of them and lay there for a little longer, marveling at the ease with which it had happened. He wondered if he should say something; what did people to say to each other once it was over? He knew in the movies they often shared a smoke. He didn't smoke and neither did she. Maybe he should ask if she wanted something to eat. Just to be polite.

"Margaret?"

There was no answer and, bending his head next to hers, he heard the gentle, rhythmic breathing that told him she was asleep. Or pretending to be. Carefully he sat up and swung his legs on to the floor. He found his pants, abandoned on a heap on the carpet, and left the room quietly, his shirt unbuttoned, and dressed out in the hall.

He opened the door and something large and furry brushed past him — Cassady the cat, home from cruising the neigbourhood. Outside it was cold and clear; the snow sparkled like miniature crystals under the street lights. A couple hurried past on the other side of the street, their arms linked, their heads down against the cold, laughing in the cool night air. Skippy pulled the zipper of his jacket up to his chin and told himself everything would be fine: Benny would come back and Margaret would have the baby and Skippy could go back to joining them for dinner and staying late to talk when Benny had left for work. It would all work out. It had to.

5.

Afterwards, when Skippy tried to work out just what had gone wrong between him and Benny, between Benny and Margaret, between Margaret and himself, he thought of it as a giant misunderstanding. He had never meant to get into bed with Benny's wife, he'd planned to call the next day, see how she was, make sure Benny had come back. And yet when he woke the next morning — early afternoon, actually, he had slept for hours and it was close to one in the afternoon when he finally got out of bed — it was as if some undefinable lethargy had overtaken him. He couldn't make himself go to the phone, couldn't pick it up and call Margaret, couldn't face hearing Benny's voice on the other end of the line.

And so he thought he might wait after all, give them a chance to kiss and make up, be sure that whatever unpleasantness had been stirred up between them had an opportunity to smooth itself out, the way things did if you waited a little. He didn't call New Year's Day or the next and by the end of the week he'd found another job working for the old man who ran the hardware store downtown and that filled his days. He spent his nights at home in front of the television set, watching the Dating Game and drinking colas. He didn't do any writing; he didn't feel like reading. His mother came into the room and asked him what was the matter, why didn't he go visit Benny and Margaret? Isn't her baby due soon? she wondered; why don't you go see how they're doing?

"I don't want to bother them," was his reply and his mother knew there was more to it than that but she let it go. What could you do when your children were practically grown? They had to work things out for themselves.

Skippy thought of Margaret and he began to be afraid that something terrible had happened. Had he done something to the baby? She was so close to giving birth, was it possible he had done something terrible by being with her like that? He wanted to know but he couldn't, there was no way to find out, and then at the end of the week the telephone rang and it was Benny's mother telling his own mother that Margaret had given birth to a baby girl, seven pounds, two ounces, and they were calling her Katherine. She had gone into labour on New Year's Day, two weeks early, but the baby was healthy and Margaret was well and wasn't it astonishing that she, a woman of not even fifty, was a grandmother? Wasn't it wonderful?

Skippy's mom said that Mrs. Carter sounded happy — "ecstatic", was the word she used, and wasn't it glorious how everything had turned out for the best after all? It just went to show you, she said, that the good Lord worked in mysterious ways and He generally had a plan for just about everything. (Skippy's mom was going through one of her religious phases again, but Skippy had told her he was a Buddhist now and, to his surprise, she seemed to accept that and didn't push him to come to church with her. As for his sister, she just dug in her heels and flat-out refused to have anything to do with religion, so her mother was on her own in this one.)

"You'll have to go see the baby," his mother said. "She'll be home from the hospital on Saturday. Take her some flowers, why don't you? People always bring something for the baby, everybody forgets about the mother and she's the one who's done all the work."

But Skippy did not go to see little Katherine, although he did think he would, one of these days. Seeing the baby would mean coming face-to-face with Margaret for the first time since — well, since it had happened, and he did not think he could do that. And there was Benny, of course. Things weren't right between them; Benny hadn't called or dropped over to the house even once since Margaret had had the baby. And it had been Benny's mother who had phoned with the news about the baby, not Benny himself. Not Margaret. If they wanted to see him, surely one of them would have picked up the phone, given him a call, told him to come over, come and have supper, what was he waiting for — an engraved invitation? But they hadn't called and with each day that he got up, went into work in the hardware store, came home and watched TV, his own ability to make the first move retreated further and further into the distance. And after a while the time to call disappeared completely and he began to face the fact that Benny Carter and Margaret, who was his wife and had been, for one brief night, Skippy's lover, were no longer part of his life. And when he realized that, when it hit him in just that way, he felt like a door somewhere had shut. He could almost hear it closing in the back of his head.

Over the next year Skippy ran into Benny on two occasions, by accident, at Billy Dee's record store. Each time they smiled and said, too quickly, their smiles too eager, Hi, how's it going? Good, great, how's it going with you? Good, great. That's great. And then one or the other of them remembered something he had to do, some place he had to be, and it was, Well, gotta go, be seeing you. Yeah, be seeing you. Yeah, right. Skippy never asked about Margaret or the baby and Benny never volunteered any information. Two acquaintances, that's what they were, who shared an interest in music. That's all.

Once, on a Sunday afternoon in July, Skippy got on the bus, number one-fifty-three, and rode past the Chinese grocery at the corner of McQuaker Street. Leaning forward, he could see the small brown frame house six doors down. The old wicker sofa was gone and a baby carriage had been carried up the front steps and left outside on the porch. Someone — Benny, most likely — had painted the trim around the windows and the door, but it was the addition of that baby carriage that made the difference, that showed Skippy things had changed, life in that familiar little house had gone on without him.

The bus pulled away from the stop and Skippy leaned back in his seat, disappointed. He'd been hoping for — what? A glimpse, perhaps, of Margaret, pushing the baby in the carriage down the sidewalk? Benny himself, all long legs and tanned arms extruding from his shirt sleeves, swinging towards him? It had been a mistake to do this, he thought; he wouldn't come by here again.

The winter of '63-'64 was a cold one — it set records for overnight lows the entire month of January. Skippy took the bus into work each morning and travelled downtown with the windows painted in thick layers of frost. It was too cold to go anywhere, do anything, and the hardware store received very few customers. Only the desperate, or the fanatical do-it-yourselfer, was willing to brave the chill northern winds in search of a screwdriver or a half dozen sheets of eighty-grit sandpaper. If it had been a regular kind of business, Skippy would have been laid off, but the old man who ran the place liked him and had known his father years ago. He kept him on, if only to have some company around the place.

The middle of the afternoon, between one and four, tended to be the "dead" time at the store; the door did not open, the phone didn't ring, and there really wasn't anything to do. When Skippy had first started working there he'd made an attempt to bring the display in the front window up-to-date, removing the old, yellowing copies of *Popular Mechanics* and brushing away decades of accumulated grime and dead flies. But the old man was against it; his customers had been coming to him for more than thirty years and they liked things to look familiar and if it was all right by his customers then it was all right by him. On the other hand, he was perfectly happy to let Skippy spend his afternoons sitting behind the counter, gazing into the still, lethargic dimness and letting his thoughts wander. He got into the habit of bringing a book to the store, for these periods, and it was while he was sitting back in the old man's swivel chair, leafing through *A Coney Island of the Mind*, which was the book of Ferlinghetti poems that Margaret had given him for Christmas the year before, that he got his big idea.

It didn't arrive full-fledged, like a bolt of lightning or a door suddenly swinging open, the way you often hear of great ideas appearing. Instead, it showed itself in bits and pieces, with first one aspect and then another entering Skippy's mind and saying, Well, why not? His first thought was, Why not open a book store? Ferlinghetti's City Lights book store and publishing house was what gave him the idea, a place where avant garde writers and dissident intellectuals could gather and share their ideas on poetry and politics and the meaning of life. But opening a book store would require an outlay of cash — he'd have to buy the books and rent store space and hire someone to do the accounts. He wasn't ready for it and he didn't have the money. And he wasn't one hundred per cent convinced that Cambrian Bay was a hotbed of radicals and dissident intellectuals. Still, he wanted some kind of place where he could talk about the kinds of things he and Benny had discussed back in high school, maybe even listen to music. A restaurant, maybe, although he knew nothing about food and had never learned how to cook.

It was the late night television news that provided the answer and when he saw it he knew that was what he wanted to do. The local television station had started a new feature, squeezed in between the final story on city council and the sports and weather. It was called "What's New?" and it was three or four minutes about something taking place in some far-away city like Toronto or Montreal or even Vancouver. On the night of February the twenty-fifth, nineteen sixty-four (he'd never forget it — it was the night one Cassius Marcellus Clay beat Sonny Liston and walked away as the new heavyweight champion of the world), the feature homed in on New

York City. Skippy was watching it with the sound off, waiting to see
if the late night sports would show something of the fight.

(He'd heard it earlier on the radio, had listened to the match,
fully expecting Liston to put this upstart in his place. This preening
young peacock of a fighter who hung out with strange, unsportsman-
like people like Malcolm X, he didn't seem to understand he was in
the presence of a champ. Dancing, hopping up and down and always
just out of range of Liston's powerful left hook, Clay was careful
not to let the big bear lay a glove on him. And then the beginning of
the seventh round and Liston wouldn't fight any more — his left
shoulder messed up and one eye bleeding, the announcer said he
wouldn't come out of his corner and Clay was crowing: "I am so
pretty!" Skippy saw it later, several times, the champ, the new
champ, dancing up and down, and Liston just sitting there, not
speaking, sweat standing out in thick white drops on his black face,
looking so much older than Clay, so much sadder. Oh, it was sad,
but he really was so pretty. It was art, was what it was, and Skippy
never forgot it.)

Now, waiting for the sportscast, the New York skyline came into
view and Skippy leaned forward and turned the sound up a little, not
wanting to wake up his mother. They were showing the Lower East
Side and the announcer was describing the tourists who haunted the
clubs where Allen Ginsberg and the other "beatniks" had declaimed
poetry for a few short years in the nineteen-fifties. Watching the
would-be hip cats nodding in the smoky darkness, it came to Skippy
that he could create a piece of the Village, a little piece of New York,
here in his own home town. He, Skippy Jacques, would open a coffee
house and, in so doing, would help to spread the word of the beat
poets and protest singers. He would bring about *satori* — enlightenment — to the inhabitants of the frigid north.

The name of the club, which came to him even before he found
a site for the club itself, was the Dharma Cafe and Coffee House and
when it was pointed out to Skippy by his mother that a cafe and a
coffee house were one and the same, he afterwards referred to it
simply as the club.

Fired with a sense of mission, Skippy prowled the back streets
of town and found he could rent the basement of an old, practically
derelict church just over the east end bridge. On alternate Saturday
nights it was used by the Ladies of Prosvita Bingo Society but they
were more than willing to have him decorate it any way he chose,
so long as he kept it "nice and respectable looking," the chairlady
told him. "None of those peace signs or writing dirty on the walls."
Skippy bought some dark black matte paint and hired a couple of

high school kids to paint the entire place one Saturday afternoon. He bought up a couple dozen small tables and stools from a liquidation warehouse and covered them with red checked tablecloths, a Chianti bottle with a candle stuck in resting on each table. Travel posters on the walls — blue and white photos of Greek islands, a shot of the Golden Gate Bridge, New York city at night. A musician he'd met who lived in the area helped him to set up a sound system and a small stage and he was set. Now there was nothing left to do except book a couple of the numerous folk groups plying their trade along the north shore, put an ad in the paper and sit back and let the money roll in.

Except it didn't, at first. Skippy spent the better part of three weeks sitting by himself in the dim church basement, the fridge full of Coca Cola whirring in the background. He was beginning to feel like the Maytag repairman. The church caretaker came down one night, an old Chinese man named Charlie Lee, and he looked around at the empty tables and the posters on the wall and told Skippy what he needed was bait.

"Like catching a fish," he explained. "You put a worm on the hook and all the little fish come to taste and bingo —" He snapped his fingers, and smiled. "You got a boat full of fishes."

Of course, Skippy thought. If he wanted the hip, cool kids to come down to the club, he needed some hip, cool kids there already. And it just so happened that he had access to one of those kids, right at his fingertips.

His sister, Mandy, was too cool to live, as his mother liked to put it. She slouched around the house in paper-white lipstick and Maybelline Thick Lash mascara, her slim figure draped in a poor boy sweater and mini skirt, her expression one of terminal boredom and contempt. She was young enough and pretty enough to make it work and the telephone never stopped ringing. If Skippy could convince Mandy and a few of her girlfriends to come and work at the cafe, the other kids would turn out like flies on a dead pickerel.

It wasn't easy but Skippy played it smart. It was important, he knew, not to come on too strong, singing the praises of the cafe, offering her good money to work there, making it sound like heaven on earth. This, after all, was the sixties; there was no way a smart young thing like Mandy was going to jump at the chance to be a waitress. And give up her Friday nights to do it? You've got to be kidding.

So Skippy sat down beside her after work one evening and pulled a book out of his back pocket.

"Here," he said, "I've been meaning to give this to you for ages.

I thought you might like to read it, if you haven't already."

In a desultory fashion, Mandy turned the book over and looked at the cover: "The Dharma Bums," by Jack Kerouac.

"You didn't read it yet, did you?" It was all part of the act, of course. Mandy had never in her life read an entire book from cover to cover unless some teacher had required it, and then she was just as likely to resort to Cole's Notes. He knew she'd probably never heard of Kerouac.

"No," she said, "not this one."

"Very cool stuff. Very heavy sort of guy. The chicks in the Village, they all dig him."

"The Village?" There was a flicker of what might almost have been interpreted as interest in her voice, and Skippy hurried to explain.

"Yeah, you know — New York City, the Lower East Side, SoHo. That sort of thing. It's where the really cool people hang out."

"Really? Well, thanks Skippy."

"It's okay. Glad to do it."

They sat for a few more minutes, Skippy apparently absorbed in the television program, Mandy leafing casually through the first few pages of the book. It was Skippy, again, who broke the silence.

"King of the beats."

Mandy looked up. "What?"

"Kerouac. The guy who wrote that. That's what they call him. Number one man for the beat generation. You've heard of beatniks, haven't you?"

She nodded. "Oh, sure. They wear black clothing and the men all have beards. And they write poetry."

"We-e-ell." Skippy stared up at the ceiling and thought how best to explain the complexities of beat subculture. "That's the general idea, I guess. A lot of them do look like that. But that stuff's just on top. Down deep, these poets are complicated and dark and nobody's really supposed to understand what they're saying. They believe in love and life and the spirit and they reject bourgeois materialism."

Mandy returned to her book, pleased in spite of herself that her older brother was finally treating her like an adult, instead of some annoying wart on the back of his hand. Suddenly, Skippy opened his mouth and proclaimed, in a loud, sonorous voice, completely unlike himself:

"I saw the best minds of my generation/starving, hysterical, naked,/dragging themselves through the negro streets/at dawn looking for an angry fix."

Closing his eyes and leaning back against the couch, Skippy

sighed, "Now that is poetry."

"That's by what's-his-name? Kerouac?"

"No, that's Ginsberg. He's a queer but he can write. Man, can he write," and Skippy shook his head with the wonder of it all. After a moment, he continued:

"Actually, I'm thinking of getting him up here. To the club, you know?"

"Who, Ginsberg?"

"Yeah, him or Kerouac or one of those guys. It's exactly the kind of place they like, good atmosphere, cool cats, groovy chicks. Although, I'm not sure but I think Kerouac's living in Florida. He's a little out of it now, out of the thick of things. Drinks too much." He shook his head, gravely. "A scary thing, what liquor can do to your brain, even a brain the size of his. But New York's full of beatniks. The streets are crawling with them."

Mandy was looking a little skeptical. "Do you really think they'd come all the way up here?"

"Are you kidding? It's right up their alley. They'll want to come and spread the word, travel to new places, seek enlightenment. No problem. They'll be here with bells on."

"Neat."

"Very neat," Skippy agreed. "I tell you, Mandy, in six months the Dharma club will be the hippest place to be in this town. In this country, practically. I swear it."

He frowned. "There's only one thing."

"What's that?"

"A place like the Dharma, you have to have very special people working there, very cool chicks. A cat like Kerouac, he can sniff a phony a mile away. He walks into the Dharma, he has to see right away that it's a cool place by the cool people working there. And where do I find chicks like that? That's the question, Mandy. That's the sixty-four thousand dollar question."

He paused, to give his sister time to consider. When, a few moments later, she suggested that maybe *she* might be interested in working at the club — just a couple of hours a night, you know, and only if she turned out to like it — he nodded thoughtfully, and agreed that that might be a possibility, she might be able to handle it, but then, she was only one person, he needed at least three or four girls like her who were just as hip, just as good-looking.

"Oh, that's easy," Mandy said. "If I do it, all my friends will want to. We know everybody who's anybody at school. I could line up a dozen girls in no time."

Again, Skippy frowned, staring down at the braided oval rug.

"I don't know," he said. "I was thinking of someone more experienced. I never thought of asking you and your friends to do it."

"Well, think of it." By this time Mandy was sitting up straight on the couch, and her eyes were shining with excitement. "We could wear black turtlenecks and miniskirts and black tights, and the college guys would all come and it would be so neat. Come on, Skippy, let us do it. It'd be such a blast."

Skippy gave in, and they shook hands on it, and Mandy gave his arm a quick, shy squeeze. "You know, Skippy," she told him, "I'm kind of surprised. I never knew you knew all that stuff, about beatniks and New York and all that. Who told you all that stuff?"

Benny, he wanted to say, but he didn't. Instead he smiled in what he hoped was a mysterious, worldly-wise manner.

"There's lots about me you don't know, Mandy. There's lots most people don't know."

The bait worked. Mandy and her girlfriends drew in the others and the word spread and the Dharma Cafe began to fill up every weekend. Of course, within a few weeks the novelty wore off for Mandy and her friends and they decided that, cool or not, waiting on tables was still waiting on tables, and they quit, but by that time Skippy had another three or four young girls waiting their turn to work there. He was philosophical about the defections; this was business, people came and went, and they were always replaceable.

He did try for Kerouac; he went so far as to send off a letter on club stationery he had specially made up to the book's publishers, asking them to pass his request along to the man, but he never got a reply. He had better luck with Ginsberg — from the poet he received a letter, short and to the point and forwarded on from San Francisco, thanking him for the offer but explaining that, due to previous commitments, he couldn't see his way to making a trip north for several years. Skippy framed the letter and put it in a place of honour just over the coffee machine. But many lesser lights did come to the Dharma, to sing, play the guitar, read poetry. Night after night the club was filled with the sounds of protest songs, Peruvian love songs, workers' songs from the 1930's.

The Dharma was open five nights a week, from Thursday through Monday. The young kids, Mandy's friends from high school, they came on Friday and Saturday, but Sundays it was an older crowd — university students who often brought their own guitars and jammed into the small hours. They made a pet of Skippy, this odd little guy who ran the place. As a regular thing he would have been outside their notice; as the owner of the Dharma they played up to him, called out to him to come sit at their tables, argued with each other over who knew him best. Myths sprang up around him: he'd been a pool shark traveling around the midwest who'd burned the wrong guy and had to hide out in Northern Ontario. He had a wife and kids but she'd run off with another guy and he supported the kids in style somewhere, living with relatives. He had dealings with the Mafia. The kids got it into their heads that the Dharma was making money hand over fist and they figured the local hoods would be wanting their share. In fact, Skippy just scraped by, his wages from the hardware store often going to pay the rent on the club or the fee for a folk trio from Windsor.

But Skippy kept his own counsel. He sat with the college kids and nodded to the music, frowned into the darkness when poets read their work, clapped approvingly when a cat came up with an especially cool line or phrase. But if there were secrets inside him, they were staying there, he was owning up to nothing. From time to time other oddball characters visited the club, standing out among the university kids with their greased-back hair and shiny suits. But they were as likely to be car mechanics as hoods and they never stayed long enough to give much away.

The hardest part in running the club was finding new groups to replenish the weekly line-up. He scoured the Toronto papers for names of acts like "The Tradewinds", "Molly and Mike", "We Are Three", small acoustic groups who performed songs by Pete Seeger and Woody Guthrie. He was amazed at the response these acts got from the kids who came to the club; personally, Skippy had difficulty telling them apart — the girls all had long dark hair and too much eye makeup, wore shapeless, sleeveless dresses and big hoop ear-rings, their bare feet in sandals, even in the winter; the boys were generally tall and hungry-looking and favoured Irish fishermen's sweaters, and if you've heard one version of "Follow the Drinking Gourd", you've heard them all. But the kids ate it up, joining in on the choruses, clapping their hands to the music and demanding encores of "Hava Nagila". And they were good audiences; for many of these groups, fresh from playing the hotel-motel circuit along the north shore, an audience that actually sat and listened to the songs was a gift from heaven.

The club opened at eight each evening and closed at midnight and then it took another hour to clear everybody out, chat with the performers, help the girls wipe down the tables and stack the chairs. By the time Skippy locked up, it was usually one o'clock in the morning and he'd stop in at the all-night restaurant on the other side of the bridge for a coffee and a toasted Denver sandwich and then put in a call to the cab company to take him home to sleep.

For the rest of the winter that was his routine — five nights a week he was down at the Dharma Cafe, listening to groups, mingling with the kids, seeing that everything was in order. If he was lonely, he was no more so than he had been for years. And if he sometimes thought of Benny Carter and wished he would come in one night and sit at a table near the back and order a coffee or a soft drink, he tried not to dwell on it. This was exactly the sort of place Benny would have loved. He would have been proud of Skippy for coming up with the idea, for carrying on the tradition they'd started back in high school. With Benny occupying a table every night or even a couple of nights a week, Skippy Jacques' cup would have been full. But Benny was unavailable these days and Skippy had no one to blame but himself.

6.

Two great changes occurred in Skippy's life in the summer of '64: he moved out of the house and he fell in love. They were unconnected, of course, but equally unexpected and devastating in their own way.

The first came about because his mother got married. This was an event which Skippy could never have foreseen, that his mother, at the advanced age of forty-three, would meet a man she liked well enough — loved, even, although that was hard to imagine — to take the plunge and get married. Not that anyone would ever replace Maurice. He'd been her first love and they'd been young together. The night she received the marriage proposal, she lay in her bed and thought of Maurice and cried to think that by remarrying she would give up his name. It seemed disloyal, somehow, and she spoke to his picture in the darkness, explaining how things were now and how she thought that, with the children being older and not needing her so much anymore, it was time to get on with her life. It was all true, it made sense, but when she got up the following morning she thought she detected a look of disapproval in her dead husband's eyes that surely had not been there before.

Her suitor's name was Joe Bruno and he looked like a Joe, Skippy thought, a big, heavyset Italian guy with a bit of a gut but still pretty good-looking, for an old guy. He was almost fifty and he worked in construction, although Skippy's mother was quick to point out that he owned his own company, with ten other guys working for him, and he owned his own house outright. She'd met him through Irene, her friend from work, who'd been cousins with Joe's first wife and had spent many afternoons at their house when Betty — the first wife — got sick, and had brought food over and washed up the dishes and generally made herself helpful. Betty had had liver disease (which was genetic, Skippy's mother explained; she'd never touched a drop of liquour) and she'd taken a long time to die — almost a year.

It had been very hard on Joe, his mother said. He'd taken it badly, had started drinking heavily in the evenings, sitting alone in the huge living room with its Danish modern furniture, downing rye whisky like there was no tomorrow. They'd never had any kids, he and Betty; something to do with Betty's "condition", as his mother put it, and now and then one or another of his buddies would drop in to spend some time with him and go home shaking their heads over the sadness of it all, this lonely man, still young, still healthy, drinking himself into oblivion, with his wife dying there in the bedroom. Once Joe had stayed late at the Legion, drinking until closing time, and got into a car accident on the way home but thank God no serious damage had been done, Skippy's mother said. It was a miracle.

Anyway, Betty eventually was taken to the hospital and died three days later and Joe Bruno drank more than ever and then one day just up and checked himself into the Brown Clinic, a detox centre up by the sanitarium. He stayed there two weeks, joined AA, and came out of the experience a new man. And a Christian. It was this fact, more than anything, that convinced Skippy's mother to marry him.

And so, early in July, on a blistering-hot Friday afternoon that would have been unbearable were it not for the light breeze blowing in off the lake, Skippy attended his mother's wedding. He stood beside her and gave her away and Mandy, who was exposed as a closet romantic, wore a long skirt made of some gauzy material and flecked with tiny yellow flowers and showered the couple with confetti on the steps outside the church.

"Isn't it cool?" she beamed, as she and Skippy and Irene and her son Norman — who at nineteen was not quite as dreadful as ever, although he did show an alarming tendency to favour pink top coats and still spoke with a lisp — stood on the sidewalk, watching her mother and her brand-new step-father drive away in Joe's shining

'64 Buick. They were heading east, for Niagara Falls, where they would stay in a hotel overlooking the falls and do, as Mandy put it, the whole honeymoon thing, which she described as "just too cute for words. I mean, at *their* age."

Afterwards, they were driving to Toronto where they'd leave the car and fly to Naples, Italy, to visit Joe's relatives and take a cruise around the Mediterranean. Neither, as it turned out, had ever had a proper honeymoon in their previous marriages: there hadn't been time for Skippy's parents with his father being shipped off to fight overseas, and Joe and Betty had simply been too poor. Joe Bruno had always planned that, one of these days, when things at work slowed down a bit, he'd take some time off and the two of them would go on a cruise or something, treat themselves to the kind of holiday you read about all the time. But work never seemed to slow down and then Betty got sick and now, of course, it was too late. So he and Skippy's mother would take the dream holiday themselves, and they were both certain that Betty Bruno would be looking down from her special place in heaven, nodding with approval that these two people had found happiness and each other. (Skippy's mother liked to think that Maurice Jacques was in a similar position, but she couldn't be absolutely sure; he'd not lived a particularly Christian sort of life but surely the good Lord would forgive the minor indiscretions of an unhappy young man and grant him a place in His kingdom. She hoped so, anyway; she didn't like to think of herself going around being so happy if poor Maurice wasn't.)

As much as Skippy was resigned to his mother's new life, it did present some problems for himself. For one thing, where was he going to live? Joe assumed they would all move into his house, the one he'd shared with Betty, and although Skippy's mother hesitated at the thought of taking over another woman's territory, it seemed to make sense in the long run. His house, after all, was beautiful; he'd designed it himself with every modern convenience — there was even an ensuite bathroom with a sunken marble bathtub. Her desire for such touches of luxury struggled with her determination to be above such worldly attachments, but still — a marble bathtub!

And because he'd built it himself, Joe felt an attachment to that house which was perfectly natural. It was roomy, as well, and Mandy was ecstatic about the large bedroom she'd inhabit, with a walk-in closet and her very own bathroom.

"Come on, Mom, you can't say no," Mandy insisted. "I could have parties there and everything. My friends would just die."

So the decision was made: upon their return from their honeymoon, they would move into Joe's house, and the other, the one Skippy and Mandy had grown up in, would be put up for sale.

Skippy couldn't see himself making the move. He liked Joe well enough, although, as is the way with the newly-converted, his mother's new husband was a bit of a fanatic about going to church and not drinking and all that. He'd expect his stepson to toe the line and he probably wouldn't take kindly to Skippy's recently acquired habit of pouring himself a vodka and tonic when he came home from the hardware store each night.

More than that, though, was the fact that he didn't want to be seen as a "mooch", sponging off his new step-father. Joe Bruno had strong opinions on moochers, a classification that included welfare bums, single parents and the steadily growing numbers of construction workers who faked back injuries to get out of doing a decent day's work. In his mind, college students were right up there with the spongers of the century. He had nothing against education, mind you — he was all for kids learning to read and write and you sure couldn't run a business if you didn't understand math — but any healthy, able-bodied young man who stayed in school past grade twelve had better have a damn good reason. A fellow who was old enough to drink, old enough to vote and with too much time on his hands was just looking to get into trouble. Which made him particularly suspicious of the Dharma club, not that he'd ever been inside. From what he'd heard, it was the kind of place where layabouts hung out, Commies, even. As he said to Skippy's mother, "I've nothing against your boy, Jean, he seems like a pretty good kid. But he's hanging around with those beatniks when he should be out doing normal, healthy stuff like dating girls and playing softball. The devil finds mischief for idle hands."

Skippy laughed when Mandy related the above conversation to him, especially the softball part. Had Joe not noticed that his stepson came equipped with a limp? He was hardly Dodgers material. Still, he'd be twenty-one in October — it was time to move out. The question was, where?

While Joe and his mother were over in Europe, Skippy spent his spare time looking through the want ads under "Apartments for Rent." There weren't many and the few he called up about didn't sound promising. Most were located in damp basements, where rules were strict concerning female guests and pets. (Skippy had never thought about getting a pet but he hated to think he'd never be allowed to have one; as for the female guests, well, as Benny would have said, that was a moot point.) Lack of availability made for high rents, and in most cases cooking facilities consisted of a hot plate and a kettle. Only once did he actually make an appointment to go and see one of these places and the landlady laid down so many rules about smoking, cleanliness and what she referred to as "visitors", Skippy just made some noncommittal remark about having to think about it, thanked her and left.

What he settled on, in the end, was a boardinghouse located in the east end of town, only three blocks from the church that housed his club. It was a nicely-kept, three-storey building, shielded by lilac trees and buckets of geraniums in the front yard and an enormous vegetable garden in the back. Here he would receive a nourishing breakfast before leaving for work each morning and a hot supper at night. There was a television in the front room where boarders, or "guests" as the landlady preferred to describe them, were welcome to sit after supper, and an electric heater available should anyone be feeling the cold. Laundry was extra, as were services such as making up the bed or changing the sheets. The landlady had nothing against pets as long as they were small and well-behaved, and guests were welcome to smoke in the front room and even drink if they wished, within reason, of course. She herself indulged in a small glass of blackberry cordial in the evening when the dishes were done. Female visitors, like everywhere else, were not permitted above the first floor, but as Skippy couldn't imagine this becoming an issue, he felt he'd found the perfect home away from home. It would be like living at his mother's house, in a way, with the added benefit that if he wished to spend the evening in his room, reading, nobody would question his right to do so. Or ask him to put out the garbage.

Skippy explained to his new landlady that he ran a coffee-house nearby and she nodded. Oh, yes, she'd heard about it, she played bingo down at the church twice a month and while some of the ladies had worried about the noise and the possibility of drinking — "or worse" — they had generally come to the conclusion that the club was a good thing and its patrons were harmless. Although she wasn't so sure about the colour he'd chosen for the walls.

"Black," she said, folding her arms under her sizable bosom, "I don't know, black is maybe not so good for a church, you know?"

Skippy pointed out that it was no longer a church and she shook her head. She disagreed. "A place that's built for a church, it's always got God in it. The people can leave, but God, He sticks around."

And so by the time Jean and Joe Bruno returned from their honeymoon cruise, Skippy had moved into Mrs. Cordelli's board-ing-house, along with his boxes of books and records and the portable record-player his mother had given him years ago. He had a trunk that had belonged to his father which held his shirts and socks and underwear and a framed photograph of Maurice when he was Skippy's age, in his army uniform, standing at ease, his legs apart, his hands behind his back. Taken somewhere in England, his mother had told him, and he looked relaxed and optimistic, as well he might: wasn't this crazy old war just created for young men like him, to give them a chance to earn their stripes, to show what they were made of? It was like this that Skippy always thought of his father although the truth was that Maurice Jacques never looked as happy or content again, once the war was over.

When he left Mrs. Cordelli's house the first time, having agreed upon the rent and accepted her offer of washing and ironing every other week (he'd do his own cleaning; he didn't relish the idea of somebody snooping around in his things), he stopped in at the hardware store and bought himself one of the novelty key rings they'd got in last week. It was in the shape of a musical note and he needed it to hold the two keys she had given him — one to the outside door of the house, and one that was just to his room. With these keys, plus the large skeleton key which gave him access to the church basement, Skippy felt he'd established himself. He was substantial, now, he had a place in the world.

The first night that Skippy spent in his new home, he lay in the bed with its clean white sheets and stared out of the window at the sky. This part of town was darker than the newer section, there weren't so many street lights and the stars were more visible overhead. They made him feel lonely, somehow, as if they were reminding him, with their cold, distant light, that he was a tiny, insignificant speck in an uncaring universe. It took him a very long time to get to sleep and when he did he had troubling dreams of wandering alone through a large, barn-like building containing many rooms, all of them empty and all of them leading only to more rooms. At one point, in one of the rooms, he caught a glimpse of his mother and father, holding hands and looking as they must have twenty years before. He hurried to catch up with them but when he did they turned around and it wasn't his mother after all but Margaret, and the man was Joe Bruno, much younger and handsome but very stern and disapproving. He woke up just then and it was early, his alarm still hadn't gone off, and he felt regretful and nostalgic but for what or for whom he couldn't have said.

Did not the Buddha teach that the path to perfect tranquillity lay in relinquishing all desires, all passions? Beneath the sal trees at

Kusinara, in his last words to his disciples, he had said, You must break the bonds of worldly passions and drive them away as you would a viper. To extinguish the fires of illusion and passion and desire — that is the remedy to the eternal succession of birth, death and rebirth. So while Skippy was lonely much of the time, he knew it was unavoidable, just as suffering was unavoidable. If he could acknowledge this and accept it, he would be miles further along the road to enlightenment than those so-called educated university students who smoked their pipes night after night in the Dharma. They might pretend to understand the pain of the human condition; Skippy lived it.

So perhaps it was a kind of Karmic joke that when the awakening did happen in his life, it arrived in the shape of everything Skippy was trying to surmount — lust, desire, passion and human weakness.

It was just after eleven o'clock on a warm Sunday evening in August when the basement door of the club opened to admit a tall, blonde woman accompanied by the notorious Arty Peach. Arty was a familiar figure in those parts; he'd grown up in the east end and had done time in Stony Mountain for breaking and entering. It was rumoured he had small-time connections with the mob but Skippy kind of liked him. He'd come in a few times when the club first started, generally on Sunday nights, and always with a girl on his arm. They'd sit up front near the band and clap appreciatively and order plenty of coffee. Skippy was pretty sure Arty laced his coffee with liquor from a secret flask, but as long as he kept it hidden and didn't get drunk and make trouble for the club, Skippy didn't mind. Arty was a little guy — Skippy sometimes thought that was why he liked him. They had their shortness in common. Arty reminded him of one of those bantam roosters you see on TV, small and feisty and ready to take on the whole farmyard. He liked him for that, although it also made him more than a little wary of him. There were stories, Skippy had heard them; Arty could be a nasty piece of work when he wanted. You didn't want to get on his bad side.

He hadn't seen him all summer; there were rumours he'd got into some trouble and had had to leave town. But now he was back and with the most beautiful woman Skippy had ever seen, outside of a movie screen or the pages of a glossy magazine. Her skin was so white it shone in the dark and her hair was a pale shade of silver that caught the light like an angel. She wore it in a French roll and piled high on top, with little curls coming forward just over her ears. She was tall for a girl, although the teetery heels she wore probably contributed to that, and her legs were slender and shapely. Her arms, too, were graceful and well-proportioned and highlighted by a series of gold and silver bangles on her wrists and a wide, shining "slave" bracelet just above her elbow. This girl, this creature, stood out among the kids and dark-haired sullen-faced singers like a bird of paradise caught in a flock of sparrows. "Radiant as an angel." Mardou Fox in ivory and silver. Skippy stared as she walked past his table and he felt the hairs on the back of his neck stand up and salute. They connected, the two of them, at that moment although he didn't know her name and she didn't know he was alive.

"Who is that?" he asked of the table at large, but the university kids just shrugged. She wasn't one of them, that was for sure, and her beauty, enhanced as it was by cosmetics and hairspray and expensive clothes, didn't interest them. The pale young girls with their long straight hair gazed at her with the thinly-disguised contempt they all felt for women who were over twenty — no longer teenagers, and therefore no longer to be considered competition. The boys were intrigued for a moment, but more for the incongruity of a woman like that coming here, into this place.

"Where does she think she is? The Ritz?" one of them joked, but Skippy saw nothing even faintly ridiculous about her appearance. She was dressed and made up exactly as she should be, like a princess, or a movie star, he thought. He could not take his eyes away from her.

Oblivious to the mild stir she was causing, the blonde found an empty table against the wall, and stood for a moment, surveying the crowd. Finally, with a small, half-smile on her lips, as if she had studied the others and summed them up for the children they were, she lay her handbag on top of the table and sat down, elegant as a queen in spite of her unaccustomed surroundings. Arty sat down beside her and as he did so his eyes caught Skippy's and he gave a brief nod of acknowledgment.

For the next twenty minutes Skippy watched as Arty and the blonde sat at their table, she perfectly still through each song, clapping politely at the end, he drumming his fingers on the table and occasionally nodding his head to the beat. The set ended — Arty glanced at his watch, leaned over and said something to the blonde and stood up, ready to leave. Slowly, with a marvelous dignity, the blonde beauty stood up and gazed around her, still wearing that small, half-smile. She reminded Skippy of a friend of his mother's who had come for tea once, a former classmate who had married well and who knew how to cross her legs at the ankles and sip her tea with her baby finger crooked.

As they walked past his table on their way out, Arty nodded once more and said, "Hey, kid, how ya hangin'?" and kept walking. Skippy longed to reach out and clutch the soft white cotton of the blonde's dress for a moment, just long enough to make her pause and notice him. And then the moment was gone; she was past him and out the door, out of his life — possibly for ever.

He thought about her all week. On the two nights when the club wasn't open he went up to his room early, before the end of the late night news, so he might get into bed and think about her. He gave her a name, "Mirabella" — "Bella" for short, because it meant beautiful and it sounded like the kind of name Kerouac might come up with, in one of his novels. In his fantasies, she came into the club the following Sunday, alone this time, and her eyes met his across the dark, smoky basement room.

"Bella," he whispered, "I need you. I love you."

And she whispered back that she, too, loved him, that she had fallen in love with him the moment she'd seen him. Slowly, gracefully, she slipped her dress down, off her shoulders (they were in his room now, standing beside his bed) and it fell to the ground and she stood next to him in her panties and bra and her high-heel shoes. He tried several variations: sometimes, when he thought about her, she kept her underwear on, which Skippy thought gave her an erotic fragility. Other times she was naked, revealed in a state of absolute perfection. Her skin was soft and pale and glowing — he imagined the golden hairs on her arms and even those excited him. Everything about her was flawless, fine, in a way no real woman could ever be. He wanted to push his way inside her, curl up within her like a baby bird in its shell, surrounded by his mother-wife-girlfriend-lover. He had to find out who she was. He had to see her again.

The following Sunday, Arty Peach came back to the club, but there was no blonde goddess on his arm. The girl who accompanied him this time was short and dark and ordinary, and Skippy wondered if the other one had simply been passing through town. He should have gone over and introduced himself the other night; she could be anywhere by now. Skippy cursed himself for being a weak, gutless fool. He didn't deserve to be happy — the Buddha had sent this beautiful woman into the club, his club, and he had done nothing about it. He deserved nothing. He was an asshole.

As luck would have it, Arty and the girl stopped by his table on the way out that night.

"Good crowd tonight, pal," Arty said. (Skippy was pretty sure Arty didn't know his name but he assumed that Skippy would know his. He was right, of course.)

"Yeah." Skippy nodded. "Sunday nights we're always pretty full, you know?"

Arty laughed, a brief, harsh bark that resounded throughout the room. "No wonder. There's eff-all to do in this town on a Sunday night, eh? It's not like you got a whole lotta competition."

Noting that Arty was in what was, for him, a very good mood, Skippy decided to go ahead and ask him. "Remember that blonde you came in with last Sunday. The blonde one?"

"Doris?"

"Is that her name?" Skippy was confounded for a moment. He'd been calling her "Mirabella" all week. But "Doris" — there was nothing wrong with that. Attached to a woman as beautiful as she was, the name suddenly took on a whole new meaning. He'd never be able to hear the name again without experiencing a shiver of anticipation. He tried to sound casual.

"So. Does she, like, live around here?"

"Around here?" Arty looked around the club, as if Skippy was asking if Doris lived somewhere in the basement, or was holed up in one of the small, dilapidated bungalows on this part of the street.

"Yeah, well, you know, I was just wondering. I mean, like, is she from here?"

Arty frowned at Skippy. What was with this kid, he seemed to be thinking? What was the big hairy deal?

Finally he replied that, yeah, Doris was from here, she'd been living in Toronto for a while but now she was back. Why?

"Well, it's just that I think I know her from somewhere. I mean, I think I used to know her. I think."

Arty was looking at him with suspicion; the friendliness, such as it was, had disappeared.

"Is that right?"

Skippy nodded. He was beginning to sweat, afraid that Arty could tell he was lying.

"Anyway," he continued, determined to see this through, "I just thought you might know how I could get in touch with her. I mean, since you know her and all."

"I might." Skippy waited, and Arty added, "And then again, I might not."

The short, dark girl was impatient to leave. "Come on, Arty," she said, "let's get outta here. I told my sister I'd meet her."

Arty turned to the girl and glared at her. "Hey," he said, "don't start with me, eh? We'll leave when I'm damn good and ready to leave, okay? You don't like it, you can lump it."

This opportunity to display his authority seemed to put Arty into a good mood once again. He turned back to Skippy and said, "Sorry, pal. You were saying?"

"Could you give her something for me?" Skippy took his wallet out of his back pocket and fished out a small rectangular card.

"Who, her?" Arty indicated the girl who was now openly sulking beside him, and Skippy said, no, he was talking about the blonde girl. Doris. The one Arty had come in with before.

"Oh, yeah. Doris. Sure, I guess."

Skippy'd had five hundred business cards made up back in February, and he almost never got to use them. In dark black letters on an ivory background, they read:

THE DHARMA CAFE AND COFFEE HOUSE
233 East Macklin Ave.
* * * Live Music * * *
Open Thu. - Mon.
Nightly 8 p.m. - Midnight
Skippy Jacques, Prop.

Now, on the back of one of them, in his neatest printing, he wrote: "When you get to the top of the mountain, keep climbing."

"Next time you see her, okay? Would you give her this for me?"

Arty took the card and read it, then turned it over and read that, too. He smiled, but all he said was, "Sure, pal. No problem." Then he turned to the girl beside him and said, "All right, we're leaving. Satisfied? Get going, for Chrissake."

The dark girl opened her mouth as if she was going to say something, then thought better of it and closed it again. There were some people you didn't push very far, no matter how short they were, and Arty Peach was one of them.

It was exactly a month before he saw her again and he had almost given up waiting. He'd thought of her constantly but had stopped expecting to see her walk in. When she did, on a Sunday night in the middle of September, he noticed two things, immediately: she was even more beautiful, if that was possible, than the first time he'd seen her. And she seemed to be a little nearsighted. She stood in the doorway peering into the dark and squinting just a little and he thought, She's here. Shit almighty, she's here.

Recovering himself, he stepped down from the stage where he'd been checking out the microphone and hurried over to her, smoothing down his hair at the back and checking that his shirt was tucked in. He wished he had thought to put on a little Old Spice, or maybe something more daring, but how could he have known that she'd eventually come back after all? Arty had been back to the club only once in the past month and he'd been in a bad mood. He'd said nothing, not hello or good-bye or anything, and Skippy had decided not to ask him about Doris. So he'd had no idea if Arty had seen her or if he'd remembered to give her the card. Knowing Arty, he might just have torn it up and thrown it away the moment he left the club. Skippy wouldn't put it past him at all, to do that. And if he had given her the card, maybe she'd tossed it into the garbage when she got home, maybe she'd written him off as some kind of weirdo.

Except she hadn't done either of those things because here she was standing right in front of him, sizing him up, trying to think if she'd met him before. A short, skinny guy with a moustache; no, it didn't ring a bell.

"Hi," he said, smiling, and then, because it was true and he was just so happy to see her, "You look great."

"I'm Doris," she said and put out her hand.

He held it and said, "I know. I gave you my card. At least, I gave it to Arty to give to you."

Opening her purse, she found the card and held it up to the light. "Are you this guy, Skippy Jacques?" (She pronounced it the French way and he corrected her, although it sounded lovely the way she said it.)

"Jacques," he said. "Rhymes with flakes." And he laughed and wished he hadn't, he sounded like a goof.

"Jacques," she repeated. "Well, Mr. Jacques, here I am."

"Right. Here you are." It was stupid but he couldn't take his eyes off her, he couldn't do anything but stand there and grin like an idiot.

Doris slipped his card into her pocket and looked around at the room. "It's quiet in here."

It was early, only just after eight. The girls who waited on tables wouldn't be in for another half hour and it would be at least a half hour after that before tonight's trio, "Song of the Wind", carted their twelve string guitars and assorted tambourines on to the stage to perform. Skippy explained and Doris nodded.

"So," she said, having made up her mind about something, "should we sit down or what?"

"Oh, sure. Come on in, have a seat, I'll get you something to drink."

Standing back to let her go first, he followed her into the room and hurried to pull out a chair for her up front, near the stage. She sat down carefully and crossed her legs at the ankles. She was wearing a jacket — the weather had turned cold overnight — and he offered to take it and hang it up, but she said she'd keep it on, thank you. Her voice was soft and husky, as though she might have a cold, although she looked healthy, if a little bit pale. She folded her hands on the table and looked up at him and he asked her if she'd like something to drink.

"Coffee? A Coke? I'm sorry I don't have anything stronger. We don't have a liquor license. I got some 7-Up, would you like that?"

"Coke's fine," she said. "With ice. Please."

Skippy hurried over to the fridge behind the counter and got a Coke and a tall glass with some ice. He would have liked to have had one of the waitresses bring it to the table, it would have looked better, made it look more like a proper business. And there was something about the place when it was empty like this that was depressing, even to his eyes. With the tables full and music playing, it felt like a club; at the moment, it felt like a church basement. He poured half the pop into the glass and carried it on a tray over to where she sat, setting it down on the table in front of her like a burnt offering.

She thanked him and took a sip from the glass and Skippy sat down at the table across from her, so he could keep his eyes on her and reassure himself that she was here.

"Is it okay?" he asked.

"The Coke? Yeah, sure. It's fine."

She gave her jacket a little tug, pulling it more closely around her, and Skippy wondered if she was cold. "Once people get here," he told her, "the room really heats up. You wouldn't believe how hot it can get by the middle of the night. Even in winter."

Doris took another sip and said nothing and Skippy wondered if he was boring her already. Whenever he talked to an attractive woman, he felt she was wishing she was somewhere else. He would try to recall the things he'd heard other guys talk about — cars and sports and getting drunk, mostly — but he'd had no experience of the first two and he hardly thought she'd like to hear about the last time he got pissed and threw up. The only woman he'd never felt that way with was Margaret. He was pretty sure he'd never bored her. If he had, she hadn't let on.

Doris took a pack of cigarettes out of her purse, found one and held it out expectantly, until Skippy suddenly realized he was meant to rise to the occasion.

"Sorry," he said. "Hang on, I'll get a light," and he got up and hurried over to the counter where he kept the matches to light the candles on each table. By the time he'd returned, she had retrieved a gold cigarette lighter from her purse and handed it to him with a smile. Feeling nervous and inadequate, he managed to get her cigarette lit, although his hand was shaking so violently she had to hold it still with her own.

Doris leaned back in her chair and blew a long stream of white smoke out through her lips, watching with a certain satisfaction while it curled to the ceiling. "So," she said, "what's the matter with your leg?"

It was so direct, the way she asked it, it took him off guard. Stumbling for something to say, he felt himself blushing and could have kicked himself for not dimming the overhead lights before they sat down. He could hardly get up now, with her watching him walk over to the light switch, paying attention to his bad leg.

"You don't have to tell me if you don't want to," she said. "I was just wondering."

"No, it's all right, I don't mind," he managed to say. "I got polio when I was a kid."

Doris nodded. "Tough," she said and took another drag on her cigarette. He thought she looked like a movie star, the way she did it, holding the cigarette at an angle, drawing the smoke in so deeply and exhaling with a curl of her lips that was almost contemptuous.

"That's really tough. I used to know a guy, back in Toronto, an American. He lost both his legs over in Korea. Got cut off right at the knee. Didn't seem to hold him back, though."

Eager to keep the conversation going, Skippy said, "Well, sure, I mean, your legs, they're just your legs, you know? There's no reason you can't still live your life, travel, whatever. Legs aren't all that important."

Doris looked at him. It was impossible to read her, to see past those gray-blue eyes. "Somebody cuts off my legs, they might just as well shoot me right there and then." She placed her index finger against her temple and mimed the action of cocking a gun with her thumb. "Put a gun to my head and pull the trigger. I'd do it myself, if I had to."

There seemed to be nothing to say to this and Skippy began to silently panic, grappling for subjects which would prove a little more fruitful. In the meantime, Doris took another sip of her Coke and looked around at the empty room.

"This your place? You own it?"

"Well, not the building, I rent the space. But it's my club, yeah, I own it."

"I heard about this place when I got back. I bugged Arty until he brought me. He didn't want to, at first. He never wants to take me anywhere. He told me I'd hate it, said I'd be bored."

"And were you?" He couldn't help asking; he wanted to know.

Doris shrugged and took another drag of her cigarette. "It was okay. I like music. I used to go to all kinds of places in Toronto — jazz, rock and roll. And I like folk music. I went to this place on Yonge Street once, the Horseshoe Tavern. You ever go there?"

He shook his head — he'd never been out of the Bay but he hoped he wouldn't have to admit it.

"Well, it was pretty good. I liked it."

This was good, Skippy thought. This was progress. She was talking now, they were having an actual conversation. Feeling a little braver, Skippy decided to ask the big question.

"Is Arty Peach your boyfriend?" he asked and the blue eyes clouded over.

"Let's just say we have a relationship," she said. And that was it.

He waited, hoping she'd elaborate a little, but instead she reached into her jacket pocket, pulled out his business card once again and held it out to him.

"Read what it says on the back of this," she commanded.

He read: "When you get to the top of the mountain, keep climbing." He didn't have to read it, he knew it by heart.

"Right," she said. "So what's it supposed to mean?"

"Well." He wasn't sure just what to say. It was something Benny used to say to him, a quote from the Dharma. If he started talking about Buddhism when they'd only just met, she might decide he was a nutcase and leave; on the other hand, she might be intrigued. He decided to go for it.

"It's Zen, from the teachings of the Buddha. That saying, it's part of the Dharma. I just heard it one time and liked it."

If Doris had heard of the Buddha, she wasn't saying. She lifted her glass to her lips and watched him over the rim. Skippy thought it might be better if he stopped while he was ahead, but then it would just be hanging there, between them. He tried to explain.

"I keep thinking about it. I think it means there's no limits, you know? Like, you shouldn't settle for something just because somebody tells you you're at the top of the mountain, that's all there is. Because it's just their word and anyway, who's to say the mountain is really there anyhow?"

Doris said nothing; she was looking at him as if she might get up and flee at any moment. Desperately, Skippy continued, "At least, that's what I figure it means, but it might mean something entirely different. And it might not mean anything at all." He laughed, nervously, and wondered if she thought he was crazy, writing something on the back of a card that might not mean anything.

And then, for the first time that night, Doris smiled. "I get it. You make your own mountains."

Skippy felt a thrill go right through him. She understood, and better yet, she instinctively found a simple way to say it. This woman was amazing — he'd been right about her all along. He was delighted.

"That's right. And if the mountain isn't there, if it's only in your own head, then you're free, you know? You can do whatever you want, because it's only someone else saying it's there or it isn't."

Doris took another deep puff on her cigarette. "You're a real thinker, aren't you?"

It was hard to tell, the way she said it, if she thought that was a good thing, or if she was being sarcastic.

To Skippy's enormous gratification, the beautiful Doris stayed at his table in the club for almost three hours. The place slowly filled up and he had to tear himself away from time to time to go talk to people, say hi to the band, make sure they had everything they needed. But the instant he possibly could, he would rush back to her table, afraid she'd gotten bored and left, relieved each time to see her sitting there, as lovely and still and peaceful as he'd left her. It was perfect, like a movie where everything happens just the way you think it should. For once.

He found, too, that as the night wore on he felt more comfortable around her. They still had little to say to each other but he was so busy there was no time to talk much anyway. And the music took up most of the evening so that he had huge long gaps when people were singing where there was no need and no opportunity to say anything. It was perfect, in its way, a perfect way to spend the night with the woman of his dreams, without having to worry about boring her or saying something stupid.

For Skippy, it was a night made in heaven. He was basking in a warmth that had nothing to do with the heat created by eighty-five bodies crowded into a small, airless room designed to hold no more than sixty. He felt his heart expanding inside him so that at times he could scarcely breathe and twice he had to excuse himself to go into the men's room and splash his face with cold water from the small, old-fashioned sink. This, he knew for certain, was love; he'd met the woman he wanted to spend his life with and the gratitude he felt was almost unbearable.

The regulars noticed and comments skittered around the room, under the cover of the guitars and the tambourine. Skippy had a girlfriend; the little guy, Mr. Mysterious, had found himself a doll.

One of the university fellows came up to him when Skippy was working behind the coffee counter, filling in for the regular girl who'd gone to use the washroom.

"Nice chick you've got there," this guy said and Skippy grinned like a little kid. He wanted to be cool about it, nonchalant, but it was impossible.

"Yeah, she's pretty nice, all right."

"Known her long?"

Skippy shrugged. "Not long."

The university student picked up his coffee and gave Skippy the thumbs up sign. "Hang in there," he said and Skippy nodded. He'd hang in there, all right; he'd hang in there for ever, if she'd let him.

It ended all too soon, of course. Around eleven o'clock, when the club was really jumping and the kids were grooving and slapping the tables in time to the beat, Doris looked at her watch and said she'd have to leave. Skippy tried to talk her out of it but she shook her head and said, No, she had to go.

So Skippy gave in and went to the counter to call her a cab. While he was there, she stood up and buttoned her jacket, taking a slow, final look around the club. When he returned to the table, she smiled at him for the second time that night. He marveled at the difference it made when she smiled — unsmiling, she was a princess, carved in ice; when she smiled it was as if she was lit from within and the beauty of it made him feel weak.

"Well, so long, Mr. Jacques," she told him, picking up her purse and slinging it over her shoulder. "Maybe I'll come back one of these days."

"When?" It sounded desperate but he had to ask it. He had to know if she was preparing to walk out of his life for good.

She watched him for a moment, as if there was something about him — or the Dharma — that she was weighing in her mind. Finally, she said, "Well, Sundays are pretty good for me. I guess I could come again next Sunday night. What do you think?"

"I think that would be great. Are you sure? I mean, you will come back, won't you?"

To his ears he sounded pathetic. He wanted to be cool, he wanted her to see him as detached, casual. Hip. Instead he was standing here in the middle of a crowded room practically begging her to turn up the following Sunday.

To his immense relief, she said simply, "Yeah, I'll come back."

He walked her to the door of the club and they went outside on to the sidewalk, to wait for the taxi. With the door shut behind them, the noise of the club was muted and the still night air seemed palpable, the way it does in September in the north. They stood side by side and Doris looked up at the sky overhead, at the cold, distinct points of light in the distance.

"When I was living in Toronto," she said, and her voice, out here in the dark, seemed more clear, yet huskier than it had, "I used to think about what it was like here in the fall and how it was so clear and made you feel so alive. I never felt like that, down east. It's just not the same."

Skippy looked at her profile outlined in the small yellow bulb overhanging the doorway and thought how perfect she was, how she existed on a plane far, far above him and how the distance between them was insurmountable — he would never touch that soft, downy cheek, never press his mouth against hers.

"Are you sorry you came back?"

He asked it because she seemed sad, suddenly, and that made him feel even closer to her. But all she said was, "No, it was time to leave."

The cab pulled up in front of the church and he held the back door open while she got in and pulled a bill out from his pocket. A fiver.

"Here," he whispered, not wanting to embarrass her. "For the cab."

She smiled and took the money and the car pulled away and he stood there and waved and before it turned the corner he called out, "Don't forget me." And then he really felt stupid because that was such a jerk thing to say, calling out like that, not cool at all.

Skippy walked slowly back down the cement steps that led into the club and he realized something: while Doris was there, he had felt like Superman, she made him feel larger than life. He had only experienced that once before that he could recall and it was the summer he was fifteen and he had been an usher at his cousin's wedding. She was marrying a Polish guy and the tables were weighed down with holopshi and pyrogies and meatballs, and someone had poured him a glass of vodka, clear, pure, and 70 proof and he had become very drunk. He had lurched around the dance floor, crashing into middle-aged men dancing with their daughters, old ladies dancing with other old ladies, bumping into long trellis tables covered with white, food-spattered table cloths. He grabbed young women who were dancing the butterfly with their sisters and boyfriends and kissed them on the cheeks; he performed a clumsy sort of polka with a friend of his mother's who laughed and crushed him against her pillowy soft bosom. Until he found himself puking into the porcelain toilet bowl of the men's room he had a great time. That's how he had felt for the past two hours with Doris and he'd had nothing stronger to drink than black coffee. He wondered if he'd wake tomorrow morning with the same skull-crashing headache, the aching throat, and the sense of complete despair that had followed his night at the wedding.

7.

There's a wildness about a northern Ontario fall: a feral taste in the air, a teasing smell of burning leaves and wet grass and the wind off Lake Superiour. The skies, which can be cloudy and disappointing in the dog days of August, clear up after Labour Day and radiate a deep, Mediterranean blue. The bush, too, transforms itself; what was once a deep, impenetrable mass of forest green shifts and shades to brown and yellow and gold, and the leaves begin their slow, graceful flight to the earth, whispering together, rustling their way into the recesses of grass and tree roots.

Life's transitory nature is never felt more keenly than in the fall, and you stop still on a sidewalk, your attention claimed by a flock of migrating geese or a thin column of smoke curling upwards from a nearby house, where someone is reducing to ashes a summer's worth of back-yard rakings. It's the period of amnesty before winter, the whispered promise of something new, something different, with the very next catch of the wind.

Skippy reached over and shut off his alarm clock and lay there for a minute, trying to think why he felt different. Excited, as if something important had happened or was about to. Then he remembered: Doris. She had come to the club last night, she had sat at his table with him, she had smoked cigarettes and drunk Coke and stayed there for almost three hours. And she had promised to come back again. Doris was in his life and his life had changed overnight.

Opening his bedroom door, Skippy peered out cautiously before venturing into the hallway. Being a weekday, the other boarders had most likely left for work already — the hardware store didn't open till ten, so Skippy was always the last one out of the house, except for the old man down the hall who didn't work and slept in till noon.

Still, it didn't pay to take chances. There was the time, after all, when he was heading to the bathroom in his jockey shorts and the door to the room next to his suddenly swung open and a chubby, dark-haired girl in a bathrobe and slippers bumped right into him. Skippy didn't know which of them was more embarrassed, especially since her eyes automatically dropped to his crotch, before she caught herself and looked away.

At least, he had consoled himself once he was sitting on the john with the door safely locked, at least he had a right to be there. He was a boarder here, he paid his rent promptly the last day of the month, Mrs. Cordelli never had to come asking for it. Not like some of the low-lifes he could mention who tended to hide out the last few days of the month, go missing for a day or two just to avoid her. That girl, whoever she was, she was lucky Mrs. C. hadn't caught her: the landlady was a strict Catholic, went to mass every day and didn't allow any of her boarders to have young ladies in their rooms.

"Now, me, I'm no prude," she had told Skippy the first day he'd moved in. "I been around. I was young once, too, believe it or not, but I tell you Mr. Jacques I always knew what was what and I didn't kid myself, if you know what I mean. When Mr. Cordelli married me he knew he was getting a one hundred percent virgin, excuse my language, but if Mama said it once, she said it a hundred times, Purity, Elena, you gotta keep yourself pure for your husband. A man is not gonna buy the cow if he's getting the milk for free. Sorry to be so forward, Mr. Jacques, but I like my young men to know where I stand. If you know what I mean."

Skippy knew what she meant. He couldn't imagine bringing a girl back to his small white room here at Mrs. C's, a room more like a monk's cell than anything with its single bed always neatly made up and little else in the room but a small bedside table and lamp and an old-fashioned dresser, no pictures on the wall, just his old portable record player and his books and records lined up in the bookcase he had created out of a couple of planks and some bricks.

He thought about the girl he had seen coming out of that room (Ahzuk Chista's room, an Armenian who worked for the railway, good looking guy but quiet, not the type you'd figure to smuggle a girl past Mrs. C. and stash her in his room for the night) and wondered if she was a regular sort of girl you might go with and want to spend the night with after a while, or if she was a prostitute. A working girl, that's what people called them.

Benny Carter had told him all about working girls, the ones he had seen in New York, how they stood on certain street corners and strolled up and down, watching the traffic, and came right up to you if you looked like you might want some company. That's what they said, it's what the girls had said to Benny that time: "Hi, good lookin', want some company?" He had smiled and teased them and said, No, thanks, darlin', as if he'd been doing it all his life. You could always tell, he said. Even when they didn't come right up to you, you could tell by the way they dressed — short skirts and high heels in the middle of winter and too much makeup with their hair backcombed high on top of their heads. Skippy had only seen women like that in men's magazines. He'd found them attractive, had imagined Mardou Fox dressed like that in something short and tight and revealing. But the idea of one of those women stepping out of the magazine and coming up to you on the street, confronting you in real life — Skippy wasn't sure he would know where to look. If he had to completely honest about it, he was sort of glad it had never happened.

And anyway, here it was different. There were no street corners where the hookers hung out, at least, Skippy had never seen them. You might see a woman walking with some guy late at night in certain parts of town, moving with the unsteady exaggerated carefulness of someone who's had too much to drink, clutching her handbag and with just enough wits about her to remember that there was a business transaction to be completed and the details had to be settled before they reached whatever tiny hotel room she was calling home for the next few hours. It always looked kind of sad, there was nothing sexy or romantic about it. And nine times out of ten the guy wasn't quite as drunk and was walking a little ahead, like he was embarrassed to be seen with her and just wanted to get to wherever it was they were going and get it over with as soon as possible.

Skippy thought that was pretty low when you thought about it. If the guy was going to spend the night with a girl like that, then at least he should treat her like a person. If it was him, and he was spending money to be with a girl, he'd treat her nicely and be grateful, that's what.

Skippy sat in the john and ran the water for his bath and thought about Doris. It was funny, the way life worked. You grow up thinking there's somebody out there for you, that some day someone will walk into your life and see you the way you really are, understand right away the kind of person you are, the kind of person nobody else can see. Like the songs say it's supposed to happen: "Some enchanted evening/You may see a stranger..." All that stuff, but it never happens and finally you give up and figure, okay, that's the way it goes, this is not going to happen to me. And the moment you really and truly give up, Whammo! It happens.

Benny would have a word for it. Benny would say it was "kismet". He used words like that all the time, fancy words that meant nothing to most people but rolled off his tongue easily. It was because of having parents who were teachers — in spite of regularly missing school, Benny had an excellent vocabulary. Skippy lowered himself into the hot, steamy water and thought how he would like to tell Benny about Doris. That's cool, man, Benny would say. That is just so cool.

If Benny and he were still friends. If Benny hadn't married Margaret. If they'd gone on their road trip together. He lay back in the tub and felt the relative coolness of the porcelain against his back and closed his eyes. Benny's car, the '59 Pontiac, nose pointed into the sunset, speeding along the blacktop of an American highway. Who knows where that car might have taken them if things had worked out like they were supposed to?

If he and Benny were still friends — he and Benny and Margaret, of course — they'd still go out to the Alex some times and after a couple of beers Skippy would mention, very casually, as if he hadn't been thinking about her the whole time, I met this girl the other night. And he'd open his wallet and take out her picture — he'd ask her for a picture the next time he saw her — and say, This is her. Doris. And Benny and Margaret would pass the picture between them and they would exchange glances, surprised at how pretty she was, and Benny might say something like, She's a pretty hot chick, Skippy, and Margaret would say, She's beautiful. And they'd hand the picture back with a smile and say, When can we meet her? And Skippy would take the picture and put it back in his wallet, handling it carefully, so as not to bend it or anything, and he'd say, Any time. Come in to the club next Sunday — she'll be there. She comes and sits with me, she likes the music. *She likes me.*

Sliding his knees up along the smoothness of the tub, Skippy let his upper body slip down until his shoulders were resting along the bottom and the water covered his ears. In the sudden silence that surrounded him, he closed his eyes and allowed himself to fantasize: Doris, here in the water next to him, on top of him, sliding her naked body along his, her sweet mouth making its way from his lips to his throat and down his chest, down to where his dick was standing straight up in the water, begging to take it in her mouth —

The doorknob rattled and there was a pounding on the bathroom door.

"Mr. Jacques, I gotta clean. I'm sorry to bother you but you're holding me up. Mr. Jacques?"

With a splash of water, Skippy sat up and reached for his towel, thinking in his confusion to hide himself from his landlady.

"Yes, Mrs. Cordelli," he called, noting with relief the door was still shut and the key was in the lock. "I'll be right out. Sorry."

"You don't wanna stay in there too long," she announced from the other side of the door. "Too much hot water is bad for your skin."

"Yes, Mrs. Cordelli. I know that. I was just getting out."

He waited until he heard her heavy footsteps retreating down the hallway, then glanced down at his naked body. His hard-on was gone; it had shriveled the minute he'd heard her voice. Landladies had that effect on most men, he figured.

A few minutes later he unlocked the door and was confronted by Mrs. Cordelli climbing the stairway, carrying a bucket in one hand and a large yellow sponge in the other. She shook her head, reprovingly.

"If you're gonna have baths in the morning, Mr. Jacques, you gotta be quick, you know what I mean? I was thinking maybe you gone and fell asleep in there." Then she smiled to show there were no hard feelings.

Elena Cordelli liked Mr. Jacques; he'd quickly become one of her favourites. He was a nice boy, well-mannered, and he didn't run after the women, which was more than she could say for some of her guests. She glared briefly at the closed door belonging to Mr. Chista and pursed her lips. That fellow, he thought he was fooling her, hiding girls in his room. Drinking, too, she was certain, although she couldn't prove it. Having a drink after work was fine — her late husband, God bless his soul, had rewarded himself with two or three beers when he came home at night, after working hard all day for the city. But drinking alone in your room, that was sneaky and not good manners and if she caught him at it he'd be sorry. So far, she had no proof, but it was only a matter of time — Elena Cordelli was not someone to be bamboozled for long.

"You working tonight, Mr. Jacques?" she asked, setting her bucket down on the hall carpet. Now that she'd reprimanded Skippy for taking too long in the bathroom, she was in the mood for some chit-chat before getting down to the morning's housework.

Skippy nodded. "Yes, but it's pretty easy Monday nights. We don't get a very big crowd. You should come some time, Mrs. Cordelli. You just might enjoy it."

She laughed. "Oh, don't you be funny. Me? In a place like that? With all those crazy people? Oh, no, I don't think so. You never get Elena Cordelli in a place like that."

He had her going now, so he continued: "Why not? A lovely young thing like you, Mrs. Cordelli. You'd fit right in. Maybe we'd even get you up on stage, get you to sing a few songs, or play the tambourine. What do you say?"

This was what Benny used to do, a gentle, teasing flirtation with older women that pleased them because they knew he didn't mean it. On more than one occasion Benny had received an extra slice of pie in a restaurant because he'd joked with the waitress. Skippy wasn't much good at it, out in public, but he found it easy with Mrs. Cordelli.

She laughed, delighted at the thought of being up on stage with all those kids. Then she picked up her bucket and pushed him aside good-naturedly. "Now you go away, Mr. Jacques, you go on down to your hardware store. You think I got nothing better to do all day but stand around talking to young men who sit in the bath all morning? Go on, you — I got work to do."

It was a glorious, clear, fall day and Skippy decided to walk to work. As a general rule, he avoided walking when he could. It drew attention to his leg, and took away from the dignity of his person. Or so he believed. But he was feeling buoyant this morning and he wanted to think about Doris. The neighbourhood was quiet, with the children already in school and most of the men already at work. The old man who lived across the street was retired and today he was out in front raking up the leaves from his lawn. He waved at Skippy and when Skippy waved back he called out, "Beautiful day." Skippy agreed that it was and kept walking; the old guy liked to talk and at another time he would have stopped to discuss the state of the world, but today his mind was on Doris. He passed the church — *his* church, he always felt, although he only had access to the basement — and noted with approval that the caretaker was there already, pulling away at the weeds growing next to the sidewalk.

"Good morning, Mr. Lee," Skippy said, stopping at the edge of the churchyard to watch.

To most people the old man was "Charlie" but Skippy always called him "Mister Lee" and he got the impression the caretaker appreciated it. Somewhere he'd heard the old guy had been a doctor once, back in China, and that he'd had to turn his hand to gardening when he came to Canada because who, after all, was going to hire a person with a Chinese degree in doctoring? The old Chinese people went to him, however, often visiting him secretly after receiving a prior diagnosis from one of the other regular, white doctors in the community. He prescribed herbs with strange-sounding names and gave them brown, murky-looking teas he'd brewed at home, which were supposed to reach parts of the body the usual doctors never even thought of. The doctors tolerated Charlie's ministrations; they did no harm, as a rule, and they certainly made the old people feel better, if only because the teas and herbal concoctions reminded them of home.

Now Mr. Lee looked up and smiled and came over to where Skippy was standing, pushing his brown fedora further back on his forehead.

"Mr. Jacques," he greeted him. "You on your way to the store this morning?"

Skippy nodded. "Getting the weeds out, eh?" he asked, just to make conversation. He always thought of this old church as kind of belonging to Mr. Lee, in a way — he'd been hired as caretaker back before the war and when the new church was built the congregation kept Charlie on to keep the place up and he did just that, for a fee that was laughably modest. If he'd been the kind of man given to expressing himself in such terms, Charlie would have said he'd done it out of love; there was a bond between the old man and the derelict church, each made redundant before his time. Now the church had a new lease on life and Charlie's salary had been marginally increased and yet it seemed that neither he nor the old building quite approved of the changes. During the daytime, the church was filled with the comings and goings of small children and their mothers, young men with sexually-transmitted diseases and assorted oldsters looking for a place to sit and play euchre, while five nights a week the rafters rang with the music of a new generation. In solitude, there had been a certain dignity; now there was bustle, and confusion, and the old man turned his back on these things as surely as he had turned his back on his homeland forty-five years earlier.

Still, he liked Skippy. They had spent several evenings, in the early days of the club, sitting in the church basement discussing the state of the world as seen from their disparate, but not mutually exclusive, perspectives. Being Chinese, Mr. Lee was of course familiar with Buddhism and the teachings of the Dharma. With Benny gone there was nobody to discuss these things with and although Skippy kept up his reading, he felt lost, most of the time, and wished he had someone to translate. Conversations with Mr. Lee were not as satisfying, ultimately, but they did make Skippy feel he was not completely alone in his quest for enlightenment.

He had been made aware, for example, that Mr. Lee had adopted a philosophical approach to his life since coming to Canada, one that seemed very much in keeping with the principles of Buddhism. With great difficulty, as he explained it to Skippy, he had had to relinquish his status as a healer, a medical practitioner, for the less lofty position as a tender of gardens, a mower of lawns. He saw it as part of his karma to resign himself to this inferior sort of life in order that he might achieve greatness in the next.

"And you see, Mr. Jacques," he declared, "I embrace the life of a gardener and I find much to celebrate. 'To see a world in a grain of sand/And a heaven in a wild flower.'"

Skippy had assumed Mr. Lee was quoting from the Buddha but the old man said no, it was one of "your people", a poet named William Blake and he'd written it about a hundred and fifty years ago. Further proof, if Skippy had needed it, that here was indeed an educated man.

Now he thought he might approach Mr. Lee about Doris: Skippy had an idea that she had been sent into his life to help him along the path, but the teachings of the Buddha were very ambivalent when it came to women. They were generally lumped under the heading "Defilements", along with greed, anger, fear and foolishness. Lusting after women was one sure way to keep yourself from continuing in the cycle of birth, death and rebirth for aeons, Skippy knew that.

And yet he'd also read that a good woman could be a helpmeet to her husband, a voice of reason and correction to turn him from the path of evil towards righteousness. Holy men in some parts of the world invited beautiful young girls into their beds to tempt their baser natures and prove that they could rise above all these things. Was that what he was to do with Doris? Somehow, Skippy had a hard time imagining that, if Doris could ever be prevailed upon to sleep with him, he would have the inner strength to reject her.

Skippy was struggling, now that he had Mr. Lee's attention, to come up with a suitable question for the old man. But he couldn't just come right out and ask if it was all right to sleep with Doris — their conversations had not prepared either of them for this kind of intimacy. Finally he thought he would ask about China, get an idea of how things worked over there, and then work his way around to the subject at hand.

"In the old country," he began, "in China, when you lived there, did men and women date like they do here? I mean, did they go out with each other and spend time alone and all that? Or was everything arranged by their parents?"

Mr. Lee took off his hat and wiped his forehead with his pocket handkerchief, giving the matter some thought. "Depends," he said, finally. "For me, my wife is chosen when we are still children. My aunts, her aunts, they make decisions, that's how it is done in the old days. I meet her one day before we get married and she is very shy, very beautiful. Forty-seven years later we are still married, still happy. The old ladies, they know what is best. Now, though, things change. Young people now, they fall in love, choose who they will marry. It's very different."

"Yeah, I guess it is," Skippy allowed. "The thing is, the way it works now, it's harder, you know? I mean, how do you know you've picked the right one?"

"Oh, you know," the old man said. "Your heart will tell you."

Then he smiled and inquired, a little shyly, if Skippy had met a young lady.

"Her name's Doris," Skippy said, anxious to talk about her to anyone who'd listen. "And she's beautiful, really perfect, you know? It's just that I've got this thing about following the path. And the teachings of the Buddha, well, they're a little confusing when it comes to women."

Mr. Lee nodded, as if he understood perfectly Skippy's dilemma. "Moderation in all things, Mr. Jacques."

"Well, yes, I've read that. But it seems to me whoever said that was never in love. I mean, how do you do that in moderation, I wonder? It seems to me the whole sex thing is so, well, all-consuming, I can't figure how there could be anything moderate about it."

Mr. Lee smiled. "Then you must go with your stomach," he said. "Your stomach is even more reliable than your heart. Many people listen with their hearts and ignore their stomachs. You must pay attention to both."

His heart and his stomach; it made sense when you thought about it. Skippy thanked him. "I guess I'd better be going," he said, and the old man nodded again and adjusted his hat once more.

"Back to work," he said, meaning both of them, and added, "Gets a little harder now. Maybe the weeds are getting stronger or maybe I am getting weak." Then he smiled and indicated the ring of silver birch trees in a corner of the churchyard. "I planted these, nineteen-thirty-nine, just before the war. I can't work any more, I get sick and die, these trees will still be here. How many doctors can say that?"

When Doris turned up at the club the following Sunday, she looked a little sleepy, as though she'd just woken up, and at first they just sat and sipped soft drinks and smoked cigarettes (she smoked, Skippy watched, fascinated — everything she did fascinated him) and after a while she began to wake up and look around her with interest.

"Who's playing tonight?" she asked and he said it was a local group, "Laura and Tom".

"They're good," he assured her. "At least, she is. She's going to be famous one of these days."

"I used to want to be famous," Doris said. "When I was a kid, you know? I even knew what name I'd use — Doris Night. Like Doris Day, you know? Only 'Night', to be different."

"Maybe you will be some day," he said and she shook her head. "No, thanks, I think I'll pass."

At that point the musicians appeared at the side of the stage and Skippy left to introduce them to the audience. This was his least favourite part of the job; he preferred to stay in the background, lining up groups, taking care of the business end of things. In front of an audience he always felt at a disadvantage — just getting up on stage was an ordeal, with his leg. And then, once there, he could never think of anything brilliant to say. He had, one night in the very beginning, attempted to tell a few jokes. It had been a disaster and now he just stuck to giving a brief welcome, introducing the act and getting the hell out of there as quickly as possible.

Tonight, as he'd told Doris, it was "Laura and Tom", and as he left the stage Skippy smiled at the singer and whispered, "Have fun." She smiled back and nervously pushed a strand of long, wheat-coloured hair out of her eyes. She was slim and tiny, just over five feet, and her partner was a heavy-set, ruddy-faced guy with the unlikely but musical name of Tom Tinker. Laura sang while Tom played the twelve-string guitar and the banjo and did all of the on-stage patter. When she wasn't singing Laura stood mutely behind the microphone, staring shyly out at the audience.

They'd only been playing together for a few weeks but already they were creating a buzz in the folk-music circles — Laura's voice was one of those originals, like Joan Baez or Mary Travers. It soared sweet and pure above the rest of the crowd and you knew as soon as you heard it that she was going to be big some day. This time next year, Skippy wagered, it would cost him three or four times as much to hire them for an evening — if he was able to get them at all.

At the end of their set, Laura and Tom came over to Skippy's table and he introduced them to Doris and ordered them coffee and a plate of sandwiches. It ate into his profits, feeding the talent, but now and then he did it when he had someone particularly special in the club. Laura McCandless was going places and it would be nice if she kept a soft spot in her heart for good old Skippy at the Dharma Cafe.

She was young and quite shy and when Doris complimented her on her singing she seemed pleased but a little embarrassed. It was obvious that all this was still new to her, the acclaim she was getting from the audience and from the two local papers, who'd each written up a favourable piece on her within the past week.

"Thanks," she said, glancing at Tom who sat next to her, watching her with open affection. "I'm glad you liked it. It's nice to stand up and sing and have people pay attention. I like it." She corrected herself: "*We* like it."

Tom put a protective arm around the back of her chair and drew his own a little closer to her. Skippy saw that they had more than a strictly musical partnership and he felt suddenly sorry for the big, good-hearted guy. He was a competent musician and displayed a certain professional bonhomie on stage but he wasn't in Laura's class, not by a long shot. Laura didn't know that, yet, but she would come to find out one of these days and when she did it would be Good-bye, Tom. It was too bad and Laura seemed like a nice person and she'd probably hate to do it, but she would do it, eventually, because that was how things worked. She was better than he was and it was natural that sooner or later she'd gravitate to others who were like her. And Tom would probably go back to playing the guitar at weddings and at the parties of his friends and some day marry a nice, ordinary sort of girl who couldn't carry a tune to save her life and live happily ever after.

Laura nibbled tentatively at a sandwich ("I can't really eat when I'm performing," she explained, apologetically. "I get too nervous.") and Tom devoured three of them and joked with people at the tables around them. Skippy, in the meantime, edged his chair closer to Doris until his leg brushed against the smooth silk of her nylon stockings. She didn't move her leg away; in fact, he couldn't say for sure if she was even aware they were touching but he was content to sit there like that, with his entire being focused on the few inches of his body that was pressed against hers. It made talking difficult, although Doris didn't appear to notice.

Tom, his arm still around Laura and his mouth full of food, wanted to know what Doris thought of the Dharma.

"I like it," she said. "It's as good as any place you'll find in Toronto."

"That where you're from?"

"Well, here, originally. But I lived there for ten years. I used to go to this place on Jarvis, just up from where we were living, called The Boardinghouse. Musicians lived there, jazz musicians, mostly, and there was a room down in the basement where the guys would come at the end of the night, you know, when they'd finished playing at the hotels and all, and they'd get together and play, just for each other and whoever happened to come by. They'd play all night long. Until morning, practically. You didn't have to pay or anything, you could just sit there on one of these old couches and curl up and listen, and leave when you felt like it. I liked it."

Skippy listened in amazement. This was the longest speech he'd heard her make in the short time he'd known her. So she would open up, given the right circumstances. And the right people, he guessed. People she found interesting. Unlike him.

"So you're a jazz fan?" This from Tom Tinker, between mouthfuls.

"Well, yeah, I guess you could say I am. I mean, some of it was a little weird. They didn't sing or anything, and they'd go off on these sort of tangents where you couldn't follow what they were doing and it didn't sound like any music *I'd* ever heard before. That's one of the things I miss, living here. Places to go, different sort of places. Where's the little girls' room?"

This last was directed to Skippy and he pointed to a door at the far end of the room, marked 'Ladies'.

"Excuse me," she said, picking up her purse. "I'll just go powder my nose."

When she had gone, Tom turned to Skippy with a smile. "Nice girl," he said, and added, "Been going out long, you two?"

"Not long," Skippy said.

"Not like us," Tom said and gave Laura's shoulder a squeeze. "Me and Laura, we've been together a long time, haven't we, honey?"

Laura, who'd said almost nothing since she sat down, looked up at Tom and smiled. "That's right," she said and he nuzzled her cheek with his beard, looking for all the world like a great big affable bear.

She looked over at Skippy and explained, "Tom and I went out together in high school. He was the first boy to ask me on a date." There was something defensive in the way she put it and Skippy realized he'd been wrong: she knew already about the difference between them. She just wasn't prepared to do anything about it, not yet.

Tom laughed and gave her another hug. "Little Laura McCandless," he said, "shyest little thing in school. Never said 'boo', did you, honey?"

"No," she said, softly. "I guess I didn't."

"Just needed me to come along and bring her out of herself," Tom confided. "And look what I found? The pretty little girl who never said nothing to nobody had a voice like an angel."

"That's great," Skippy said, feeling some comment was called for. "You make a nice couple."

The look she gave him now was downright hostile, although she recovered quickly and forced herself to smile. "Thanks."

Tom hugged her again and Skippy thought once again he looked exactly like a bear — with a fragile, frightened rabbit in its grip.

Doris came back to the table just after the next set had begun and he asked if he could get her anything. She shook her head no, and for a few minutes he attempted to find things they could talk about. Finally, she turned to him and suggested, not unkindly, that they just listen to the music, which is what they did for the rest of the set.

Afterwards, Doris seemed more cheerful. She asked him how long he'd had the club and if it made any money and he in turn asked what she did for a living.

"Well," she said, "you won't believe this but I used to be a model. When I was living in Toronto."

"No kidding. I believe it."

"You do?"

"Well, sure. You're beautiful. You'd be a terrific model."

This seemed to please her. She smiled and lit another cigarette. "It's a very tough business. Very competitive. But I guess I did all right."

"What kinds of things did you model?"

"Oh, the usual. Dresses and things for the catalogues, some magazines. I was in Chatelaine once."

"You were?" He knew that magazine, his mother got it all the time.

"Uh-huh. They were going to use me on the cover and then they used another girl instead. But there were three whole pictures of me inside."

"I wish I'd seen them."

"I still have them. I'll bring them in some time, if you want. I mean, if you're interested."

"Of course I'm interested. I'd really like to see them."

"Well, okay. I'll bring them."

"Do you still model?"

She shrugged. "Now and then. The work's not really here, not like it was back east."

"So what do you do?"

"Oh, this and that. I guess you could say I'm sort of between jobs right now but that's okay. Something will come up pretty soon."

In the meantime, Doris watched a lot of TV. Johnny Carson was her favourite. She grew animated when she spoke of him and offered to tell Skippy a secret.

"I have this thing, this fantasy, you know? About Johnny. I pretend I meet him at a party, in Toronto or some place, and he comes up to me and tells me I'm the most beautiful girl he's ever seen and asks me to go out with him. And he takes me on his sailboat — he has one, you know, I read about it — and we sail around the world and go to all these great places and hang around with all these famous people. Funny, huh?"

"It's not so funny," Skippy declared, loyally. "I bet he would fall in love with you, if he met you." *I know I have*, was what he wanted to say next. It was on the tip of his tongue.

"Well, anyway, I am going to see him one of these days. In the flesh. I plan to take a trip to New York, that's where they do the show, and I'll get tickets and be in the audience. A friend of mine, she went to see the Beatles when they were on the Ed Sullivan show, you know, the second time? She stood in line for ages to get in and it was all dumb kids and they screamed so loud you couldn't hear anything. Well, I told her, Sheila, I'm sorry. I would not cross the street to see the Beatles. You couldn't pay me. But one of these days I am going to meet Johnny Carson."

Throughout the rest of that fall and as winter set in he and Doris established a pattern that never varied. She arrived at the club every Sunday around eight o'clock and left just before eleven. Skippy would phone for a cab, then wait outside with her while she had a final cigarette. When the taxi arrived, he helped her into the car and gave her the money for the fare. She would take it with a smile, lean back into the seat and drive away. And that was it.

Sometimes, he thought of trying to kiss her good-night. If she ever gave him even the smallest signal, some indication that it would be all right to do so, he would have pressed his lips against hers and lived on that kiss for the rest of the week. He dreamed of coming home at night after closing down the club and finding her there, in his room at Mrs. Cordelli's, waiting for him. He imagined her in bed, already asleep, while he crept quietly into the bedroom, leaving his shoes at the door and taking off his shirt and pants without waking her up. Then he would slip into bed beside her, warming himself against her body, nuzzling the back of her neck until she murmured in her sleep and turned towards him, sleepily opening her arms to welcome him in and adjusting her body to fit his.

He never mentioned any of this to her, of course. There was something in Doris that kept him from completely opening up to her. Once she had told him, apropos of nothing in particular, that she was not the romantic type.

"I never have been," she said. "It's just not me."

That was all right. There was plenty of time for romance. And in the meantime, he had Sunday evenings and Doris and his dreams.

8.

"You're in a good mood these days."

It was Sunday afternoon and Skippy was at his mother's house — Joe Bruno's house, although his mother was slowly putting her stamp on it. He came most Sundays, in time for dinner; his mother liked it and Joe liked anything that made Jeannie happy. His sister Mandy regularly tried to beg off and find an excuse not to attend these family gatherings but her mother was uncharacteristically adamant about Sunday dinner: Mandy would sit down and eat and pretend, at least, that she was part of the family.

Now Mandy sat across from her brother and picked at the food on her plate. Pork chops, mashed potatoes and gravy. Could her mother have come up with a more fattening meal if she'd tried? Her comment about Skippy's mood was not meant as a compliment; his cheerfulness was an insult and a deliberate dismissal of her own injured feelings.

Before Skippy could reply, his mother added that yes, it was nice to see him looking so happy these days.

"Are things going well at the club?" she asked.

But it was Joe Bruno, of course, who hit it dead on. Well, being a guy, he would — it's the first thing most guys would think of.

"I think Skippy's got a girlfriend," he said, as if Skippy was no more than twelve and this was some kind of adolescent crush. "Eh, pal? What do you say? Found yourself a little lady friend out there?"

"Is that right, dear? Have you met somebody nice?"

Before Skippy could respond, Joe declared, "Well, of course he has, Jeannie. Just look at him. Come on, son, let's hear all about it. Who's the lucky girl?"

Deciding it was probably easier just to tell them and get it over with, Skippy helped himself to two scoops of mashed potatoes and set the bowl down in the middle of the table. Then, picking up his fork, he acknowledged that her name was Doris Pantoniak and he'd met her at the club.

"At the club?" His mother sounded uncertain, although she tried not to show it. What kind of a girl, after all, would he have met at the club? One of those beatniks with the long hair and no shoes?

"She came in one night with a friend and we've been seeing each other ever since."

Well, it was true, wasn't it? They did see each other, even if it was only once a week at the coffee-house.

"What does she do, dear?" There was just the slightest emphasis on "do"; he knew his mother was hoping that what she "did" was respectable. Not wanting to admit that, from what Skippy could tell, she mostly sat around and watched TV, he decided to take the easy way out and lie.

"She's a teacher."

"Oh, a teacher." The relief in his mother's voice was audible. Teaching was an honourable occupation. She might have been a teacher herself, if she hadn't had to go to work right after high school.

"That's wonderful," she told him. She looked around the table for approval. "Isn't that wonderful, Mandy? Your brother's met a teacher."

"I don't see what's so wonderful about it," Mandy remarked. Teachers were not among her favourite people.

"Being a teacher's a very good job," Joe Bruno pronounced, between bites. On his honeymoon cruise he'd met a doctor who convinced him that chewing each mouthful twenty-five times was a way of ensuring you didn't overeat. He hadn't lost any weight by doing this, so far, but it certainly took him much longer to finish a meal.

He swallowed and continued. "Especially for a woman. You'll never get rich, but it's steady work and people respect you. And you can always fall back on it. You should give it some thought." This last was directed at Mandy, who glared at him and appeared about to make a smart remark, then thought better of it and kept quiet.

"What grade does she teach, dear?" his mother wanted to know.

"Five and six," he replied, surprising himself at the ease with which he was able to come up with this stuff. "It's a mixed class. At John A. Macdonald."

"Five and six," she repeated. "Those are difficult grades. Especially together like that. She must be quite good at what she does."

"She is," he said, keeping his eyes on his plate and concentrating on his potatoes. "She's very good."

"So when do we get to meet this paragon?" Joe asked. (Besides deciding to get into shape, Joe was working on his vocabulary: he now subscribed to Reader's Digest and was improving his word-power.)

"Will you be bringing her around to meet us?" his mother asked.

Skippy shrugged. "I guess so. I just met her. It's not like we're getting married or anything."

"No, dear, of course not."

Without thinking, he added, "She used to be a model."

Mandy suddenly showed interest. "A model? Really? That's neat."

"But I thought you said she was a teacher?" His mother sounded alarmed, now, and glanced across the table at Joe, methodically chewing his food.

"She was. She is." He was beginning to feel distinctly uncomfortable. This was getting complicated; he wished the subject had never come up. "She's a teacher now, but when she was living in Toronto she did some modelling."

"She must have been very young," his mother said, trying to keep any trace of concern from her voice. "I mean, if she's in her twenties now — is she your age, Skippy?"

"It was when she was going to high school," Skippy said, side-stepping the age issue. The fact was, he didn't really know how old Doris was — it just hadn't come up. "She modelled part time, to make money, you know? She was in Chatelaine."

"Oh, Chatelaine." His mother's face brightened. That was a name she knew — like teaching, it stood for decency, reliability, good old-fashioned virtues. "Did you hear that, Joe? Skippy's friend modeled in Chatelaine."

Joe wasn't convinced. He'd read about models and he'd always thought they weren't always the most respectable girls in the world. There'd been a guy who worked for him, one of his daughters had left home to be a model. Word had got around that she was working in a nightclub, somewhere in the States, had a baby out of wedlock, the whole bit. Still, this girl of Skippy's had worked in Toronto and Chatelaine was a family magazine. They probably didn't get up to that kind of stuff here in Canada. He decided to adopt a benevolent attitude; after all, it was Jean's only son and God knows she'd been praying he'd finally meet somebody some day. Maybe this girl was the one. He swallowed and smiled at his stepson.

"Well, that's just great, son. Sounds like you hit the jackpot."

"Yeah. Well, I just met her," Skippy repeated. "Don't start planning the wedding just yet."

Afterwards, Skippy called a cab to take him to the club. "Fifteen minutes," the dispatcher said and he went into the living-room and settled himself on the couch to wait. Mandy joined him as he leafed through an issue of National Geographic magazine and paused at a pictorial essay on the Bushmen of the Kalahari, with shots of young, half-naked women carrying their children on their backs.

"Don't you think it's weird," Mandy began, "how it's okay to show pictures of African women with no clothes on but if you do it with white women, it's like, considered disgusting. Don't you think that's kind of two-faced?"

"It's natural for these people," Skippy said. "That's what they do, they live like that. We don't."

"Some of us do." Mandy glanced behind her, to be sure that her mother and step-father were still safely in the kitchen, washing up the dishes and listening to *The World Tomorrow* on the radio. They were; the voice of Garner Ted Armstrong could just be heard behind the closed door, announcing the imminent destruction of California with special punitive measures in store for Hollywood.

Lowering her voice, she continued, "You know Irene's son, Norman? Well, he has these magazines in his bedroom about nudist camps and they're full of these men and women, some really old ones, too, and they're all playing volleyball and golf and bowling, all completely naked."

"That's different." Skippy pictured, for just a moment, an elderly white woman hitting a golf ball in the nude and grimaced. "That is disgusting. Anyway, what are you doing hanging around in Norman's bedroom, looking at dirty magazines? That guy is weird."

"Oh, he's all right. I kind of like him, if you want to know the truth. He knows all about hair and makeup and stuff."

"I bet he does."

"Norman says I should be a model. He says I have fantastic bones. Which is why I want to ask you something. Was that true what you said in there? About your girlfriend being a model?"

"Doris? Well, yeah." Which was true. It was practically the only true thing he had said about Doris. "She was, anyway. Back in Toronto."

"Do you think you could introduce me to her?"

"Why?"

"Because I want to ask her about it, get her to give me some tips. I mean, I think I should take a course or something but Norman says I should just head to Toronto when I graduate and get some pictures taken and start doing the rounds. What do you think?"

"I think you shouldn't be getting career advice from Norman, that's what I think."

"Anyway, will you?"

"Will I what?"

"Introduce me to your girlfriend."

Skippy tried to imagine himself suggesting to Doris that she come over and meet his sister and tell her how to get into modeling. Somehow, he couldn't see it.

"I wouldn't bug her or anything, Skippy. But it would be so neat to meet a real live model. And if Mom met her and liked her and everything, then she wouldn't think it was so awful if I wanted to do it. I can't even talk about it with her right now, she just says, Stay in school, get a good education. And Joe thinks I should be a nurse." She pronounced "nurse" with such absolute derision you'd think her step-father was promoting a career in the U.S. marines.

"I thought he wanted you to be a teacher."

"Oh, he changes it every day. Secretary, teacher, anything boring where I won't get into trouble and they'll make me wear long skirts and no makeup. But, like, if you invited your girlfriend over for dinner one time, they'd meet her and see that modelling's not so bad after all. Please, Skippy. You'd be doing me a huge favour and I'd owe you for ever. I mean it."

"I don't know," he began, but his sister cut in.

"Skippy, please. I never ask you for anything, you know that."

It was true; she never did. And she had spread the word about the Dharma and worked for him for almost two months before getting fed up and quitting. It probably wouldn't hurt just to mention it to Doris, just to see what she said.

"Okay," he said. "I'll ask her about it. But give me a while, okay? I'll wait till the time is right."

Mandy grinned. "You are the greatest, Skippy. You really are."

When Doris arrived at the club that night, she seemed upset. Her eyes were red and swollen and there was a mark on her right cheek, a sort of graze as if she'd been hit with something sharp. She wouldn't say anything at first, just asked him to get her a soft drink, and when he came back to the table she'd slipped her coat off and lit a cigarette.

"Doris, are you okay?" he asked. "Is everything all right?"

"I'm fine." Her voice was even huskier than usual and it occurred to him that she had been crying.

"What's the matter?" he asked. "What happened?"

At first she said nothing, just smoked and looked away into the distance, silent and unhappy. Finally, she revealed that she and Arty Peach had had a fight.

"Did he hit you?" He was ready, right there and then, to go and find Arty and have it out with him. If she just said the word, he wouldn't hesitate. The thought of that thug, that little punk, hurting Doris, making her cry — it was unthinkable.

"Doris, if he hit you —"

"Don't worry. I hit him back even harder. He won't do it again. I'm just mad about my TV."

"Your TV? What about it?"

"He smashed it. Stuck his foot right through the front of it, just kicked in the glass and then threw it against the wall. He said television's for morons and I'm a moron because I watch it all the time. And he won't pay for a new one. And when I yelled at him he hit me and I hit him back. And then I came here."

Setting her cigarette down on the ashtray, she reached for her purse and began rummaging around in it.

"I must look terrible. Have you got a Kleenex or anything?"

Skippy went to the men's toilet and brought her back a bunch of toilet paper. While she wiped her eyes and checked her makeup in her pocket mirror, he made up his mind about something.

"Doris, if it's just the television that's bothering you, don't worry about it. I'll get you a new one tomorrow."

"Oh, you don't have to do that," she said but he could see her face beginning to clear already.

"Well, I want to," he told her. "I want to do something for you. What kind was it, anyway?"

"A little black and white portable but the picture wasn't very good. What I'd really like is a colour set, like I used to have back in Toronto. It was a Panasonic, with a twenty-six inch screen and everything. I'd love to have another set like that."

"Well, then you'll have it," he told her, feeling momentarily drunk with power. "I'll get it for you."

And if he'd had any faint pangs over the cost of such a gift, they were obliterated by the rare, sweet smile that lit up her face as she said, "That's really sweet of you, Skippy. Thank you."

Feeling braver than usual, he reached a tentative hand towards her cheek and touched the mark where Arty had hit her.

"You shouldn't ever let a person hit you, Doris. Nobody has the right to do something like that."

She said nothing and after a moment he removed his hand. She picked up her cigarette and took a drag and the moment was over.

That night when he walked her to her cab she suddenly stopped before getting into the car and gave him a quick hug. "Thank you," she whispered and kissed him on the lips, a soft brush of her mouth against his, and it was so unexpected he said nothing and it was over almost before he knew it had happened. He stood and watched the taxi disappear down the road and for the longest time he was sure he could still feel her mouth, lightly pressed against his.

The Christmas Skippy was thirteen, he had wanted a bike, but not just any bike: he'd wanted a tri-coaster Glider bicycle, with a burgundy frame. He'd seen it at Eaton's, on display in the big corner window, and had gone into the store and casually walked around the bike two or three times, coolly assessing the whitewall tires, the leather seat, the glistening newness of the frame. Fifty-eight ninety-five — more than his mother took home in a week. It was beyond thinking about, yet he couldn't stop thinking about it. Maybe, just maybe, he'd come down the stairs Christmas morning and the Glider would be propped up next to the tree. He'd stopped saying his prayers when he was a kid, but for a month before Christmas Skippy got down on his knees and prayed every night for that tri-coaster Glider with the burgundy frame.

Skippy got a lot of presents that year, he got a Gene Autry cowboy shirt and a Black Diamond baseball glove (grade A genuine cowhide) and, best of all, a Kodak Ultra Modern Bull's Eye camera, but there was no bike.

When he had opened all his presents he made his mom and his sister come and stand outside on the steps in the cold so he could take a picture of them with his brand new camera. And then his mother took a picture of Skippy and his sister and then he went out into the middle of the street so he could take one of their house and get it all into the frame. He fooled around with that camera for hours and made a really big deal about it, and that night his mother came into his room to kiss him goodnight. She sat on the bed next to him and he showed her how he had stored the camera on his bookshelf, up high where it wouldn't get hurt.

"I'm sorry about the bike," she said. "It was just too expensive."

And Skippy grinned and told his mother to forget it, he didn't give two hoots about a silly old bike that he couldn't ride in the snow, anyhow. Who cared about a bike? He didn't, that's for sure. And for the rest of the winter he avoided going into Eaton's and would cross the street to avoid the corner window until the spring came and the snow melted and the bike finally disappeared.

Doris was thrilled with the TV set. A Panasonic 26-inch, just like she wanted, with remote control and automatic fine-tuning. Skippy paid to have it delivered and when she turned up at the club the following Sunday night, she rewarded him with another hug, and there was a warmth in her voice he hadn't heard before.

"It's terrific, Skippy. I stayed in Monday night and watched television until one in the morning. Everything looks better on it, even the commercials."

She went very quiet and for a moment she looked away, as if she wanted to say something but wasn't sure how to put it.

"You don't know what it means," she said, finally, "to have a guy give you something so nice, and for nothing. To give you something that cost a lot of money and not want anything in return —"

"I don't, Doris, I don't want a thing."

"I know that. You're the first guy I ever met who didn't want something from me."

And so Skippy screwed up his courage to ask her to come to dinner. He put it to her in an offhand way, like it was no big deal, so she wouldn't think he'd be devastated if she said 'no'. Doris thought about it for a minute and then she said, "When were you thinking of?"

"Oh, any Sunday. Any Sunday at all. Whatever's good with you." In spite of himself, he could feel his hopes rising. Maybe she wasn't going to turn him down after all.

"Well." She seemed to be considering, working something out in her mind. "I usually eat supper with Dolly on Sunday."

"Dolly" was Doris' mother. Skippy knew very little about her, except that she wasn't much of a mother and she had lousy taste in men. "So I come by it, naturally," Doris had said, smiling to show it was sort of a joke.

Skippy forced himself to keep the disappointment out of his voice. "That's okay, don't worry about it."

"But I guess she could eat alone for once," Doris said. "It wouldn't kill her."

"So you'll come?"

"Sure. I guess so."

"Would next Sunday be okay? Could you come then, do you think?"

"All right."

"That's great." But there was one more thing, one more detail to settle. Feeling stupid, Skippy confessed the lie he had told his parents. "I said you were a teacher."

"A teacher?"

He nodded. "I'm sorry, I don't know why I said it. But they think teachers are so great and when I thought of it I didn't know you'd be coming over and — well, it was a really dumb thing to do."

She considered for a moment. "What grade do I teach?"

"Five and six. Mixed class."

"Where?"

"Sir John A." He couldn't look at her, the whole thing was just so absurd.

"Well, that's good, anyway. That's the school I went to. At least I know it."

"Yeah? That's great. So you don't mind? Pretending you're a teacher, I mean?"

"It could be worse. You could have said I was a brain surgeon."

And so it was settled. Doris Pantoniak would come to his house — his step-father's house — and spend an evening with his family and she would talk about teaching. They would sit at the table together and afterwards move into the living-room and watch TV and he'd sit next to her on the couch and maybe they'd hold hands or he'd put his arm around her, very relaxed and natural, like it was no big deal. And when it was time to leave, when he had to go down to the club, they could share a cab, and maybe she'd come with him, or he'd drop her off and kiss her good-night and make a date to take her to a movie or something the following Saturday. And one of these nights, when the time was right, and in spite of Mrs. Cordelli, Doris would come back with him to his room at the boarding house. She would walk up the stairs with him and come into his room and sit down on the bed. "Skippy," she would say, in that soft, husky voice full of promise, "come sit down beside me." It was simply a matter of time.

Doris had told him not to pick her up the following Sunday.

"Just give me the address," she said. "I'll get there."

So just to be sure, Skippy turned up at his parents' house a full hour before she was due and planted himself at the huge picture window overlooking the street. It was cold out, and overcast, and the day had a brooding, unsettled feeling about it. As he watched, the wind whipped the pages from somebody's newspaper along the silent streets and the enormous elm tree that dominated the front yard fought to hold on to the very last of its leaves. The temperature had dropped overnight — an Arctic front was moving in, the radio announcer had said — and the cabby on the way over had worn a toque and complained that the roads were like ice.

In spite of the warmth of the overheated living-room, Skippy's hands were cold, and he shoved them into his pockets and wished he'd insisted on picking her up, after all. It was a lousy day to be out; attendance would be down at the club tonight. For the past couple of weeks the numbers had been dropping but he knew it was that way all over town. The cold weather was keeping people at home, for a while, but eventually they'd get sick of staying in and would come out looking for a good time, somewhere to get warm and forget about winter. He'd picked up some portable heaters on sale back in the summer and had stored them in a back room at the church. Tonight he'd set them up around the club and get the place good and warm before the first set.

His mother came into the room, looking for somewhere to set a vase of dried flowers. "I found these down in the basement," she said, setting them down on the coffee table, then stepping back to assess the effect. "Fresh would be nicer, of course, but they cost an arm and a leg this time of year. What do you think, honey?"

"They look nice, Mom. Really nice."

She was making a special effort in honour of Doris and Skippy was grateful. She always wore a dress on Sunday, of course, but he saw that she'd applied lipstick and a little rouge and he thought he caught the scent of cologne. This could have been for Joe's benefit, of course — she was still newly-married and, according to Mandy, they were always "grabbing at each other and giggling like kids." It was disgusting, his sister felt, but Skippy thought it was kind of sweet. He'd never given much thought to what it must have been like for his mother, widowed in her twenties, but she certainly seemed to glow these days. Watching her, a suspicion of what might be causing that glow entered Skippy's head and he turned his head away, embarrassed. He was glad she was happy; he didn't want to know more than that.

Now she was smiling at him, fondly. "You can sit down, you know. Hanging around the front window isn't going to make her get here any sooner."

"I was just looking out at the roads," he said, feeling a little foolish. His mother knew how much all this meant to him — they all did. It made him wish he'd had more experience with women and bringing them home to meet the family.

"They look pretty bad. Maybe I should call the cab company and see that they send someone reliable. Some of those guys, you know, they think they're A. J. Foyt."

"Why don't you come give me a hand with the dinner?" his mother suggested. "It'll take your mind off —"

She didn't finish the sentence and after a moment he nodded and followed her into the kitchen where she put him to work peeling potatoes and cutting them into quarters. Once she was sure that he was settled at the table and knew what he was doing, she turned back to the counter and began rolling out dough to make pie crust. Blueberry. His favourite and, as a lucky coincidence, it was also her husband's. She and Joe had picked the berries the last weekend in August, driving out along an old logging road till they came to a place Joe knew about, and had pulled off the road and stayed in the car for a while, necking like teenagers. She had felt young and silly and inordinately happy and retrieving the plastic bag of dark purple fruit from the freezer this morning had brought back the remembrance of that hot afternoon in a very physical, tangible form. They had picked as much as they needed — more than they could possibly use, if they ate nothing but blueberries all winter — and then he had found a soft, shady spot and pulled her down next to him and they'd made love right there, in the open, something she'd never done before. And something else: Joe had put his head down, put his mouth on her private parts, and it had been almost painful to receive such a pleasure and she'd been embarrassed at first and tried to lift his head up, but he persisted and she'd eventually given in to the sweet, dark sensation and let it happen, even pushing him further, harder into her, until finally she had had to push him away. Maurice had tried that once, and she'd stopped him, shocked. She'd been so shy about some things, so fearful, in some ways. Well, she'd been young, they both were. And now, here she was, behaving like a hoyden, lying out in the woods like a loose woman, not caring if anybody saw her or not. Was this something that came with age, she wondered? Where had it come from, this freedom?

On the way back in the car, she was shy at first and sat a little apart from him, turned towards the passenger door. So after a few miles he pulled the car over and made her look at him.

"Jeannie," he said, his arm around her, his hand stroking her cheek, "anything between a married man and woman that gives pleasure is a joy to God. There's nothing wrong with it. It's okay."

And she nodded, looking away, looking down at her fingers twisting together in her lap, and said, "I know," not believing it, but then, having said it, she found she did believe it, after all, and she still felt shy but she felt better. And since then he had done it again, and other things, and she, too, was reaching out for him in bed, and he laughed and said he'd created a sexpot, but he said it with affection and she laughed, too, and told him to come here and quit talking and get to work.

All of this had come about without planning; it was as if she'd accepted a gift and opened it and found all these other unexpected pleasures. Like those little wooden dolls she'd had as a girl, the ones from Russia, which fit inside each other, one by one, and you'd never know, from looking, that one round, chubby little doll could hold so many others inside it.

Afterwards, they would lie in bed, their arms around each other, and talk before going to sleep and it was then that she sometimes spoke about Skippy and how she worried about him, how he had always been alone and she had thought it would change, one day, and now she was beginning to think it never would. He insisted on living in that boarding house when he could be here with his family and he had no close friends, not even Benny Carter, now that something had happened, she wasn't sure what, and Benny didn't come around any more. Something to do with Benny's wife, she thought. Skippy had talked about her a lot, what a nice person she was and how they discussed poetry and writing together. And then the baby had been born and Skippy hadn't even gone to see her, hadn't called or sent a card or anything, which was so cruel, so unlike him. And this club — it took up his evenings, he got home late and then had to get up and go to work in the store and he'd never make any money, it wouldn't lead to anything. When was he going to get married and settle down? When was he going to find somebody?

"Kids these days," Joe would tell her, in a mood to be charitable, having just made love, "they take longer to grow up. They're always talking about finding themselves. They're all like that. He's no different than anybody else."

But he was different; he was her son and he'd been hurt early in life — first, losing his father, then the polio. It had marked him, set him apart, and she wondered if it was possible that there was any woman out there who would see the good in him and take care of him. As she had. As she still would, if he'd let her. If society didn't have this ridiculous, hurtful notion that a mother had no place in her son's life once he was grown.

At any rate, the impossible had happened — he'd found a girl and she sounded too good to be true. A teacher, and pretty into the bargain. It occurred to her, briefly, to wonder what a girl like that would want with Skippy, but she pushed that thought away immediately. She saw what his mother saw, obviously: a good, kind, sensitive boy with a great deal of love to give, to the right girl. She hoped, without knowing she hoped, that this Doris was the right girl.

Rolling out the dough with practised strokes on the floury wooden board, she told her son about watching her mother do this when she was very small, just able to stand on her tiptoes and clutch the table and watch.

"It looked like so much fun," she remembered. "I wanted to try it and she gave me a small piece of dough for myself and I sort of squished it around for a while and then she sprinkled it with butter and cinnamon and put it in the oven with her pies and didn't I just think I'd done something terrific? I remember my father coming home and making a big fuss over it and telling me I was going to be a wonderful cook someday."

She smiled and peeled the circle of pastry from the boards, laying it gently in the pie pan. Taking the large, red-handled scissors she kept just for cooking, she snipped away at the edges of the crust and added, "I did the same with you when you were little, remember? And your sister Mandy. I wanted you both to know how to cook. But Mandy, I don't know. It didn't seem to take with her. She can't stand to even be in the kitchen. I don't think that girl knows how to boil an egg."

Skippy was peeling away at the potatoes, thinking how similar the motions were to whittling wood. An image of Benny came into his mind, sitting on the verandah of the little house, carving away at a piece of wood he'd brought home from the mill. Benny's long, sensitive fingers manipulating the block of eastern white pine, caressing the surface, exploring the tiny fissures like a blind man, all the while carrying on a conversation about — what? Poets? Politics? That book he was reading about how the pesticides were destroying the planet? And music, of course, always music, always a window open to hear the radio on in the background, Ray Charles and Elvis and the music Margaret liked, the songs she would turn up the volume on her transistor radio and sing along with, forgetting about Benny and Skippy outside on the porch — the Crystals and Gene Pitney, the Shirelles and the Four Seasons. "He's a Rebel" — that was Benny, and "Johnny Angel" — that was Benny, too, under another name. They were all about Benny and her, they all sang to her heart.

As if she knew what he was thinking, his mother closed the oven door and turned around to face him. "Why don't you see your friend Benny any more? I never hear you talk about him these days or that nice girl he married. Don't you miss them?"

He kept his eyes on the potato he was peeling and shrugged. "I don't know. I see him around sometimes."

"You were friends for a long time," she commented, keeping any trace of criticism out of her voice. They didn't like you being judgmental, young people; they hated it if they thought you were finding fault, laying blame. She waited and he said nothing, so she brushed the flour from her hands and changed the subject.

"So. We have a guest for dinner. I hope she likes what we're having. Do you think she likes roast beef, dear? And gravy?"

"Of course, Mom." Skippy smiled, putting thoughts of Benny out of his mind. "Everyone likes roast beef, who wouldn't?"

"Well, you never know. Look at your sister. She always acts as if I'm trying to poison her. And models are often picky eaters. They worry about keeping their figures and all that, she might prefer something else — a soufflé, or an omelet or something."

"She's not a model, Mom. She's a teacher. She *used* to be a model, when she lived in Toronto."

"Oh, yes, that's right. Mind you, old habits die hard. She might still *think* like a model. Well, I'm not going to worry about it. I'm sure it will all work out just fine."

"I'm sure it will," Skippy agreed and wished he really believed it.

At ten minutes to six his mother came out of the kitchen to where he was sitting in the living-room, staring out at the darkened streets.

"What time did you tell her, dear?" she asked, deliberately casual, unconcerned.

"Five-thirty," he said and didn't look up. "I told her we ate at five-thirty, and she said she'd be here by five."

"Well. I'm sure she'll turn up. She's just been delayed, that's all."

"Yeah." He kept his head turned away and eventually she went back to the kitchen.

At twenty past six she came out and suggested he phone her.

"I don't have her number," he said, knowing it was hopeless. She wasn't going to come.

"But you know her last name, dear, couldn't you —"

"She lives with her mother and I don't know her mother's married name. Or her address. There's no point."

There was a silence. Then his mother, trying to sound cheerful and fooling no one, said they'd wait until seven, she could keep supper warm until then.

Seven o'clock came and went and his mother and Joe and Mandy sat down in the dining room and started their dinner. Skippy said thanks, but he'd wait in the living-room, just in case. He wasn't very hungry. His mother wanted to insist, to argue that he must eat, he needed to eat, but Joe spoke to her in an undertone — "Leave the boy alone, Jeannie, just let him be" — and so she sat down at the dining room table and passed the basket of rolls to her daughter. Their conversation was subdued, desultory; the presence of the lone figure in the living room lingered over the meal. His mother had difficulty swallowing — she felt angry, humiliated. She had worked hard over this meal, put herself out for this girl, this — this *model,* and now she didn't even have the good grace, the pure, common decency to call and apologize for not turning up. It was easier, somehow, to believe it was she, the mother, who had been slighted. It was preferable to see herself as the victim here rather than face the hurt she knew had been inflicted on her son.

At seven-forty-five they heard him pick up the telephone and make a short call. A minute later he came to the doorway of the dining-room and said he'd called a cab. He had to get to the club; he had to be there by eight.

His mother wanted to say something, wanted to tell him she was sorry, but she could see by the look on his face there was nothing to say. Joe stood up to walk him to the door, but Skippy said, no, he'd wait outside, the guy said it would just be a few minutes. And when the door shut softly behind him, she and Joe exchanged glances, but it was Mandy who expressed what they were feeling:

"What a bitch, eh, Mom? Someone should give her a good kick in the ass."

And her mother didn't even remonstrate with her for using bad language. For once, she agreed with her daughter.

9.

Doris did not turn up at the club that night and the week that followed was the longest of Skippy's life. He came up with a new plan a half dozen times a day and dropped it just as quickly, rejecting every scheme to find a way to contact her as unworkable or undignified or both. He could, for instance, call up the cab company that took her home every Sunday and see if the dispatcher would give out her address. Was there some kind of driver-customer confidentiality among cabbies, he wondered, the kind that existed between doctors and their patients, or lawyers and their clients? And if he did find out where she lived, what then? Was he to turn up on her doorstep like some kind of avenging angel, all outraged sensibility because she'd stood him up? Women did that all the time — they were changeable, ambivalent creatures. It was his own fault for not having arranged to pick her up in the first place.

Which was what it had come down to. Even as he left his mother's house that Sunday night, huddled in the back of the taxi like some wounded bird, he had begun to make excuses for Doris. She'd been sick, got the flu or some other such thing, not serious enough to warrant hospitalization but enough to force her to stay in bed, a box of Kleenex by her side. Or it was her mother who had gotten sick and Doris, the dutiful daughter, had to stay home and take care of her. She couldn't have phoned; he had provided her with a street address, that's all, not a phone number or his step-father's last name. He'd been a fool not to give her more information — she'd had no way to contact him.

He was willing to believe almost anything, he told himself any of a thousand things might have happened, that she had forgotten, even — she didn't write it down, something else came up, it was painful to admit it but it was possible she had forgotten all about it. The one thing he did not — *would* not let himself believe was that she had simply decided not to come. She had entered his life such a short time ago, they had been together less than two months, it couldn't possibly be over so quickly.

Maybe, he thought, she was testing him. Maybe she wanted to see how he'd react, to see if he was the jealous, angry type who'd shout at her, call her names, hit her in the face like Arty Peach. Well, if that was the case, he'd show her. If she turned up at the club the following Sunday, there'd be no recriminations, no wasting precious moments demanding an explanation. He'd be pleasant and smiling and unconcerned, as if nothing had happened. And when she apologized, when she explained what had happened, about her mother being sick and there being no way for her to get hold of him, he'd be completely understanding and tell her not to worry about it, it was no big deal, he was just glad to see that she was all right. That would show her the kind of person he was; she'd see he was a lot more mature than some people he could mention.

She walked in the following Sunday and relief surged through his entire body, as if he'd been holding his breath for a week. Standing in the doorway, as usual, squinting slightly in the dim light — she did need glasses, she'd admitted, but was too vain to wear them — she appeared uncertain of her welcome and that gave him a momentary feeling of power. He had the power to forgive her or turn her away; he'd never felt that towards anybody before in his entire life. It was exhilarating, even erotic, this sense of control, and it propelled him towards her with a confidence which was unusual for him.

She saw him and smiled and the feeling evaporated immediately: it wasn't power he wanted, when it came to Doris, unless it was the power to hold and protect her. The authority was all hers — she could do anything with him, anything, as long as she continued to come to his club every Sunday.

Before she had a chance to say anything, he told her it was good to see her.

"I'm sorry about last week," she said, loosening the belt of her camel-hair coat and removing the scarf she'd tied loosely around her throat. "We were supposed to get together, weren't we?"

"For dinner," he said, grinning like an idiot, he was just so happy to see her.

"Something came up," she told him. And then, "I couldn't get away."

"Don't be silly, it doesn't matter. It wasn't important."

Guiding her through the room, he brought her to the table — their table, the one near the front where they always sat, helped her off with her coat and pulled out the chair for her.

"You've done something to your hair," he said, sitting down across from her, and she instinctively reached up to touch the blonde strands, as if reassuring herself that they were still in place.

"Do you like it? I had it cut." It was straighter and cut just below her ears, she'd had her bangs cut as well. The effect, he thought, was to make her look younger.

"It looks nice," he said and it did, although he realized with a pang of regret that his fantasy of taking the pins slowly out of her hair and letting it fall down past her shoulders was not going to be realized. "It shows off your eyes," he added.

She nodded, as if this affirmed what she already knew. "Yeah, I thought it was about time."

There was something else that was different as well; she was sporting a new watch, a small, square face on a thin gold strap. Skippy didn't know much about these things but it looked expensive.

He smiled. "New watch?"

Her reaction was unexpected. She looked startled and almost guilty, he thought. She told him it was a present from her mother, who'd paid only twenty dollars for it, and wasn't it amazing how it was so cheap when it didn't look it, did it? No, he said, it didn't.

"She was in the States," Doris said, opening her purse and pulling out a slim, silver cigarette case. "She got me this there, too. You can get all kinds of deals, down in Minneapolis."

Like the watch, the cigarette case, too, looked like it had cost a lot of money and he wished he had thought to buy something like that for her. It was exactly the kind of thing she should have, he thought, even if it wasn't as expensive as it looked. If ever there was a girl who should have nice things, it was Doris.

She waited while he lit her cigarette, took a long, deep drag, then held the silver case out to him.

"Sure you don't want one?"

"No, thanks." He hesitated, then finally said, "I was worried when you didn't show up."

"You shouldn't worry about other people. It's a waste of time."

She snapped the case shut and dropped it back in her purse. Then she took another pull on her cigarette and tapped it against the ashtray, watching him.

"So now what?" she said. "We're going to sit here all night and you're going to make me feel bad for not turning up last Sunday. Is that it?"

"No, I wouldn't do that. I would never do that, Doris —"

"It wasn't my fault, you know. I told you, something came up."

"I know that, I wasn't blaming you."

"You don't own me," she said. "I don't have to answer to you if I change my mind about something."

He knew he should shut up, it was getting him nowhere, talking like this. But he had to get to the bottom of it. "So you changed your mind. That's why you didn't come."

She stared at him defiantly for a moment, then suddenly her shoulders sagged and she looked tired and unhappy. "Oh, shit, Skippy. Look, I'm sorry about your mom and all. But that's me. I don't like people expecting things of me. It just makes me nervous. You should never have asked me."

He said nothing and the defiant look came back.

"Forget it," she said, stubbing her cigarette out in the ashtray. "I've got better things to do than sit around feeling guilty because I missed out on Sunday dinner with your folks."

He watched, helplessly, as she angrily thrust her arms into her coat and stood up. "I'll tell you something, Skippy. I did you a favour, not coming over that day. It wouldn't have worked, believe me."

"Doris, don't go." But she wasn't listening.

"I don't even know why I agreed to it. Sitting around the dinner table, pretending I'm a teacher, pretending I'm your girlfriend. I must have been crazy."

"Doris, I promise, I'll never ask you again."

"You know why I come here? Because I feel sorry for you and because I've got nothing better to do in this one-horse town on a Sunday night. And if you think I need to sit around with your parents while they size me up and decide if I'm good enough for their son, well, you've got another think coming. I may not be perfect but at least I'm not a cripple."

The word, coming out of her own mouth, had the same effect on her that it had had on his mother years ago, when he'd been the one to say it. Doris was standing there, clutching her purse against her chest, and now she suddenly stopped and looked at him, as if she'd only just realized what she'd said.

"Oh, Jesus." She let the words out in a long, soft breath and sank back into her chair, still cradling her purse in her arms. And then, after a minute, "Jesus, I'm sorry, Skippy. I shouldn't of said that. I didn't mean it. I don't know what got into me."

"It's okay." He sounded a little hoarse, he had trouble getting the words out, but that was due more to relief that she had stopped shouting at him, that she was sitting down again, that she wasn't leaving. The word itself had not totally lost its power to hurt, after all these years; he felt something that might be described as pain, in a distant part of himself, but he could choose to ignore it. Benny Carter had done that for him — he had taught him how to take an insult, a thoughtless phrase, and render it harmless. Or at least stow it away where it could do no damage.

"Make it into a poem, Skippy," he'd said. "Cripple, ripple, stipple, dripple. Limp, gimp, pimp, simp. It's just words, that's all. Say them twenty times and they stop making sense, they don't mean anything any more. They're just words."

Now Doris was looking at him as if she might cry and he reached out and touched her hand and gently pried it away from her purse.

"Don't go," he said again and she shook her head, still watching him, still horrified by what she had said.

"No, I won't." He held her hand in his, stroking it, marvelling once again at the slender, fragile perfection of the bones. It was like holding a small bird and he thought he could write a poem about her hand — just her hand. There was enough poetry in that one small piece of her anatomy to fill a book.

After a moment she asked, softly, the way a small child might make a request, "Do you think I could have a Coke?"

"Sure," he said and reluctantly let go of her hand. When he returned with her drink, she took a sip and then, in that same, childlike voice, she said once more she was sorry.

"I don't know what got into me, Skippy," she repeated. "I don't usually say mean things to people. I guess —" She stopped, took another sip and then, looking away from him, she said only that sometimes things got to her, she wasn't sure why, and she'd taken it out on him.

"I don't mind," he said and he didn't. "You can take it out on me whenever you want to. That's what I'm here for." He laughed; it was meant to be a joke but he knew it was true, in a way.

Doris didn't laugh. She seemed a little sorrowful and told him he shouldn't say that. "Nobody has the right to be mean to you," she told him. "You shouldn't let them. Not even me."

"I just meant it's okay if you blow up sometimes, that's all. I mean, everybody gets mad now and then."

She smiled. "Except you."

"No, I get mad. Lots of times."

"Really?" She didn't believe him.

"Sure. Hey, I'm only human."

Doris didn't say much for the rest of that evening and neither did he. It was busy, for one thing — the kids had begun coming out again and he had three acts performing tonight. One was a poet from Toronto, not very well-known outside certain circles, but he'd been published several times and Skippy considered it a coup to have got hold of him and persuaded him to read. He was aloof and unfriendly for the most part, in town for six weeks to teach at the college, and his manner on the phone had been skeptical and slightly amused, as if he found the whole idea of "performing" a little distasteful.

"Like a trained seal, is that it?" was the way he put it, but Skippy thought his attitude had more to do with the fact that the Dharma was in a small town in the north, rather than downtown Toronto. Still, he had persisted with the poet because in spite of the guy's condescension and rumours of his drinking, he was good and someday he'd be famous. Well, as famous as you got if you were Canadian and wrote poetry. And Skippy would be able to say he'd met him — hired him, even, when he was young and on the way up.

The poet turned up late, smelling of liquor but not too drunk to read, accompanied by a student who was obviously thrilled to have been chosen by the great man and just as obviously destined to be dumped at the end of his college contract. She looked to be in her third or fourth year at the university, Skippy thought, which made her all the more vulnerable: by that time most girls were hoping to have snagged a husband, which for many was the whole point of college in the first place. Well, if she thought this guy was going to make the situation more permanent before he left, she was about to be disappointed. Still, she'd have the memory of a brief, romantic liaison with an actual poet to keep her going for the rest of the winter and at the very least he'd no doubt present her with a copy of his most recent book, with a special message inscribed that could be interpreted as meaning more than it seemed.

His thoughts running along these lines, Skippy was startled to realize how cynical he was becoming about some things. Surely he hadn't always looked at life this dimly? It had been less than a year since he'd started the club and at that point he'd still been in awe of writers and musicians — anyone with a "creative" bent. He still got a kick out of the music and filled his room at Mrs. Cordelli's with paperback books of poetry, old and new, but meeting some of these people in the flesh was often a let-down. It was just as well, he thought, that he'd never been able to nab Kerouac or Ginsberg; he'd hate to discover that those two, the giant gods of the movement, were as vain and petty and downright ordinary as most of the people seemed to be who took their turns on stage at the Dharma.

He got up to greet the poet and brought him back to the table to introduce him to Doris, the student hovering in the background at a distance that was at the same time respectful and yet indicative of some ownership. She watched her man — her trophy — suddenly turn on the charm in the presence of this beautiful woman. He took Doris' hand and instead of shaking it, he bowed slightly and pressed it against his lips. Then, without relinquishing it, and keeping his eyes fixed on hers, he recited:

"She walks in beauty, like the night/Of cloudless climes and starry skies;/And all that's best of dark and bright/Meet in her aspect and her eyes."

If he was expecting Doris to be overwhelmed by this, he was disappointed. Men had been paying her compliments on her looks all her life, although most of them, she'd have to admit, expressed themselves in terms that were a little more prosaic.

She smiled and gracefully retrieved her hand. "That's pretty," she said, picking up the cigarette she'd been about to light. "Did you write it?"

Skippy reached for the lighter but the poet was there before him. He struck the flame and held it for her while Skippy and the student watched, each of them feeling rather displaced. "No, I didn't, I'm afraid. It was written by Lord Byron some hundred and fifty years ago, but he had you in mind when he wrote it."

"Did he?" Doris took a drag on the cigarette and smiled once more. "Gee, and here I hardly knew the guy."

Skippy was proud of her. She was holding her own with this guy, even putting him in his place, letting him know that while naive college students might be impressed with him, she wasn't. The poet was angling for an invitation to sit down so Skippy told him he was on in a few minutes and he had a table set aside for him — and his friend, he added, intending to remind the man of his romantic obligations — and if he wanted to take a seat there, Skippy would have one of the girls bring them a couple of cups of coffee.

The poet shrugged; she was a pretty girl, prettier than most he'd encountered in this godawful place, and she'd obviously been around more than the students he'd been mixing with here. It would have been pleasant to dump the other one and spend a night in bed with this one and not have to worry about sneaking her out of his room on campus at some ridiculous hour of the morning and hoping the dean of arts wouldn't find out, at least not until he was safely back in Toronto.

If it had been later in the evening and he'd had more to drink, he might have pressed the point. But he was here to earn his pittance — actually, it was a good deal more than they paid for these readings back home but he wasn't about to admit that — and get out of here and back to his small, cell-like chamber, where the student would massage his back and other, more intimate parts and worship at the shrine of the poet he was and the laureate he would one day become.

He retreated to his table, to the immense relief of the student, and Skippy sat down again across from Doris and took hold of the hand that had recently been kissed by the poet.

"He thinks he's something, doesn't he?" she said.

She wasn't impressed; Skippy felt he could afford to be generous. "He's very good, you know," he told her. "He's had three books published and he's not even thirty."

"Is that right? Well, I hope his writing's better than his pick-up line."

Skippy didn't want to talk about the poet. He wanted to sit and hold Doris' hand and marvel that she was here, she'd come back into his life and nothing, as far as he could tell, had changed. The way she'd erupted earlier, well, she'd been upset, these things happened. It hadn't destroyed anything between them; in fact, if you looked at it in the right way, it had brought them closer. He'd seen a part of her that lots of people, probably, hadn't. And she, in turn, had seen that his feelings for her were so deep, so loving, that nothing she could say could change them. He gave her hand a gentle squeeze and she smiled and squeezed him back.

"I'm glad you're here," he whispered, feeling the need to say something of what was in his heart.

"Are you?" She smiled and then, as if she was surprised to hear herself saying it, she added, "So am I."

The poet finished his reading just before eleven and as he came down from the stage Doris glanced at her watch and asked Skippy to call her a cab. He left the table to use the telephone and when he returned he saw that the poet had usurped his chair and was leaning across the table, talking to Doris in an intense fashion while the student sat forlornly across the room, watching.

Skippy approached the table and the poet looked up and smiled.

"You abandoned your lady," he said, and Skippy replied that yes, he had, for about thirty seconds.

"I was telling Doris," the poet continued, turning back to her, "that she reminds me of Teresa, the Countess Guiccioli. She ran off with Byron when she was nineteen and he was thirty-one. Left her husband and lived with him for years. She changed his life."

Doris was smoking a cigarette, watching the poet and saying nothing. Her expression was unreadable. Skippy stood helplessly between them, feeling suddenly like a fifth wheel, and the poet turned back to him, still smiling.

"He had a club foot, you know, Byron. It profoundly affected his writing."

Skippy felt he should say something. "Really? Well, that's interesting." It sounded ridiculous; he should have shut up and said nothing.

"Would you like a ride home, Doris? We could continue our discussion."

"She doesn't need a ride," Skippy began but Doris interrupted him.

"What about your little friend?" she asked, indicating the student across the crowded room.

"Oh, we'll drop her off, of course," the poet replied. "I would never abandon a lady."

Doris seemed to make up her mind. Stubbing her half-finished cigarette into the ashtray, she stood up and smiled at Skippy. "You can cancel the cab," she said. "Your friend here will see me home."

As Skippy stood there, watching, the poet helped Doris into her coat and let his hands rest, just for a moment, on her shoulders. It was a small gesture but it was enough. Then he looked over at Skippy — she's mine, the look said, I win, you lose. But all he said was, "Great gig, man. Let's do it again some time."

Over my dead body, Skippy thought, and watched while the two of them made their way towards the door. As they passed the table where the student sat, the other miserable witness to this little drama, the poet stopped and leaned down to speak to her for a moment. She nodded, slowly, and stood up. Doris and the poet continued towards the door, the student following dejectedly a few steps behind, and before they disappeared, Doris turned and smiled and blew a kiss to where Skippy was standing.

Two weeks before Christmas, Skippy walked into the hushed, luxuriant recesses of Martin's Fashion Fur Shoppe and paid fifteen hundred dollars for a full-length mink coat.

"Your fiancee is a lucky girl," the sales lady told him.

This was the very best kind of mink, a once-in-a-lifetime purchase. Carefully, aware that for the first time in his life he had something someone else might want to steal, Skippy carried the large silver box home to Mrs. Cordelli's and stowed it under his bed. Each night when he got home from the club, he pulled the box out from under the bed and lifted the lid to check that the coat was still there. He ran his hand along the fur and imagined Doris wrapped in this magnificent garment; the very best, he told himself. Only the very best for Doris. He lifted a sleeve to his face and closed his eyes and breathed in the rich, animal smell. This was what sensuous women wore, women with white skin and soft, full lips. A coat like this was more than a piece of clothing: it was a statement, a declaration, an exotic invitation.

He'd had to borrow the money to get it. Earlier in the week he'd approached his stepfather and asked for a short-term loan, "for a business project," he told him. Joe'd made up his mind about Skippy: he liked him, in spite of the coffee house and the weirdos who went there. He was a good kid and he deserved a helping hand in life. And if Joe could provide it, he was happy to do so.

He wrote out the cheque and handed it to Skippy with a flourish, regretting only that he couldn't tell Jeannie what he'd done. She was crazy about the boy and she'd have been thrilled to know Joe was helping him out. But Skippy made him promise to say nothing to Jean and a promise was a promise. Joe Bruno was a man of his word.

On the Sunday night before Christmas, Skippy arrived at the club earlier than usual and was too nervous to sit still. He darted between the stage and the front door, checking and re-checking the lights, the sound equipment, opening the fridge and counting the bottles of pop, the bags of coffee. That afternoon he had written a poem, "To Doris", all free-form and anarchy, and he considered it the best thing he'd ever written. He hadn't actually sat down and composed a poem since the winter he'd spent with Benny and Margaret, although snatches of verse went through his head from time to time. But today he had suddenly felt inspired and had sat up in his room and written the entire poem in one unbroken, three-hour stretch.

Perhaps Doris was his muse, he thought; all great poets and writers had a muse, some beautiful woman who brought out all that was good and creative in them. One day he would write a great epic poem, in the same class as "Howl", and he would dedicate it to Doris. He might even write it and then die very young and he and Doris would both become famous, the Percepied and Mardou of a younger generation. He had written his poem on two pages of foolscap paper and folded it carefully and put it in his inside jacket pocket. Sitting down at a table near the stage — "their" table, where they always sat when she arrived — he took it out and read it over again, just to see if it was as good as he'd thought it was when he was writing it. It was. Better, even. It had poured out of him without hesitation, as if somebody else was directing his hand, a greater force was guiding his pen across the paper. Tonight he would give her the coat and ask her to stay until the club closed and come back with him to his room. And then, when they were alone together, he would read her the poem. It would be the most perfect night of his life.

At nine o'clock "Kin of the Wind" appeared on stage for their first set of the night and the applause of the crowd distracted Skippy from thinking about Doris, who was now almost an hour late. "Kin of the Wind" was the former "Laura and Tom" with two additional guitar players and Tom standing to the side, looking vaguely bewildered. It was happening already, Skippy realized. Laura was changing, coming into her own, but either unwilling or unready to push Tom aside just yet.

In the three months since she had first appeared at the Dharma, Laura had increased in poise and confidence — even her voice, which had been thrilling before, was better, more controlled. Normally deep, it could suddenly leap an octave or two and hit a high note and sustain it effortlessly for what seemed like a minute or more. Perhaps it didn't really matter who accompanied her; once she opened her mouth nobody in the audience was paying any attention to the guys on the guitars and the banjo. She was the star.

Laura and her back-up group (which was how Skippy found himself thinking of them) had finished their first set and left the stage when Doris finally made an appearance, looking rushed and distracted and not her usual serene self. She apologized for being late, something had come up, and Skippy was so relieved to see her and thought she looked more beautiful than ever.

"Be a sweetheart and get me a Coke, okay?" she asked him. "I'm parched."

He helped her off with her coat and saw that she was settled at the table, then hurried off to find her a soft drink. When he returned she had lit a cigarette and was looking a little more relaxed.

"Merry Christmas," she said and handed him a parcel done up in green and gold paper. "It's a sweater," Doris added, as he lifted it out of the box. "I should lie and say I made it myself but knitting's not one of my talents. I'm not the most domestic person in the world. Do you like it?"

"Of course I like it," he said, holding it up to the light. "It's great. It's perfect." People around them were watching, he knew, but he didn't care. It was only the second time in his life he'd been given a gift by anyone other than his family — the first was Margaret but that was different, he hadn't been in love with her — and he didn't know what to say. He had known he would give Doris a present for Christmas; he'd never imagined she'd get something for him.

"Try it on," she said. "Go ahead. I want to see if it fits you. I can take it back if it's too small. Go on."

It was a perfect fit, a turtleneck, the type favoured by the guys who played here at the club, and Doris was pleased with the effect. "It suits you, you know that? You can wear that classic sort of stuff. I knew it'd look good on you. I have an eye for that kind of thing."

"I have something for you, too," he told her, "but I don't want to give it to you here in front of everybody."

"Why, what is it?" she teased. "Sexy underwear? A see-through nightie?"

He was embarrassed. "No, nothing like that," he said and suggested they go into the small room behind the stage where the performers kept their instruments and sometimes hung out between sets. Laura McCandless and her group were just finishing their break when Doris and Skippy entered and the guys smiled and stubbed out their cigarettes in the ashtray on the counter.

"Great crowd, man."

"Yeah," he agreed. "Not bad at all." And he added, specifically to Laura, "You sound terrific tonight."

She thanked him, glancing at Doris, and then back at him.

"We're off to Winnipeg next weekend," she offered. "A TV folk show. A kind of hootenanny sort of thing. They're taping it at the university."

"Really? That's great."

She nodded. "And then maybe down to the States, if Steve can line it up."

Steve was one of the new guys; he'd begun to take over as manager from Tom.

"I've got some connections with the bluegrass people," he said. "There's very big things happening, south of the border."

A snort was heard from the corner of the room where Tom sat, slumped into a rickety wooden chair that looked about to collapse under his weight.

"Connections," he repeated, like the word was slightly obscene. "It takes more than connections to make it big in the States, Stevie boy. It takes talent. And timing. And the right breaks."

Unperturbed, Steve turned to Tom and explained, as patiently

as though he were telling it to a child, "We have the talent, Tom —
we have Laura. And we'll make our own breaks."

Tom said nothing; it was obviously not the first time they'd had
this particular argument and Laura, for one, was eager to get back
to the stage where things were simpler and people weren't struggling
for control. She stood up.

"It's time, guys," she announced and the others immediately got
up and picked up their guitars. The men might argue all they wanted
behind the scenes but when it came to performing, Laura was front
and centre and they took their cues from her.

"Break a leg," Doris called out as they left and Laura smiled
and swept out of the room, the men trooping single file behind her.

As soon as they were alone, Skippy gently shut the door, then
turned to Doris and told her to sit down and close her eyes.

"What is this, Skippy?" she asked, intrigued. "What are you up
to?" But she did sit down, rather gingerly, on the edge of an old,
paint-spattered chair in the middle of the room. When her eyes were
closed, Skippy placed the box on her lap.

"Okay," he said, "you can look now."

"What a big box." She pulled at the tape that held the paper in
place. "Is it something to wear?"

"You could say that." He was enjoying this beyond measure.
He wished he had the power to extend the moment indefinitely, so
that this state of expectancy could last for ever. All too soon, she
lifted the lid of the box, pushed aside the tissue paper, and discovered
the glistening fur pelts.

"Oh, Jesus," she whispered and sat there, not touching it, not
lifting it out of the box.

"Here," he said, reaching for the coat, "I'll help you." And he
took the box from her and set it on the floor and held up the
magnificent coat in front of her.

"It's mink," he said, "wild mink. Try it on."

Still seeming a little dazed, Doris stood up and shed the coat she
was wearing. Then, with Skippy's help, she put on the mink and
when it was on there was a transformation. Standing there, clasping
the coat to her body, she merged with the coat, she and the coat
became one. If ever there was a woman born to wear mink, it was
Doris; you would never think, to look at her, that she had ever worn
anything else. He wanted to reach out his hand and stroke the fur
but it was too much. In this coat, Doris was untouchable — he could
never imagine approaching such glamour.

She looked up at him and he saw in her face that she, too, was
in awe of the sheer extravagance of such a gift. "How do I look? Is

it gorgeous? I wish I had a mirror, I wish I could see."

"It's beautiful," he told her. "You look amazing."

She did a brief pirouette and hugged herself with pleasure. "I feel amazing. It's wonderful. It's absolutely wonderful."

With a note of concern in her voice, she said, "It must have cost a lot," but she gave another twirl and lovingly caressed the thick, dark fur.

"It's good quality. I've seen a few mink coats and this is the very best."

"That's what the saleslady said." He couldn't take his eyes from her. The fantasies he'd had of Doris in this coat, the pictures he'd conjured in his mind — nothing had come near the woman that stood across from him now, in this room. He had known the coat would look good on her; what he hadn't known was that it would turn her into royalty.

"Touch it," she said, in her soft, husky voice, and he reached out and placed a hand on the collar of the coat. Doris took hold of his hand and guided it down through the soft bristles of fur. He felt the shape of her body underneath and she closed her eyes and stood completely still while he ran his hand all over the coat, all over the glorious softness wrapped around her. She took his other hand and gently directed it underneath the coat, placed it around her waist, and pressed herself against him.

"Kiss me," she told him, her eyes still closed, and there was a note of command in her voice that thrilled him. He kissed her, heavily, on the mouth, and she didn't pull away. For a moment they stood in this embrace and finally it was he who lifted his face from hers and told her that he loved her.

It wasn't how he planned it, he hadn't meant to say it there and then, but the words came out spontaneously and there was no taking them back. She said nothing and he wondered if she hadn't heard him, so he repeated it, and this time she opened her eyes and smiled.

"I know," she said. "Thank you, Skippy. It's the best thing anyone's ever given me."

Now, he thought, he would ask her to stay, he would ask her to come back to his room, to spend the night with him, but when he started to speak, she interrupted him.

"Skippy, I'm sorry but I can't stay. I'm going on holiday tomorrow — for three weeks. Phil, my mom's boyfriend, he's taking Dolly and me to Las Vegas. We're driving down in his car. Didn't I tell you about it? I thought I did. We're leaving first thing in the morning and I still have to pack and everything. I have to go."

He couldn't let her see how disappointed he was. He put his arms around her again and held her but after a moment she pushed away again, gently, and repeated that she had to go.

"Call me a cab, will you? And then, come back here. We'll wait here, for the taxi."

He nodded, miserably, and went out of the room to the counter where the telephone sat. When he returned, the door leading to the toilet was closed.

"I'm in here," she called out to him. "I'll be right there."

When the washroom door opened, she was still wearing the coat, holding it closed with both hands. She was smiling and before he could say anything she said, "Come here, Skippy. I've got something to show you."

As he approached, she let go of the coat and it fell open and for a moment he wondered if he was dreaming. She wore her high heels and the coat and a tiny gold cross on a chain around her neck. And that was all.

"Come here," she said again and reached out to take hold of his hands. Pulling him towards her, she wrapped the coat around the two of them and pressed her naked body against his. Unwilling to close his eyes, he ran his hands along her bare back, her hips, the curves of her bum, and she stood there and let him, barely moving, her warm breath brushing against his cheek. Eventually, she slowly pulled away once more and did up the buttons of the coat. Retrieving her clothes from the bathroom, she shoved them into the pockets of the coat and smiled.

"Deep pockets," she said. "That's good."

"You're going home — like that?" he whispered, still feeling dazed from the touch of her skin.

"Sure. Won't it be nice for you to think of me, sitting in the back seat of that taxi wearing nothing but this coat? And only you and me will know, Skippy. It'll be our little secret."

Outside the church door, the taxi was waiting. Doris pulled the coat more tightly around her and turned to him.

"Merry Christmas," she whispered. And she was gone.

It was only after the cab pulled away and turned the corner, out of sight, that Skippy remembered the poem, still folded in the pocket of his shirt. He had forgotten all about it.

10.

January was cold but there was nothing new in that. Business at the club had picked up — students were always looking for someplace warm and cheap to spend the winter evenings. And business at the hardware store was slow. So Skippy had his nights to rush around and see that the coffee urn was working, the ashtrays were emptied and the musicians turned up on time, and his days to sit behind the high counter at the store and read and ponder his feelings for Doris.

The three weeks she'd been away had been interminable; he was convulsed with anxiety the whole time that she might not come back. But she did and turned up as usual on a Sunday night with postcards of Caesar's Palace and stories about the famous people she had seen, onstage and at the betting tables. She had come "this close" to seeing Johnny Carson, she said; a woman next to her in the washroom told her Johnny was playing roulette but by the time Doris got to the table he had left. She was bitterly disappointed, she told Skippy, but still, it was something to know that she'd even been under the same roof as her idol.

Phil, her mother's boyfriend, had taught her to play Blackjack and she'd had beginner's luck, which Phil maintained was partly because the dealer took a shine to her. Her mother had stayed with the one-arm bandits but Doris preferred to hang out at the tables where you could see people and mingle. One wealthy Texan played every day they were there; he called Doris his good luck charm and before he left he gave her a diamond bracelet, which she proudly displayed in the dim light of the Dharma.

"I don't dare show it to Dolly," she announced, admiring the way it sparkled on her wrist. "She'd pawn it the next time she needed some cash. She's done it before."

"What about the mink?" Skippy asked her, suddenly worried that the beautiful coat — his coat, the one he went into hock to afford — would turn up on some middle-aged matron with blue-tinted hair. "Won't she pawn that?"

"She wouldn't dare. She knows if she tried to take that coat I'd kill her. I let her try it on, just once, and that's it. I think she's jealous, you know that? She calls you my rich beatnik boyfriend. Because of the club and all that. You know."

The thing was, though, except for the night he'd given her the coat, Skippy never saw Doris in it. She told him she wouldn't wear it just anywhere — it was too fancy for the club and she wouldn't want to get it dirty — but she promised that, one of these nights, she'd wear it again, just for him.

And if Skippy had hoped that the mink would be his passport to establishing a more intimate relationship with Doris, well, that, too, had not panned out. Five months into their relationship, Skippy was no closer to having sex with Doris than he had ever been. Apart from that one night in the back room of the club, when she had shown herself naked and let him caress her, demonstrations of affection between them were few and far between. She let him hold her hand at the table in front of the stage and allowed him to kiss her, briefly, at the end of the evening. She side-stepped all suggestions that they get together outside the club, go to a movie or have dinner somewhere when he wasn't working.

"This is nice," she once told him. "I like coming here Sundays and sitting with you like this. It's relaxing. Don't spoil it, okay?" She said it with a smile but there was a note of warning in her voice: Watch your step, she was telling him. Push me too hard and you'll lose me for good.

But he wasn't giving up hope. She might not want the relationship to be any more than it was, right now, but she kept coming back each Sunday, didn't she? She turned up one night a week and surely she wouldn't do that if she didn't feel something for him.

Occasionally, there were evenings when she simply didn't show up. He would keep one eye on the door all evening, not giving up completely until almost eleven; only then would he admit to himself that she was definitely not coming. And then he had seven long days and nights to endure until he saw her again. He always left the club completely crushed on the nights she didn't appear, he felt utterly defeated.

Doris told him it was her mother's fault. She'd gotten sickly, over the winter, and when she was feeling low she'd want Doris to stay with her.

"It's all in her head," she confided to Skippy. "She never gets sick when there's a man around. It's just when she knows she's going to be on her own for a few days, then she gets all soppy and doesn't want me to leave. She's just scared to be alone."

Doris was in his thoughts continually. He dreamt about her most nights, although sometimes the dreams were distinctly unpleasant.

One was his old childhood nightmare of being chased along the top of a snowbank by a dwarf wielding a large, curved knife who threatened to carve him up "like a turkey." Now the dwarf had the face of Arty Peach and Doris stood there in the background, not laughing, but not doing anything to help either.

After one of these dreams, Skippy woke up in a sweat and a story came to him, something he'd heard a couple of years back about what Arty had done, once, to a guy who owed him some money. According to the story, the guy didn't have the cash so he headed out to the bush to hide out in an old trapper's cabin. Arty tracked him down and held him at gunpoint for over an hour while the guy sweated and pleaded and finally got down on his knees and begged for his life. Arty never did kill the guy, in the end, but he'd taped the whole thing and he got a kick out of playing that tape in bars and listening to the poor guy go through the whole process all over again. And letting everybody else hear it, too. Arty thought it was the funniest thing he ever heard; the guy left town after that and no one ever heard from him again.

There was no reason, of course, for Arty to want to kill Skippy. They had no quarrel with each other. As far as Skippy knew, Doris never saw Arty any more — hadn't seen him since the time he'd kicked in her TV. At least, she hadn't mentioned him since then. But then, she never talked about other men at all, except for occasional stories about some she had known back in Toronto. As far as he could figure, Doris spent most of her free time with her mother. Which was absolutely fine by him.

It's hard to say how long things might have gone on like this, with Skippy seeing Doris most Sunday nights down at the club and spending the rest of the week thinking about her, if the telephone hadn't rung one bitterly cold winter afternoon while he was working at the hardware store. The old man called out from the small room at the back, the crowded cubbyhole he referred to as his office, that there was a call for him, he could take it back there.

Skippy picked up the phone and said, "Hello?", avoiding the censorious stare of the old man who did not approve of "personal" calls being made on company time. It was his mother and she sounded breathless as if she'd been running or was extremely excited.

"Your Uncle Gill," she was saying, "your father's older brother."

Gill, short for Gillaume. Skippy had been named for him, "William", the anglicized version, although he never thought of it since nobody ever called him that. He'd never even met Uncle Gill, but he'd seen pictures of him and had heard how he'd left the bush in the late 'forties and gone out west to work the oil fields in a place called Leduc, Alberta. A taller, stringier version of Maurice, with none of the soft boyishness Skippy had always connected with his father. But he, of course, hadn't died young; he'd lived and worked outdoors all his life and was bound to have been hardened by the experience. And something else, some disappointment, Skippy thought, was associated with this uncle — he'd gone to seek his fortune and it hadn't quite worked out.

"He's passed away, dear," his mother said, lowering her voice out of respect for the dead, although she'd hardly known Gill, had met him just twice — once at Maurice's parents' place, the night they got married, and one other time, after the war, when he'd come by to say he was leaving, going to make his fortune in Alberta. Grim, rugged, not much of a talker, he'd seemed exactly like the cowboys you saw in the movies, just the right type of man to do well in a world of prairie fields and no women.

"That's too bad," Skippy said, wondering if his mother was proposing he go to the funeral. "When did it happen?"

"Two months ago. He had a heart attack out in a field somewhere, that's what the lawyer said."

"Lawyer? What —"

"He's left you some money, Skippy," and now all thoughts of the dear departed were discarded in the excitement over this, the real news, the reason for the phone call. "The lawyer for his estate called me just a few minutes ago, and he says Gill mentioned you in his will. In fact, you're the only person he mentioned. Well, of course, he never got married, at least I don't think he did, and he didn't have any children and so you would be his nearest next of kin. You and Mandy, although the lawyer didn't say anything about her. Maybe you could give her a little of it, Skippy, just to be nice? What do you think?"

Skippy finally managed to interrupt his mother. "How much, Mom? How much did he leave me?"

"Five — thousand — dollars!" his mother replied, spacing the words dramatically, to give the answer its full effect.

Five thousand dollars. It was more than he'd make in a year working at the hardware store. It was enough to pay back his step-father for the mink coat, enough to do whatever he wanted, as long as what he wanted to do was within reason. And it came to him, right there with the telephone receiver in his hand and the old man indicating it was time to hang up the phone and get back to work, it came to him what he wanted to do: he wanted to take Doris and go on the road. Just like he and Benny had planned almost three whole years earlier. He wanted to pick up the plan where he and Benny had left off. Who was to say that a road trip had to take place between guys? If he could get Doris away from this place, away from her mother and Arty Peach and whatever other ties she had to this town, if only for a few weeks, he could show her that he was more than a funny little guy who ran a coffee-house. He could take her to New York, show her the places he and Benny had talked about, read poetry to her at night under the stars. They would stroll through Central Park, eat egg rolls in Chinatown, go see the Rockettes at Radio City Music Hall. There is a rose in Spanish Harlem. Little Italy. The Lower East Side. They could even go see the Tonight Show with Johnny Carson — she would be thrilled to finally see her hero in person. This was a gift he could give her, thanks to his dead Uncle Gill.

His mother was saying something on the other end, something about papers to be signed, and he said yes, he'd come over after work, and yes, it was wonderful, who'd have thought that Uncle Gill would have remembered him, after all this time? And then he said he had to go, he had to get back to work, and placed the receiver back in its cradle.

"Well," said the old man, "I hope that was important."

Skippy nodded, and said that it was, and the old man raised an eyebrow in question. But Skippy was caught up in his own thoughts and walked out of the little room, back to his seat behind the counter where he spent the rest of the afternoon considering the machinery of fate: an uncle he had never met, had scarcely heard of, even, had gone and died and left him just enough money to fund a plan to bring him together with Doris — and at exactly the right time, as well. The symmetry of it overwhelmed him: it was destiny, part of the gigantic cosmic dance, and it only proved all over again that he and Doris were meant to be together.

June was the best time to do it. The first Saturday in June, in fact, when it would be warm and she would feel the heat of the road on her face, she would see it as a celebration. She would love it; hadn't she told him how much she'd enjoyed the trip to Las Vegas, passing through all the small towns and stopping at roadside restaurants for burgers and strong coffee, the kind the truck drivers drank? And she loved to drive; she'd got her license years ago but had hardly ever driven when she was living in Toronto because you didn't need to, you could walk or take the streetcar everywhere. She'd do the driving and he, Skippy, would sit in the passenger seat and navigate.

The thing was, he couldn't come right out and ask her. If he put it to her that he wanted them to take this trip together, she'd have a million excuses — she'd brush him off the way she always did when he tried to get her to commit to anything other than their Sunday night visits. No, it was he who would have to take charge, he who would make the decisions, sweep her off her feet so that in the end she would have no chance to say no, no chance to turn him down. And then, once they were on their way, she'd be so happy, so grateful, and everything would be perfect.

And so, on his own, he planned the route and made the preparations. He bought a brand new Rand McNally Road Atlas and marked it all out in pencil: Highway 61 south to Duluth (it meant going west a little and in the long run it would take more time than heading east around Lake Superior and crossing the border at Sault Ste. Marie, but he wanted to get into the States as soon as possible). From Duluth it was south on 35 to Minneapolis-St. Paul, they could get just south of there by the end of the second day — they wouldn't get much further than Grand Marais the first day since they wouldn't be leaving till night time when Doris came to the club. Then back onto 61, which wasn't as great a highway as 35 but he liked the idea of following the Mississippi down to Dubuque, Iowa. (Hawkeye State. Capital city: Des Moines.)

Just south of there, the great river veered to the east, and they could take 52 and 67 to Clinton, then cross the river into Illinois (Land of Lincoln) and head east for the long drive across the state to Chicago. (City of big shoulders. The windy city. Home of the Great Fire, Al Capone, John Dillinger and the St. Valentine's Day Massacre.) Just the sight of the map of Illinois and all those towns crowded next to each other excited him. Unlike the big, white, empty country to the north, the U.S. was throbbing with people — in places like Sterling, Rock Falls, Rochelle, De Kalb, Wheaton, Elmhurst and Oak Park, which weren't really towns at all but suburbs of Chicago. Then along the northern part of Indiana into Ohio to Toledo, and following the southern shore of Lake Erie through Cleveland and up to Erie, Pennsylvania (historic Gettysburg, a pity to miss it, but it was too far out of the way, maybe they could catch it on the way back), and then north to Buffalo (home of two U.S. presidents — Grover Cleveland and the obscure Millard Fillmore and site of the assassination of President McKinley in 1901) which was just a hop, skip and a jump from Niagara Falls, the American side (not as spectacular as the Canadian side but Skippy had never seen either and it would be romantic to stand at the foot of the falls and hold hands with Doris behind the curtain of falling water). Highway 90 east through New York State. (The Empire State.

Capital city: Albany. Highest point: Mount Marcy, 5,344 ft.) Right through Syracuse and maybe up into the Adirondack Mountains (more than 200 lakes of irregular shape, spectacular gorges, waterfalls, lakes, ponds and swamps, first sighted by Samuel de Champlain in 1609). From Albany south on 87, through the Catskill Mountains where Rip Van Winkle napped, across the Hudson to West Point, world famous military academy, south to Yonkers, the Bronx, and into Manhattan. It was amazing to look at the blue and yellow lines criss-crossing these pages and think that soon, in just a few months, he would be an invisible speck on this map, he and Doris, making their way along the unknown highways (unknown to them, at any rate), a couple of free spirits. Adventurers. Lovers.

They'd see it all, soak it all up like a sponge, like a pair of sponges, he as navigator, Doris doing the driving — he'd look through the classifieds when it came nearer the time and find a good deal on a second-hand car. And maybe get Joe Bruno to pick it up and drive it down to the club for him. Or back to the boardinghouse. So they'd take off in a convertible, a '57 Chevy, maybe, the top down and the wind blowing through Doris' beautiful blonde hair. And when they'd had enough of New York, they'd get back in the car and head north, through Vermont, and explore all the small towns and villages of his mother's family: Chester, Westminster, Granville, NY. Names his mother had pointed out to him written in delicate, long-ago handwriting in her old family albums. He and Doris would walk hand-in-hand through churchyards and search out the old gravestones with the names of men, women, tiny children, sometimes whole families buried together. The ghostly romance of the graveyard with its gentle reminder of ashes to ashes, dust to dust, but not just yet, thank God, not for a little while yet.

He wouldn't abandon the club, of course. That would be unthinkable. The Dharma had changed his life, had given him a purpose, a reason to get up in the morning. He'd find someone to manage it for him while he was away. And when he came back he and Doris could run it together. He imagined her in a close-fitting black dress, welcoming people into the club, introducing the acts. She'd be so much better at it than he; she could move into the limelight and he could retreat into the background where he belonged.

And eventually, with Doris there to help him, he could finally sit down and write. Poems, maybe even a novel. Who knew what he could accomplish, with the beautiful Doris as his muse?

II.

The spring in northern Ontario flirts like a teenager: just when you've given up hope of ever seeing the snow melt, for a day or two in late March or early April there'll be a sudden lightness in the air and you'll hear the ground beneath you humming with excitement, the rustling of leaves about to bud. And then it's as though spring has changed her mind, a petulant party girl who doesn't like the dress she's wearing and won't come out, after all, and the skies darken and the biting winds return. A few more days, sometimes a week or two, and then another appearance, long enough to set the creek waters running and create a thick muddy mess of the roads and the ditches beside them. Some years, if you're lucky, she sticks around this time, stretching herself out in the long grass, luxuriating in the new, wet smell of the earth. You tell yourself then that spring has really come and you take the chains off the tires, toss the parka into the very back of the closet, along with the high rubber galoshes and the heavy gloves. Seven more months, eight if you're lucky, before you have to face the snow and the sub-zero temperatures and anyway, when the weather is this perfect, isn't it just possible winter will never come again?

But Mother Nature in this part of the world is part benevolent goddess, part Merry Prankster, and she can take it into her head to pull the blanket of green out from under you with a toss of her leafy head. A flick of her wrist and winter is back, its cold, white body spread-eagled across the landscape, smothering the shoots of grass, the tiny shrubs, and whipping its tail in an icy fury at having been pushed aside so easily. And you feel cheated, as if you had some right to expect, even in this frigid part of the world, a normal, Leave-it-to-Beaver type spring and summer. Basketball hoops and hopscotch and little girls in pigtails linking arms and roller-skating down the sidewalk. That was the Canadian dream, fostered by American sit-coms, that was why we paid our taxes.

Friday afternoon, the last day of April. It had been raining in the morning and now, at four o'clock, the sky was still overcast and the mountain overlooking the city was shrouded in a mantle of cloud, its lower slopes exposed, barren of leaves as yet, this early in the year. Skippy pulled up in a cab in front of Mrs. Cordelli's, paid the driver and struggled up the sidewalk with four large shopping bags inscribed in lavender script, "Anderson's Ladies' Wear," and, in smaller print underneath, "Apparel for the Style-Conscious Woman." In spite of the coolness of the weather, he was sweating; small beads of perspiration flecked his forehead and his shirt was damp under his jacket. The last hour had been spent buying clothes for Doris and in the scale of ordeals it rated up there with going to the dentist and getting up to dance in public — sober.

The problem he'd foreseen was in the surprise element of the road trip: Doris would arrive at the club expecting to sit down with him as usual, smoke a few cigarettes and listen to a little music, also as usual, and then look at her watch around eleven o'clock and ask him to call her a cab. She was unlikely to come packing a toothbrush and a change of underwear. So it was up to him to take care of all that. Borrowing a department store catalogue from his landlady, he made up a list of things he thought a girl might need for the first few days on a road trip and headed downtown to the two-storey brick building across from the Bank of Montreal.

Anderson's was the oldest women's clothing store in town; he used to be taken there regularly on Saturday afternoons when he was out shopping with his mom. In the days when he was too young to know it wasn't hip to be hanging out with your mother, he had looked forward to these excursions, enjoying the cool, clean air of Anderson's, with its big-bosomed clerks tapping briskly along the hardwood floors in their shiny black pumps and the racks of shimmering dresses in all the colours of the rainbow.

At the very far end was the special section, the one he would think about for hours afterwards, once he was back home and tucked in bed for the night: ladies' lingerie, crowned by armless torsos wearing Wonderbras and panty girdles and rows of high-stepping legs doing the Can-Can, each in a different coloured nylon stocking. There was something unspeakably erotic about these plaster body parts, unencumbered by heads or arms or anything that didn't speak directly to the matter at hand. When he was six he thought of asking for one of those legs for his birthday but never managed to quite get up the nerve.

Sometimes these visits to Anderson's were brief, just a hurried march up and down the aisles, the clothes a blur of fabric and smell and colour, his mother urging, "Come on, Skippy, don't dawdle, I'm in a rush," and no time to linger in the caress of a luxurious fur coat or stroke the silky skirt of an evening gown. Just a cursory inspection of the new stock, with Skippy hurrying to keep up and wondering how she could sort anything out when she was moving so quickly, and then all too soon back out into the street with the cold wind snapping at his cheeks. Other days, though, when his mother was out to buy something, or had time on her hands to try things on, she'd disappear behind a curtain while Skippy perched on a straight-backed chair next to the change room, keeping an eye on the groceries. This was where they parked the men while their wives squeezed themselves into underwire bras and figure-pinching girdles or changed into slim Chanel suits and party dresses with cinched-in waists and full skirts, coming out to be zipped up and asking the men, "Do you think it makes me look fat?" And there was never an acceptable answer to that; "No, of course not, you look wonderful" earned a frustrated shake of the head and a search for someone more reliable — a woman — to ask. And a reply in the affirmative was simply unthinkable. Skippy, not wanting to be caught watching but unable to turn away, was captivated by the intimacy of the men helping their wives with zippers and buttons, their large, clumsy fingers slow at the job, the women generally growing impatient and pulling away with "Oh, here, let me do it."

When his mother pushed back the curtains it was his turn and he jumped up to fasten a loop at the top of her collar or fumble with a bow that tied at the back.Close to his mother like this, Skippy was aware of her in a different way, taking in the scent of her cologne, the faint salty smell of her sweat, the sharp sting of her hairspray. He struggled to slide the zipper all the way closed and wondered what it would be like to be this close to the girls at school, to stand near enough to them to see what they smelled like, to touch their clothes, their hair, their skin with his fingers. He got in trouble, once, for doing just that. In grade three he sat behind an exuberant firecracker of a girl called Rebecca, "Beccs" for short. She crackled with energy and laughter and seemed born knowing how to do somersaults and cartwheels and how to skip Double Dutch. She had no use for Skippy, even back then skinny and underfed, no matter how many peanut butter sandwiches he ate. He was a quiet, withdrawn child, not so much shy as unequal to the task of making friends or keeping up with the politics of the playground. All of these children from all sorts of backgrounds — Ukrainian, Italian, Polish and Finn — mingling together at recess and after school and Skippy always standing on the sidelines and watching them dart about, the girls in circles and small groups with well-defined rules (there was always an order in their movements, a regularity in the way they arranged themselves), while the boys were anarchic, restless, forming roving gangs that collided with the girls, creating momentary confusion and laughter and shrill, excited accusations, and then moving on to wreak havoc somewhere else as the girls returned to their games.

"On a mountain, stands a lady/Who she is I do not know/All she wants is gold and silver/All she wants is a fine young man."

Beccs was always front and centre in these games, the best skipper, the first to be captured when the boys chased the girls, the first to break away. Skippy spent most of that year watching her, her long auburn hair streaming out behind her while she chased around the school yard, even in class it twitched from side to side, rippling with excitement. One morning she came into the classroom with her tiny pointed chin held higher than usual. She'd had her hair done — a "French braid", she called it. "My sister did it," she said. "She's a hairdresser in Winnipeg and she came home last night and did my hair like this and it took for ever." And she flounced into her seat in front of Skippy and her slim neck with its soft downy hairs were revealed and he saw that the Peter Pan collar of her dress was unhooked. Without thinking, he leaned forward in his desk and grasped hold of the hook and she screamed. She screamed bloody murder and the more she yelled the more terrified Skippy was and he couldn't let go and the teacher had to come and pry his hands away from Beccs' collar and Beccs was taken to the nurse's room to lie down till she stopped being hysterical and Skippy's mom was called at work and she had to ask for time off to come to the school and get him and take him home and before he could go back to school she and Skippy had to meet with the principal. And Skippy never could explain, not to Mr. Havermeyer or to his mother, why he took hold of Rebecca's clothing and why he couldn't let go.

On this particular Friday afternoon, Skippy took the bus down to the corner of Broadway and Main Street, and crossed the street to the bank on the corner. When he came out fifteen minutes later, he carried a small leather satchel containing the last of the money left to him by his uncle. Thirty-five hundred dollars. He'd given five hundred to Mandy and tried to get his mother to take the same, but she'd refused. In the end he'd pushed a hundred dollar bill into her pocket and insisted she go get herself something nice.

"But I don't *need* anything, Skippy," she told him. "I have everything I need."

"I know that," he said. "Go buy something you *want*."

Placing the wallet carefully in his inside jacket pocket, he crossed the street again and walked half a block to the two-story sandstone building that was Anderson's Ladies Wear. As the large glass doors swung shut behind him, he felt like he'd stepped into a no-man's land where a man needed a wife or a mother or at least a steady girlfriend as his passport. On his own, he was trespassing.

A group of young women stood behind the counter next to the cash register, talking and laughing and he hesitated, waiting to be noticed, not wanting to have to approach them. He was suddenly conscious of the missing button on his corduroy jacket, wrinkled from the twenty-minute bus ride, and in a mirror to his right he saw that his hair, damp from the light drizzle, was sticking up at the back, in a sort of misplaced cowlick. Where, he wondered, were the comfortable matrons, soaked in Yardley and Evening of Paris, who had ushered his mother down the aisles in his youth? The ladies with double chins and thick ankles and hair tinted impossible shades of gold and silver and blue who acted as surrogate grandmothers and offered him pale oval mints from a small dish to the side of the counter? The salesgirls he saw here now were his own age or younger, fresh from shampoo and toothpaste ads, little gold crosses dangling from their ears, charm bracelets clanging on their slim white wrists. If he could have, Skippy would have turned around and fled, but he had a duty to Doris: he couldn't drag her away from her home and her belongings with only the clothes on her back. He had to provide her with a temporary wardrobe at least and it was the thought of Doris that gave him the courage to stand his ground when one of the salesgirls detached herself from the group and came towards him, her gum stashed neatly under the counter.

"May I help you?"

Skippy smoothed his hair back and held out his list and the girl took it from him gingerly, as if it might explode in her dainty, well-manicured fingers. She read it in silence, then looked up at him, frowning.

"You want all these things?"

He nodded and then remembered what he'd planned to say. "It's for my sister, she had to fly to Toronto for an operation and she gave me a list of stuff to get for her." He waited and then added, "It's got her sizes and all, it's all written down."

It sounded fake, even to him, even though he'd rehearsed it in front of the bathroom mirror, practicing a sincere, brotherly kind of emphasis when he referred to his sister and the operation in Toronto. Now, it just sounded weird; what was he doing here anyway, who did he think he was fooling?

The salesgirl didn't appear to notice, however. Studying the list, she turned on her heel and headed towards the back of the store, reading the items aloud as she walked: "One nylon peignoir, blue or pink, size 10, with matching nightie." For the next twenty minutes

Skippy followed her around the store as she picked up blouses, skirts, a pair of Bermuda shorts, and held them up for inspection: "Is this what she'd like, d'you think? Does she go for the mod look or what?"

In almost every case, Skippy simply nodded or responded with, "I don't know. She likes a lot of things. Whatever you think will be fine." He felt foolish. It was taking much longer than he'd anticipated and the salesgirl seemed to think he should know things like, did his sister look better in pink or blue, did she have shoes to match this outfit?

Eventually the girl gave up and just made the decisions herself. He was, after all, a man; he'd probably never looked twice at what his sister wore.

"She'll like this," she said, picking out a pink linen jacket with matching skirt. "It's a Dior copy. Looks just like the original. You'd never know the difference."

At the counter, tapping the figures into the cash register, the salesgirl remarked, "Funny that she didn't bring any of this stuff herself, when she went into the hospital."

Skippy had thought of this and was ready with a reply.

"She couldn't. It was an emergency. She only found out a few days ago she had to have the operation and they flew her down there the other night." He added, "And then there were complications, you know, and now she's going to be in for a while."

The girl stopped ringing up the items and looked at him with some concern. "Gee, it sounds serious. Is she gonna be okay?"

Skippy shook his head and shrugged. "I don't know. It's not too good, that's for sure. The doctors can't quite figure it out."

"Really?"

She was interested now and wanted to hear more. Skippy was wishing desperately he'd kept his mouth shut about the whole thing or at least looked up some medical condition in the dictionary and memorized the symptoms. He cleared his throat and told the salesgirl it was some sort of virus, like the flu, only worse.

"The doctors say they've never seen anything like it." He remembered a line from a recent doctor show on TV and added, "They're completely baffled."

"It's not catching, is it?" She looked alarmed, as if she was afraid Skippy was going to infect her right there in the clothing store.

"Oh, no. It's more of an intestinal thing, probably from something she ate." He held out a handful of bills, willing her to take them and let him get out of there in one piece.

"Something she ate? Jeez, that's awful. You mean, like Chinese or something? You couldn't get that sick from eating regular food, could you?"

He shook his head, trying to think. He was beginning to feel a little sick himself, coming up with all this stuff. Why was it, he wondered, that every time he mentioned Doris to anyone outside the club, he ended up lying about her?

"No, she was in Mexico, on a holiday. That's where they figured she got it."

"Oh, Mexico. I've heard you can get really sick from the food down there. The water, too. They say you shouldn't drink the water, either."

"Yeah, I guess that's right. So this comes to —?"

"And you're out buying her all these clothes. It's amazing she'd want you to get her this stuff when she's so sick."

"It takes her mind off her condition. And I guess it sort of gives her hope. I mean, hope that she's going to get better and get a chance to wear them." Please, he thought, please take the money and let me shut up.

The salesgirl was impressed. "Boy. You are some brother, you know that? You're a really good guy, doing this for your sister. I can't imagine my brother doing something like that for me." To Skippy's relief, she finally took the money from his outstretched hand and put it in the drawer of the cash register. As he picked up his parcels, she reached out and gave his hand a squeeze.

"You take care, okay?"

He managed a small, foolish smile and headed towards the door. Just as he reached the exit, the salesgirl called out, "Give your sister my love, all right? And tell her she's got one hell of a brother."

12.

Mrs. Cordelli stood in the hallway, her arms folded across her chest, immovable and forbidding, and she frowned and pursed her lips in disapproval.

"Now, Mr. Jacques," she said, "you've always been a good boy, a good boarder, and it seems to me you've been happy here. Am I wrong? Was I wrong to think Elena Cordelli was providing you with a good home all this time?"

Skippy stepped back and leaned against the banister of the stairway. He'd dreaded this part, telling his landlady he was moving out, even though he knew he didn't need to feel guilty. It's just that it had dawned on him that after the road trip, when he and Doris came back to Cambrian Bay, they would already be started on their new life. Nothing would be the same as it had been. And that meant she would not be living with her mother and he wouldn't be coming back to Mrs. Cordelli's. They'd live together or at least they would as soon as they could arrange it. So he figured on telling the landlady now, well before he left, in order to let her have plenty of time to find another boarder.

According to Mrs. C., there were legions of young men calling her every week, looking for room and board. She was always turning away customers. "In this town," she had said, "you gotta look pretty hard to find a place like this, nice and clean and food that's good for you, not some kind of garbage out of a can like some people I could mention." (His landlady waged a silent war with her colleague Antonia Schevek who kept the boarding house at the end of the street; Mrs. Schevek was a soft, plump Polish woman with slovenly habits, rumoured to top up her housekeeping money by providing her boarders with little extra services from time to time. This was only rumour, mind you; nothing had ever been proved but you only had to pass her on the street with her red hair piled high and catch the scent of her perfume to know she was comfortable with the needs of men. For her part, Mrs. Schevek looked down her nose at Mrs. Cordelli for her "tight-ass" ways and the moustache on her upper lip. Not that she would dream of saying such things to Mrs. Cordelli's face: the two women fired their shots only in the presence of others; they were unfailingly polite to each other when they met and would in fact stop and chat about the weather, the cost of groceries and the family of East Indians that had moved in across the street. They were competitors when it came to the boarding house business, but they closed ranks against newcomers.)

Without waiting for an answer, Mrs. Cordelli continued, "And a month, thirty days notice only! You think nice boys from good families come through this town every day of the week? It costs a lot of money to run a house like this and feed hungry men all day long."

She turned and walked towards the kitchen and then thought better of it and came back. "Is it Mr. Wilson? You have another fight with that old man?"

Wilson was Mrs. Cordelli's longest resident. He had worked as a logger all his life, first around Seattle when he was young, where he joined up with the Wobblies and got himself beat up a few times in workers' demonstrations. After the war he had come north and worked in the bush until hurting his back ten years ago. Now he lived on disability and spent all day in front of the TV in Mrs. Cordelli's front room. Just before the other boarders got back from work, he'd leave the house and walk down to the Frontenac Hotel on Front Street and drink, coming back sullen and silent around eleven. Mrs. Cordelli would keep his supper warm for him in the oven and he'd eat it in front of the television, alone except for Skippy, who, on the nights he wasn't at the club, liked to watch the late night news. Skippy prided himself on the fact that he read the newspaper from front to back every evening and watched the news whenever he could. It was important to keep up with things, to be informed. There were university kids who came to the Dharma who didn't know there was a war going on in Vietnam, who'd never heard of Senator Barry Goldwater, who wouldn't have been able to tell you that the World's Fair was taking place that very minute in Flushing, New York.

He liked watching the news at night because by then Mrs. Cordelli and the others had gone to bed. He had the place to himself except for Wilson, who generally just grunted "Evening" and sat down on the armchair near the door and ate his meal in silence. Sometimes, though, the old man came back in a talkative mood and these were the times Skippy hated, because he would have something to say about every story on the news and expected Skippy to respond. The worst night, the night Mrs. Cordelli was referring to, they had got into an argument about the Queen of England. She was visiting Ottawa with her husband, the Prince, and a shot of her being handed a bouquet of flowers by a little girl in a frilly white dress filled the old man with rage.

"Did you see that?" he said, pointing to the screen with his fork. "See the way that little girl curtsied like that, bowing down to that corrupt old bag of bones? Did you see that?"

Skippy usually knew better than to say anything but he was in a good mood that night and he thought he'd humour the old man.

"She's not that old."

"What? What did you say?"

Skippy smiled. "I said she's not that old. She's in her thirties or something, isn't she?"

"Oh, excuse me." Wilson sounded offended and Skippy wished he hadn't said anything. But it was too late now. "I didn't realize I was in the presence of a monarchist."

Trying to brush it off with a laugh, Skippy replied, "I'm not a monarchist, Mr. Wilson. I just said — "

"I heard what you said, all right. I heard exactly what you said. You think she's special, that woman, because she happened to be born a queen rather than a common, ordinary working man like me. That makes her a better person, eh?"

Skippy couldn't help himself. "A princess, actually."

"Eh?"

"She was born a princess, Mr. Wilson. She didn't become a queen until her father died."

"Oh, I see. Oh, excuse me. Excuse me so much. I didn't know I had an expert in the room beside me. I'd better watch what I say, I might make some more mistakes if I'm not careful, having this queen expert here in this room."

"Mr. Wilson —" But the old man wouldn't let him finish.

"No, no, I understand. I know your kind, I've met them before. Royalty lovers, queen lovers, people who think that a woman like that can come into our country, into our houses even, and tell us what to do. Make rules for us, make us bow down to her. And you think that's all right. You like that, don't you? Well, here, let me make you feel right at home."

And he put his partly eaten meal down on the floor and stood up straight at attention and began to sing: "God save our gracious Queen,/Long live our noble Queen ——"

Skippy tried to interrupt. "Mr. Wilson, please!"

" — God save our Queen./Send her victorious —"

His voice was booming out now, he was standing stiff as a poker and shouting out the song and Skippy was terrified he'd wake up the whole house. He jumped up and took hold of the old man's arm, trying to get his attention.

"— Happy and glorious —"

"Please, Mr. Wilson, be quiet, you'll wake everybody up." He was holding on to Wilson's arm and Wilson was trying to shake him off, still singing: "— Born to reign over us —— Let go of me. Get away from me, let go of my arm."

The old man pushed at Skippy with his free arm and Skippy, nervous and upset and not thinking properly, pushed back. The old man was strong as a bull, bad back or no bad back, and he took a swing at Skippy that would have broken his jaw if it had connected. Luckily it didn't, but suddenly they were both swinging at each other, pushing and shoving and knocking over the coffee table. It's hard to say what damage they might have done if Mrs. Cordelli hadn't suddenly burst into the room and shrieked at the top of her lungs.

"My God, my God, what are you doing? Stop, stop, are you crazy? Stop or I'll call the police."

Skippy was on the floor with Wilson on top of him. The old man halted in mid-swing and looked up at his landlady, looming above him in her housecoat and her hair hanging down past her shoulders.

It gave her the appearance of one of the crones out of "Macbeth" and it must have struck Wilson that way, too, because he stared at her blankly, for a moment, unable to understand why this apparition was hovering over him in a rage. Skippy, for his part, had his arms over his face to ward off the next blow and peered out at Mrs. Cordelli in extreme confusion.

"In the name of God what are you doing you two? Fighting like animals, like drunken sailors, here in my home, in my front room, making enough noise to frighten the dead. Are you out of your minds? Get up or I'll get my broom and beat the two of you to death, I swear it."

Wilson slowly got up from his knees and returned to his armchair, not looking at Mrs. Cordelli, not looking at Skippy. Skippy stayed where he was for a moment, relieved to have the pressure of the old man's body off his chest, and then he, too, got up and stood where he was, swaying slightly from the exertion of the last few minutes. Mrs. Cordelli looked at the two men, and shook her head.

"Thank God Mr. Cordelli died before this day. It would have killed him to see something like this happen in his own home. He would have dropped down dead in a minute, I swear it."

Skippy mumbled an apology but the landlady wasn't listening. Now that order was restored, she was enjoying the drama of the scene. She shook an accusatory finger at Skippy.

"Fighting with an old man like that, old enough to be your father, to be your grandfather. You want to kill him? You want to give him a heart attack? He's not a strong man, you know, he's got a bad back. It could go like that, snap, break right in half like a twig. Is that what you want? You want to kill a man like that, a man like your grandfather?"

Skippy had just enough spirit left in him to reply that the old man was nothing like his grandfather but that was it. He felt a sense of shame steal over him and he wished he was upstairs in his room with the light out. Wilson had picked up his plate had gone back to eating, silently, as if he, too, wished he were somewhere else. Mrs. Cordelli turned her attention to him and said, "And you, you crazy old man. What are you, some kind of a nut case? You gotta start a fight with some young boy just to show you're still big and strong? You wanna kill yourself? I tell you right now, in twenty-five years I never had nobody die on me, in my own front room, and I'm not gonna start now. You behave yourself, you hear?"

She waited and Wilson continued to eat, staring down at his plate. Finally he knew she wasn't going to leave him alone until he said something, so he grunted in reply and she pulled her housecoat together, satisfied that she had, as usual, come out on top.

"All right then," and she turned back to Skippy. "Now you pick up that table and those magazines and you thank your lucky stars nothing got broken and get to bed. I don't wanna hear a thing out of you two the rest of the night. Good night."

She swept out of the room, leaving Skippy to set the table upright and tidy up the room. This took a few minutes and the whole time he wondered what, if anything, he should say to the old man. He decided he should apologize, even though, to be absolutely fair, the fight hadn't been his fault. Still, it takes two, his mother had always said, and it would be a big thing for him to do — make the first move, show there were no hard feelings. Mrs. Cordelli had compared the old man to Skippy's grandfather; Gaston Jacques had been a tiny, white-haired man with cloudy blue eyes who worked as a telegraph operator for the railroad. He'd died when Skippy was three and all he remembered of him was the little wooden figures he used to carve for him, funny little men and women the size of clothespins. Wilson really was nothing like his grandfather but he was probably some-body's grandfather. Somebody loved him, or did once, and climbed on his lap and gave him hugs. Did a man like that deserve to be caught in a fist fight over the Queen of England? Skippy stood in front of him and put out his right hand.

"Sir?"

The old man looked up, a knife in one hand, a fork in the other.

"Sorry about the fight, Mr. Wilson," said Skippy, his hand still held out in friendship. "I guess we both got a little carried away." He waited for Wilson to say something and then repeated, "Sorry."

Wilson said, "Go fuck yourself," and turned back to his meal.

Since then the two men had not spoken to each other and Skippy turned off the television and went up to his room the minute he heard the old man come in at night. He missed the late night news and thought about getting himself a small, portable television to watch it in his room — there would have been enough, from the money his uncle had left him — but every dollar spent on such luxuries meant a few hours less spent on the road trip with Doris.

So when Mrs. Cordelli demanded to know if he'd been fighting again with Wilson, Skippy quickly said no, he'd been fighting with nobody. "I really like it here, Mrs. Cordelli, this is a great place."

"So why're you leaving then?"

"I want to travel. I want to see the world. You know, I've never been to New York, to Times Square. I've never been anywhere, Mrs. Cordelli."

The face of his landlady softened and she reached out to him.

"Come," she said, "give Elena a hug."

It was the last thing Skippy expected and the last thing he wanted to do but he could see no way out of it without hurting her feelings. Reluctantly, he stepped into her embrace and she held him tightly for several minutes — you wouldn't think an older woman's arms could be that strong. He patted her on the back once or twice, unsure what to say. Something seemed to be called for on such an occasion but he was damned if he could figure out what it was. Finally she released him and when he stepped back he saw that her eyes were wet with tears.

"Just like my boy," she said, and drew a large white handkerchief out of her apron pocket. She blew her nose and smiled at Skippy. "My son Vito, ten years ago he says to me, Mama, I wanna see the world. And that's it. He goes travelling and once, just once, he comes back to see me. One Christmas, and then he's gone again. Now he lives in California, has a wife, a baby girl, and never comes back to this place. Too busy, too many things to do to come home and see his mother."

"Why don't you go visit them? Go down to California yourself?"

She shrugged and put the handkerchief away. "Who can do that, get away long enough to go all that way? My husband's dead, who's gonna take care of this place?" She smiled. "You think I should kick everybody out for a month, tell them to find somewhere else to live for a while so I can take a holiday? I don't think so. Mrs. Schevek, she'd snatch them all up in a minute and feed them too much rich food and — well, other things I'm not gonna mention, and then how am I gonna make a living? No, no holidays for people in my business. Maybe when I retire, then maybe I go down and live in California and get to know my granddaughter. You think that's a good idea, eh?"

"I think it's a great idea, Mrs. Cordelli. Be sure to send me a postcard."

She laughed, delighted at the thought of mailing off a postcard to Skippy, some ten years down the road. "Yeah, sure, sure, that's a good idea. I send you a postcard from California, you send me a postcard from New York. How do you call it, pen pals? We'll be pen pals, you and me, eh?"

That night the club was more hectic than usual. For one thing, two girls had called in sick, which left him with just a single waitress and himself to do everything: wait on tables, pour coffee, make sandwiches, introduce the musicians. And early in the evening he'd had to ask a couple of guys in black leather jackets to take their quarrel outside. They were members of the local motorcycle gang and they could have wrecked the joint, if they'd wanted to. Instead, they left, taking their buddies with them, and Skippy gave a quick, fervent sigh of relief before turning to the next item on the agenda, which was an overflowing toilet in the ladies' washroom. There was a full moon — he'd noticed it earlier, on his way to the church — and he decided that cab drivers were right: all kinds of crazy things happened when the moon was in this phase of its cycle.

He'd just finished with the toilet and was making his way across the room towards the counter when a familiar voice spoke just behind him:

"Skippy? Is that you?"

He turned, expecting to see one of the regulars. A slim, dark-haired woman stood against one wall, her arms wrapped nervously around her, clutching her purse to her chest.

"Long time no see," she said. "It's so dark in here, I wasn't sure it was you."

He found his voice and greeted her, glancing automatically behind her to see if anyone was with her.

"Hello, Margaret," he said, unsure whether to take her hand in his, give her a hug, whatever. It had been so long.

"I'm alone," she said. "Benny's at home with Kate. Have you got a minute?"

Placing a hand on her elbow, Skippy guided her to his table near the front, the one he shared Sunday nights with Doris, and offered to take her coat. She shook her head.

"No, I can't stay long. I have to get back."

"Would you like a coffee or anything? Or a Coke?"

He couldn't take his eyes from her, couldn't shake the feeling that she wasn't really here, that he was imagining it. It had been such a long time — more than two years — he had almost forgotten what she looked like. Surely she was thinner, now, and shorter than he remembered. But that was probably because she was so much different from Doris. Where Doris' eyes were blue-gray and full of light, Margaret's were dark and troubled. He thought of the last time he'd seen her, climbing into bed with her, making love from behind, then leaving almost immediately, frightened he'd hurt the baby, afraid Benny would come home unexpectedly. He'd been so intimate with her at one time; now she sat across from him, looking about her as if the surroundings alarmed her. She was out of her depth in this place. He reached out and patted her hand, to reassure her.

"It's all right," he told her. "I'm glad you came."

"I went to your house," she said, not meeting his eyes. "Your landlady said you'd be here."

The girl who was waiting on tables rushed by, a tray in her hand, looking harrassed and distracted. He shouldn't be sitting here, there were things to be done, but Margaret had come to see him. He couldn't just get up and leave her, just yet.

"How are things?" Skippy asked her. "How's the baby? And Benny?"

"They're fine."

She didn't seem to want to talk and yet there must be something she wanted to say. She'd come all this way to find him and now she just sat there, fingering the clasp of her handbag and watching the people around them. He wanted to tell her he was sorry, he wanted to explain his behaviour, but there seeemed to be no way to lead into it. She was closed off, silent, unapproachable.

Just as he was thinking he'd have to get up and help the girl wait on tables, Margaret leaned forward and looked him right in the eyes, for the first time since she'd arrived.

"I came to ask you a favour," she said and it took him aback a little, her finally coming out with it, just like that.

"Well, sure, Margaret, anything. What is it? What do you want?"

There was a sudden burst of sound from the stage as the musicians entered and picked up their instruments. He'd have to go in a moment, he'd have to introduce the set.

Margaret shook her head and said, "Not here. I want you to come over to the house."

"To your house?"

She nodded and he asked, "When?"

"Saturday. In the afternoon. I thought you could come maybe around three?"

He thought about Benny, about running into him like that, and he knew he wasn't ready. As if she knew what he was thinking, she added, "Benny won't be there. He always goes out on the weekends."

Skippy hesitated. "Are you sure?"

Margaret nodded and for the first time a small smile played at the corners of her mouth. All she said was, "I'm sure."

So it was settled. Skippy would come over the following Saturday and they would talk. About what, he wasn't sure. He knew what he would say if he had the nerve but he wasn't sure it mattered any more. He wasn't sure she cared to hear it.

Once she had his promise to come, Margaret stood up to leave.

"Can't you stick around?" he asked. "It's a good group tonight. From Windsor." Now she was here, he wanted her to stay and see what he'd created, listen to the music and be part of his world, for a while.

But she said no, she had to get going. And she didn't want him to call a cab, she'd get the bus, thank you. There was a reserve about her that had never been there before; it might have been shyness at not seeing him for such a long time but he guessed it was deeper than that. Margaret had changed in the past couple of years; he didn't really know her now.

The following Saturday Skippy took the afternoon off and caught the bus across town to the west end, passing the once-familiar shops and warehouses along the route. The bus driver had the radio on and it was tuned to a popular phone-in show, one he remembered from high school. One of those afternoon shows that attracted bored housewives and unemployed mill-workers who welcomed a chance to rant about vandalism in the parks, overpaid garbage collectors who left the lids off the garbage cans and children who couldn't read or write and what were we paying our taxes for, anyway, to turn out a generation of illiterate delinquents with no respect for the law or their parents or anybody?

"Mouth-breathers," Benny had called them. He was fascinated by them, the same people calling in each and every day. When he and Skippy were both still living at home and going to school, they'd skip out sometimes in the afternoon and come back to Benny's and hide out in his bedroom, the radio tuned to the talk show station. They had names for the regulars: "Sexy Sonia", "Miss Crank", "Buffalo Bill". Sexy Sonia was in her late twenties with long blonde hair and huge breasts. Married but unhappy.

"You know what she does, don't you?" Benny'd offer, lying on his stomach, his feet on his pillow, sorting through his records while they talked. "She calls from bed and she's lying there wearing one of those see-through nighties and she's playing with herself while she's talking on the phone."

"Yeah," said Skippy. "She's in love with the D.J. because her husband doesn't know how to satisfy her. He's too old, that's the problem, but he's got money. So she's trapped."

Buffalo Bill liked to rant about corporal punishment. Said when he was a kid he got beaten regularly by the teachers and he didn't get where he was today not getting beaten and what your average juvenile delinquent needed was a good, swift kick up the backside.

"Good old B.B.," Benny exclaimed when the announcer finally managed to get rid of him. "He was better than ever today. Don't you think he would've made a good Nazi?"

This afternoon it was an old favourite: fluoride in the water supply. Too boring, unless one of those really paranoid types got on, the ones who saw fluoride as a Communist plot to render us all sterile and wipe us off the face of the earth, but unfortunately the callers this afternoon all sounded fairly sane. Skippy wondered if the radio station had started screening the people who phoned in, making sure they had something intelligent to say before putting them on the air. If so, it was too bad, he thought; the old callers had been a lot more entertaining.

The bus pulled up in front of the Chinese grocery and Skippy got off and walked slowly down the street towards the small brown stucco house with the pale pink trim. Now that he was actually here, he was shy about climbing the familiar wooden steps and ringing the doorbell. What if Benny was home, after all? What would he say? How would he explain his presence after such a long time?

He could lie, of course. He could say he just happened to be in the neighbourhood and thought he'd drop in to say hello. And if Benny shut the door in his face, well, it would be too bad but it would get him off the hook. He'd done what Margaret had asked, he'd come to the house to see what she wanted. It wouldn't be his fault if he had to turn right around and go home.

It wasn't Benny who answered the door; it wasn't even Margaret. A small child in overalls and a frizz of curly, dark hair stood before him and stared up at him with Benny's eyes. She held a half-eaten sandwich in one hand and clutched a cloth rabbit to her chest with the other. Skippy realized that this must be the baby, not a baby any longer, it had been — he did a quick calculation in his head — almost two and a half years since she was born.

"Hello," he said, awkwardly crouching down to bring himself more to her level. "You must be Katherine. I'm a friend of your mother's."

The little girl backed away a few steps, then turned to flee, just as Margaret came down the hall from the kitchen.

"Who is it, Kate?" she called, then stopped and stood there for a moment, her face giving away nothing. Then she smiled and came forward to let him in.

"You came," she said and he saw she had thought he might not. He had, in fact, considered staying away, lying in bed the night before, unable to sleep, weighing his choices, deciding finally that if he didn't come he'd never know what might have happened, what he might have been able to accomplish.

Nothing had changed yet it felt very different. The house was more lived in now, things that had felt temporary three years ago had become permanent, fixed. The rental atmosphere had gone; this was a place where people lived, a family had taken root in this house. The furniture which had perched on top of the carpet was now sunk in at least an inch or two, as if to tell the world, "We belong here, this is our home." And there was no longer a place for Skippy; when he sat on the couch it didn't make way for him as it had in the past — it resisted his weight, rising and falling in other places to fit the bodies of Benny and Margaret and their child.

Katherine, in the meantime, had taken refuge behind her mother and peered out at him with a disapproving scowl.

"I don't think she likes me," said Skippy, because it was he who didn't really like children or, rather, was uncomfortable around them, always felt he was being judged in their eyes, back in the playground again. Waiting by the monkey bars at recess.

Margaret laughed. "Don't be silly. Kate likes everybody, don't you, Katie? She's just a little cranky right now. Time for your nap, isn't it, sweetie? Time for a little sleepy-bye."

She took the child's hand and led her to the stairs.

"Do you like the name?" she asked him.

"Kate? Sure. It's pretty."

"We named her after Benny's mother." He knew that but didn't say so. "He insisted on it, don't you think that was funny? I wouldn't have thought he'd even care about something as ordinary as a name. It was okay by me, though. We named her Elizabeth as well, for my own mom. Katherine Elizabeth. My mom would have liked that."

Skippy felt something was called for so he said, "She's great. She seems like a great kid."

"She's her father's child," said Margaret and the way she said it, it didn't sound like an entirely good thing.

Margaret took the little girl upstairs to bed and Skippy waited and leafed through a copy of *Life* magazine he'd found on the coffee table. After a while, Margaret came back downstairs and slumped in the chair across from him, her eyes closed. Skippy wondered if he should leave, did she care that he was there, would she rather he left? Just when he had pretty well decided to make some excuse and go, she opened her eyes.

"Sorry," she said. "This time of day, I'm exhausted. She never stops. I'm the one who needs the nap, not her."

There was a pause, while she stared at him as if she was trying to work out who he was, or who he had become. And then she said what she had said the other night: "So. Long time no see."

This was his opportunity. He hesitated, then said, "I wanted to come by, Margaret, and say I was sorry. I should've come before."

He thought she might say, "Sorry for what?", but she didn't.

What she did say showed him she remembered exactly what had happened and had thought of it often. As he had.

"You could have phoned," she said, "or at least come to the hospital. Didn't you care what happened to me?"

He began: "I wanted to —" Skippy couldn't say any more. What else was there to say? He'd acted like a jerk. Why try to dignify it with some half-hearted excuse?

"Can you imagine how I felt?" She sat there and watched him, sounding more tired than angry. "Having sex, having a one night stand with my husband's best friend while I was pregnant. I felt like the worst kind of tramp in the world. I felt like a slut, like a cheap little slut."

"Margaret, please, don't say —"

"I hated you." The words shocked him, all the more because of the way she said them. She didn't raise her voice, didn't even look at him, just sat slumped in her chair, looking away now, speaking to the floor. "I hated you and I hated me and when I went into labour the next morning I thought I was going to die and I thought I deserved it. I figured I deserved to die, I was such a bad person."

"I'm sorry." It was a whisper, she probably didn't even hear it, which was just as well, it was such an inadequate response, it was less than nothing. And yet he was sorry: at that moment he would have given anything not to have gone upstairs that night, not to have climbed into her bed. He said it again. "I'm sorry, Margaret. I wish it hadn't happened."

At this she looked up at him and he saw that she believed him. She smiled. "Me, too. I guess you wouldn't have a cigarette on you, would you?"

"You don't smoke, do you?"

"Sometimes. It relaxes me. But you don't, do you? I forgot."

She stood up and walked over the window, looking out at the scraggly tree in the front yard. "That thing's dying. I keep wanting Benny to cut it down but you know him, he wouldn't hurt a single living thing. Except me."

"Was he angry? When I stopped coming around?" He must have been hurt, he must have wondered why Skippy stopped spending night after night at the Carter household. But he had never called to ask, never come over and confronted Skippy about it. He simply seemed to accept that the friendship was over.

Margaret said nothing, just stood there looking out the window, and Skippy began to talk, to explain things. He wanted to retrieve himself in her eyes, at least — Benny was lost to him but he could make it up with Margaret, he thought. He told her he had been afraid to come around that first year. He had known he would not be able to look at Benny and bear the judgement in his eyes. The judgement that would be there even if it was only Skippy who saw it, even if Benny himself knew nothing of what had happened. And then he'd started work at the store and got the club going and there seemed to be no time: on the nights he wasn't working, he was at home going through the books, sending off letters to folk groups, listening to tapes and records. It was a full-time job, running the Dharma, there was no time for sitting around friends' living-rooms talking and drinking wine and discussing poetry.

And of course, there was Doris, but he didn't mention her. There seemed no point in it, now. Margaret had changed, he could see that as he spoke. She didn't listen to him in the same way, there was something critical in her demeanour, something judgemental. He thought of the woman he'd known back before the baby was born. She'd seemed very sustaining in those days — she took care of him and Benny as if they were children. He'd written about that in the poem he'd given her, using words like "earth-mother" and "well-spring" and "fountainhead".

And now, sitting here, he saw that it was different. *She* was different. Maybe it was having the baby that had changed her; maybe she gave all her nurturing to the little girl now and there was none left over for grown men who were supposed to be capable of caring for themselves.

That sadness, too, surely that had never been a part of the Margaret he'd known. She must be lonely, here in this house on the edge of town, surrounded by Poles and Ukrainians, most of whom spoke little English. Who would she have to talk to, except the little girl? He tried to remember what friends she had, if any, but the only one that came to mind was Linette, the ugly girl who'd been part of the wedding party and had gone back to live in New York. The whole time she was pregnant, it had just been the three of them, Benny and her and Skippy, and she seemed to like it that way. Well, she still had Benny; she was crazy about him and now she had his baby.

"Benny at work?" he asked her, and she shrugged.

"Saturday afternoons, Benny goes to the mountain. He's got a girlfriend on the reserve. At least, that's what they tell me."

"Who's 'they'?"

"People who call in the middle of the day to make sure I know what's going on. People who tell me they're my friends but won't say their names. You'd be surprised how many people there are like that in a town this size."

She saw his reaction and smiled. "Poor Skippy, you're shocked, aren't you? You didn't come to hear any of this. You thought we'd have a nice little visit, catch up on old times. And now you see an unhappy wife with a husband who's fooling around on her and who's probably even more miserable than she is. Depressing, isn't it? Do you want something to drink?"

What he wanted to do was leave but he couldn't. It was early in the day to be drinking but she obviously wanted one. So he accepted the offer of a drink and followed her into the kitchen where she found him a beer in the bottom of the fridge.

"I hate the taste of beer," she told him. "What I like is rum and orange juice. Ever try it? It sounds awful but it leaves a nice feeling in the pit of your stomach. Makes everything all warm and orangey."

They carried their drinks out the back door and sat outside on the steps, in the warm spring sun. The back yard was tiny but neat with a crabapple tree in one corner and a huge lilac bush in the other. In between, against the back fence, someone had dug a vegetable garden and there were neatly carved rows with empty seed packets on sticks at each end. It didn't seem such a bad part of town, sitting out here; you couldn't see the train tracks and the noise of the traffic was filtered out by the trees and the sparrows and starlings overhead. Whether it was the sun or the rum and orange juice, Margaret began to cheer up and asked him if he still read poetry.

"Sometimes," he said. "What about you?"

"Sometimes," and they laughed. "I don't know, Kate keeps me pretty busy. There never seems to be time for stuff like that."

"What about Benny? Does he still read as much as ever?"

That was a mistake, bringing up his name. "That's about all he does, when he's home. Sits in Katie's bedroom and reads and listens to those damn, depressing records of his. He won't sit in the living-room because he can't stand the TV being on and I need some sound or I'll go crazy. I've told him, if he'd just talk to me now and then I wouldn't need the damn TV but he just goes into her room and shuts the door. Oh, shit —"

She began to cry and Skippy was horrified. He had no idea what to do, he could hardly carry on talking and pretend not to notice. Finally he set his beer down on the step and tentatively put an arm around her shoulder.

"It's okay," he said, hoping this was what was required. "Don't cry, Margaret. It'll be all right."

Somehow this just seemed to make things worse. She was sobbing now, really crying out loud, and she didn't seem to care that anybody might hear her, out here on the steps with neighbours on either side.

"Margaret," he said, "please don't cry. What's the matter? Tell me what's wrong."

She said something which he couldn't make out, as her face was buried in his shoulder and she was crying so hard.

"What? What is it, Margaret? What did you say?"

She lifted her head and looked at him, tears streaming down her face. "Everything. That's what's wrong. Absolutely everything."

This was awful, seeing her so sad like this. "Is it Benny?" he asked. "Is something wrong with him? Is he sick or something?"

"He hates me," she whispered so softly and with her head lowered almost to her lap so that he had to bend down to catch the words.

"What?" He'd heard her but he couldn't believe it. Benny'd never hated anybody in his life. He was the nicest, most easy-going guy ——

She lifted her head and looked him straight in the eye, defying Skippy to contradict her. "He hates me."

"But that's crazy. Why would he hate you? He loves you."

"Because I told him, Skippy. I told him about you. About us. That's why."

There are moments in a person's life when everything stops, when the world freezes and you experience everything around you in slow motion. You can feel the hairs on your arms stand up, feel your heart pounding against your chest, hear the blood rushing past your eardrums. Skippy had once turned a corner at night and found himself face to face with some high-school bullies, four miserable thugs who didn't like the look of him. In the brief space of time between recognizing the bullies and feeling the shock of a fist against his nose, Skippy had experienced this cold, terrifying place; now, he felt it again.

13.

"The soul of Jonathan was knit with the
soul of David, and Jonathan loved him
as his own soul."

"About us? What did you tell him about us?"

Skippy found himself in a fog; his mind was blank, he couldn't think, and yet when he spoke to Margaret the words came out calmly, without emotion. Someone else was talking now, someone who didn't care about words like betrayal, or friendship, or infidelity.

"The truth, Skippy. I told him I loved you, that I could talk to you. I told him you felt the same way. Everything."

Now this was something he had to understand. She was saying something important here; he had to get out of the fog surrounding him and make himself understand.

"Everything." He said it again but he didn't understand the word, he didn't know what it meant. What she meant.

"Yes. That's why he left." Now she saw she would have to explain and she moved closer to him, placed a gentle hand on his knee, spoke to him as she would to a child.

"Skippy, when you came over that night, Benny was gone, remember? He left because we'd had an argument. Well, not really an argument. I was the only one who said anything. Benny never fights, he never shouts back. I felt guilty, I didn't want to sleep with him any more, I was thinking about you all the time. About us. And finally I just had to tell him. I couldn't pretend any more."

The warmth of her hand on his knee — Skippy could focus on that and when he did the mist began to lift. Her left hand it was, the one with the plain gold wedding band on the fourth finger. He had held that ring, kept it in his inside jacket pocket for safe-keeping, bringing it out when the minister gave him the nod. He had been the best man.

"You told Benny we were in love. Is that right?" He spoke slowly; he had to be absolutely sure what he was saying, what *she* was saying.

"Yes. And he got upset and left and I didn't think he was coming back. But he did. He came back the next morning, after you left, and we had a huge fight and this time he did shout and my labour started and he took me to the hospital and I was in labour for thirty-six hours. It was awful, Skippy. I thought I was going to die, I thought I was going to lose the baby. But I didn't. I had her and she was beautiful and Benny was crazy about her."

Margaret paused to take a sip of her drink and held the glass up to sun for a moment, admiring the way it gleamed in the light, the colour of the sun.

"You should have seen his face, Skippy, when he came into the room to see me after I woke up. He'd been to the nursery and he said he'd picked her out right away, before the nurse even held her up to the window. He said the two of us had produced a completely perfect human being. I'd never seen him like that about anything. So I thought everything was okay. I thought that was it, it was all over. Except that when I came home from the hospital with Kate and I took her upstairs to put her to bed in the nursery, I saw that everything was different. All his things were gone from our bedroom — his clothes, all his books and magazines, his records, he'd taken everything and put it into Katie's room. He'd even put a mattress for himself in there, on the floor next to her crib. And when I came downstairs and asked him about it, he said from now on he was sleeping in Katie's bedroom. And that's the way it's been ever since."

She set her glass down on the step next to her and began to fiddle with her wedding band, sliding it back and forth along her finger. The ring moved easily, as if it were loose, as if the finger that wore it was thinner than it used to be.

"For a long time," she continued, "I thought he'd get over it. I thought he couldn't stay mad for ever. And he loves Katie, he loved her right from the beginning. So I kept telling myself things would get better. And then I started getting these calls — one of them, I'm pretty sure, was from her, the girl on the reserve. She kept telling me to leave, she said I should pack up and take my baby and move back to New York, Benny didn't love me, he couldn't stand to even look at me. After a while, I stopped answering the phone."

Skippy wanted to say something but he didn't know where to begin. All of the things she was telling him, about Benny and some girl from the reserve, he had imagined none of this. He had assumed that Margaret and Benny had gone on as before — only without him, is all. He had never pictured anything like this.

As for being in love with Margaret — was it possible? He had cared for her, of course. Maybe, just for a very short while, he had been a little in love with her, but that was because of Benny. Because she was Benny's wife and Benny was his friend. And there'd been no one else in his life then, no Doris with her cool blonde hair and her deep, husky voice, sitting across from him at the table in the club, holding a cigarette between her perfect fingers.

Margaret picked up her glass, took another sip and continued: "I was really jealous of you, you know. That's what it was all about in the beginning."

"Jealous? Of me?" She was jumping too quickly from one thing to the other, he felt he couldn't keep up.

"Well, of course. You and Benny were best friends, you'd been friends all through high school. And you had these big plans to go on the road, to see the world. And I wrecked them."

"You didn't wreck them —" Skippy began, but she interrupted him.

"Yes, I did, but Benny told me it was okay, he said the baby and getting married was more important but that one of these days you and him might decide to do it, after all, and I wasn't to get upset if it happened or think he was abandoning me or anything, because he'd always come back."

"I thought —" Skippy stopped and stared out over the tiny back yard. The crabapple tree was in bloom and a small brown sparrow flew up from behind the fence and perched on one of its branches, almost hidden by a sprig of white blossom. He cleared his throat and said, "I never thought he'd still want to go, not with being married and having a baby and all."

"I think he felt he owed it to you."

"The trip?"

"Yes, but it was more than that. I mean, he wanted to go, too, but I think he figured you'd get a kick out of it. I mean. Well. You know."

He did know. Benny had thought, Poor old Skippy, he's never going to go anywhere if I don't take him. Poor sap.

"He felt sorry for me." The words came out more roughly than he'd intended and Margaret glanced at him quickly and shook her head.

"No, I didn't mean that. He cared about you, that's what I meant. And that's why I was jealous, at first."

"And after that?"

"Well, after that I got to know you, I guess, and I could see why Benny liked you and why you two got along like you did and I felt like I was part of it. Which was nice. It was like finding a family again, just the three of us. And then you gave me that poem, remember?"

He remembered. Twice in his life he had written a really good poem, each time for a woman. He still had Doris' in a dresser drawer in his room — one of these days, when the time was right, he'd give it to her.

"I still have it, you know. You gave it to me when I was pregnant and fat and ugly and it made me feel like the most special person on earth. I felt beautiful when I read it. I felt like you thought I was beautiful."

Margaret turned to him with that steady, serious stare that seemed to be looking deep within him. Benny had the same look; it was funny, but it had never occurred to Skippy until just now that they each had the same way of looking inside a person and weighing up what they had found.

"Do you remember what you wrote? Do you remember how personal it was, the things you said? It was a love poem and I'm not sure you even knew it. I should have read it and then burned it or put it away somewhere safe, but I didn't. I kept it on me, I carried it around with me and every now and then I took it out and read it all over again. And of course, finally Benny saw it and asked about it, wanted to know what it was. So I told him. I told him it was from you."

"Did he read it?" Skippy asked.

"He wouldn't. I wanted him to but he wouldn't. He said it was none of his business and then he said he was going out for a walk. I didn't want him to. I wanted him to read it, I wanted him to see what it said. I wouldn't let him out the door, I stood in the way holding that poem, waving it in his face, telling him, Go on, read it, see how your best friend feels about me. He loves me, Benny, that's what I said, and I told him I loved you, too, I said we loved each other and it was all in this poem and if he wasn't such a coward he would read it and see. I told him that I couldn't wait for him to leave for work every night because then I could sit with you and talk to you and feel close to somebody, for a change, not like I was with a stranger. I said terrible things, Skippy. I said every single thing that came into my head. It was awful."

Margaret was crying now and Skippy put his arm around her once more and tried to comfort her. Her shoulder was soft, her skin was warm under his hand, beneath the thin cotton of the housedress she wore. He began to remember what it was like, being with her, being in bed with her that night, and he held her more closely and pressed his mouth against her hair. He closed his eyes and rocked her, gently, and she relaxed against him and wept, until finally she sat up and wiped her cheek with the back of her hand.

"God," she said, "I must look awful. I just feel so bad when I think about it, you know? It just makes me feel so sad."

"I know," he said and he did. He knew exactly how she felt; it was the way he felt whenever he happened to go past the big old house out by the golf course where he and Benny had spent so many hours in that upstairs bedroom, listening to records and reading Billboard magazine. A feeling of loss, that's what it was. And now there were two of them, him and Margaret, and they'd both lost the one person they'd really cared for.

Margaret wiped her face with the hem of her dress, the way a small child would do, and took another sip from her drink. She made a wry face and said, "This stuff probably isn't helping any. I always feel like crying when I drink."

Skippy took a swig of beer and winced as it went down his throat. He wasn't much of a drinker anyway and the bottle had been standing in the sun long enough to lose the chilly edge that was necessary if he was going to enjoy it at all. He set it back down on the step and wondered if she still wanted to talk. It was nice out here in the sun but after what she had said he didn't want to meet up with Benny and he thought maybe he should be going. And then Margaret had another sip of rum and orange juice and began speaking again and he thought he'd wait, hear her out. Let her get all the talking out of her if that's what she wanted.

She was telling him about being in the hospital, about being in labour. She was telling him about wanting Benny:

"I kept calling for him," she said. "The pain was so bad and it went on for such a long time and they kept saying, Hush, now, you're going to be fine, and they wouldn't let him come in. He would of, if they'd let him, I know that. If he'd known how bad it was for me, he would of pushed his way in, I know he would of. He was mad at me, but he'd always do the right thing."

She sighed, remembering, and took another long sip of her drink. The glass was almost empty and she rattled the ice cubes in it absently while she was talking.

"That's when I knew it was him. He was the one I wanted there, I knew if he was there with me, I'd be all right. I'd live and the baby'd live and everything would be okay. I remember grabbing on to the nurse's arm and just begging her to go get him, let him come in with me. And I prayed, too. I said, Please, God, get me through this and I promise I'll make it up to him."

She laughed, self-conscious, and brushed a strand of hair from her forehead. "Silly, isn't it? But I meant it. I was going to make it up to him, I was going to show him it didn't mean anything, all those things that I said. But he won't talk about it. I tell him I'm sorry, I've told him a thousand times, I say, Benny, I didn't mean it, I was upset, I was a little bit crazy. And he won't say a word. It's like he's walking around with this huge sore thing inside of him and he won't share it with anybody. I want him to come back to bed, I want him to talk about it, but he won't. Sometimes I just flip out and say, Jeez, Benny, it's been two and a half years. This is too long to punish a person. And he looks at me like he's completely amazed and he says, I'm not trying to punish you. And I say, Well, what do you call it, what you're doing? And he says, Simplifying. I'm just simplifying my life. What's that supposed to mean, Skippy? Will you tell me what the hell that is supposed to mean? Because I can't figure it out."

Skippy thought he knew but he also knew that it was just Benny Carter's way of protecting himself and no explanation was going to make Margaret feel better. What she wanted was to go back to the way it had been before the baby was born and Benny would never go back. He could go on but he could never go back.

Margaret got up and stood inside the open doorway, listening for a moment. "I thought I heard Kate," she explained. "She wakes up sometimes, needs a drink of water before she goes back to sleep." There was no sound from inside the house and she decided she was wrong. She also decided she needed another drink.

"What about you, Skippy? Would you like another beer?"

He shook his head. His beer sat on the step next to him, untouched after that first unpleasant taste. He waited while she went into the kitchen, listened to the sound of ice cubes, then a splash of rum, then orange juice, being poured into her glass and glanced up at the sun in the pale spring sky. It was getting late; ten past four, his watch said. Benny could be home at any time. He should go.

But he was reluctant to leave just yet. Not until he got what he came for, although he couldn't have said what that was just at the moment. It had something to do with Benny, something to do with being forgiven, he thought. Because it was now clear that absolution, if it was coming, was not to be gained through Margaret, who was drained and exhausted; it was Benny who maintained the power to forgive, to forgive the two of them. But it was forever beyond him to approach Benny, to come right out and ask for it.

Margaret returned and sat down beside him again. "The good thing, I guess," she said, as if they had been talking all along, "is that I finally worked out what was happening between you and me."

"Between us."

"Yes. It wasn't love I felt for you, Skippy." She glanced at him and said, "You don't mind, do you? I mean, it's been a long time and I have to be honest."

He shook his head. No, he didn't mind.

"I liked you a lot because you were Benny's friend and because you were so good to me. But a lot of it was because I was pregnant and Benny — well, he was so shy with me, you know? Because of the baby and all, he was afraid of hurting her. He never wanted to — well, you know." She took a sip of her drink, suddenly shy, and Skippy said quickly that he knew, grateful that she wasn't going to go into detail about that.

"And he hated working at the mill," she continued. "He still does, I know he does, but he wouldn't complain or say anything about it because he didn't want me to feel guilty. But I felt guilty anyway. And then you came here every night and talked to me about poetry and books and things that were happening in the world and it made me feel special. So I thought I was in love with you."

"But you weren't."

"No, and you weren't in love with me, either. It was Benny, we were both in love with Benny, that's what I think. And now he hates me and you don't come over any more so it's all just a big, huge, shitty mess."

She took a long sip of her drink and he tried to think of what to say now, how to respond to what she'd said about being in love with Benny. He decided it was better not to respond to it at all; instead he asked her when it was she knew she wasn't in love with him.

"Right away, I guess." She held the glass next to her cheek and rolled it softly back and forth, cooling her skin. There was a breeze now in the back yard and with the sun sinking lower in the sky, Skippy was beginning to wish he had kept on his jacket. But Margaret, he saw, looked hot: her cheeks and forehead were flushed and he wondered if it was the rum that was causing it.

"I didn't want to admit it to myself," she said, "but after we — you know, after we did it and you left, I was lying there in bed and I felt awful, I felt like I'd made the world's worst mistake and it was too late to do anything about it, because I'd said all that stuff to Benny and now he was gone for good. Except he wasn't. He came back and I thought everything was all right again. But it wasn't. I was wrong."

She laughed. "Confusing, isn't it?"

Skippy saw that she was feeling better; when she laughed she sounded like her old self, except she took another drink right away and he thought that maybe she was getting drunk. She shouldn't get drunk, should she, when her little girl was upstairs asleep and Benny could come home any minute? What would he think if he saw the two of them like this, sitting on his own back step, getting drunk in the middle of the day? Maybe she did this often; maybe she poured herself a drink every time Kate had her afternoon nap, maybe it was something she was used to.

He thought how he didn't really know her any more, this woman sitting next to him. There had been a time when he'd told her everything and he'd never thought of her being unhappy — she'd seemed content, she and Benny both. Now he wondered about Benny, as well: if she had changed so much, would he find that the same thing was true about Benny? Was his old friend, the only one he'd ever had, lost for ever, changed by marriage and work and having a kid? And unhappiness?

But what could *he* do about it? What did he know about marriage and family and putting things back together when they were so obviously broken beyond repair? He lived alone in a room in a boardinghouse, slept in a houseful of men who lived in similar rooms, all of them isolated for one reason or another, not one of them up to the task of living a fully evolved sort of life where you made commitments, got tangled in the complicated skein of families and friends and community. He saw now that, if it hadn't been for Doris, he would have remained in that cloistered state for ever, most likely. She had rescued him just in time.

"Skippy, I need to ask you something. I need you to do me a favour."

Up until this moment, Margaret had been sounding a little drunk, her words tumbling over each other in a rush to confide, to tell everything. But now she was sitting up very straight and the look on her face was serious; this was something big, this was why she had come out to the club the other night. This was important.

"Sure. If I can."

"Will you talk to him? He'll listen to you. You're his friend, at least you were. He always cared what you thought. He never cared what I thought, not really. He never asked me my opinion about books or people or anything. We weren't friends that way, but you were. If you talked to him now, I think he'd pay attention. I think it would help."

Talk to him. Talk to Benny Carter, who had been his friend for four and a half years, had showed him how to smoke a joint, how to wear his off-white Levi 501's slung low at the hips, how to comb his hair back into a ducktail, the way Elvis did before he went into the army. Benny had introduced him to the world beyond Cambrian Bay; it was because of Benny that he had opened the club, because of him he'd met Doris. Everything that he, Skippy, was he owed to

Benny Carter. Margaret might as well have told him to go talk to God.

"What do you want me to say?" He was stalling for time, hoping there was an honourable way out of this, hoping she'd relent and let him off the hook.

But Margaret wasn't going to do that. She knew exactly what she needed from Skippy, she knew just how he could help her.

"I want you to tell him it was all a mistake, I was never in love with you, we were just friends and you took it the wrong way. Tell him I was all mixed up, being pregnant and all, I wasn't thinking straight, and you wanted to comfort me and you talked me into it. Tell him you were mixed up, too, and not thinking straight, either, and you just kind of pushed me into it. But tell him it was him I loved, not you, and you knew it all the time."

"You mean —" He couldn't continue. She was telling him that Benny knew, he knew about what had happened that night. She had told him.

"Tell him it was a mistake," she continued, her cheeks flushed, her dark eyes lit with some intense, inner fire. "You came upstairs, you thought I wanted you, we just got carried away. It's the one thing I never should have told him, it's the one thing he can't get over."

"You want me to say I raped you." It was a statement and she nodded, eagerly, as if the word meant nothing more than giving someone a push, a momentary lapse of courtesy between friends. He wondered if she'd gone crazy, sitting in this house day after day, or if she was only drunk.

"I don't think —"

"It's the least you could do," she said and there was a bitterness in her voice that showed she knew exactly what she was asking and she didn't mean to let him say no. It was a phrase his mother had used when he was a kid, the final, guilting sentence, used when other forms of coercion had failed. He'd accepted that the hardest things in life — going back to the corner store and returning the candy he'd taken, apologizing to Mrs. Barrie next door for chasing her cat through her vegetable garden — these were always the least he could do and so they had to be done.

And now Margaret thought the least he could do was lie to his former best friend Benny Carter, tell him he had raped his wife, had pushed his way into her against her will, ignored the fact that she didn't love him, didn't want to be with him. She was asking him to take what had been between them and turn it into something dirty so that Benny would forgive her. And hate him. Because if Benny Carter didn't hate him now, he surely would after that. There would be no going back, no clasping hands in friendship ever again, assuming Benny even let him leave the house without beating him to a pulp. It was outrageous, what she was proposing, yet she thought it made perfect sense.

She saw his reluctance and it hardened something within her. "Look," she said, sounding nervous but determined. "You slept with me, Skippy, you came upstairs and got into bed with me when I was pregnant and we made love. You don't deny that, do you?"

No. He didn't deny it.

"And then you left and you never called, never visited, nothing."

He tried to say something but she continued: "I was angry about that but I knew you were ashamed because of what happened and so was I, so I understood it, but it means you owe me something. I'm not saying it was all your fault. I wanted — it was my fault, too, and I know that. But Benny doesn't have to know it. You can fix it."

Margaret set her drink down on the step beside her and took both his hands in hers and pressed them tightly. Her fingers were cold from holding the glass and stronger than he expected. She would hold him there in her woman's grip until she got what she wanted from him.

"Remember what you told me about karma? You said what you do in this life shows up in the next one. You called it the moral energy of your actions. You see? I remember. I remember everything we talked about. I've been unhappy in this life, Skippy, so many bad things have happened to me, I think I must have been a very bad person in another life. You, too, maybe. You've never seemed very happy, you know that? Maybe we both did awful things in our past lives. But now I'm making up for all that. I have Kate and I love her and take care of her. I'm a good mother, even if I do sometimes have a drink in the afternoon, just to get through the day. But no one can say I don't love her, no one."

She glared at him, defying him to contradict her, and he assured her he knew that, he could see she was a good mother.

She nodded and the grip on his hands lessened, just a little. "That's right. And because I made a mistake once I shouldn't have to be punished for the rest of my life. If you talk with Benny, if you explain what happened, that would be an act of good karma for you, wouldn't it? Something like that, it would make up for what we did. It would help, Skippy. Do you understand?"

He was overwhelmed. She still held his hands in her own; she was not going to let go until he'd agreed. And why not agree? What other choice did he have? She was right; he had behaved badly, climbing into bed with her and then avoiding her afterwards. He'd behaved like a pig — she must have hated him for it. And now she was offering him a chance to make things better, get the past all sorted out before leaving, with no unfinished business.

He tried one last time, made one final attempt to dissuade her.

"He'd kill me," he said, sounding like a coward and hating himself for it. "At least, he'd never speak to me again. We'd be enemies for ever."

"No, you wouldn't, Skippy. That's where you're wrong. He'd be upset but you and him were friends for a long time, he'd forgive you. I know he would. He'd be mad at first, I guess, but he's already mad. It's eating him up, feeling like this. But if you talked to him, it'd give him a chance to get over it. Especially when he saw you were telling the truth. He'd see how much courage it took to do that and he'd forgive you."

"Except I wouldn't be telling the truth, would I? I'd be lying."

"Would you?" she said. "Didn't you come upstairs and get into bed with me when you knew I was unhappy that night, you knew Benny and I'd been fighting? Can you sit there and tell me you didn't take advantage of the situation, Skippy, just a bit?"

He could not. "All right," he said, looking down at the flattened, brown grass beneath his feet. He did not want to meet her eyes.

"You'll do it?"

He nodded. "Sure. It's the right thing. I'll talk to him."

She said nothing but pressed his hands tightly in hers and he thought for a minute she was going to kiss him. Instead, she simply said, "Thank you. You won't regret it."

Releasing him, finally, she picked up her glass from the step, drained it and tossed the ice cubes into the dirt at the side of the house. "I have to start getting supper ready now. Katie'll be getting up soon."

"Will Benny be back for supper?"

She shrugged. "Who knows? But I make it just in case. Anyway, Kate and I have to eat. You'd better go."

At the door she handed him his jacket and helped him on with it. "I remember this," she said. "Your leather bomber jacket. It was Benny's, wasn't it?"

"Yeah, it didn't fit him. He said it made me look like James Dean."

"When are you going to talk to him?"

"When should I?"

"During the week," she suggested. "He gets home for supper around six, could you come after that?"

Skippy said he'd come Tuesday. The club was closed, he could come by around seven.

Margaret said she'd go out with Kate once he arrived, so it would be just the two of them, like in the old days, and it would be easier to talk.

Just as she was about to close the front door, Skippy remembered something. "Where's Cassady?" he asked and she looked perplexed until he added, "The cat, remember? I don't see him around."

"He ran away," she told him. "Just after Katie was born. I guess he didn't care much for babies."

The air was cooler now than it had been; a sluggish cloud blotted out what remained of the sun and the wind had picked up. He walked half a block to the bus stop and waited next to a couple of elderly ladies in head scarves, carrying brown paper shopping bags and discussing the state of the world in some language he didn't understand. They looked over at him and he saw them glance at his leg and then at each other. Tsk, tsk, they were probably saying. Poor boy, got a bad leg. At least the old ladies looked directly at him, not like the people he passed who looked the other way and pretended not to see him altogether. He heard his mother's voice in his ear: "Feeling sorry for yourself, Skippy? Just remember, people don't think about you nearly as often as you think they do. In fact, most of the time, they're not thinking about you at all." This, somehow, was supposed to cheer him up. It never did.

Anyway, right now he had more pressing things to think about than the state of his leg. Now that he was out of the stuffy little house, away from Margaret and her sad brown eyes, pleading with him, making him feel guilty, he began to feel better. Why should he put himself through the pain of contacting Benny? It was over, wasn't it? Wasn't it better for all of them if he stayed out of Benny's life? She couldn't force him to come over on Tuesday and if he wanted, he could manage to avoid her phone calls for the next few weeks. He'd wait until he and Doris were on their trip, somewhere across the border, and then drop her a post card along the way. *Something came up*, he would write. *Sorry I couldn't make it but I'll sort it out when I get back.*

He found a seat near the back and sat there, brooding, as the bus headed north across the railway bridge and passed a run-down, scrappy little park behind the high school where he and Benny had hung out the summer Benny got his license. It was a favourite place of theirs that summer — why, Skippy couldn't recall. It just seemed like a good place to go to hang out, was all. And he remembered how this one night, just as they'd been getting ready to leave, they'd seen this guy start hitting his son. For no reason, it seemed, the guy just began shouting at this kid and smacking him hard against the side of his head. The kid didn't even try to run away, he just stood there, taking it, although he flinched each time the older guy made contact and you could tell that it hurt. It must've hurt like hell but the kid didn't make a sound and this seemed to make his father (because it must have been his father — you weren't allowed to beat the shit out of anybody who wasn't your very own kid) even angrier, because he hit even harder and when the kid finally fell to the ground, he started yelling at him, calling him names, like, "You bastard," and "Get up, you lousy little fucker. Get on your feet."

There were some people around; two women with very young children stood next to the swings and watched and shook their heads in disgust but nobody made a move. It was then, when the kid was on the ground, that Benny made his move. In a moment he was behind the guy and put his hand on the guy's shoulder and turned him around.

"What do you want?" the guy said and then, without waiting for a reply, he told Benny to mind his own business.

But Benny had hold of the guy and he wasn't letting go. "Leave him alone," he said and the guy swore at him and tried to push him away.

Benny said it again and this time the older guy took a swing at him, which Benny blocked, holding him firm so the guy couldn't get away. The kid just lay there on the ground, saying nothing, looking up at Benny and his father. Benny let go of the guy to reach down and help the kid to his feet and that was when the guy hauled off and gave Benny a kick right in the ribs. Benny staggered forward and almost fell, then turned and punched the guy and you could hear it connect, right across to where Skippy was still standing by the car. The guy fell flat on his back and the kid took off without looking back even once and Benny walked back to the car, rubbing his side where the guy had kicked him.

He got behind the wheel and started the car and Skippy got in the passenger side and they drove off, the wheels of the car kicking up loose gravel and dirt from the road leading into the park. Skippy asked if he was okay and Benny said, Yeah, he was fine and Skippy said he guessed Benny showed him, meaning the guy, and all Benny said was, No, he'd probably made it worse, the guy'd probably beat the hell out of the kid when he got home because of what Benny had done. There was no way out of it, though, Benny had added, sometimes you just gotta do stuff.

Now he saw that the same rusty swings were still in place, the same young kids — or younger versions of those kids — were hanging around, having a few laughs, razzing each other the way kids do, and he remembered how good it felt to prop yourself against the hood of a car and know you were never going to have to do anything but watch, never going to have to get involved. It made him feel old just thinking about it. Sometimes you just gotta do stuff, Benny had said. He leaned back in his seat and closed his eyes, resigned. He'd talk to Benny, after all. He'd given his word.

14.

The bus let him off just before the East End overpass and Skippy stood on the sidewalk and thought about where to go next. It was bingo night at the church, which meant the club was closed and he felt at loose ends, like he always did on these nights, but more so right now with the conversation with Margaret repeating itself in his mind. He wanted to think. And he was hungry — he hadn't eaten since breakfast and the tepid bottle of beer he'd consumed earlier sat uneasily on his stomach.

The familiar odour of greasy chips and burgers reached his nostrils, emanating from the small Italian restaurant two doors down. He pushed open the door and the girl behind the counter looked up and smiled.

"Hey there," she said and brought a cup of coffee over to the booth by the window.

He'd been coming in here for almost a year now, ever since he moved into Mrs. Cordelli's, and she'd come to know his habits.

"The usual?" she asked and he nodded.

"Please," and in a few minutes she returned with a toasted Denver on white bread, and two large slices of pickle on the side. He was probably imagining it but he often thought that the pickles on his sandwiches were larger than those he noticed on other people's orders. Which might not have meant anything — it was the short-order cook in the kitchen who made the sandwich and he was pretty sure the cook wasn't going out of his way to please him. Still, the waitress might have asked the cook to put extra big pickles on his sandwich, that wasn't beyond the realm of possibility.

Back when he first started coming in, he'd thought about asking her name but was too shy. Now it was too late; it would sound stupid after all this time. But there was something about her he liked: she was quiet, but not mousy, just not loud-mouthed like lots of girls who waited on tables, and she always looked pleased to see him when he came in. Last summer he had thought about this girl and imagined that he might ask her out, one of these days, if he could figure how to lead up to it. But that was before he met Doris, of course; he hadn't thought of the waitress in that way since then.

There were only two other customers in the place while Skippy was eating and when he had finished half of his sandwich, he remarked, "Slow this afternoon, eh?" and she nodded. It was, she said, and she liked it that way.

"But it'll pick up. Saturdays always get busy around six o'clock. Sometimes I can hardly keep up. Still, I guess I shouldn't complain. I mean, if it wasn't busy, I wouldn't have a job."

Skippy agreed that no, she probably wouldn't, which pretty well depleted his fund of conversational topics. But it was nice, anyway, sitting here drinking his coffee and eating his Denver in silence while she wiped tables and hummed a little now and then.

A car went by with the top down — first of the season, a sure sign summer was on its way — and his thoughts turned to Doris and the road trip and the need for a good used car. A thousand bucks or under, that's what he was looking for. He'd paid Joe Bruno the thousand he still owed him and if he laid out no more than a grand for the car, that would leave him just over two thousand dollars for the trip which was more than enough. They could go a long ways on two thousand dollars, chalk up a lot of miles on the speedometer. More than likely, he'd come back with some cash in his pocket, but if he didn't, that was all right by him. This money from his uncle was a windfall; he hadn't been expecting it, and it just seemed like fate that it had arrived for the precise purpose of giving him a chance to get Doris to himself. If it hadn't been for her and this trip, the money would most likely have just stayed in the bank. He had no need for it; aside from Doris, there was nothing he wanted.

He finished his second cup of coffee and considered whether or not to have dessert: he wasn't hungry, he was sure he couldn't eat another bite, but a piece of pie or some angel food cake would give him a reason to hang around a little longer. Then the restaurant door opened and a family — mom, dad and two noisy young kids — entered, and he decided to give dessert a miss. He left a tip for the waitress — he always tipped her extra, just like she always gave him slightly bigger pickles — and called good night to her on his way out.

"Take care of yourself," she said. "Don't do anything I wouldn't do."

Skippy smiled and let himself out the door, thinking how people always said that. If it was a guy saying it, the guy would always add, "And if you do, name it after me," which was coarse and not something you said to a girl, anyway, but it made you feel like you were sort of a wise guy even if you weren't. It was just one of those things, that's all. Skippy never said them, himself, but he liked it when other people did.

The boardinghouse was quiet when he got back with only the front porch bulb burning and a dim light on in the hallway. It was always like this on a Saturday night. Mrs. Cordelli claimed it as her night off and headed down the street to play bingo, which meant that if you wanted something to eat you had to go out for it. She made an exception for Mr. Wilson and kept his dinner warm for him in the oven, but the others were expected to fend for themselves. The Armenian in the next room usually had a date and the other three had a long-standing poker game across town at Brewster's Taxi Company, in the back room. Which left Skippy and old Mr. Wilson who would be drinking down at the Frontenac Hotel, as usual.

Skippy went up to his room and stretched out on his bed, on top of the covers, staring up at the ceiling. What he was thinking about, what had been haunting him since leaving Margaret's, was the thought of sitting down across the table from Benny and telling him he'd raped his wife.

Perhaps everybody in this world was afraid of at least one other person. He'd never really thought about it before, but Skippy knew that there was a part of him that was afraid of Benny Carter. It wasn't really a physical thing, although there had been that one night back in high school when it had been made clear that he was a coward and that his best friend could hurt him, if he chose.

It was the week before Christmas and they were in Benny's room with the door shut, doing some last minute cramming. Two exams the following day, physics and French, and Skippy was lousy in both of them. History and English, those were his good subjects, and geography too, if it had to do with maps. He liked to study maps of Europe and Asia and South America and memorize the names of the towns and rivers, imagining himself there, under a palm tree or next to a pyramid. When they studied Greece he took extra books out of the library and read up on the city-states of Athens and Sparta and the Peloponnesian wars. After every semester he filed the information away in his head, another country to be visited once he had finished school and was free to travel.

Physics, though, that was another matter. He didn't get it and he didn't understand how it came so easily to his friend. But then, most things came easily to Benny. He did lousy in school because he didn't care about it very much and because he was always taking off and missing a week here and there. But when he put his mind to it, he soaked up information like a sponge; once he had read something, or heard it, he almost never forgot it. He told Skippy it was just a case of opening up the door.

"You don't remember things because you don't want to remember them," he said, "or you think you won't be able to. Human beings only use one fifth of their brain power, we don't even try to use the rest. But it's all sitting there, waiting to be used. You just have to learn to tap into it."

Easy, right? Well, it was if you were Benny. In terms of being a best friend, Benny Carter really only had one fault and it was this: he didn't understand that everybody's minds didn't work like his. When kids at school weren't hip to the beat poets, or the blues, or T. S. Elliot, Benny figured they were just being stubborn. How could anyone read "The Waste Land" and not be knocked out by it, not want to stand up and salute the beauty of those words? Didn't everybody think Kerouac was a genius? Didn't the whole world think like him? Continually, every single day, maybe every single hour, Benny was confronted with the fact that just the opposite was true, that most people didn't think like him, that almost nobody thought like him except Skippy Jacques and Skippy was really just a poor disciple. Benny stood alone and walked alone and Skippy limped along a step or two behind him.

"Come on, man," he said, that night in the upstairs bedroom. "Think about it. This stuff is just common sense. It's about inverse relationships — one goes up, the other goes down."

Skippy was fed up. "Forget it," he said, sitting up and slamming his text book shut. "I'm not going to get it. It makes no sense."

Benny sat up and leaned towards him, placing a hand on his friend's shoulder. He was grinning and shaking his head. "You're closing your mind. You're telling yourself you can't do this. Open up, man, let it in."

Let me in, he might have said. In fact, Skippy wasn't entirely sure he hadn't said that.

There were times when Benny was so sure of himself, when his brown eyes glittered with the excitement of making a point, that he became almost overbearing. Even a disciple needs to get out from the shadow of the master now and then, if he's not going to be swallowed up entirely. Skippy pushed at the hand gripping his shoulder but Benny wouldn't let go. Instead, he pressed his fingers deeper into Skippy's flesh and it hurt.

"Stop it," he said but Benny wasn't listening.

"Open up." Skippy glanced at his friend and saw that he was still smiling, but he was deadly serious and was steadily applying more pressure to Skippy's shoulder. He tried to pull away but Benny was stronger.

"Boyle's law," he said. "The pressure of a gas varies inversely as its volume at a constant temperature. P times V equals K. K is the constant. Concentrate, Skippy. You can do this, man."

By now Skippy was sliding off the bed, struggling to get away from the hand that held him, and Benny moved with him on to the floor, pinning him to the carpet and pressing his fingers into Skippy's flesh until it felt that something would break, some bone, some blood vessel, and Skippy was pushing against his friend, mortified and in pain and struggling not to cry.

"P times V equals K. Say it, Skippy, tell me you understand. Come on, man, do this for me. Say it."

And Skippy finally said it, angrily, spitting it out with a hatred he would not have expected he could feel for anyone, let alone his best friend. Immediately Benny let go and left the room. In a moment he was back with a cold, damp cloth. He knelt on the floor beside Skippy and pulled down the shoulder of his T-shirt, revealing the raw, red imprint of his own hand. Skippy was turned on his side, ashamed of himself for hurting, angry with his friend but angrier with himself. He pushed Benny's hand away but Benny was just as insistent as he had been earlier, although much more gentle. He placed the cloth on Skippy's flesh and held it there and then got up and fetched some ice cubes from the kitchen and held them in place until the throbbing died down and Skippy told him it was okay, he wanted to get up.

He stood up and tucked his T-shirt into his jeans, not looking at his friend, then retrieved his jacket from the back of the chair where he'd dropped it a few hours earlier. When he turned to get his book, he saw that Benny had already picked it up and was standing in front of the bedroom door, holding the physics text out to him like a peace offering.

"I'm sorry, man, I didn't mean to hurt you. I just wanted to show you."

Skippy practically snarled at him. "Show me what? Show me that you're some big tough guy who likes to push people around? All right, you showed me, okay?"

He pushed past Benny and out the door and turned to face him, his voice shaking with anger.

"You're an asshole, you know that? You call yourself a friend but you don't even know what it means. You don't know fuck all."

Then he turned and headed down the hall and just as he reached the top of the staircase, Benny called out, "Hey —"

Skippy turned around and he saw something in Benny he'd never seen before. He looked confused, completely bewildered, as he stood there in the doorway. He looked like he'd just lost his best friend.

"It's all right," said Skippy and his voice was steady now, the anger was gone. "Forget it, man. It's okay. I'll see you tomorrow."

Skippy turned on his side and closed his eyes, the memory of that baffled look on Benny's face as distinct now as it was three and a half years ago. Neither of them had ever mentioned the incident again and it had never been repeated.

But Skippy never forgot the look in Benny's eyes. That, he knew, was why he'd avoided him all this time. He didn't want to see that look again, he didn't want to have that kind of power over Benny Carter.

He must have fallen asleep; when he awoke it was late, the room was dark and a street light shone through the open window. There was a sound somewhere, downstairs in the room below him — the muffled voices of the television and the slide of a kitchen drawer, the rattle of silverware. He was wide awake; sitting up, he saw that it was just gone eleven, the late night news would just be starting.

Out of habit, he reached one hand under the bed and felt for the metal foot locker he kept there. It had been his dad's and it contained his father's discharge papers from the army, a few old photos, his poetry notebook and an ancient, unopened package of condoms. More importantly, though, it held the leather wallet with his money for the trip. He liked the idea of having it on hand like this. It made the trip seem more real, somehow.

The box was still there. And the key to the lock was tucked safely in among his socks in the top drawer of his dresser.

Making his way down to the living room, he passed the kitchen and caught a glimpse of Wilson getting his supper out of the oven. Nobody else was around; Mrs. Cordelli would be home by now, for sure, and was probably in bed. The others would still be out playing poker — the Armenian was most likely with his girlfriend. Lately, Chista was gone from Friday night until Monday morning and Skippy guessed he'd found himself a sort of permanent relationship, on weekends, anyway.

Skippy took a seat in front of the television set and in a few minutes Wilson padded into the living room, a plate of food in one hand and silverware in the other. He stopped short when he saw

Skippy and seemed to be unsure whether to stay or to retreat upstairs and eat his supper in his room, on a tray. Making up his mind to stay, he placed his meal on a TV tray and sat down heavily in the armchair nearest the door. Silently, he picked up his knife and fork and began to eat, his eyes fixed on the television screen in front of him.

Since the night of the fight, here in this room, Skippy and Wilson had said nothing to each other. They avoided each other whenever they could and when, as was the case tonight, they had to be in the other person's presence, they adopted a policy of appearing unaware that the other even existed. It was a game and a silly one and Skippy was suddenly tired of playing it. Why should he hold a grudge against this old guy, especially when he was leaving soon anyway? Why not mend fences, as his mother would have said, or — in another of her phrases — extend the olive branch?

"It takes a big man to admit when he's wrong," she would tell him. "Especially when it isn't his fault." Which made no sense, really, but he knew what she meant.

Skippy waited for a commercial — Condition by Clairol: Do you have to hide your hair to look prettier? — and turned to the older man.

"Mr. Wilson, can we talk about something?"

Wilson looked up from his dinner, surprised. He stared at the kid, trying to focus on his face, trying not to seem drunk, although he was. He always was, this time of night. Quietly drunk, staggering just a little as he walked along the quiet city streets, feeling a little edgy by the time he arrived home. (Mrs. Cordelli's boarding house had been "home" to Wilson for six years, the longest he'd lived anywhere since he'd left his wife.)

"Mr. Wilson, I'm leaving at the end of the month —"

The old man said nothing, just looked at him and continued to chew, and Skippy wondered if he might be too drunk to understand anything.

"The thing is, I was hoping we could shake hands and let bygones be bygones."

Wilson turned back to the television and Skippy thought about dropping it. But he'd made up his mind to mend fences so he figured he'd keep on going.

"You know, sir, I really feel bad about that fight. I didn't know you had a bad back. How is it, anyway?"

"Eh?"

"Your back. How is it?"

"It's lousy. My back's been lousy for twenty years and every year it gets worse, okay?"

"What happened to it?"

"You writin' a book or what?"

"I'm just curious, that's all."

Wilson considered this, then he said, "War wound. Got shot in the back at Dieppe and spent six months in hospital learning how to walk again. And then ten years ago I got in the way of a harvester, got hit in the very same place and when I came out of the hospital that time I was finished for the bush. Don't know how to do anything else so here I am. Sitting on my arse all day with just enough disability pension to get good and drunk every night. If I had any balls I'd take a gun and shoot myself in the head and get it over with. But I don't."

"Gee, that's awful."

"Yeah, it's awful, all right. Awful pathetic." It was said in a tone of voice that inhibited further conversation and Skippy turned his attention back to the television, unable to think of anything else to say. A few minutes later, he tried again.

"Do you have any family, Mr. Wilson? A wife or children or anything?"

The older man gave him a disgusted look. "Yes, I have a wife, I have children. What do you think, I'm some kind of weirdo that never got married? Think I'm so horrible to look at no woman would have me? Is that what you think?"

"No, sir, I didn't mean that at all."

"Oh, you didn't, eh? Then what did you mean? Or maybe you're just a nosy little asshole, is that it? Poking your nose in other people's business for no good reason. Is that it?"

Skippy thought he'd better try to explain himself before the old man got himself worked up into a state and they had another fist fight, right here on the carpet.

"Mr. Wilson, it's nothing like that. I'm not trying to be nosy. It's just that I'm leaving, like I told you, and I'd sort of like to make things up before I go."

"Leaving, eh?" Wilson gave a disgusted shrug, as if there was no use trying to explain the actions of some people. "Don't know what you think you're going to find. It's all the same out there, once you get to it. No difference. Might as well save your money and stay put."

The national news ended and the local guy came on, leading with a story about an accident at the local amusement park. Some woman had stood up in one of the rides and had fallen off and was killed. They had a file shot of the ride, twisting and spinning in the air and filled with young people screeching with happiness, and then a shot of the woman, in her late twenties, pretty good looking, Skippy thought, and that made it sadder. The picture of the woman was blurry, the way photos in newspapers and magazines always are when they're of dead people, and then they went to the spokesman for the midway who explained how good their safety record was and how this was a "freak accident" and under normal circumstances it was impossible for anybody to get hurt. The implication was that the woman had been drunk, but of course, nobody came right out and said it. Then the announcer came back on and said the woman was married with two young children and funeral services would be held on Tuesday.

Wilson spoke up as the programme broke for another commercial. "Three kids," he said. "All boys. Last I heard two of them were still living in Sudbury and the third was running a pansy joint on Yonge Street in Toronto. There. Satisfied?"

"What about your wife?" Skippy asked.

"Boy, you're a real Mr. Interviewer, aren't you? A real Walter Cronkite. Well, since you ask, I don't know where my wife is, haven't heard from her in years. Oh, I guess I could find her, if I had to. She wouldn't thank me for it, I can tell you. She made that pretty clear when she kicked me out. Handed me my dad's old leather suitcase and my one good suit on a hanger and told me she never wanted to see me again. Said she was tired of raising three kids on her own ten months out of the year and if she was going to be alone she might as well have the good times that came with it. So I said good riddance to bad rubbish and came up to the Lakehead. That was ten years ago — no, closer to fifteen, I guess." He shook his head, and said it again. "Fifteen years. Good God almighty."

The rest of the news was pretty uneventful, mostly city hall stuff and the opening of a new wing at the hospital. Skippy was getting tired but he always watched the whole newscast, just in case something important happened, he wouldn't want to miss it. Right before they went to sports, the announcer said, "Finally in the news, city police are launching a crackdown on prostitution. Staff sergeant Blaine Cooper says in the past three years the number of young women plying their trade on our city's streets has doubled and the situation is close to being out of control." Then they went to a shot of one of the city streets at night, with two women in tight skirts and high heels standing on a dark corner, their faces turned away from the camera.

"See someone you know?" The old man was looking at him with a smile, and Skippy felt the blood rush to his cheeks.

"No, I just —"

Wilson laughed. "Hey, I know, you just want to look. Listen, I can't do anything but look so consider yourself lucky." He put his plate down on the floor and stood up. "Come on," he said, "I want to show you something."

Skippy hesitated, but the old man was insistent. And he had suddenly changed towards him — all hostility was gone and he appeared friendly, even excited. What could it hurt to go upstairs with him for a minute, Skippy asked himself? He was a harmless old guy, probably didn't have a friend in the world. He'd humour him, go up to his room, show him there were no hard feelings.

Wilson's room was down at the far end of the hall from Skippy's, right next to the bathroom. Skippy had never been in it, in fact, he'd never been invited into any other room the whole time he'd lived here. He was curious, in spite of himself, to see what it looked like. It turned out to be pretty bare, decorated only with a large, colourful calendar on the wall, showing brown-skinned people in bathing suits running along a white, sandy beach. "Portugal," the old man said, when he saw Skippy looking at it. "The Algarve, the most beautiful place in the world. People aren't much to look at, don't let that picture fool you, but the beaches are God's gift to mankind."

There was an old oak dresser against one wall, next to the window, with a piece of clean white linen draped over the top and two photographs in small, oval frames. One was of a turn-of-the-century couple, stiff and unsmiling, probably Wilson's mother and father. The other was more recent, a head and shoulders shot of a young woman with short dark hair and a shy, tentative smile. That, Wilson told him, was his wife.

"Pretty girl, eh? That was taken before we were married, she went to a professional photographer and sent it to me in England, where I was stationed. I kept that picture with me for four years, all through the war. After I got hit I spent six months in hospital in France and I'd take it out and look at it and say, That's what I'm fighting for. And when I got back to the States, I married her. Here, have a drink."

The old man had taken two shot glasses and a bottle of Hiram Walker out of a dresser drawer and poured them each a drink. "Here's mud in your eye," he said, and drank it down in one gulp.

Skippy sipped his drink and studied the photo of the former Mrs. Wilson. "She looks young," he said, and the old man nodded.

"She was. A hell of a lot younger than me, twenty years, almost. I never did figure out why she wanted to marry me in the first place. Father figure, I guess that's what Freud would say. She wanted a dad and she got me. And I didn't want a daughter and I got her. Neither of us were very happy."

They stood in silence for a moment, looking at the picture of the woman who was too young, who had tired of her too-old husband and told him to leave, when suddenly there was a noise, a sort of rustling from a corner of the room, that caused Skippy to jump. The old man laughed.

"That's Jack," he said. "I guess you haven't met him."

"Jack?"

"Sure. Jack the rabbit. Come on, I'll introduce you."

He led Skippy to where a large brown and white rabbit with impossibly long ears crouched in a cage in the corner. The animal had yellow eyes, one very bright and alert, the other dull and glazed over, and he regarded Skippy with disfavour.

"He's a French lop," the old man told him, unlatching the top of the cage and lifting the rabbit out of the straw. He held him up so Skippy could get a good look and the animal's hind feet pawed fiercely at the air, struggling to get away.

"Now, Jack," said Wilson, "this is Mr. — what's your last name?"

"Jacques," said Skippy.

"How do you spell that?"

Skippy told him and the old man stared at him in astonishment.

"Well, would you believe it?" he said. "Jack, this gentleman has the same name as you. So you're both French and you're both called Jack. Amazing, wouldn't you say that was an amazing coincidence?"

Skippy reached out to pat the rabbit, but pulled his hand away when it snapped at his fingers.

"Now, Jack," said Wilson, "you behave yourself." To Skippy, he added, "He's a little antisocial, like me. Doesn't see too well, being blind in one eye, and it makes him a little nervous of anybody new. All right, fella, we'll put you down and let you go back to sleep." He placed the rabbit back in the cage and closed the top. "He gets cranky when you wake him up. These days he sleeps a lot, a sign he's getting old, I guess."

Skippy finished his drink and set the glass down on the dresser. "Well, sir, I guess I should go —"

But Wilson stopped him. "Now hang on just a minute, I want you to see something. You'll like this, just hang on a minute."

The old man stooped down and reached under his bed, pulling out a photograph album. More pictures of the ex-wife, Skippy thought. He should find an excuse to leave.

Wilson sat down on the bed and opened the album. His white head bent over the book, he began to turn over the pages, taking great care not to bend the corners or disturb the pictures pasted inside. Without looking up, he said, "The worst thing about getting old is the women. They get old, too, and you think about climbing into bed with someone your own age, her body all worn out from too many kids and her tits all hanging down and wrinkled, and you think maybe you don't want it so bad after all. Maybe you'd rather not. Maybe you're lucky to be on your own at this age and the only decrepit old body you gotta look at is your own. Know what I mean?"

He looked up at Skippy, standing beside him, working on a way to get out of the room without hurting the old guy's feelings, and he laughed. "No, I guess you don't. But you will, I tell you, boy, you will."

Skippy marveled at the turnaround in such a short time; Wilson had gone from being surly and noncommittal to being a real chatterbox. Here it was almost midnight and he was going on like he could rattle away till morning. Skippy guessed he was lonely, living up here with only a half-blind rabbit for company — he probably wanted to tell his newfound friend the story of his life.

"Now sit down, boy, you're going to love this. Here," and he held the album up so Skippy could see it, "what do you think of that?"

It took Skippy a moment or two to adjust to what he was looking at, it was just so different from the family photos and nostalgic snapshots he was expecting. A page of colour photographs of women, young and not so young, mostly naked, lying spread-eagled on beds, draped over tables, sitting on chairs with their legs apart and their hands cradling their breasts. The photos had been placed five to a page, held in place by those little sticky corners you buy at the five and dime.

Skippy turned the pages in silence and there was page after page of the same sort of thing. The photos showed everything — well, they would have, except that they were blurry, obviously taken by an amateur, and the women themselves did not look much like the professional models in the men's magazines. Some of them had small breasts or fat thighs — one had a purple appendix scar spreading across her belly. Only a couple were actually beautiful to look at; in most cases they looked like girls Skippy had grown up with, or their older sisters, smiling broadly at the camera. It was incongruous, really, to see faces that belonged in a high school yearbook on such completely naked bodies.

Wilson wanted a response. "Well," he repeated, "what do you think?"

Skippy felt he had to say something but what he really wanted to do was drop the book on the floor and get out of there. Here he was, sitting in a room with a man old enough to be his father — his grandfather, even — looking at dirty pictures of young girls. It was obscene, he hardly knew the guy.

"Who are they?" he asked, finally.

"Hookers." It was announced triumphantly, gleefully, satisfied that Skippy never would have guessed. "Every last one's a hooker. Been taking these photos for almost five years now. I guess you could say it's my hobby. Some men collect stamps, I collect whores. Photos of 'em, anyway. It's really something, don't you think?"

Skippy nodded. "It's something all right." He continued to turn the pages, becoming interested in spite of himself, and he noticed something. "They're all brunettes," he said.

"Well, I guess you could say that." Wilson chuckled and leaned closer to Skippy, exuding a powerful odour of alcohol and some pungent brand of hair cream. "Fact is, if you look, I mean if you really look, you'll notice lots of them aren't brunettes at all."

Skippy looked again at the photos and saw that some of the girls were natural blondes, and redheads.

"It's a wig," Wilson confided. "A black wig. I get them to put it on and then I take the picture. I like it better that way. Even the ones who are natural brunettes, I still like them to wear the wig. Otherwise, it doesn't feel right."

Skippy started to close the book but the old man stopped him. "Wait," he said, "I want to show you my favourite. Right at the back. Go on, skip right over to the end."

It was more of the same, two pages of naked girls kneeling on chairs, stretched out across beds, posing in doorways. Then he saw that there was a similarity: "It's the same girl."

"Aha!" Wilson positively cackled, he was so delighted. "You got it, fella, you hit it spot on. It's the same girl, eight pictures of the very same girl, can you believe it?"

"I guess you must like her," Skippy said and the old man slapped him across the shoulder.

"Like her? I damn well love her," he said. "She's an angel, this girl. I met her last fall and I told myself, Wilson, this is it. This is where your collection stops. You've found the perfect girl."

Skippy was curious, in spite of himself.

"Why? What do you like about her?"

"I'll tell you something. I've thought about this myself, wondered what it is about this one that puts you off ever wanting to take a picture of any other girl. And it's this." Wilson grew very solemn, and Skippy had a feeling he was about to learn something. It was the same kind of feeling he used to get when Benny had been away and had come back, brimming with some new, secret information.

"Every other girl I've had, they go along with it, put on the wig, take their clothes off, lie back on the bed and pose — up — to — a — point." He stared Skippy in the eye and waited to see the effect his words were having. "Only up to a point, get it? They'd do it, well, they had to do it, didn't they? I mean, they were getting paid to do what I asked them to so they couldn't very well say no. But you could tell they didn't get it. Well, this girl, she gets it. You see what I mean?"

Skippy wasn't sure he saw it at all and he wasn't sure he wanted to. The old man was sitting too close to him, his breath smelled, his hair stank, and Skippy was feeling trapped, like poor old Jack the rabbit asleep in his cage.

The old man continued. "She got it right away. Didn't have to explain a thing. She saw what I wanted and you know what? She not only did it, she made it better."

He took one of the photos out of its corners and held it up close to Skippy's face. "Look at her," he said, "did you ever see such a pretty face? Did you ever see such an angel?"

The photograph wavered a few inches from his nose, a slim, pretty woman in a black wig pointing her breasts at the camera. And the smile — wasn't there something familiar about that smile that shone through the blur of the camera lens? Skippy took the picture from Wilson and studied it; then he looked down at the open pages on his lap. It was her. There was no doubt. The woman in the wig was Doris.

He began to feel sick. The face in the photo album, repeated over and over, smiling up at him from bedspreads, over the backs of chairs, teasing him among the cushions of a couch. He stared at her face and heard himself asking, "Do you — do you do it with her?"

"Screw her, you mean?" Wilson laughed. "Hell, I wish I could. No, I'm afraid that harvester put an end to any good old-fashioned fornicating for yours truly. Besides, that's not the point of the exercise."

"It's not?" His voice was dull and hoarse and he couldn't look up at the old man. He wanted to be away from this place, he wanted only to get out of this room and back to the safety of his own, but he was bound to the bed, unable to move.

Wilson stood up. "I'll show you."

"What?"

"Close your eyes. Just for a minute, it's all right. Close your eyes and I'll show you what I mean."

Skippy shut his eyes and heard the old man open a drawer. After a minute, Wilson told him, "All right, you can look now."

Skippy looked. The old man had donned a short black wig, a woman's wig, the one in the pictures, and he was smiling just like one of those girls. Just like Doris.

"Watch," he said, "this is what happens."

Wilson shut his eyes and then, very slowly, he began to sway from side to side. He hummed a tune, softly, almost under his breath, and while Skippy watched in horror, he began to stroke his own arms, his chest, running his hands up and down his hips and thighs. With slow, graceful movements he began to undo his shirt buttons with one hand, still stroking himself with the other, his eyes closed, his face lifted up towards the unseen camera. Skippy was afraid to speak, almost afraid to move, as the old man continued his obscene strip tease, removing his shirt, revealing his pasty white shoulders and the gray chest hairs showing above his undershirt. Slowly, he undid his fly and then turned his back to Skippy, still swaying, still humming, and fumbled with his belt. After a moment he turned to face him, triumphantly swinging the belt in the air. His khaki workpants began a slow, deliberate slide to the floor and the old man stepped out of them, deftly flinging them to one side with his foot. He dropped the belt and stood there in his undershirt and shorts, his socks and his shoes and began to roll his shirt up, revealing his hairy belly inch by inch.

The skin on his neck was wrinkled like a chicken's, red and rough, in contrast to the rest of his body which had remained covered up and hidden for some seventy years. Freckles, or maybe they were age spots, sprinkled his arms and the backs of his hands, and when he pulled the shirt completely over his head the wig came off with it and his white hair stood up like a rooster's comb. This, it seemed, was the finale, for the old man threw his arms up over his head in triumph and stood there, his eyes still closed, beaming ecstatically. Then, he dropped his arms to his sides and sat down on the bed next to Skippy, panting slightly from the exertion.

"That's it," he said. "And then I take her picture."

He retrieved his shirt from the floor and began to dress and Skippy closed the photo album and stood up.

"Well," he began, and stopped.

He tried again: "Well, I better be going, I guess."

"Now, son, don't rush off. Have another drink. I'm having one."

"No, thanks, I'm pretty tired. I should be going to bed."

The old man, his shirt half-buttoned and holding his pants in his hands, accompanied Skippy to the door. "Well, any time you want a little company, feel free to drop by. You're a fine young man and I'm sure glad we got to know each other."

He held out a hand and Skippy, after a moment, took it. Wilson had a powerful grip for an old guy. "Yes, well. So am I. Good night."

Wilson stood out in the hall and watched as Skippy walked the dozen or so yards to his room at the far end. He called out, softly, so as not to wake the others, "Sleep tight. Don't let the bed bugs bite."

Skippy nodded quickly, afraid that somebody might come out and see the old man standing in the hall half-naked. "Right, sir," he said. "I won't."

It must have been some twenty minutes later, when Skippy had undressed and got under the covers and was lying there, staring up at the ceiling, that he heard a noise at his door and the sound of something being slipped through the crack underneath. He waited a moment, then turned on the lamp by his bed. It was an envelope and he considered ignoring it, pretending he hadn't seen it. But then Mrs. Cordelli would find it when she made her housekeeping rounds the next morning and that might be worse. So he got out of bed and retrieved the envelope. The old man had written on the front, in an elegant, old-fashioned hand-writing:

"For Mr. Jacques, who will Appreciate It"

Somehow, the sight of that laboured, ornate script made him feel sick and apprehensive. He knew what he would find and didn't want to find it but could not resist opening the envelope. So he did, and stood there looking at the face of his beloved Doris, naked and stretched out across a bright green shag rug, wearing Wilson's wig, smiling Wilson's smile.

15.

Doris Pantoniak was thirteen years old when she became aware of the fact that she was attractive to men: older men in general, her step-father and his friends in particular. These men did not attract her at all; in fact, Doris was a tomboy at that age and preferred climbing trees and playing baseball to wearing dresses and pretending to be a girl. She liked boys if they were good at sports and didn't try any funny stuff but she had no use for romance and despised the girls who played up to them and vied for their attention.

So when Doris realized her mother's husband was looking at her chest and following her around the house and making excuses to brush past her, she wondered if it had been going on for a long time and she just hadn't noticed.

"Ted's looking at me," she told her mother, who laughed and continued brushing her hair in the bathroom mirror.

"Fifty-three, fifty-four," she counted the strokes. "Don't be silly, who'd want to look at you? You're just a kid."

"He comes into my room in the morning, when I'm getting dressed."

"Oh, for God's sake, Doris, what do you think? You're some kind of knockout in your undershirt and panties? Think you're Lana Turner or somebody? Trust me, kid, you'll be lucky the day a guy like Ted takes any notice of you at all. Now get out of here and let me finish getting ready for work."

Doris' mother worked in the office of the local brewery, typing letters for the district manager and answering the phone. She'd worked there before the war, and after Doris was born and Doris' father went missing in action, the manager gave her back her old job and her mother took care of the baby. Doris was always closer to her grandmother than she was to her mom; after she died Doris walked up and down the street in front of her house and told herself that if she made it all the way from one end of the street to the other and back without once stepping on even the teeniest crack, her grandmother would come out the front door and call her in for supper.

Doris' mother's name was Delores but everybody called her Dolly, even her daughter. Dolly insisted on it.

"Jeez, kid, give me a break," she'd say whenever Doris would forget and call her 'Mommy' or 'Ma'. "Don't make me feel ancient."

Dolly had blonde hair and long painted fingernails and she went out on dates a lot and just wasn't around very much. She was a terrific dancer, everybody said so, and she and her dates made the rounds of the clubs and the hotel ball rooms, dancing night after night to 'The Original Stylings of Roy Jamieson and his Orchestra' or 'Big Al and the Stomphouse Four'.

If it wasn't dancing, it was the movies; Dolly loved the musicals the best — *Singin' in the Rain* with Gene Kelly and Debbie Reynolds, Doris Day and Danny Thomas in *I'll See You in My Dreams* — and especially, oh absolutely above all, *An American in Paris*, with the extravagantly wonderful music of George Gershwin. Nothing Dolly ever saw after that lived up to that seventeen-minute ballet sequence between Gene Kelly and Leslie Caron, but there were others that were fun, too, and had their moments: *My Blue Heaven, On Moonlight Bay, Tea for Two, April in Paris*. In the back of Dolly's mind there truly was a place where men and women stopped in the middle of the street and burst into song and the rest of the citizens joined in, perfectly in pitch and knowing all the words.

There was no point in Doris saying anything to her mother about all this going out. Dolly would simply put her hands on her hips and say, "Listen, miss, I gave up a lot to bring you into this world. I think I deserve a little fun when I can get it."

This was in reference to her mother's career as an actress — the career she could have had, to be exact. Long ago, before she was married, Dolly Pantoniak (who was Dolly Ahtila in those days) had been approached by a genuine Hollywood casting agent. He'd come up to her at a dance and given her his business card and told her to look him up if she ever came to California.

"You could be big," he'd told her. "Very big."

It was a true story; Dolly kept the card and Doris had seen it many times. But she'd married Doris' father and then the war had come and she'd had a baby and of course after that it was too late.

"Remember," she'd remind Doris from time to time, "I could have been a movie star. A big one. So you'd better be grateful."

Doris thought her mother could still be a movie star, she had such long, beautiful hair and her face was so pretty. She told Dolly that sometimes when she was getting ready to go out for the evening and Doris was sitting on the back of the toilet, watching and sitting on her hands so she wouldn't bite her fingernails. (Dolly painted them with red nail varnish, trying to get her to quit chewing on them and it would work for a day or two, but, sooner or later, Doris would forget and start nibbling away as usual.)

"If we moved to Hollywood, I bet you'd get a part in a movie right away," Doris would say. "You could be another Betty Grable."

Dolly laughed and told her she was crazy — what, an old bag like her, don't be silly — but she would smile into the mirror as she gave her hair a final brush and you could tell she didn't really think she was an old bag at all.

When she was finished putting on her lipstick, she'd stand back and take a good look at herself.

"What do you think?" she'd ask Doris. "Will I pass?"

"You look beautiful," Doris always told her and her mother would smile and reach up to pull the light switch.

"I guess I'll do," she'd say. Then, "Come on, you, get yourself into bed and stay there. And if you need anything, you know Grandma's number."

After Dolly left, Doris would climb into bed and hug Raggedy Andy for company.

"When I grow up," she told him, "I'm going to buy a big house for us all to live in, me and you and Dolly and Grandma. And my mom will never have to work ever again."

By the time Ted McGillvray entered the picture, Doris still bit her nails but she had stopped keeping her mother company while she got dressed and Raggedy Andy was relegated to the top shelf of the closet in her bedroom. And she'd forgotten all about the big house; she and Lindy Folgram were going to buy a ranch when they got out of high school, and raise horses.

"You're a big girl," Ted told her the first time he came over for supper.

"Who do you like best," she asked him, "Joe Louis or Rocky Marciano?"

"Gee, I dunno," he said, "I don't follow boxing a whole lot."

"He's a lover, not a fighter," Dolly piped up and she and Ted laughed and Doris ignored them.

"Bobby Matthews says Marciano's going to be bigger than Louis ever was but I say Joe Louis is still the best. Bobby Matthews is full of crap."

"A pretty girl like you shouldn't be thinking about boxing and stuff like that," said Ted. "You want to think about how you're going to make some lucky man happy some day."

Dolly shrieked. "Her! This one'll be lucky if some guy ever looks at her, let alone marries her."

"I don't know about that," he said. "She's got beautiful eyes," and he looked directly at Doris and she didn't like it.

"She's got my eyes," Dolly said. "Come on, you two, let's eat before the damn pot roast gets cold."

The next day Dolly wanted to know what Doris thought of Ted.

"He's okay, I guess. He doesn't know much, though. He didn't even know that Joe Louis is the one-round kayo champion of all time."

"He wants to marry me, Dodo." That was Doris' baby name and her mother hardly ever used it any more, unless she had a special favour to ask.

"So? Tell him to take a hike."

"He's got a good job," her mom said. "He works in the sales office at Northwest Builders and they really like him. He's only been there six months and he's already had two promotions. He could be running the place in a few years."

"But you've got lots of boyfriends, Mom, you don't need him."

"Lots of boyfriends. Right. Married guys who tell you they're leaving their wives, except they never do. Mama's boys who run away the minute they see a real live woman. Drunks who want to go out with their buddies every other night and re-live the war. Yeah, I've got lots of boyfriends. I guess I'm just the luckiest girl in town."

To her horror, Doris saw her mother's eyes fill with tears.

"It's okay, Mom," she said. "You go ahead and marry Ted. He seems like a nice guy. It'll be all right."

"You think so?"

Doris didn't think so, not really, but it was awful to see her mother so upset. "Sure, Mom. You marry Ted and everything will work out fine. You'll see."

So Dolly dried her tears and married Ted and they had a pretty good time, all things considered. The job at the builders' office didn't pan out in the end — the manager's nephew finished school and was brought in to take over the place and Ted said no way was he taking orders from some kid who was wet behind the ears, so he quit and found another job at Arnie's A-1 Auto Sales. At first he really liked it and Arnie thought he was great and took him out Friday nights to the Legion Hall to have a few drinks after work. The only thing is, the cars were junk, really, and he finally said that to Arnie one of those Friday nights and pretty soon he was selling commercial air-conditioning equipment instead and he would have kept that job permanently if the company hadn't gone bankrupt. But no matter how many jobs he lost, it was never more than a few days before he found another, and Dolly was unflinchingly loyal and always maintained that it was only a matter of time until the perfect job came along.

As for Doris, she didn't find herself growing any more fond of her step-father as the months went by. He continued to stare at her all the time and now and then his poker buddies came by to play cards and they hung out in the kitchen, smoking and drinking beer and eating the sandwiches Dolly made them and making coarse jokes that ended with them all laughing, her mother most of all: "Oh, you fellows are awful. Honest, Ted, aren't they awful?"

If Doris came down to the kitchen to get a drink from the fridge or make herself a sandwich, Ted would always say something like, "It's little Princess Doris, come to visit the peasants. Say hello to the Princess, boys."

And they'd all say in unison, "Hello, Princess," and watch her while she poured her drink or spread peanut butter and jam on her bread and make some comment about what a big girl she was getting to be, just like her mother, and then Ted would make some reference to her mother that would make Dolly laugh and say, "Ted, watch your mouth, you dirty old thing." And Doris would get out of there just as quick as she could.

It was the Monday morning after he'd lost the air-conditioner job that Doris opened the bathroom door to find Ted leaning against the wall, blocking her exit.

"It's all yours," she said and tried to push past him but he put out his arm to stop her.

"What's your hurry?" he wanted to know, standing so close to her she could smell last night's whiskey on his breath and almost taste the Brylcream in his hair.

"Excuse me," she told him, "I have to get to school."

Abruptly, Ted took hold of her and pulled her towards him.

"You're just a little tease, aren't you? Walking around here with your tight little blouses, showing yourself off like that. You think you're hot stuff, don't you?"

"Hey —"

And then he kissed her and she tried to push him away and he just kissed her all the harder, and forced his tongue into her mouth so that she could hardly breathe. When he came up for air she yelled at him to stop, to let her go, and he kissed her again, and the taste of him made her sick to her stomach.

"There," he said, finally, and laughed. "That's what you needed, wasn't it?"

He let go of her and her hand immediately came up and slapped the side of his face. She didn't think about doing it, she had never slapped anybody before in her life, but she did it instinctively and she did it hard, and almost before she had time to realize what she'd done, he hit her back, right on the face, and she saw a white flash and felt nothing for just a few seconds.

Slowly, she slumped down on to the floor, and he stood over her and said, "Don't you ever do that again, you hear? Nobody hits me and gets away with it. Nobody. You ever do that again and I'll kill you. I mean it, I swear I'll kill you. I fought in the war and I killed men and I wouldn't even think twice about killing someone like you."

He stepped over her and into the bathroom. Just before shutting the door, he said, "And don't you say anything to your mother about this, either. Or you'll really wish you hadn't."

Doris was late for school that day and when she did arrive her teacher made her go to the principal's office for a late slip. The secretary behind the counter took one look at her and said, "Good grief, Doris, what did you do to your face?"

"Fell down the stairs," she muttered and grabbed her late slip and left. One side of her face was all swollen and she thought her nose might be broken. It wasn't, as it turned out, but she was pretty much of a mess for few days after that. Lindy was all over her at lunchtime, wanting to know what happened, and when Doris told her, too, about the stairs, she looked like she didn't believe her, but she didn't say anything more about it and she told Bobby Matthews and the other kids to mind their own beeswax.

When her mother came home from work Doris told her she'd got into a fight with the school bully, so of course Dolly gave her a lecture about how it was time she grew up and stopped acting like a hooligan, she was a young lady now, for Heaven's sake. And Ted just sat there all through dinner watching her with a smirk on his face. Not that she looked at him if she could help it; she kept her gaze fixed on her plate and wouldn't talk and finally Dolly got exasperated and told her to leave the table if she couldn't at least be sociable. Doris didn't have to be told twice.

She went to her room and lay on her bed and looked at the pictures she'd cut out of old issues of Boxing Illustrated and taped on her wall: Joe Louis standing over a kayoed Billy Conn, Louis in the ring with Max Schmeling — the second time, after he was the champ — Louis in uniform in 1941. Before she went to sleep that night she took the pictures down, rolled them up and stashed them in her cupboard, on the top shelf, right next to Raggedy Andy.

Doris avoided Ted as much as possible after that, leaving the house early in the morning when her mother left for work, not coming home until she knew Dolly would be there, too. And by the end of the month Ted got another job and the house was livable again, since he had to be at work at seven and he and her mom were out every night, now he had money coming in again. Still, he'd pinch her behind whenever he got the chance, and make little kissing faces at her when Dolly wasn't looking. It was revolting, but bearable. What Doris couldn't bear was ever to have those lips on hers again or to taste that tongue of his in her mouth. As long as he didn't try that again, she could stand it.

It was early in December, a few months after the tongue episode, that Doris came home from school to find Ted lying on the living room couch, asleep or passed out. She stood just inside the front door, wrapped in her heavy winter coat and scarf and wearing her galoshes, and gazed at him with loathing. He's been fired again, she thought, and he's spent the entire afternoon drinking in some bar. How sweet it would be to pick up the cushion that had fallen to the floor and just hold it over his face until he stopped breathing. She would be doing the world a favour — one less drunken creep to deal with. Then things would go back to the way they used to be, just she and her mother having a perfectly good time on their own. The way it used to be.

She figured she'd go into her room and change out of her school clothes and go hang out at Lindy's until her mother came home. Better not be around just in case he woke up and got any ideas. If she wasn't ready to kill him, then she'd better just stay out of his way.

Doris had just hung up her dress in her closet and was rummaging around in a dresser drawer, looking for her western shirt, the checked one she liked with the little lassoes on the collar, when she heard a sound at the door and turned around. Ted stood there, his face puffy from sleep, his shirt hanging outside his trousers. He was staring at her, his mouth hanging open just a little, and she felt her heart begin to pound against her chest.

"What do you want?" she asked him and her voice didn't sound like her voice at all, it sounded like the voice of a very small girl, a very small, frightened girl.

He said nothing, but came further into the room and she backed away and said it again: "What do you want in here?"

Now he smiled, as if he'd only just heard her, and said, "I think you know what I want. Don't you?"

"You better get out of here. I'm getting dressed." She was right back against the bed now, Ted was blocking the door. She thought of the window behind her and wondered if it was big enough to let her climb through it. Probably not; she had grown several inches in the past year — she and Lindy had measured themselves in her mother's kitchen and she was almost five foot four. And anyway, it would mean turning her back on Ted, and she couldn't do that.

Slowly, he walked towards her and she waited till he was almost there then tried to duck around him. He reached out and caught her and held her tightly, while she twisted and pulled and struggled to get away.

"It's about time for another kiss, don't you think?"

"Let me go," she cried, "let go of me."

He pulled her close to him and held her next to his chest.

"Say please," he said and he stroked her hair and nuzzled her ear with his lips.

"Please," she said and waited, her knees like rubber, her heart pounding. Please, she thought, let me go.

He placed his hand under her chin and forced her to look up at him. For just a moment their eyes met and then she looked away and he said, "No, I don't think so."

He kissed her again, like the other time, and she thought she'd gag with that tongue of his in her mouth, practically in her throat, and she tried to pull away but this time she didn't hit him because she knew he'd hit her back, he had said he would kill her and she believed him.

Finally, he raised his lips from hers and she gasped for air and tried to free herself, but he pushed her down on to the bed. She watched in disbelief while he fumbled with his suspenders and the zipper of his pants and wondered, was he going to show her his thing? She had seen Bobby Matthews' thing years ago, touched it even, because he asked her to, but she hadn't thought much of it. And she'd shown him hers, because fair's fair, and he'd touched it, and then they'd pulled up their pants and come out of the bushes across the back lane and gone to play baseball. It had been nothing, nothing at all, they'd even laughed about it and said, "Is that what it looks like? Who cares about something like that?" It felt like a hundred years ago.

Ted pulled his pants off and stood over her, confused, trying to remember what it was he was he was doing in her room in his rumpled shirt, his boxer shorts and his socks.

"Please," she said, which was a mistake, because his face cleared and he remembered and smiled at her.

"Little Princess," he said and climbed on to the bed, kneeling over her on all fours. "Little tease." He stroked her face where he had hit her and he said, "Had a bad boo-boo, didn't you? Daddy gave you a bruise on your little face. You were a bad little girl and Daddy had to hit you, didn't he?"

"You're not my dad," she muttered but he just smiled and continued to stroke her face.

"You're not a bad girl now, though, are you?" he said. "You're a good little girl for Daddy now, aren't you?"

He moved his hand down her face to her neck, along her throat to her chest, running his fingers along the top of her cotton undershirt.

Summoning her courage, she told him he'd better stop or she'd tell her mother.

"Oh, no, you won't." He put a large, sweaty hand against her throat. "You say anything to Dolly and I'll break your little neck."

Silently, not making a sound, she started to cry, the tears forming in the corners of her eyes and spilling down her cheeks.

"Such a good little girl," he said and pulled her shirt up, revealing her small breasts. "Doesn't even wear a bra, just a little princess." He bent down over her and took her breasts in his mouth, first one, then the other, and she closed her eyes, willing it to be over, trying to think of something else. Anything else.

"Now it's your turn," he said. "Now you be nice to Daddy."

And he took her hand and placed it on top of his penis and she felt his flesh on her fingers and pulled her hand away in shock. Firmly, he put her hand back and told her to hold on to him. She kept her eyes closed and thought of snakes, of giant worms, and she was terrified to open her eyes in case she saw it, in case she had to look right at the horrible thing she was holding in her hand. And then, while she held on to it, he started to move, to jerk up and down and she let go of it and he yelled at her and made her take hold of it again. He moved faster and faster and suddenly he cried out and stiffened and something warm and dreadful spilled all over her hand and she pulled it away and he swore at her and grabbed her hand and held it there until it stopped and he groaned and rolled off her and was still.

Doris opened her eyes and she saw that he was lying on his side, turned towards the wall and she wondered if he was asleep. The awful, messy stuff was all over her and there was a wet spot on the bed next to her where some of it had spilled over. She had just decided to take a chance on trying to get out of bed without waking him when he sat up and swung his legs across her on to the floor. He reached for his pants and pulled them on without saying a word, stood up and pulled up the zipper and adjusted the suspenders. Then he looked down at her where she lay, rigid, afraid to look at him, her bare legs and arms covered in goosebumps.

"That, my dear, is what's known as a hand job," he said. "Practice and you might get good at it."

16.

Skippy had no idea when he began walking where he was going to end up. He had no goal, nothing but an overwhelming need to escape the tyranny of his room at Mrs. Cordelli's. If he could just get some air, clear his head, he would be able to get things back into some sort of perspective. If he could just think.

The night air was cooler than he had expected and he wondered if he should go back to his room and get his jacket. But then he'd run the risk of waking up Mrs. Cordelli; his landlady slept with one ear open to any unusual comings and goings and he would have no explanation for being up and about at this time of the morning. He would walk and walking would keep him warm.

A cat ran across the path in front of him, not a black cat, not bad luck, just a lean old tabby used to prowling at night, off on some business best carried out under cover of the dark. It disappeared into the hedge guarding somebody's front yard; a soft rustling sound, then silence. In the distance he heard the high-pitched whine of an ambulance, stopping as suddenly as it had begun, as if conscious of disturbing the silence. There was no moon and even the streetlights in this part of town were subdued, their pale circles of light heightening the gloom of the neighbourhood.

He turned a corner and came in sight of the church, dark and abandoned, its domed roof outlined against the night sky. A single yellow bulb had been left on just over the side door. The bingo ladies had long gone home, the floor would have been swept, chairs and tables stacked and put away, ashtrays emptied. Bingo ladies smoked heavily, it was part of the game. Not even the university students with their pipes could smoke up a place like fifty old ladies playing bingo. Sunday mornings after a bingo game, Skippy would get up early and go down to air the place out, put the chairs and small, round tables back in place, restore the look of a coffee house. He wished it was morning now, that he was busy arranging things in the basement of the church, this night over and done with.

He stood at the front gate of the church and saw that a small tree, a bush, had been newly planted not far from the sidewalk. It hadn't been there the day before, he was sure of it; Mr. Lee must have planted it earlier today, digging up the soil in this spot and patting it into a small, raised mound around the plant, protecting the roots. There was something almost painfully optimistic about the act of planting such a tiny tree when the man who planted it could not expect to be around to see it grow much bigger. An act of faith was what it was. Appropriate for a church which had outlived its parishioners.

Skippy pushed open the gate and walked around to the side entrance. He fished the skeleton key from his pants pocket and slipped it into the lock. It was tricky, this, especially in the dark, hard to see where the key fit, but it slipped into place, suddenly, and the door swung open. He stepped into the basement and switched on the overhead light, the one that illuminated the tiny foyer, and shut the door behind him.

There were moments, now and then, when Skippy would suddenly get this feeling that the club really belonged to him. The musicians in full voice, the audience attentive, clapping along and joining in on the chorus, the smell of coffee and tobacco chasing away the dankness of the old basement. He would look around at the faces, the posters on the walls, and think, *I did this. I made this happen.* He might not sing or play an instrument or have anything much to say, unlike the poets who took their turn on the small, makeshift stage. But he had created something here, he had given all that talent a place to grow, to blossom. Like Charlie Lee, he was a gardener, of sorts. He'd left his mark.

Skippy had planned to just stop in for a moment, check that everything was all right, nothing left spilled on the floor or burning in a waste paper basket. But he walked further into the room, all the way up on to the stage at the far end. There was a switch on the wall behind him and when he flicked it on it created a spotlight effect directly overhead. The view from here was different. Standing on this stage, he was suddenly important, the focus of attention. He imagined the club full of people and the hush that came over the room as they realized he was there at the microphone, getting ready to speak.

Skippy reached into the pocket of his shirt and brought out the piece of paper he'd taken just before leaving Mrs. Cordelli's. It was the poem he'd written, the one for Doris, the one he'd planned to read to her at Christmas. He'd taken it with him, thinking that the words from that poem might counteract, in some way, the effect of the photograph. Now seemed like a good time to read it.

He sat down on a stool and leaned into the mike. The power was off but it didn't matter. This audience wouldn't complain. He cleared his throat. And then, feeling a little foolish at first, but gradually gaining confidence, Skippy began to read:

> *"Goddess nymph*
> *untouchable*
> *heart-catching mind-snatching*
> *bury me inside you."*

There were fourteen verses and Skippy read them all and his voice was unsteady at first, but it quickly grew stronger, gaining confidence. When he finished it seemed the silence in the empty club had taken on a heaviness, like the moment right after a reading when the audience is waiting to be sure it's over before breaking into applause. He waited, then carefully folded the paper and returned it to his pocket.

"Thank you," he said. "Thank you very much."

He switched off the overhead light and got down from the stage. The audience, invisible but appreciative, parted to let him through and he turned and stood at the back of the room, savouring the moment. For a few minutes up on that stage he'd felt like a poet. He'd felt important — he'd felt larger than life. The feeling was still with him as he turned off the light and left the club, closing the door quietly behind him.

The experience of performing had lifted his spirits. He was keyed up, now; he didn't want to go back to his room. He felt like he did on nights when the club had been really moving, the music hot. He was stirred up, excited.

Instead of turning back towards the boarding house, he headed west and in ten minutes he'd crossed the overpass bridge and was once more in front of the Italian restaurant, the one where the nice waitress worked, the one who was always glad to see him. The place was still open but she would have left work by now — put on her jacket, picked up her purse, said good-bye to the cook in the back and left for home. He imagined her getting on the bus, making her way to an empty seat somewhere near the back, another busy Saturday night over and done with.

Or did she have a boyfriend, some guy who worked at the shipyards or down at the mill, who came by each night just before she was finished, waited for her in his souped-up jalopy, revving the engine impatiently if she was late? She was a pretty girl — not as pretty as Doris but sweet, nice looking, she'd have a boyfriend. What would she think if she knew he was in love with a hooker? Would she be shocked?

This was the first time he'd said it in his mind: hooker. Doris was a prostitute. She did things with men for money. He thought of Benny's stories of the whores on the New York street corners, his easy camaraderie with them. Take it easy, man, he could hear Benny's voice in his ear: Be cool. She's just a working girl, just trying to get by. Like the rest of us. Don't sweat the small stuff, *amigo*.

But this was Doris — the woman he wanted to marry. The woman he'd put on a pedestal and worshipped from the moment he'd seen her walk into the club. Put her up there without question, without caring to know anything about her, really, knowing only that he'd met the woman of his dreams. And after all this time, after eight months of weekly meetings, what did he know of her except that she watched a lot of TV and lived with her mother? Oh, and she hated the smell of lilacs, she'd told him once. Couldn't bear them anywhere near her. And that was about it.

He shivered and began to walk more quickly, around a corner and on to Front Street with its all-night restaurants and pool halls, a few run-down hotels with the curtains always closed and the names spelled out in neon. The Plaza. The Olympia. The Frontenac, where Wilson was a regular. It was not a nice part of town but it had been there for ever, one of the oldest streets in the city. It had enjoyed a certain gentility once upon a time, but that was so long ago there was nobody alive anymore who remembered. Now it was a street of rough men and unhappy faces and drunks lurching out of doorways, even in the middle of the day. A car approached and he heard the sounds of a Beatles song blaring through the open window, then disappearing into the night.

Next to the Frontenac was an empty lot, a relic of a sporadic attempt at urban renewal, bearing a sign that read "Future Home of Seniors of Tomorrow — Sponsored by Ontario's Department of Housing." The sign had been there for years, put up to fulfill an election promise that had not come to pass, and had been faded by the sun and the winter storms to the point where its message was almost unreadable. Appropriately enough, the seniors of this particular neighbourhood had taken to tossing their empty wine bottles and assorted garbage into this lot, to the extent that the site was in danger of becoming a health hazard. Still, no one was likely to complain, least of all the occupants of either of the decrepit old hotels which overlooked it.

Skippy stopped in front of the Plaza Hotel and sat down on the cement step, just to catch his breath. His leg was hurting and he had to rest it, just for a minute. He had come here once, with his mother, to find his father sitting out here, slumped over, his head resting on his arms. He must have been just a kid, five or six, maybe, and his father would have been about thirty, prematurely worn down, his face lined with disappointment and his fingers stained with nicotine. He remembered asking his mother why his father was sleeping there on the sidewalk, and the pained, drawn look on her face as she told him to wait there by the curb while she walked towards her husband and put her hand on his shoulder.

That would have been a year, two at the most, before the accident at the plant. There was some talk his father had been drinking on the job but it was never proved and Skippy never heard anything like that, not till he was much older. He and his mother and his grandmother stood outside on a windy spring day and Skippy looked up at the clouds scudding across the sky over the mountain while they buried Maurice Jacques. (His sister was only two and considered too little to attend a funeral, even one for her father. Especially one for her father.) His dad was in that box and he wasn't ever going to come out of it. It wasn't a joke and he wasn't playing hide and seek and in a minute he wasn't going to lift the lid and peer out and say "Boo!" like he did some nights when he'd come home from work and Skippy's sister was already in bed and he and his mom were sitting at the kitchen table listening to the radio. That wasn't going to happen. Skippy could keep his eyes on those clouds as long as he liked, especially the one that looked like a bunny, and cross his fingers behind his back, all ten of them and say eenie, meenie, miney, mo to himself over and over again and his father wasn't going to be alive again, ever. He knew that, he really did. He wasn't hoping for anything. And when he got home that night and had to get undressed to go to bed, his fingers were sore from keeping them crossed like that all afternoon and he could hardly straighten them out, they hurt so much. But that was okay because he knew it wasn't going to happen. He just wanted to do it, that's all.

A police car cruised towards him, trawling for "troublemakers", and the two cops slowed down as they approached him, peering out the window and almost coming to a stop. Skippy nodded at them in what he hoped was a friendly manner, stood up and began walking again, his eyes fixed on a point about a mile away where the street curved into Broadway Drive and the city's downtown began. The police car accelerated and continued on down the street and Skippy let out the breath he'd been holding and found that he was shivering. He rubbed his arms, trying to warm them up; but if he went back for his jacket it would be too late to come out and start all over again. His leg would never hold up all that way. He should have called a cab; he could always hail one, but the only one that came along had its light turned off and the driver was speeding along the street, eager to get home to bed.

It was just as well. What would he say, if a taxi did pull over and stop for him? What directions would he give? He was walking, that's all, out walking on a spring night, but his leg was beginning to throb and there was nowhere in this area to sit for a moment and get his bearings. There were no benches at the bus stops, no wooden seats with wrought iron legs and armrests like the ones that were scattered in the city's parks. Here, if he wanted to rest for a moment, he'd have to sit on the curb, his feet in the gutter, like some bum with no place to go. He passed another all-night restaurant, its lights. on and music coming from a juke box at somebody's table, that song about the guy who's got plenty to do now that his girlfriend's left him, counting flowers on the wall, playing solitaire, watching Captain Kangaroo. Skippy thought he'd go in for a coffee, sit in one of the booths for a few minutes until his leg felt better, but when he felt for his wallet it was missing. Then he remembered he'd left it in his dresser, top right hand drawer, where he always put it when he was getting ready for bed. He hadn't thought to retrieve it when he left the room. In his pocket, where he usually kept his wallet, there was only the envelope, addressed to Mr. Jacques.

Down the street a burst of noise as two men spilled out of the side door of the Manhattan Tavern. A poker game, most likely, in a room at the back. Penny-ante stuff, with some shady types taking part now and then, would-be Mafiosos who ran bawdy parlours and had illegal dealings connected with the construction and trucking industries. The Armenian, Azhok Chista, he'd taken in a few of those games. He told Skippy that Arty Peach was a regular, came in and threw his weight around but kowtowed to the heavies from out of town. Arty talked tough but he knew his place. He knew enough to be afraid of the right people.

The two guys got into a big black Buick and took off down the street, tires screeching, laying rubber for a good quarter mile. Maybe the game hadn't gone so well; they seemed to want to get out of there pretty fast. Or maybe it had gone too well and the big boys, the out-of-towners, weren't pleased. Chista had told him that when these guys condescended to take part in this bush-league stuff, they generally expected to win.

Just ahead was the Olympia, its large vertical letters flashing out the name of the hotel in pink neon. The "I" was missing, he noticed. O-L-Y-M-P- -A. And this was where Front Street came to an end. Broadway Drive to the right, a few warehouses and miles of train tracks to the left, and then the waterfront. He'd stop for a moment and rest his leg; the cop car was nowhere around. He could sit on the steps and get his bearings. With a sigh, he settled on to the cold concrete of the step and leaned back, stretching his leg out ahead of him as far as possible.

Above his head, a window opened and somebody said, "This place stinks. I bet they never change the sheets."

Immediately, Skippy pressed himself against the wall of the hotel, hoping that whoever was moving around up there wouldn't look out and see him hanging around on the sidewalk. Then another, deeper voice said something that he couldn't quite make out, and Skippy found himself listening, trying to follow the conversation.

Deep Voice spoke up again, more loudly, and Skippy heard him say: "Close the curtains, Michael. Do you want the whole world watching?"

Voice number one, which Skippy determined belonged to a young guy, maybe younger than him, came so clearly and close by he must have been hanging out the window: "You know your problem, Frankie boy? You are paranoid, that's what. Neurotic and paranoid and ugly into the bargain. Not a great combination."

Inside, someone laughed, and it took Skippy aback: it was a girl. So there were three of them up there, at least, two men and a girl.

The girl said something and then the young guy said, "Shit. Look at this place. Two o'clock in the morning and the town's deserted. Even the drunks have gone home to bed."

The girl's voice, now, closer to the window: "Come on, Michael, let's get this over with. Let's not take all night, okay?"

A half-smoked cigarette fell from the window and the young guy said, "All morning, you mean. Time to get up and go to church, in a few more hours."

He must have moved away from the window because the next time he spoke, Skippy couldn't make out what he said. He stood up and moved out on to the sidewalk, looking up at the open window, the one with light on. The curtains were closed and he could see nothing, but he could hear the sounds of a scuffle of some kind, as if there was a fight going on. A silence, and then what sounded like a slap and somebody cried out. Skippy strained to hear but he couldn't get a handle on what was happening. A scraping sound, a table being moved or a chair pushed aside, and then more grunts and muffled cries.

Someone was being hurt. The girl again, crying out in pain, he was sure of that. Skippy suddenly knew that those men were hurting her; she was in trouble. It could be Doris, for all he knew — maybe it was Doris. Might she not be up in that room with a couple of perverts, men who had paid their money and were expecting something extra, something she hadn't bargained for? He had to do something. He searched the street for a sign of a car, a taxi, anybody who might help. Where were those cops now that he needed them?

He hesitated another moment and then he heard Deep Voice say something, give an order, perhaps, and then the young guy, clear as anything: "Kneel down, you bitch. You asked for this."

That was it. Skippy flung himself through the hotel door and into the lobby, frantically looking for a security guard, somebody. The place was deserted but there was a bell on top of the counter, with a hand-written sign Scotch-taped underneath: "Ring bell for service."

Skippy slapped his fist down on the bell two or three times and waited impatiently for someone to appear. He was just about to ring again when the door behind the office opened and a sleepy character in a wrinkled shirt came out, doing up his collar button as he approached. He looked extremely unhappy at having been disturbed and for a moment Skippy lost his nerve.

"What the hell do you want?"

Skippy wondered if he should ask him to call the police and then he thought that if it was Doris, if she was the girl who was upstairs being hurt, she might not exactly welcome the constabulary. And anyway, by then it might be too late. Something had to be done right now.

The man behind the counter stared at Skippy with pale, hooded eyes. A small plastic tag was pinned to his shirt with the name of the hotel and "DENNIS" printed in capital letters. There were shadowy patches under his eyes that stood out against his pallid complexion and he appeared not to have shaved for several days.

"You want a room, I only got singles left, and you gotta pay for the whole night."

Skippy found his voice. "Somebody's being hurt."

The man continued to stare at him. "What?"

"Upstairs, in one of the rooms. Somebody's being hurt. I think they're hurting a girl."

The hotel man — Dennis — smirked. "Yeah, well, I'm sure everything is hunky-dory, fella. Don't you worry about it. It's none of your business and it's none of mine neither, long as they pay their bill."

He turned to leave and Skippy said, "The police might not think so."

Dennis turned back to stare at Skippy and now the smirk was gone.

"What did you say?"

"If you don't help me, if you don't come up there with me, I'm going to call the police."

"Now look, buddy, I don't want any trouble. There's no need to bring the cops into this. Don't be doing anything stupid."

There seemed to be a threat in that last statement but Skippy stood his ground. "Are you going to let me use your phone?"

The desk clerk stared at him for another moment, then seemed to make up his mind. "What room is it?" he asked, finally.

"Right upstairs. Right above us, facing the street."

Dennis picked up a set of keys from a hook on the wall behind him and came out from behind the counter. He nodded towards the stairway. "Well, come on, Mr. Knight-in-shining-armour. Let's go save the fair maiden."

On the landing, the desk clerk stopped and turned to watch Skippy struggling to manage the stairs.

"You okay?" he asked, looking pointedly at Skippy's leg.

Skippy grunted a reply and kept on going. Dennis shrugged and continued on to the top. When he got there, he waited for Skippy to catch up. His face was impassive; this was not someone who felt pity for or even much interest in his fellow man. Still, as Skippy made it to the top of the stairs and paused to catch his breath, the clerk remarked, "Elevator's broke," before turning to survey the double row of closed doors leading off the corridor.

"Okay. So which room is it?"

"It was right over the front door, looking out to the street."

For some reason, Skippy had expected it to be obvious which room it was. The noise of a fight, perhaps, or the sound of voices behind a particular closed door — he had thought that, when he got to the top of the stairs, he would know.

But it was quiet in the corridor, not a sound, and he suddenly thought, Maybe it's all over. Maybe they — maybe they've —

He didn't want to finish the sentence, not even in his mind. If anything had happened to Doris — if those men had hurt her, or worse — he'd have to kill them. He'd have no choice. His whole life was being weighed at this moment, in the hallway of this seedy hotel, with its smell of damp wood and toilets that hadn't been flushed. If he went into one of these rooms and saw that the unthinkable had happened, he would have to act. And he would be acting alone, he knew that. It was pretty obvious that this Dennis person was not about to risk his own safety for the life of a prostitute, no matter how good-looking.

The clerk studied the doors in front of them and said, "Right over the front door, eh? Well, that could be one oh five or one oh seven. Guess we'll have to knock on both —"

There was a noise from behind the door directly in front of them, a dull thud, followed by a sound that could have been a cry.

"One oh five it is," said Dennis and rapped sharply on the door.

There was no response and he knocked again and called out, "Open up. This is the desk clerk."

A pause, and then the door opened, just a crack, with the chain still on. Skippy couldn't get a good look at whoever stood on the other side, not with the clerk blocking his view.

"Yes?" Skippy recognized the deep voice of the older man.

"We've had a complaint," Dennis said. "About the noise."

"Oh, I'm sorry," said the older man. "We'll keep it down."

"Is everything okay in there?"

"Well, of course. I'm just entertaining a friend, that's all. Nothing to worry about."

"A little late for entertaining, isn't it?"

Skippy craned his neck to see around the clerk but he got only a shadowy impression of a large man with gray hair wearing a white collar of some kind. Doris — if it was her — must be hiding somewhere.

"Ask to see the girl," he whispered to the clerk.

The older man was mumbling his apologies again and attempting to shut the door but the clerk's foot was in the way.

"Excuse me," Dennis said, doing a pretty good imitation of a courteous hotel employee, "but we'd just like to check that the young lady is all right."

"Young lady? I don't know what you're talking —"

Dennis dropped the attempt at decorum. "Look, fella, there's a guy here says something weird's going on in this room, and unless you want the police called in, maybe you better just let us have a look. Okay?"

"Well, for —" The older man stopped, shut the door and removed the chain. When he opened the door again, Skippy saw that he was wearing a priest's collar and shirt, a heavy wooden crucifix, black socks that were held in place by garters and shiny patent leather shoes. And that was all.

It occurred to Skippy that for the second time in one evening he had seen two half naked old men. And he'd never had a desire to see even one.

The older man, who was obviously a priest or dressed up to look like one, didn't seem particularly embarrassed. What he did appear to be was annoyed and he regarded both Skippy and the desk clerk with unconcealed contempt.

"I am Father Francis Duvalier," he announced, still standing in the doorway, "and I am having a little discussion with a friend of mine. You have no right to barge into my room and disturb my privacy, and I'll thank you to remove yourself immediately."

The desk clerk wasn't at all discomfited by the lecture or by the fact that the man who was haranguing him wasn't wearing pants. He pushed past the priest into the room, saying, "All right, Father, hang on to your hat, we're just checking, that's all."

Skippy followed the clerk and looked around the room for the girl, afraid of what he might find. But there was no girl; just a very young man, younger than he'd sounded, sitting back in a chair near the window, one leg crossed over the other, wearing jockey shorts and a T-shirt. He smiled at Skippy and said hello. He was so casual and relaxed that Skippy felt embarrassed. Still, there had been a girl in here, he knew that, and she wasn't here now.

"She's gone," he said to the clerk and then, to the priest, he demanded, "What have you done with — what have you done with the girl?"

With a wry smile, Dennis, who must have had some experience in these matters, headed directly to a door next to the foot of the bed. Opening it with a flourish, he said, "Come on out, sweetheart," and

Skippy saw the outline of a young girl, dressed in tight leather pants and a bra, crouched in a corner of the closet.

Skippy's first emotion was relief — it wasn't Doris. Then he noticed that she was young, outrageously young. And tough in a way that was almost scary.

The clerk stood, holding the door open, and finally Father Francis spoke up: "It's all right, dear, these aren't the police. You can come out."

Only then did the girl stand up and emerge from the closet, looking straight ahead at the priest and ignoring Skippy and the desk clerk. She was tiny and very thin and came not even close to filling the leather bra clasped around her chest. She wore a pair of leather gloves with the fingers cut out of them and in one hand she was holding a bullwhip. Her skin was pale and lightly freckled and if Skippy had seen her on the street or at the beach he would have guessed she was no older than twelve or thirteen. Here, even in her leather pants, high-heeled boots and outlandish make-up, she looked about fifteen. Sixteen, tops.

There was something so solemn about the way she stood defiantly in front of them all, standing straight and tall and hanging on to that ridiculous whip, that made Skippy want to cry.

"All right," said the priest. "Are you satisfied? Nobody's hurt, everyone's fine. Right?"

"You planning to use that thing?" Dennis asked the girl, referring to the whip. She gave him a quick, contemptuous glance and turned back to stare at the priest.

Father Francis stepped past the desk clerk and put his arm around the girl's shoulder. "Ruby, dear, these men just want to know that you're all right. Go ahead and tell them."

Only then did she speak. In a flat, impassive voice, she said, "I'm fine."

"There, you see?" said the priest. "She's fine. We're all fine. Now will you please leave?"

The clerk seemed to be fascinated with Ruby. With difficulty, he looked away and addressed the boy, still sitting in the chair, now picking at his toenails.

"You okay?"

The boy looked up and smiled and Skippy saw that he was a better-looking, more filled-out version of Ruby. Older, too, although he probably wasn't more than twenty.

"Me? I'm fine. Peachy keen." Indicating the other two and the room at large, he added, "We're just having a little late-night communion session, eh? Confessing our sins and saying our Hail

Marys and all that."

"Michael —" The priest's voice was stern, sounding a warning, but the boy just laughed and went back to picking at his feet.

The desk clerk turned back to the priest. "Okay, Father, I guess we'll get outta here. Sorry to disturb you."

"I should think so," said the priest. "You'd think you'd get a little privacy, even in a place like this."

"Yeah. Well, keep the noise down, that's all." The clerk headed out into the hallway, with Skippy right behind him. He turned back and said to the room in general, but looking at Ruby, "I'll be right downstairs if you need anything."

Ruby turned away, with a scornful look on her face; Dennis was beneath her contempt.

"How reassuring," said the priest, shutting the door on them and replacing the chain.

"Satisfied?" said the clerk and Skippy didn't know what to say. The image of that young girl, Ruby, standing there in that weird get-up, bothered him almost as much as the photographs of Doris. He couldn't have said what he was expecting to see when they entered that room but it certainly wasn't a girl younger than his sister in the kind of costume he'd only seen before in some of the stranger men's magazines. And there had been that time, years ago, when the exhibition had come to town, and he and Benny had stood outside the sideshow tent watching a woman in leather pants brandish a whip and taunt the men in the crowd with promises of exotic, unspeakable pleasures if they paid five dollars to come inside. But that woman was old — she looked almost fifty under the makeup and the dyed red hair, and Skippy kept thinking how she was probably somebody's mother or even grandmother, and felt bad for her. She was nothing like Ruby. Ruby was just a kid; she should be tucked up in bed in her p.j.s right now, in a pretty white room with dolls and girls' stuff all over the place, not strutting around in leather bras and playing S and M games with some old man.

The effort it took to get back down the stairs and out to the front lobby drained Skippy of the last of his strength. He was exhausted and wanted overwhelmingly to stretch out on a bed, any bed, and go to sleep. He felt extremely depressed; Ruby and that young guy who looked like her brother and the old priest walking around without his pants on — it was all just too sad for words.

The encounter had just the opposite effect on the desk clerk. He was wide awake now and appeared to be in a great mood, expansive and almost friendly. When they got downstairs he invited Skippy to sit down on the overstuffed leather couch near the counter and offered him a cigarette. Skippy declined the smoke but he did sit down and sank back with relief into the comfort of the large, plush cushions. The desk clerk lit a Rothmans and sat down on a stool behind the counter, running a hand through his smooth, dark hair, checking that every oily strand was in place. He smiled at Skippy, revealing a set of very yellow, very crooked teeth, and Skippy thought that maybe that was why the clerk was usually so dour: maybe he didn't like to smile a lot and show off his bad teeth.

"Takes all kinds to make a world," he offered and Skippy nodded in agreement.

"I guess you see now why working the desk in a place like this ain't exactly the glamour job it looks."

Skippy had never thought that in the first place but he agreed that it must be difficult.

"Mind you," the clerk continued, "it's a people job, and I like people. I'm good with them, you know, I know how to deal with them. That's why Uncle Mel gave me the job in the first place."

"Your uncle owns this place?" Skippy was deadly tired but he was trying to keep up his end of the conversation. After all, the clerk was letting him sit here. Maybe he could talk him into letting him lie down for a few minutes, just till his head cleared.

Dennis nodded. "Melvyn Shoemaker. You know him? Ran for city council last fall but got beat out by the broad from the school board. I told him next time, let me be his campaign manager and he'll win by a landslide. If anybody can dig up a little dirt on the opposition, it's me. He says he'll think about it. Anyhow, Uncle Mel owns this place and the Plaza down the street and the Villa Fiesta. You know the Villa Fiesta?"

Skippy knew it. Girls met their clients there. It was that kind of place. It was very likely that Doris had met Wilson at the Villa Fiesta. Doris in a wig, posing for Mr. Wilson. He would get up in just a minute and leave. Just as soon as his bad leg stopped throbbing.

Dennis continued, pleased to have someone to talk to now that he was wide awake. "Uncle Mel's into real estate, eh? Let's see, he's got two apartment buildings, a house up on Church Street and an office building downtown. Besides the hotels, eh? This place is the worst of them, it's the only real dump. But I figure I do my time here, make the most of it, and he'll give me something better coupla years down the road. Makes sense, don't you think?"

Again, Skippy nodded. He was too tired to talk; what he wanted to do, for just a few minutes, was close his eyes and go to sleep. If he could just sleep for, say, twenty minutes, he'd be fine. A half hour at most, that's all he needed.

Dennis laid out his plans, what he was going to do once Uncle Mel put him in charge of the apartment buildings and he got a little cash together. When he was ready, when the time was right, he would look around for a deal, a way to really make some "serious" money.

"The thing is," he was saying, apparently happy to do all the talking himself, "the most important thing is not to be greedy. I got pals who saw their chance and took it without thinking and you know where they are now? You know where those guys ended up? Stony Mountain, that's where. Doing time in the pen because they were greedy. And do I feel sorry for them? Shit. Who do I look like — Schweitzer?"

Dennis laughed and took a quick, nervous drag on his cigarette. "I tell you, pal, I got no time for some jerk with no brains who thinks he can walk in and just take what he wants and live like a king for the rest of his life. They should lock people up and throw away the key, just for being stupid. You know what I mean?"

The night clerk continued to talk and the words melted into each other, as Skippy's head fell back against the couch and the green grass rose up around him, long, waving shards of green from his childhood, soft, silky whips of grass. He lay there with the sun beating down on him and Doris came up to him, wearing a short, black wig and a flowing white dress like a bride's gown, the material so thin he could almost see through it, and she was smiling and holding a bouquet of flowers, just for him, hand-picked wild flowers, and she kneeled down beside him and whispered in his ear, "Get up, come on, wake up, fella. It's morning, you gotta get up."

Skippy opened one eye and saw that a blurred figure was standing over him, a sallow, unshaven face inches away from his own, emitting a dank body smell mixed with cigarette smoke. He sat up quickly and then flinched as a sharp pain pierced him in his left side. He was stiff from leaning over that way for — what? An hour? Two hours? Longer than that; the sun was peering in through the ancient stained glass window, high above the lobby of the hotel. It was morning. He was in the lobby of the Olympia Hotel and he'd slept all night. And the person standing over him was Dennis, the desk clerk.

"You're awake. Good."

Skippy sat up and pushed his hair back from his face. There was a sour taste in his mouth and his left cheek was damp from where it had rested against the leather arm of the couch.

"What time is it?"

Dennis pointed behind him to a clock hanging slightly off-centre on the wall: seven twenty-five. "I'd let you go on sleeping," he said, "but the day guy comes on at eight and he ain't as sociable as me, you know what I mean?"

He watched as Skippy slowly raised himself from the couch and stood for a moment, getting his bearings. "You got a place to go to?" he asked and Skippy didn't answer right away. He did have somewhere to go; he knew that now. He had woken up knowing exactly what it was he had to do. The few hours on the couch, as brief and physically uncomfortable as they were, had crystallized something in his mind. He knew what he had to do.

The clerk stuffed a bill into Skippy's shirt pocket.

"Here. I called you a cab. Go home and get some sleep. You look like you could use another forty winks."

Skippy thanked him — "I'll pay you back" — and reached for the door. Then he stopped and turned back.

"The old man," he said. "The priest and the young girl. And the guy. Did they —?"

"Left about an hour ago," Dennis told him.

"All three?"

The clerk nodded. "All three."

"Right." Skippy waited but there didn't seem to be anything else to say. "Well, thanks again," he said and pushed open the hotel door.

Dennis followed him and stood in the doorway as Skippy made his way down the stairs and on to the sidewalk. It was a clear, warm morning, too early for anyone to be up and about, especially on a Sunday. Dennis stretched and yawned and shook his head, trying to wake himself up.

"Spring's here, you can smell it," he remarked and Skippy agreed with him.

"You know," said the clerk, "you ever need a job, just give my Uncle Mel a call. You can use me as a reference. He'll find you something."

"Thanks," said Skippy. He felt something more was called for so he repeated, "Thanks a lot," and tried to put a proper amount of gratitude into his words.

Dennis shrugged. "No problem. Well, keep your nose clean," and he turned and went back into the hotel.

17.

Doris opened her eyes as the bus shuddered to a stop and the driver's voice came over the intercom: "Sault Ste. Marie. Half hour stop, folks. We'll be pulling out at oh-nine-hundred hours. That's nine o'clock in plain talk."

She had drifted off somewhere east of Marathon, although it was hard to tell when you were driving through the bush at night, stopping every fifty miles or so to take on new passengers or deposit them by the side of the highway. She'd had a seatmate at the beginning of her journey, a young Indian girl who told Doris she was going home to spend the summer with her family on the reserve.

"I can't wait," she said in her soft, shy voice. "I'll see my mom and my sisters and my oldest sister's new baby."

When Doris woke up the seat beside her was empty and she wished she'd thought to ask the girl for her address, if only to have had someone to write to once she got to Toronto.

The restaurant where the bus had stopped was a self-serve cafeteria and Doris bought a couple of postcards and some greasy French fries, smothered in a viscous brown gravy whose only redeeming feature was that it was hot, much hotter than the fries which had been sitting under a warming lamp for some time. To this she added a dollop of ketchup and a generous sprinkling of salt and washed it down with a vanilla milkshake that was much better than she had a right to expect, in a place like this. The food settled in her stomach in a thick, comfortable ball, filling the anxious gap that had been troubling her ever since she'd got on the bus and she began to feel happier, more positive than she had all week. Here she was, on her way to the big city with nobody to tell her what to do and almost a hundred dollars in her pocket.

The money was her mother's, tucked away in a dresser drawer, her "rainy Monday" money she called it. Doris had taken it, along with Dolly's brand new, powder blue suitcase, while she and Ted were at work. They owe it to me, she thought. They kicked me out and they don't care if I live or die. The least they can do is pay my way to Toronto.

Rummaging in her bag, she found a pen and spent the next ten minutes filling out the postcards. One to Lindy Folgram, of course, and one, after a few moments' thought, to Bobby Matthews. He was only a boy and he could be pretty dumb but she thought she'd like to let him know she was gone. In case he asked or anything.

It had been a long winter. Her stepfather had taken to coming into her bedroom once or twice a week, always late at night, after Dolly was asleep. He would lie down beside her and make her touch him and then he'd leave, always warning her what would happen to her if she so much as breathed a word of it to her mother. He told her it was her fault, anyway, for "flaunting" herself around him — she was to blame for what happened.

She'd thought about running away but she had no money and besides, where would she go? There was no one to take her in and anyway, Ted had convinced her that nobody would believe her story, if she tried to tell it.

And then Lindy's older sister had come home for Christmas and the two younger girls sat up in her bedroom, watching her put on her makeup and listening to her stories about rich boyfriends and the big cars they drove and the nice things they bought her. The sister's name was Candace but everyone called her Candi, and she was nineteen and had been living in Toronto for over a year, working in a restaurant that was sort of a nightclub, and she made tons of money. You could tell by the way she dressed and the jewelry she wore that she was doing okay. She showed the younger girls a real gold lighter and said it was a present from a boyfriend, and she gave Lindy a friendship ring with four genuine cultured pearls. When Doris admired it, Candi smiled and said she'd give her one, too, the next time she was in town.

"I'd love to come live in Toronto," Doris told her and Candi smiled and leaned closer to the mirror to inspect her lipstick.

"Well, you be sure to give me a call if you come," she said. "Lindy's got my phone number. You call if you ever need a place to stay."

And then the doorbell rang and she stood up and ran her hands quickly over her skirt and adjusted a stocking.

"Gotta go," she trilled. "Ciao." And the younger girls watched while she sauntered out of the room, swinging her hips with a confidence they could only dream of.

"Are you really going to go to Toronto?" Lindy wanted to know and Doris surprised herself by saying, Yes, she was, as a matter of fact.

"When? Right now?'

Doris thought for a moment. "In the fall," she said, finally. "I'll get a summer job and save up, and in September I'll go."

"But what about the ranch? What about raising horses?"

Doris gazed at her friend for a moment. She felt years older than Lindy, somehow, although there was less than a month between them.

"We can still do it," she said, wanting to be kind. "When you finish school we'll go out west and get a place. But first, I have to get a job."

In the end, it happened sooner than she'd planned. It was the fifteenth of April and dark clouds had been gathering overhead all afternoon. The storm broke at night, a crashing, mind-shattering thunderstorm, the first of the year, and she didn't hear Ted come into her room. She was conscious of the smell of him before she knew for certain he was there — he'd been drinking, as usual, and he and Dolly had come in shortly after midnight and gone straight to bed. The storm must have woken him; flashes of lightning showed him, ragged with sleep, hovering over her.

"Move over, Princess," he whispered. "Make room for Daddy."

She closed her eyes and ordered herself, as she always did, to be somewhere else, anywhere, anywhere but here. It wasn't her hand wrapped around that awful snake-like thing of his; it wasn't her mouth he was kissing, slobbering all over with his disgusting, horrible tongue; she was somewhere else while this was happening. He couldn't hurt her — he couldn't lay a finger on the person who was Doris.

He had just begun to jerk and writhe next to her, grunting and groaning as usual, when she heard him cry out in a shrill, frightened voice. It was more of a wail, like the sound a wounded animal might make, and it went on and on and Doris opened her eyes and realized it wasn't Ted who was making this sound, it was her mother, there in the room with them, silhouetted in the light of the open doorway, her mother standing there screaming at them, at her, calling her name, and Ted, still writhing and groaning and not knowing anything except his own body pressed against hers and his great, huge need pushing and pounding inside him and so he kept moving until he suddenly stopped and collapsed beside her and the sight of him finally at rest seemed to galvanize Dolly into action. She grabbed him by the hair and yanked him off the bed and on to the floor and then she literally threw herself at Doris and began hitting her, slapping her hard on the face, against the side of her head, over and over again. Doris tried to escape from her mother's blows; she ducked under the covers but Dolly punched at the form huddled on the bed, hitting her again and again and all the time crying and calling her names, horrible names, and who knows how long she might have gone on like that if Ted hadn't finally pulled her away from the bed and held her while she tried to hit him and finally collapsed, crying, in his arms.

"Ted," she wailed, "Ted, how could you? How could you do this to me? How could you?"

And he held her and soothed her: "There, there, sweetheart, it's okay, don't cry. It's all right, baby, everything's gonna be fine."

He stroked her hair and kissed her face and she stood there in his arms and let herself be calmed while the thunder rolled on into the distance, and after what seemed like a very long time, she turned to where Doris was lying on the bed, still huddled in a ball, tears running down her face as she watched her mother in Ted's embrace. When Dolly spoke, her voice was flat and harsh and she didn't sound like her mother. She didn't sound like anybody Doris knew.

"You'd better get out," she said. "Tomorrow morning, I want you out of here."

And then she turned and she and Ted left the room, together.

When Doris finished writing her postcards, she went to the pay phone and called long distance to Candi Folgram, letting the phone ring almost a dozen times before there was a click and a sleepy voice said, "Hello?" Doris had to explain three times who she was and why she was calling. Finally, the older girl seemed to get the idea, and told Doris to come by when she got in — she'd be out but there'd be a key under the mat.

Returning to the bus, Doris saw she had a new seatmate, a tired, somewhat haggard-looking older woman who nodded briefly to her as she clambered into her seat, then sat back and closed her eyes as the Greyhound shifted into motion and nosed out onto the highway. A thick book lay open on her lap and Doris smiled when she saw the title: *You Can't Go Home Again*, by a man called Thomas Wolfe.

Candi's apartment was on north Jarvis Street, on the very top floor of a decrepit old mansion called "Sutton House", built in the final years of the nineteenth century and shaded on all sides by towering maples and elm trees. It was like something out of a movie, Doris thought. A horror movie, starring Vincent Price. Four storeys tall, it was capped by two tower rooms surrounded by iron railings and rickety-looking fire escapes protruding from the sides.

The apartment itself was cheerful enough, although messy — Candi was not much of a housekeeper. And it was stuffy, even with the windows open. There was a small kitchen which contained a profusion of dirty dishes and an ashtray full of cigarette butts but very little food, and a tiny bedroom with a bedspread and pillows in an almost violent shade of rose. The bed was unmade and looked as though it had been that way for quite a while. Doris thought Candi probably didn't have much time for housework, what with working and having lots of boyfriends and all.

The noise from the street was relentless. Heavy-set women in kerchiefs hauled shopping bags down the sidewalk and stopped to shout across the street at other women doing the same. Now and then Doris made out what they were saying but for the most part they shrieked at each other in some foreign language — Italian, Doris guessed, judging by their long black dresses and head scarves. Occasionally the sound of a horse's hooves punctuated the din of the traffic and a rickety old cart made its way up the wide old street, bearing fruit and vegetables or an assortment of rakes, shovels and brooms. And directly across from Sutton House was a block of tenement houses with crumbling foundations, missing steps and yards littered with trash and grubby young children playing "kick the can" and tag.

It was exotic, in its own way, but much dirtier than Doris had imagined. She had anticipated smartly-dressed, good-looking men and women striding purposefully down sunny sidewalks, characters straight out of her mother's favourite musicals. She had not expected the grittiness of her new surroundings; if there were riches here, they must be kept hidden behind closed doors in other, more affluent parts of the city.

Candi accepted Doris' presence with a good-natured shrug, asking few questions and offering little advice, except to suggest that she might want to give it a couple of weeks and then go back home again.

"This is no place for a kid," she said. "And anyway, shouldn't you still be in school?"

"I thought I could work, get a job somewhere. I don't eat much and I have some money. I won't be any trouble, I promise."

Candi smiled and reached for a bottle of nail polish. "Stick around for the summer," she suggested, "and see how it goes. I don't mind some company — it can get lonely sometimes, here in the big city. Just don't go stealing my boyfriends," she added, with a grin to show she was kidding. And Doris grinned back, relieved that she could stay, thinking that the last thing on her mind, then or ever, was stealing anybody's boyfriends.

She got a job within two weeks of her arrival. Waitressing, six days a week, in the coffee shop of the old Westwood Hotel on Jarvis

Street, one of the more genteel establishments in the area. She had lied about her age, told them she was almost sixteen, and said she was finishing her high school by correspondence. The woman who ran the coffee shop looked skeptical, but in the end agreed to take her on from nine in the morning till two, on probation. If she worked out she could stay for the summer. After that, they'd see.

She was given a black uniform to wear, with a white apron and cap that had to be washed and ironed on Sundays, her day off. She had to wear black shoes with flat heels and no nail polish or rouge, although she could wear a little lipstick, which was good as it made her look older. And Candi showed her how to put her hair up in a bun, a "French roll", she called it, and how to apply just a little mascara and eye shadow so it could hardly be noticed.

"There," she said, when she was finished, "you look like a million bucks. I better be careful bringing any men around here. They see you and they'll go crazy."

Doris smiled, shyly, and inspected her new, made-up self in the bedroom mirror. The girl who looked back at her could have been seventeen or eighteen, and was so transformed from the tomboy of half an hour ago as to be considered almost beautiful. Candi had also taken a needle and thread to Doris' uniform and made a few calculated alterations, raising the hem by an inch and a half, and taking it in at the waist and the bust.

Not enough to raise the suspicions of her boss, but enough to show her figure off to its best advantage.

"What do you think?" Candi wanted to know. "Are you gorgeous or what?"

"I'm pretty gorgeous, all right," Doris said and they both laughed.

"I'll tell you one thing," said Candi, putting her mascara and eyebrow tweezers back in their basket on the dresser, "you won't go broke waitressing, anyway. They may not pay you much at that place, but you're going to make a fortune in tips."

Waitressing, Doris learned, was hard work, harder than anything she would ever do again. After fifteen minutes on the job, carrying trays and rushing back and forth between the kitchen and her tables, she was ready to drop, and she still had over five hours to go. She had to carry pots of hot coffee without spilling a drop, and balance white china plates of turkey sandwiches and little jugs of cream, and remember who ordered what. And do it all with a smile and never get mad when an old lady told her she was a "silly, sloppy girl" for spilling tea on the tablecloth or when a businessman made a joke about her and dangled her tip just out of reach, telling her to "come and get it." All of this for seventy-five cents an hour, plus tips, except that only the businessmen tipped and you had to put up with so much rudeness on their part, as they showed off in front of their clients, that you wondered if it was worth it.

Still, no matter how tired she was at the end of the day, she always put on a cheerful face when she arrived back at the apartment on Jarvis. Candi was pushing her to go back to school and since Doris wasn't going to tell her the real reason she wouldn't go back, she'd have to at least pretend that this job was everything she'd hoped it would be.

Once, she asked Candi about putting in a word for her to the owners of the Capri, the place where Candi worked. But the older girl shook her head and told her she was too young.

"You have to be twenty-one to serve liquor in Ontario," she said and when Doris argued that Candi wasn't, she wasn't even twenty, Candi said the owners looked the other way because their customers wanted to look at pretty young girls, not old bags who were almost thirty.

"Anyway," she added, "you wouldn't want to work there. You wouldn't like it."

"But you make such good money."

Candi nodded. "Yeah, well, that's true. But — well, it's not for everybody. I mean, there's some nice fellows, all right, but there's creeps, too. Anyhow, you're going to go back to school and make something of your life. You're not going to waitress all your life."

As for *her* life, what Candi wanted, what all the girls wanted who worked at the Capri, she explained, was to meet a really nice fellow — "with money" — and quit work and get married. It happened, she told Doris, it wasn't just a pipe dream. Why, just last summer one of the girls had met the son of a big brewing family one night, right there in the club. He'd come back a few times, asked her out and the next thing everyone knew she was getting married and moving to Montreal. Candi had even met her; she'd started work at the Capri about a month before.

"So if it could happen to her, it could happen to anyone. She wasn't even that cute or anything. But she did have a good figure."

Candi had set her sights on one of the owners of the Capri, a French-Canadian named Jean-Paul, or J.P., as everybody called him. J.P. was already married — he had a wife and three kids back in Montreal — but he spent most of his time in Toronto and he and Candi had been seeing each other for almost six months.

"It's not a real marriage," Candi explained. "He and his wife don't do things together, like most people. She just wants to stay home with the kids and she doesn't care about how she looks or dressing up nice or anything. He's going to ask her for a divorce, one of these days. He's just waiting for the right moment."

There was something about the way she said this that made Doris think it wasn't as wonderful as Candi made out, going out with a married man and all. Still, Candi was practically a grown woman, living in a big city; what might have been shocking in Cambrian Bay was probably normal in a place like Toronto.

In spite of the age difference — or maybe because of it — Doris and Candi got along well, living together. Doris got up every morning at eight in order to be at the coffee shop by nine o'clock and by the time she finished and walked home from the Westwood, Candi would be just getting up, still in her dressing gown, reading the afternoon paper. She liked the show business column and the social pages and she read snatches of them aloud to Doris, along with her own spontaneous, slightly obscene commentary:

" 'Miss Francine Ridley has sailed for Europe to visit Italy, France and Switzerland.' Switzerland, eh? Maybe good old Francine is planning a little visit to that nice old Swiss doctor who does abortions for the jet set. Nothing about that, I see."

Or: " 'Mrs. James Pearcy is opening her home on St. Clarens Avenue for a garden tea June 20th, sponsored by the Toronto Women's Liberal Association.' No mention of the little mess *Mister* James Pearcy got himself into, having an affair with his confidential secretary. My girlfriend knows a fellow who's a reporter at Queen's Park and he told her all about it. The missus stood by him, of course. That type always does."

As for Doris, she favoured the comic section of the paper: Mary Worth, Gasoline Alley, Mark Trail and Blondie. She skipped Henry, which had no words and was boring, and Pogo, which had too many words and was too much work. They both liked to see what was happening at the movies — Candi often went to a matinee with one of her girlfriends, while Doris spent her evenings at the double features. In her first month in Toronto, she saw Walt Disney's *Peter Pan*, the latest Francis the Talking Mule comedy with Donald O'Connor, *The Girl Who Had Everything* with Elizabeth Taylor and Fernando Lamas and *Roman Holiday*, with Audrey Hepburn. That one she saw three times and began to seriously consider dying her blonde hair black. She made a point of avoiding musicals, however; they reminded her of Dolly.

Candi turned a page and said, "Will you listen to this?" She began a lot of conversations that way, when she was reading the paper. It was usually in reference to some tiny story on the third or fourth page — Candi wasn't much for headlines, regarding the exploits of the world's politicians as tedious compared with the scandals revealed every day in the divorce courts and the crime pages. But she had an eye for the unusual and the healthy skepticism of the true agnostic. She would have made a good journalist, if she'd been willing to accept the cut in pay.

"'A-Bomb Tests Linked to Tornadoes?'" she read. "'The Atomic Energy Commission, the weather bureau and just about everybody else said today that the Nevada atomic tests had nothing to do with the recent series of disastrous tornadoes.' Ha! I'll bet. Listen to this: 'Representative James E. Van Zandt, a member of the joint congressional atomic energy committee, originally told a reporter he was convinced the tornadoes definitely were connected with the nuclear tests. Several hours later he told another reporter he didn't mean that at all.' So what do you think about that?"

"I don't know," said Doris. "Nothing, I guess."

"Nothing?" Candi was incredulous. "It means they got to him."

"Who's they?"

"The CIA. Eisenhower. The whole gang. These A-bomb people have incredible power. Look what they've done to the Rosenbergs."

"Who are the Rosenbergs?"

"Who are the Rosenbergs?" Candi repeated. "Honey, don't they teach you anything in that school you're going to?"

Doris corrected her — she wasn't going to school anymore — and Candi said, Well, we'll see, and then went on to explain that Julius and Ethel Rosenberg had been convicted of selling secrets about the bomb to the Russians and if the President of the United States didn't step in soon they would die in the electric chair that summer. They'd been offered life in prison instead, if they'd only confess, but they wouldn't, which was proof they were innocent, according to Candi.

"And it's not just me who thinks that," she added. "Hundreds of thousands of people all around the world have written to the White House, asking for mercy. But it's no use. They just won't listen."

Doris wanted to ask who "they" were and why it was no use but Candi had turned the page and was on to something else.

"Listen to this: 'Polio Cases This Year Above Usual Number.' They're saying that so far the number of polio cases in Canada this year is almost twelve hundred, and that's up from last year and the year before."

"Do you think that's because of the bomb tests, too?"

"Listen, sweetheart, I can't prove anything, and even if I could, no one would listen to me, anyway. But I'll tell you something: ten years from now they're going to look back on the atomic bomb and see how it's changed the world and they're going to be amazed they just sat back and let it happen. And I'll be sitting right here, saying 'I told you so.' If I'm still alive, that is."

Doris laughed. "Of course you'll be alive. You're not that old."

Candi put down the paper and looked at Doris with some concern. "Honey, don't you read anything? Don't you know what's going on in the world? I'll be lucky to see thirty and I hope you're not counting on being a grandmother because it ain't gonna happen. The men — and I mean men — who are in charge of this world are working just as fast and just as hard as they can to blow the whole place to smithereens. Anybody who tells you different is either stupid or a liar. So if you want to spend what time you've got slaving away in a coffee shop, sucking up to some fat old biddies and wiping ketchup off the floor, you go right ahead. But I plan to enjoy my life, what I've got left of it."

In later years, Doris would look back at that first summer in Toronto and marvel that she managed to keep it together. She was so young; her friends back home were all still in school, getting ready to graduate from junior high. Lindy and Bobby Matthews had been on the prom committee, making plans for the big dance. She, too, would have been making paper flowers and putting up posters and selling tickets, if she'd been there — dumb kid stuff, really, and yet when she thought about it, when she caught a passing glimpse of herself in the long, low mirror opposite the coffee shop counter, she felt a sudden pang of homesickness and wished she was back in the Bay and things were simple again.

The fourth of July, the night before her fourteenth birthday, Doris was walking home from the Westwood, enjoying the warm summer evening and ignoring the whistles and catcalls from the fellows who drove by. She was tired; one of the girls had called in sick and the manager had asked her to work a double shift. Her feet were aching and she wanted to get back and soak in a nice, hot bath.

But nothing could spoil this evening for her; she had an envelope in her pocket containing her week's wages and a handful of change from the day's tips. And tonight, after she had her bath, she was going to make herself a birthday cake, an angel food cake, with European chocolate icing. She'd bought the ingredients from the corner grocery store yesterday afternoon and left the eggs out on the kitchen counter this morning to warm to room temperature. Candi, lo and behold, actually owned an angel food tin — a tube pan with a removable rim — and an electric mixer. Doris had found them both tucked away under the sink and even Candi seemed surprised to see them. She figured they must have been left there by a former tenant:

"I never made an angel cake in my life," she said and added, pointing to the mixer, "I'm not sure I'd even know how to operate that thing."

Doris did all the cooking, now — she liked it, and it made her feel like she was helping out. Candi had told her several times that it was nice to have company in the apartment; "I hate coming home to an empty place," she'd confided one evening. "Before you came here, some nights I'd get so low I'd phone up the bootlegger for a bottle of rye and just sit up drinking all night till it got light out and I could finally fall asleep."

Tonight, Doris told herself, she could soak in the tub as long as she liked. Candi had a date with J.P., they were going out to dinner and then to a show and Doris would have the place all to herself. It was nice, sharing with another girl, but it was also pleasant, sometimes, to be alone.

She was thinking about the cake and turning fourteen and when she opened the door to the apartment she didn't notice, at first, anything out of the ordinary. The voice of Frank Sinatra was crooning gently from the radio in Candi's bedroom and the lights were on, which was strange because Candi should certainly have left by now. She would never leave without turning off the lights — in spite of her haphazard approach to housekeeping, Candi was a martinet when it came to the electricity bill. When Doris first moved in, she had told her to be sure to turn out the lights whenever she left a room and never leave the radio on when she was out of the apartment. She must have been in a rush, Doris thought, and just forgot to turn everything off before she left.

Doris went into the bathroom to run her bath and remembered the jar of green bath crystals Candi kept on her dresser. Surely she wouldn't mind if Doris borrowed a handful, just this once.

The older girl was asleep on the bed, still in the fluffy pink housecoat she'd been wearing when Doris had left. She was turned over on her side and the bed was in its usual state of disarray.

Doris tiptoed over to where the radio was warbling from the top of the night table and switched off Sinatra in mid croon. What had happened? Had J.P. broken their date? He did that sometimes, called at the last minute and said something had come up, or just forgot to call, period. It was only eight-thirty; Candi wouldn't have gone to bed yet. Maybe she was sick.

Doris approached the sleeping figure and touched her gently, on the shoulder. "Candi? Are you okay?"

There was no response and Doris began to feel afraid. She said her name again, louder this time, and when the older girl didn't respond she sat down on the bed beside her and struggled to lift her to a sitting position. Candi was like a dead weight in her arms, her head lolled to one side. It was then, as she sat on the bed beside her unconscious friend, holding her upright, that Doris noticed the bottle of Seagram's, almost empty, on the floor next to the bed and the small plastic bottle lying beside it. Doris let Candi fall back against the pillow and leaned down to pick up the bottle. "Valium, 10 mg," she read. "Take as prescribed." The bottle was empty.

18.

It was a short cab ride back to the boardinghouse. Skippy got out of the back and asked the driver to wait: "Five minutes," he said. "I just have to grab a few things."

His landlady was already up; she'd been awake since six and had attended early mass. Now, as Skippy unlocked the front door and let himself in, she came out of the kitchen, wearing her Sunday best black dress and stockings and her thin gold chain and crucifix, the only jewelry she allowed herself since her husband died.

"Mr. Jacques, you give me a scare," she told him, a spatula in one hand and a frying pan in the other. "I'm just starting breakfast. I didn't hear you go out."

There was no time to talk, to explain things. Quickly, conscious of the meter ticking in the taxi outside, Skippy told her he was going away for a few weeks. Something had come up and he had to leave earlier than he'd planned. His rent was paid up for the month, he'd take a few clothes and get the rest of his stuff when he got back.

"What, now?" Mrs. Cordelli said. "You're leaving now, just like that?"

"Yes. I'm sorry." He headed towards the stairs, calling out to her over his shoulder, "Don't worry, Mrs. Cordelli, everything's all right. I'll send you a postcard."

"But what about breakfast? You gotta eat something."

He shook his head and made his way up the staircase. "It's okay," he said, "I'm not hungry."

At the top of the landing, he stopped and turned to look down at her, still standing in the hallway, looking troubled.

"Mr. Jacques," she said, "are you in trouble? Something bad happen to you?"

"No, Mrs. Cordelli," he said with a smile. "Something good. Something very, very good."

The clothes he'd bought for Doris had been packed for a week; it was just a case of throwing a few essentials into a suitcase, grabbing his toothbrush and shaving kit and leaving a note for Margaret. The talk with Benny would have to wait; he'd write a short, explanatory letter and ask Mrs. Cordelli to mail it in the morning. Margaret would understand. She'd have to.

What he'd realized, upon waking up in the hotel lobby, was that if ever Doris needed him it was now. She was pure and beautiful and perfect but there were forces around her — forces like Arty Peach and the Wilsons of this world — who were out to sully her, take advantage of her beauty. Only he, Skippy Jacques, loved her with a passion that was clean and unadulterated: he loved her with his soul, with his entire being, and the time had come to prove it. He had spent the first twenty-one years of his life passively accepting whatever came his way. Now was the time for action.

He opened the top drawer of his bureau and took out a book of matches: on the inside cover, in her round, childish handwriting, Doris had written, "Four-thirty-one Maplewood Crescent." This was her address — her mother's address, really, but Doris lived there now. She'd been staying there since she came back to the Bay, in one of those new subdivisions out by the highway. The kind of places being built all over the country to house low-income families with too many kids. Instant slums, Joe Bruno called them.

But Doris didn't care. "It used to matter to me where I lived," she told him one night. "I used to buy stuff for the apartment, put up nice curtains, keep things looking pretty. Now, as long as it's clean I guess I just don't notice. One day, when I have the money, I'll buy a place out in the country, and I'll have a garden and fix it up just the way I like it. Until then, it's just not important."

Skippy put the matches into his shirt pocket and looked around the room to see if he'd missed anything. His books and records, of course, but they could stay there until he got back. Other details, he could take care of them once he was on the road. At some point he'd have to find a phone and make a few calls — arrange for one of the girls to come into the club early tonight and open up, there were two acts scheduled and it was too late to cancel. Tomorrow morning he'd call the musicians, explain he was closing temporarily, for a couple of weeks, a month, maybe, he was sorry to give such short notice but this thing had come up and he had no choice. The old man, too, at the hardware store — he'd have to call him and make some excuse. And his mother; shit, he'd forgotten to call his mother. It was Sunday and she'd be expecting him to come by for dinner. Maybe they could stop by the house on the way out of town and he could go in quickly and explain.

It was too bad to do it this way, everything in a rush, when he'd spent so much time planning it all, working the details out so carefully, but that's just the way it was. He saw now what had to be done and there was no putting it off, not even for a minute. Whatever Doris had done in the past, whatever kind of life she was living right now, none of it mattered. Fortune had brought her into his life; he must act quickly if he wanted to keep her there.

At the last moment he suddenly remembered the money. Reaching under the bed, he pulled the metal box towards him and set it on top of the mattress. Stupid, really, to keep so much money in his room. What if the box had been broken into, what if the money was gone? All his plans would go up in smoke and he'd have no one to blame but himself.

The money was there: thirty-four one hundred dollar bills, crackling fresh from the bank. Enough to make this the trip of a lifetime. Grateful to whatever god had forgiven his foolishness and kept the money safe, Skippy put the bills back in their wallet and put it carefully into his inside jacket pocket, where it bulged reassuringly against his chest.

He was just locking the door of his room, his suitcases beside him in the hallway, when Mrs. Cordelli called up to him that there was somebody on the phone, downstairs. His first instinct was to ask her to take a message — he was in a rush, the taxi was waiting — but as he came down the stairs she handed him the receiver and said, "It's a lady."

It was Margaret and when he heard her voice he immediately began to explain that something had come up, he had to leave town, he'd written her a note all about it. But she was telling him something, something about Benny, and finally he shut up and sat down on the chair in the hall, prepared to listen.

"He's gone," Margaret was saying and her voice was flat and tired-sounding, as if she'd been up all night.

"He came home last night and packed up his things and said he was moving out. It's the girl on the mountain, I think, but I don't know for sure. He says it's not anybody else but the address he gave me is on the reserve. He said that's where he'll be staying, for now.

He wasn't drunk or angry or anything. He just came into the bedroom and told me, very calmly, that he was leaving. He said not to worry, he'd take care of me and Katie, he said he'd always be her father and he'd never abandon her. But he said he couldn't do this any more, he couldn't go on being my husband and living in this house, he said he couldn't go on being a hypocrite. And then he kissed me good-bye and he left."

She was silent then and Skippy struggled to think of the right thing to say.

"What will you do?" he asked, feeling inadequate. As always.

"I'm going back to New York," she said. "My friend Linette's never seen Katie, she's always asking about her, she's always saying we should come and visit. I guess we'll go stay with her for a while. I don't know. I can't stay here."

"No," he agreed. "I guess you can't."

After a moment he added, "I'm sorry," but she didn't respond, maybe she didn't hear him. At any rate, there seemed to be nothing further to say.

"I just thought I should tell you," she said. "You know, so you wouldn't come around Tuesday night. We won't be here. I'm getting the bus this afternoon."

"To New York? You're leaving already?"

"To Toronto," she said. "We change in Toronto and get a bus to New York. I phoned already. There's one leaving at three."

"Margaret, is there anything — can I do anything? Do you need any money?"

"No. I don't need anything. I'm okay." She didn't sound okay, she didn't sound like anything at all, but there was something in her voice that made him afraid of giving offense. He waited and before he could say anything else, she added, as an afterthought, "He asked about you."

"Me? What did he say?"

"He asked if I ever saw you around."

"What did you tell him?"

"I said, Sometimes. And he said the next time I saw you I should say hi. From him."

"That's it?"

"That's it."

There was a pause while Skippy digested this information. It was such a small thing, really, it might not mean anything. And then, again, it might. He wanted to ask Margaret what she thought, what she figured Benny had meant by it, but this was the wrong time. And so he said nothing and after a while Margaret said that she had to go,

Katie was up and wanting her breakfast and she had to get packed, so he said he was glad she'd called, which he was, although it had left him feeling unsure of himself, unsure of what was expected. And then he said he was sorry not to see her before she left and she said nothing and he thought of telling her he'd be in New York, too, with Doris, but somehow he didn't want to get into that, and so he fell silent, as well.

"Well, I'd better go," she said, finally. "Take care of yourself."

"You, too." He thought she was wanting something more of him but he couldn't think what, and finally she said good-bye and hung up and he was left sitting on the chair in the hallway, holding on to the phone.

Mrs. Cordelli came out of the kitchen and gave him a look. She didn't miss much. Outside, the taxi driver leaned on the horn and Skippy replaced the receiver and stood up.

"Well, I guess I'll be going."

His landlady stood in the doorway and watched as he picked up his suitcases. They felt heavier than before; he was aware of a sudden, unexpected weariness overtaking him. He opened the front door and saw the cab parked at the curb and felt the morning sunshine on his face.

"You be careful," said Mrs. Cordelli. "Stay out of trouble, okay? Don't pick any fights with old men."

She was making a joke, an inside joke, between the two of them, and he grinned to show he appreciated it.

"I won't," he told her. And then, because he wanted to say good-bye to someone, he set his suitcases down on the step and gave her a quick hug. This pleased her and she followed him outside and stood on the porch and watched while he hauled the bags down to the cab, got in himself and drove off; just before they turned the corner he turned and looked out the back window and saw her standing there still, like a sturdy, miniature saint, dressed in black.

19.

Candi made two attempts to take her own life that summer and each time Doris got her to the hospital in time. The doctors would pump out her stomach, give her more tranquilizers and send her home. By the end of August she began to seem more like her old self; she and J.P. went back to seeing each other when he was in town and Doris thought that maybe whatever had been bothering her had got fixed. Then, three days before Christmas, Candi checked herself into a room on the seventeenth floor of a downtown hotel. She drank and took pills and dialed J.P.'s number in Montreal, hanging up at first when his wife answered, then breaking down and crying to speak to him. Finally he picked up the phone and told her to stop being silly and the next time she called he refused to pick it up at all and just let it ring. And ring. Around two o'clock in the morning, Candi sobered up enough to get dressed, brushed her hair and put on fresh makeup and left her handbag on the end of the bed where it would be sure to be found, along with the note she had written on a piece of hotel stationery. And then she opened the large window overlooking the street and jumped.

It was Doris who had to go down to the morgue and identify the body and it was she who made the necessary telephone calls to Candi's mother and to the Capri, and Mr. and Mrs. Folgram came down to Toronto to arrange for Candi's broken body to be flown home for a memorial service and when they had gone back Doris sat in the empty apartment with the lights off and stared at the piece of paper she was holding. It was too dark to read the words, but she knew them by heart: "Dear Doris," it read. "Sorry about all this. I guess I'm just having a bad day. Rent's paid till the fifteenth of January. Keep the lighter. It's in my purse. Love, Candi."

J.P. arrived the day after Boxing Day and brought her some fruit and cheese from the farmer's market and a loaf of crispy white bread from the bakery down the street.

She didn't want to see him. She hated men, she'd decided. All men, but J.P. more than anybody.

"Go away," she said, refusing to unlock the door. "Get out of here."

He persisted and made his way into the apartment, telling her she shouldn't be alone. "It's unhealthy, sitting around here in your housecoat, all by yourself. It won't help."

Doris' blue eyes accused him. "She loved you. She did it because of you."

J.P. shook his head. "She would have done it anyway." He sighed and set the food down on the kitchen table, looking around for a knife. "She wanted the wrong things, she wanted life to be a fairy tale. All around her bad things were happening and she wouldn't see them for what they were. Believe me, Doris, she would have found a reason to do it eventually."

"Do it." They couldn't speak the words, not even J.P. who was a realist and had no illusions.

"I should have been there." Doris felt her eyes fill with tears and knew she was going to cry again. She'd been crying all morning; she felt she'd never be able to stop.

J.P. found the knife, cut two slices of bread and made her a cheese sandwich.

"Here," he said, handing it to her and pouring her a glass of milk. "Eat, and then we'll talk."

When she had eaten most of it — there was a lump in her throat, and it hurt when she swallowed — he sat down at the table across from her and asked her what she was going to do.

"You know what you should do, don't you? You should go home. You're just a kid, Doris. You should go back to school, finish your education. You don't want to end up like poor Candi."

She thought about going home. Going back to Ted and her mother. No, she couldn't go back. There was no "back" to go to.

"I'm staying here," she said. "This is where I want to be. I've made up my mind." He didn't try to argue with her. Instead he nodded, as if he'd expected her to say that, and took a cigarette from a pack in his pocket. Tapping it lightly on the table top, he smiled at her and leaned back in his chair.

"Well, if you're determined to stay in the big city, we'll have to find you a job, eh? If you are going to afford to live here."

Doris said she already had a job but J.P. shrugged that off — a coffee shop waitress, for seventy-five cents an hour. That was not a job, that was slavery. He would find her a real job and in the meantime he'd see that she didn't go hungry.

"I don't want your money," Doris told him but he pressed a folded twenty dollar bill into her hand and told her to take it.

"For Candi," he told her and she saw he was serious. "She would want me to take care of you. I owe it to her."

Which was the only time in the years she knew him that J.P. came close to admitting responsibility for anything.

That night she slept for the first time in the bed with the pink sheets and pink pillowslips, the bed that belonged to a dead girl, and it was a very long time before she fell asleep. When she did she dreamt she met Candi walking towards her on Jarvis Street, arm in arm with an older couple with dark hair and tight, sad little faces. "These are the Rosenbergs," she told Doris. "We've become very good friends."

J.P. became part of her life after that, calling her on the phone when he was in Montreal and turning up on her doorstep when he was back in Toronto. Candi had given him a key to the apartment and often he would simply be there, lying on the couch, reading the paper, when Doris got back from work. He came bearing gifts of food and small, funny ornaments he thought she'd like, little offerings of friendship. He was putting himself out to make her like him, which was unusual for J.P., she thought. She'd known him to be cold and aloof, much of the time, and downright nasty when he wanted to be. Once, when she'd come home from work, she'd found the two of them, Candi and J.P., arguing in the kitchen. She heard what sounded like a slap and Candi had come running out of the kitchen, past Doris, her hand to her face, and slammed the bedroom door. J.P. had come out right after, picked up his coat and hat from the couch and smiled at Doris, completely unperturbed.

"Your roommate is behaving like a spoiled little girl," he said, adjusting his tie in the mirror by the door. "She needs a spanking and the next time, I promise, I'll give her one. Tell her that for me, will you, Doris?"

But he'd never hit Doris; he never put a hand on her except to pat her on the shoulder or kiss her lightly on both cheeks when they met. She began to think it was possible that J.P. looked upon her as a daughter and she slowly began to relax around him and trust him, just a little. She told him about her troubles getting to sleep — since Candi's death she never just dropped off anymore, but lay there tossing and turning, sometimes until the early hours of the morning. He gave her some pills, but they were too strong and she felt heavy and listless the next morning. And so he suggested she try something else, something the musicians in the club used when they needed to loosen up, to relax. Marijuana, it was called, and she was nervous about trying it but J.P. insisted and it worked — for the first time in weeks she fell asleep before midnight and slept right through until morning. And, even better, her sleep was deep and dreamless.

She came to depend on the dope, as he called it, and would ask J.P. to leave her a couple of sticks when he went back to Montreal, enough to last her for the rest of the week. He always obliged and she portioned them out carefully, just one or two a night, not enough to get hooked or anything, but enough to let her relax and fall asleep and not think about anything. Once J.P. was detained in Montreal for an extra day and she had nothing to smoke and sat up in bed all night with the light on, unable to calm the panic rising in her chest. After that, she always made sure she had four or five sticks extra, just in case.

It was a Sunday afternoon, two months after Candi's death, and J.P. had stopped by to take her to a show. He rummaged through the cupboards, looking for something to eat, and when she told him there was nothing, she'd had to pay the rent on Friday and had no money left, he took her by the hand and led her into the living-room.

"Sit down," he told her. "I think it's time we had a little talk."

She watched as J.P. began to pace the rug in front of her, fingering the dark green stone of his tie pin. "What do you make at that place?" he wanted to know. "That coffee shop, what do they pay you? Forty, fifty dollars a week?"

"Nowhere near that," she said.

"You know how much your friend Candi made in an hour? Fifty dollars, sometimes sixty. Sometimes more."

Doris was astounded. "I don't believe you. Nobody makes that much money working as a waitress, not even in a nightclub."

"You're right," J.P. said. "She didn't. Not as a waitress."

And that's when J.P. explained to Doris what Candi really did, how she really made her money. The Capri, it turned out, was more — or less — than a nightclub. The customers came for other things besides a few drinks and entertainment. And the women who worked there, they provided the "extras."

Doris wouldn't believe it, at first. But in the end, she knew he was telling the truth. He had no reason to lie to her and why would he make up stories about a dead woman? Still, it wasn't a pleasant thing to hear.

"Why are you telling me this? I don't want to know things like that about Candi. I don't want to think about it."

"I'm telling you this," he said, sitting down next to her and taking her hands in his, "because I want you to know there is money to be made out there and you could be making it. A girl that looks like you shouldn't be working as a waitress, not for that kind of money."

Doris stared at him, unable to believe what she was hearing.

"You want me to do what Candi did," she said. "You want me to be a — a whore."

He laughed at the way she pronounced the word: "hoor", the way the boys back in junior high had said it. J.P. shook his head and touched her cheek lightly. The diamond in his pinky ring flashed in the light.

"It's not pimping I'm talking about, Doris. It's photography."

J.P. arranged everything. The following Saturday he drove her down to an old office building on Yonge Street and walked her up to a small, cramped studio on the third floor. He introduced her to the photographer, Hank Waterman, a middle-aged, balding man who specialized in lingerie shots for "Titter" and "Wink" and "For Men Only". He'd been happily married for over thirty years, according to J.P. — Doris couldn't be safer.

Hank handed her some costumes and showed her where to change and J.P. told her he was leaving but he'd be downstairs to pick her up at three o'clock. Left alone in the studio with Hank, Doris was shy at first and wished she hadn't agreed to do this, no matter how much money it paid. Feeling silly, and a little embarrassed, she came out from behind the screen wearing a short, see-through nightie, her arms crossed in front of her chest.

Hank smiled and pointed to a velvet, tiger-striped couch against one wall.

"Have a seat," he said, as if she was dressed in nothing more revealing than a T-shirt and jeans. "I'll just take a few minutes to get set up here and then we'll get going. There's Coke in the fridge if you want some. Help yourself."

With patience and a quiet sense of humour, Hank showed her how to pose, indicating that she should arch her back or point her toes without once ever actually touching her or making her feel uncomfortable. She knelt on bearskin rugs and against romantic painted landscapes and Hank told her to pretend she was alone in her room with the camera, and the camera was her very best friend.

"It's play-acting," he said. "Have fun with it."

And, eventually, she did. In this small room with only Hank and the lights and the camera, she felt sheltered, protected; even Hank faded into the background as she concentrated only on the lens of the camera, shifting positions according to the gentle instructions that came out of the soft darkness beyond the light. The three hours were over before she knew it, and when Hank turned off the bright lights and asked her if she was tired, she shook her head: she was exhilarated, she could have gone on much longer.

Hank paid her and shook her hand and Doris left the studio delighted with herself, feeling light as a feather as she walked down the steps to where J.P. waited for her on the sidewalk. The poses had been provocative, but innocent; Doris sensed she would have gone further if Hank had requested it. Quite a bit further, she guessed.

After that first Saturday afternoon, Hank Waterman used Doris regularly and gave her name out to other photographers looking for new, fresh young faces — and bodies, of course. She preened and posed and postured in hundreds of baby-doll nighties, spaghetti-strap negligees, merry widows and Victorian corsets and black net stockings. She stood upright in high heels and brandished whips for the dominatrix look; she perched demurely on swings in white cotton panties, licking lollipops, the child seductress. Sometimes the costumes and poses were so outrageous that she and the photographer both laughed and she found it difficult to arrange her features into the proper sultry pout required for the eternal temptress.

"Do fellows really like this stuff?" she asked Hank one afternoon, staring doubtfully at herself in a drastically abridged version of Little Bo Peep's costume, holding a shepherd's crook and a stuffed lamb.

"You'd be amazed," said Hank, peering at her through the viewfinder. "Men like just about anything that moves as long as it has breasts and wears skirts."

"Or doesn't wear them," she said and he looked up at her and laughed.

"You're right," he agreed. "Especially then."

It was a challenge to find a new way to turn her head, a new way to bring out the right feeling for the outfit — like acting, she thought, and wondered if maybe she'd inherited some of her mother's flair for performance. But that would mean going on stage, saying lines in front of all kinds of people, and she knew she'd never have the nerve for anything like that. Here, in Hank's studio, it was safe; he and the camera were the only onlookers and they supported and encouraged her to do her very best. Three months into the posing she was so confident of her ability to make money this way, she gave up her job at the coffee shop. Never again, she thought; she'd never take another order, pour another coffee or suck up for another tip as long as she lived.

Early in June of that year she got a letter from Lindy Folgram, the first she'd had since Candi had died. Mrs. Folgram had suffered some kind of nervous collapse and she was sending Lindy to her aunt's in Oakville for the summer and she'd agreed, reluctantly, to let her daughter spend a week or two with Doris. It would be a scream, Lindy wrote — they would go to all the shows and shop at all the big stores. She could hardly wait, she was just so excited.

Doris was excited, too, as she read the letter out to J.P. She and Lindy were almost fifteen now, practically grown up, and it would be great to see each other again and hang out and do grown up things. They could go to movies and make fudge and stay up late talking every night. And Lindy could tell her about Cambrian Bay and give her all the news from home.

"Tell her not to come," J.P. said and Doris stopped in mid-sentence, not quite comprehending what he had said.

"What do you mean?" she asked and he repeated it, slowly, as if she was a little girl, and not very bright.

"I can't do that," she replied. "And besides, I don't want to. I really want to see Lindy again, and J.P., honestly, you'd like her, she's the nicest person —"

Taking hold of her hand, J.P. interrupted her, smiling and speaking in a very gentle voice, "Doris, listen to me. What do you think you're going to tell her, if she comes? She's going to want to know what you're doing here, what your job is, how you're making all this money. You want to tell some girl from your home town that you're modeling for skin magazines and have her go back and spread the word to everybody you know? You want your mother to know that?"

"I don't care what my mother knows," Doris said, but she was beginning to feel uneasy, her joy in Lindy's letter quickly fading.

"Yes, you do. I know you do."

He stood up and went to the closet to get his jacket. As he put it on, he said to her, "You sit down and write your friend Lindy and tell her you'd love to see her, but you can't this summer. Write her a nice letter and I'll mail it."

"I wouldn't know what to say," she said, knowing she'd already given up the fight.

"You'll think of something," he assured her. "You're a smart girl, I know you'll come up with something. I have to go now, I have an appointment."

Lightly, he brushed her cheeks with his lips and gave her shoulder a squeeze.

"Go ahead, now, write a nice letter. Do it right away, before you forget."

Miserably, she watched him leave. After a few minutes she got up from the couch and rummaged in her purse for a notepad and pen.

"Dear Lindy," she began, "How are you? I'm fine. It was swell hearing from you and I'd love to see you this summer but I can't. I'm really sorry but I'm going to be away for July and August...."

Doris had been modeling for two and a half years, without incident, when she took a cab over to Queen Street, the night of Hallowe'en, 1956. An evening shoot wasn't unusual — a lot of the photographers had day jobs and did the naughty stuff at night — and although the photographer was one she hadn't worked with before, Hank Waterman had told her all about him. His name was Gary, he was in his late fifties, and, like lots of the photographers, he shot for the men's magazines on the side — weddings and bar mitzvahs were his main source of income. Hank told her he drank pretty heavy, which is why he'd never gone to the top.

"But he's good and he could have been big time if he'd wanted to. He could have shot for the big fashion magazines if he'd stayed off the booze. He doesn't drink when he's working, though; you'll be okay."

When Doris arrived at the studio that evening, the first thing she saw was that Hank was wrong — Gary had been drinking. In fact, he still was; a bottle of dark rum stood on a stool next to the tripod, most of it already gone. Gary greeted her from a corner of the room and he looked like he'd been on a bender. His sweater and pants appeared slept in and he didn't seem to have shaved for the past few days.

She turned to leave — a cardinal rule with her, never work with a drunk — but he stopped her, said it was a special assignment, lots of money, not to worry, everything was going to be just fine.

Against her better judgment, she took off her coat and walked over to where he was arranging some pillows on the floor.

"How much money?" she asked.

"A thousand dollars." He was agitated, nervous. There was definitely something funny about this shoot. "Five hundred for you, five hundred for me."

Doris wasn't convinced.

"What do I have to do?"

He told her and she put her coat back on.

"No, thanks. I'm not interested."

She made her way to the door, which was locked, and when she turned back to Gary, she saw he was no longer alone. There was somebody standing behind him and in the dim light of the studio she could see it was a man, but couldn't make out his features.

"This is Mr. X."

"Mr. X" stepped forward and Doris gave a gasp of fright: his face was hidden by a grotesque rubber mask, a gorilla mask. Apart from that, he wore only a wristwatch and a pair of boxer shorts.

"Mr. X, I want you to meet Doris."

The man in the mask walked towards her, and she shrank back, unable to move, unable to take her eyes away from the loathsome, exaggerated features of his disguise.

"Don't be afraid, Doris," the gorilla man said, his voice deep and partly muffled. "This is going to be fun."

Without taking her eyes from the masked man, she spoke to Gary. "Unlock the door, please. I'm not doing this."

Gary said nothing, and now the other man took hold of her hand, and held her in a firm grip. "They were right, Doris. You're a beautiful girl. And very young."

"Gary?"

Gary wouldn't look at her; he walked over to his where his camera stood on a tripod and began to fiddle with the settings. Something in Doris gave up, at that point. It was obvious that Mr. X was in charge here, not Gary. Keeping his arm firmly around her, the man in the mask led her over to the screen and knelt down on the pillows, pulling her down beside him.

"Doris," he said, "if you relax and just leave things to me, you'll enjoy this. I'm not going to hurt you and I won't get you pregnant. Is that what you're worried about? Are you afraid you'll get pregnant?"

She shook her head, unable to speak.

"I'm not going to come inside you," he continued. "I promise you that. We're going to do lots of things, nice things, that can't get you pregnant. You haven't done any of those things before, have you, Doris? You're young and sweet and unspoiled. So you just do what I tell you and you'll see how nice it will be. Why don't we start by taking off your clothes? Here, let me help you."

If I can see him, she thought. If I can just see his face. Suddenly she reached up and took hold of the mask, giving it a jerk. Immediately he pulled away and raised his hand, as if to strike her. But he said only, in that calm, dangerous voice, "Don't be a silly girl, Doris. I don't want to hurt you."

Once she was naked, the man turned her over on to her stomach and told her to look up at the camera.

"Now smile, Doris," he said. "Show us how much you're enjoying it."

She gasped as he began to enter her from behind and in spite of herself, she turned her head and asked him not to hurt her.

"Hush now," he said, pushing himself further inside her. "We want to see your face, Doris. We all want to see your lovely face. Turn around and smile at the camera like a good girl."

She turned back and looked up towards the camera and the photographer began to take pictures.

20.

There was not a maple tree of any kind within shouting distance of Maplewood Crescent. If there had been, the noise and exhaust fumes from the large trucks that rumbled along the highway nearby would have smothered it in its infancy. The street itself consisted of a row of perfectly square two-storey red and yellow brick houses, each with a couple of concrete steps leading up to an aluminum storm door. On each side of the door a rectangular window overlooked a bleak little patch of lawn and the parking lot across the street. A tin shed in the corner of the lot bore the sign:

TENANT PARKING ONLY
Unauthorized motor vehicles
towed away at owners' expense
By-law 23-1964
Section 3(a)

Outside each house were one or two children's bikes propped against the wall, while a half-ton pickup truck was parked in front of the house next to the corner. Cardboard boxes, small tables and children's toys were scattered across this particular front yard: someone was moving — in or out, Skippy couldn't say, but he hoped for their sake it was out. Further down the street, a motorcycle leaned against an unpainted wooden fence and an assortment of towels, underwear, shirts and pants were hung out to dry on a makeshift clothesline.

As the taxi pulled up in front of number four thirty-one, two young girls approached, one pushing the other in a shopping cart. The girls stopped and watched as Skippy paid the fare and stood looking at the house while the cab drove away.

Somehow, he'd thought there'd be something distinctive about number four-thirty-one, something to set it apart from the others. At least its front yard was tidy and bare of clutter, which was more than you could say for most of its neighbours. Upstairs, two windows, curtains closed, overlooked the street; one of them, he hoped, contained Doris.

"You don't live here." It was the bigger girl, the one who was doing the pushing, who spoke up, while her friend simply watched him with solemn brown eyes.

"No, I'm just visiting."

"Told ya," the girl remarked to the other. "He's just a boyfriend. Aren't you, Mister?"

Skippy didn't know how to respond. But he decided he didn't like the implication. "No," he said, "I'm not a boyfriend, I'm a friend."

"Same thing. You're a boy and you're a friend, so you're a boyfriend." The bigger girl was evidently pleased with the logic of her reasoning; she smirked and stood with her hands on her hips, ready to prove to him once again, if he needed proof, that she was a force to be dealt with. "Got any gum?"

"No. Sorry. Why did you think I was a boyfriend?"

"Mrs. McGillvray has lots of boyfriends." And then, in a sort of sing-song manner, like a chant: "She has round heels, my mommy says so." With what was meant to be a winning smile, she added, "Me and Lucy really like gum."

They waited to see if Skippy would respond but he was digesting this last piece of information: Doris' mom had lots of boyfriends. Was she — did she do it as well?

Picking up his suitcases, he walked up the sidewalk to the door and was about to knock ("Out of order. Please knock" was taped under the doorbell) when the girl, the one that was not called Lucy, cried out, "Hey!"

Skippy turned around and the girl said, "What's the matter with your foot?"

"Nothing," Skippy said, which was true.

"Well, you sure walk funny," was the rejoinder and Skippy thought there was a lot to be said for the days when little girls were too shy to talk to strangers.

He knocked on the door and the sound of his own knocking gave him a start. What was he going to say when Doris or her mother came to the door? He had never tracked her down like this before, he'd never even spoken to her anywhere but at the club. Would she be angry when she saw him standing on her mother's front steps, here without an invitation, without any kind of warning?

As he raised his arm to knock again, the wallet full of money swung against him, its pressure restoring his confidence. He knocked once more and a woman's voice called out from within.

"All right, all right, hold your horses. Give me a minute, for Heaven's sakes."

When the door eventually swung open, an older, rather frayed version of Doris stood in the doorway, dressed in a pink nylon robe and toeless sandals. Her hair was blonde, like Doris', but it was what his mother would have called "bottle blonde" and it was done up in rollers. She had Doris' blue eyes and delicate features but there were deep lines around the mouth and under the eyes that betrayed her age. You could see she had been an attractive woman, once; most likely she still was to a man in his forties or fifties. Guys that age, well, they obviously wouldn't have the same expectations as a younger person. They'd be satisfied with less.

"Yes?" She was frowning when she opened the door and she gave Skippy a once-over that plainly said she didn't think much of what she saw. "What is it? What do you want, banging on the door this time of the morning?"

"Mrs. McGillvray?" he asked and the frown deepened.

"Now, look, if you're with the Mormons I've told you people before I'm not interested. I may not be a regular church-goer but I have my own beliefs, all right?"

"I was looking for Doris."

"What do you want with her? Is she in some kind of trouble?"

Skippy shook his head and tried to look as non-threatening as possible. "No, I'm just a friend. Really. I just need to talk to her."

"Well, who are you, then? Is she expecting you?"

"My name is Skippy Jacques." He put out his hand and when she made no move to take it, he let it drop to his side. "Doris knows me but she's not expecting me. But if you could just tell her Skippy's here to see her, I'm sure it would be all right."

Unconvinced, Dolly McGillvray leaned her head out the door and looked past him, up and down the street. The two girls were still standing at the foot of the sidewalk, watching the scene in the doorway with profound interest. This, you could be sure, would be relayed eventually to the bigger girl's mother, as one more proof of Mrs. McGillvray's reputation for "sleeping around."

Dolly glared at the girls, then turned back to Skippy. "I'm Doris' mom," she said, finally. "If she's in some kind of trouble, you can tell me."

"Oh, no, Mrs. — Mrs. McGillvray. There's no trouble. And I'm really sorry to bother you. I just need to see her for a minute."

She noticed the suitcases and frowned. "What are those for?"

"I'm just on my way out of town. I just stopped by to see Doris first."

Her face softened. "Well, I'm sorry, dear, but she's fast asleep. When she wakes up I'll tell her you stopped by."

She was getting ready to shut the door.

"Please," he began, and stopped.

"Well?" She was losing her patience. It was far too early on a Sunday morning to have to deal with some poor lovelorn friend of her daughter's. And she'd have to speak to Doris about giving out this address.

"It's just that, I took a cab here, and it's sort of a long way, and I really would like to see her, Mrs. McGillvray."

She waited a moment, considering, then shrugged and stepped back from the door. "All right, then, I guess you better come in," she said, rather ungraciously. And then, to the two little girls on the sidewalk, she called out, "Run along, you two. Didn't your mothers ever tell you it's not nice to stare?"

The girls held their ground, however; the older girl made a face and stuck out her tongue and Dolly gave up and slammed the door shut behind her.

Skippy could not have said what he was expecting the interior of the house to look like but it most certainly was not the extravaganza that assaulted him the moment he stepped inside. Where the outside had been bleak, dreary, washed-out, the room he walked into was a riot of colour. A red shag carpet covered the floor wall-to-wall and the walls themselves were painted a shade of pink only slightly more muted in its intensity. Pink lampshades criss-crossed with lace and silk flounces hung from the ceiling and there were orange velvet drapes at the front window. Tiny occasional tables bearing every sort of knick-knack ever offered at the local five and dime were placed at strategic intervals and at least three wall mirrors captured the reflected opulence of the place. It looked exactly like a magazine picture Skippy had seen once of a bordello in New Orleans, under the heading "Louisiana Ladies of the Night."

But what really made you sit up and take notice were the clowns. They were everywhere. Framed paintings of clowns were hung all over the walls — sad, happy, standing on their heads, clutching balloons — while the clown theme was repeated in little figurines set along the windowsills and embroidered on cushions scattered on the couch.

Skippy stood in front of one of the paintings, a sad clown with a tear flowing down one cheek, and Dolly McGillvray came up behind him.

"I did that," she told him. "I painted all of these."

"They're very good," he said.

"Well, thank you." For the first time he detected a note of friendliness in her voice and guessed, rightly, that no matter how absurd anyone else might find these paintings, they were Dolly's pride and joy. "That's very sweet of you to say — What did you say your name was?"

"Skippy Jacques," he said and held out his hand again. This time she took it and held it for just a fraction longer than was absolutely necessary.

"Skippy," she said. "What a sweet name. Well, Skippy, you can call me Dolly. That's what my friends call me."

Was it his imagination or was there a hint of something else in the way she said "friends"? He found it hard to believe but it appeared that Doris' mother was flirting with him.

"Do you paint a lot?" he asked her, wanting to find something else to talk about, something to divert his attention away from the fact that she was standing next to him and she smelled very good, for an older woman.

"Just paint by number," she said. "It keeps me busy. Keeps my mind off things. I took it up when my husband died, two years ago. I never would've painted them if Ted was still alive. He hated art, said he couldn't see any point in it. Still, why paint when you've got the real thing, eh?"

She pulled her robe more tightly across her chest and he noticed that she had a very shapely chest. For an older woman.

"What about you, Skippy? Do you paint?"

"No, I don't have any talent, that way." It was a simple thing to say but she smiled as if he had said something clever.

"Oh, I see. Well, I just bet you have other talents, eh? Am I right?"

Skippy had no idea what to say. She was flirting with him, there was no doubt about it, but his capacity to flirt with women was limited at the best of times — it was practically non-existent when it came to a woman old enough to be his mother.

To his relief, Dolly finally turned and headed across the room towards the kitchen.

"Are you hungry, Skippy?" she asked over her shoulder. "I make the best scrambled eggs. My late husband used to call them orgasmic."

He told her he'd already eaten and added, "I really should talk with Doris. I can't stay too long."

"My goodness, you're an eager beaver, aren't you?"

Skippy had no response for this and he stood in the door of the kitchen while she took a can of tomato juice out of the fridge and poured herself a glass. Then she brought out a half-empty bottle of vodka from a cupboard and emptied a healthy portion of it into the tomato juice. Giving it a quick stir, she held it out towards him with a smile.

"Like a taste? Hair of the dog that bit you."

"No. Thanks."

"Well, bottoms up."

Dolly took a swig and sat down on one of the two red vinyl kitchen chairs, patting the other with her free hand. "Come sit down," she said. "It's 'way too early to wake up Doris, just yet. Sit down and have a chat and let's get to know each other." When he hesitated, she added, "Come on, now. You've woken me up. I won't be able to fall asleep again for ages."

Feeling he had no other choice, Skippy sat down on the chair she offered and made a show of looking at his watch.

"I can't stay too long," he said. "I have to get going pretty soon."

Dolly ignored that. The "pick-me-up" was beginning to take effect and she was in the mood for a little conversation. Sundays were boring days at the best of times; her married boyfriends generally spent them with their wives and Phil never came by till after eight. Until then, she had a whole day to get through so she might as well enjoy what company there was, even this early in the morning.

"Now, Mister Eager Beaver, why don't you tell me how you know Doris? I don't recognize the name; you're not one of her usual friends, are you?"

"I'm the one who owns the club. The Dharma."

Dolly's face brightened. "Oh, yes. Now I remember. You're the beatnik." She eyed him critically, and shook her head. "I thought you'd look different. Somehow I pictured you with a beard. And taller. Never mind, I'm sure you've got other attractions. You know what they say, don't you? Good things come in small packages."

This time there was no mistaking what she was getting at. Skippy was flustered and said again that he couldn't stay long, he really should go and see Doris.

She smiled. "Oh, dear, I've embarrassed you, haven't I? I'm sorry, I'm really terrible sometimes, just saying whatever pops into my head. What you see is what you get with Dolly. What did you say your last name was?"

He told her and she shook her head. "I don't think I know anybody by that name. Is it Irish?"

"French. You spell it the French way, J-A-C-Q-U-E-S."

"I knew a Frenchman, once. He was a terrific dancer. Dressed to the nines, too. I was crazy about him." She laughed. "And who do I marry? A Uke who gets killed in the war and a Scotchman who can't hold a job for more than a month at a timet. That's me all over. I never had any luck with men. Always made the wrong choices. I guess Doris has told you all about me, huh?"

"Well, no. Not really."

Dolly considered this, and took another sip of her drink. "We've never really been close, you know. Not the way mothers and daughters are supposed to be close, anyhow. I don't understand why. God knows I've tried, but it's like she doesn't really trust me or something. I find it very hurtful, if you want to know the truth."

Skippy searched for something to say, and finally came up with, "I'm sure she trusts you. She probably just likes to keep things to herself."

"I thought it would be different, if she came back here to live. I thought, well, we haven't seen each other in all these years, she must've changed, she's grown up by now, we'll have lots in common. But we don't. We don't seem to have anything at all in common. We don't even like the same movies."

There was a pause while Dolly took another sip of her drink, and stared moodily into her glass. It seemed like a good moment to remind her that he was there to see Doris, but when he suggested waking her up, Dolly placed her hand on his arm, restraining him.

"Hang on, dear. Keep me company for a little while. Now, I asked you how you knew Doris and then we got talking about other things, didn't we? So you go ahead now, dear, tell me all about yourself."

"Well, there's really not much to tell."

"Oh, now I don't believe that, Mr. Skippy Jacques. I don't believe that for a moment."

There was absolutely no doubt now; this woman was out-and-out flirting with him and it was not his imagination. As if to confirm his suspicions, she edged forward in her chair so that her left thigh was pressing against his knee and her right foot was nudging his. And then — there was no mistaking this, this was not an accident — her hand brushed his leg, just a quick, light touch, and then came back to rest on the top of his thigh. Slowly, very slowly, her fingers began to stroke the material of his pants, her long nails pressing deliberately into the fabric.

Skippy looked down at the table — he couldn't meet her eyes.

"Mrs. McGillvray —"

"Call me Dolly, dear."

"Dolly. I — I really wish you wouldn't do that. If you don't mind."

To his enormous relief she suddenly pushed her chair back, stood up and made her way over to the sink. Turning on the tap, she reached for a silver percolator on the counter and dumped the contents into the sink, then held it under the running water and gave it a rinse.

Skippy was confused. "Mrs. McGillvray —"

"Dolly," she corrected him, turning off the tap and rummaging around in a cupboard.

"Dolly, I really need to see Doris."

"Now, I'm going to make you a cup of coffee," she said, matter-of-factly. "You can drink it while I have a cigarette and then we'll go upstairs and wake up Doris. All right?"

She turned to face him and he saw that she appeared calm and self-composed; she did not look like a woman who'd just tried to make a pass at her daughter's boyfriend and had been turned down. Unless she did this kind of thing often and was used to it — being turned down, that was.

"All right?" she repeated and he nodded. Anything, just as long as she didn't try to feel him up again.

Once the percolator was plugged in, Dolly came back to the table and reached into her dressing-gown pocket for her cigarettes. Skippy recognized the silver case when he saw it: it was exactly like the one she'd bought Doris, the time Doris hadn't turned up for dinner.

"I see you bought one for yourself," he remarked, striking a match and holding it steady while Dolly bent her head and touched the tip of the cigarette to the flame. She said nothing until it was lit, then raised her head and took a deep, satisfying drag, exactly as Doris would do, the first cigarette of the evening.

"What do you mean, dear?"

"The cigarette case," he explained. "I see you bought one for yourself, as well. Doris told me you got it for her last winter when you went down to the States."

Dolly looked slightly amused. "This?" She held the case up to the light and he saw the two of them reflected within it. Sitting down at the table across from him, she informed him that the cigarette case belonged to her daughter.

"Arty got it for her, down in Minneapolis. They went down for the weekend and he picked this up somewhere. He says it's pure silver but I have my doubts. Arty wouldn't know the truth if it sat on his face. Anyway, she says she's trying to quit so she gave it to me. Too much of a temptation to keep smoking, with this around."

"Oh." So she'd gone with Arty Peach, that weekend back in November. She'd stood him up for Arty. And she'd lied about it.

In what he hoped was a casual tone of voice, he asked if Doris went on a lot of trips with Arty. Dolly shrugged.

"A few. Down to Duluth, mostly, or Minneapolis. And he took her to Las Vegas over Christmas. Arty loves to gamble — well he would, wouldn't he? — and he says Doris brings him good luck. Which I never understand because he never seems to win anything. At least, he never has any money on him. He's always borrowing from Doris. I don't know why she puts up with it."

Keeping his tone deliberately light, unconcerned, he asked, "So you don't like Arty very much?"

"Like him? Oh, Arty's all right if you know how to handle him. I just think Doris could do better, that's all. And he has an awful temper, you know. He broke her television set, did you know that? Oh, yes, of course you did. You bought her the new one. I'd forgotten about that. It's a lovely set, Skippy, it was very sweet of you. And that coat. Now that was beautiful. Your club must do very well, Skippy, for you to spend that kind of money."

"Not really. I mean, it does all right, I guess. But Doris is worth it."

"Is she, dear?"

"Well, sure she is. I think Doris — well, I think she's worth it."

For a moment they sat in silence, Dolly smoking, Skippy listening to the coffee beginning to bubble in the pot. So Arty was still in the picture. Arty took Doris to Minneapolis, took her to Las Vegas last Christmas. That whole story, about going there with her mother and Phil, it had all been a crock. The cigarette case was from Arty; the watch, too, most likely. The times she'd not turned up on Sunday nights, because her mother was sick. She'd gone away with Arty, most likely. And when Arty broke things, it was Skippy who'd picked up the pieces. She'd used him. And he still loved her.

It made him almost sick to think how much he loved her when she would treat him like this. He knew it should matter, the untruths, the casual taking for granted of his affection. But it didn't. Nothing mattered but Doris, being with her, taking her away. In spite of what he had learned, it seemed that going away with Doris mattered now more than ever.

"Dear." Dolly was tapping his arm with a long, pointed fingernail. "Are you all right?"

He nodded, and she said he'd looked like he was a million miles away.

"I was just thinking," he replied.

"How old are you, dear? Twenty? Twenty-one?"

"I'll be twenty-two in October."

"Twenty-two. And how old do you think Doris is? Do you want me to tell you? She's twenty-five. She'll be twenty-six in July. Now, I'll bet you didn't know that, did you? I'll bet you thought Doris was twenty-one or twenty-two, didn't you? Does it make you wonder just how well you know her? Well, dear, don't feel alone — nobody really knows Doris. I don't. I'm not sure even she does. She's a closed book, that girl. Closed the book and threw away the key."

There didn't seem to be anything to say; Dolly passed a hand across her eyes as if she were suddenly tired, and disappointed, somehow. Her face in repose, the mouth turned downwards, the chin beginning to recede into itself, seemed like that of a much older woman. Older and worn out.

"I was eighteen when I had her. Just a child, really. Babies having babies, that's what that was. I didn't know anything. I didn't want to know. I was young, I was pretty and I wanted to have a good time. I did not want to be stuck at home with some little brat, making cookies and cutting out dress patterns. So there I was, the original party girl, married to a big, dumb guy who went off and got himself shot in the war. By his own men, too, can you believe it? Friendly fire, they call it. Didn't even get killed by the Germans, got in the way of one of his own guns."

Dolly shook her head at the stupidity of it all and stubbed out her cigarette in the ashtray — bright green glass with "Welcome to Reno" written in gold around the rim, a souvenir, no doubt, from her daughter's vacation. She reached for another smoke and struck a match, seemingly unaware of Skippy's presence; at least, she lit her own cigarette this time, rather than waiting coyly for him to light it.

"I didn't even cry when they told me. It sounds awful to say it and I feel bad about it now, but I didn't cry. It was as if he was some man I'd known for a little while, a stranger, really, and now everybody was coming around to the house, bringing food and saying how sorry they were and looking at Doris like she was an orphan or something, feeling sorry for her because they knew what I was like — I had a bit of a reputation, you know. And I just wanted to take their casseroles and their home-made jams and throw them against the wall."

She suddenly looked up and smiled and said she guessed it must sound pretty awful, hearing her say something like that.

Skippy found his voice. "It must've been pretty bad, I guess."

"The thing is —" Dolly leaned forward and lowered her voice. "The thing is, when they told me he was dead, all I could think was now I could go out again, now I could start dating and having fun again, because I wasn't married any more. I could get out of the house. All the old biddies were shocked, I can tell you, they thought Dolly Pantoniak was one loose woman all right, running around with men, having a good time. But I didn't care. My mother used to say, Dolly, people will talk, and I used to tell her, Then let's give them something to talk about."

She laughed and glanced at Skippy to gauge his reaction. "I was wild," she explained, unnecessarily. "It's just the way I was. Marriage didn't change me and having a baby didn't change me. And you know what? I'm still wild. I still say to heck with the neighbours, to heck with all the fuddy-duddies who say you've got no right to have a good time because you're over thirty and your husband's dead. They're just jealous. I'm out there enjoying life and they're staying home being miserable. They're jealous."

Skippy was thinking about Doris. He wondered what it had been like for her, having a mother who went out every night, a mother who was determined that nothing was going to stand in her way. His own mother'd been left in a similar situation — widowed young, two kids to bring up. She'd never dated, never even seemed to have a personal life, a life apart from that of her children's, until last summer when she suddenly up and married Joe Bruno. Until that moment she'd lived for her kids; in some ways she probably always would.

Dolly seemed to be reading his thoughts. "I suppose you think I'm a pretty bad mother," she said, her smile belying the accusation in her words. "Well, you're right. I am. At least, I was. And Doris suffered for it, I guess. There was a long time when we didn't speak to each other, she didn't write me, she wouldn't even take my calls. And I didn't really blame her. I mean, how could I? It was her grandma raised her, not me. She was the one who put Doris' hair into pony tails, read her books every night, took care of her when I was out with a fellow. I always remember my mother telling me when I was pregnant that when you have a child you feel this sort of *surge*. That's how she put it. She said you look at the baby in your arms and you think, This is my child, this is a part of me. Well, it didn't happen to me. I lay in that hospital bed and they put Doris in my arms for the first time and I looked at her and I thought, Who the hell are you? And you know what's funny? She looked up at me as if she was thinking the very same thing. And I don't think either of us has ever figured it out. Ever."

"But she came back to live with you."

"Well, there comes a time when every girl needs her mother, I guess. Even a poor excuse for one like me. I suppose, after Ted died, we just needed each other. So she came to live with me. But she won't stay for ever."

"No?"

Dolly shook her head. "She's been away too long. There's nothing in this town for her and I think she probably knows it. She came back to find something, that's what I figure, and I think it probably was never there in the first place. But that's just my opinion.

What do I know, hey? I'm only her mother."

The coffee had stopped percolating and Dolly stood up and stretched and rubbed her forehead as if she were trying to clear away the fog. "Goodness, listen to me. Here I am, going on like a real chatterbox. I must've made that drink a little stronger than I thought." She smiled down at Skippy and there was something in the way she looked at him that reminded him of his mother. Perhaps she had more of the maternal instinct than she gave herself credit for, he thought. Or perhaps it was just that most women over forty reminded him of his mother.

She poured him a cup of coffee and set it down in front of him and he curved his hands around the cup, feeling the need to warm himself, to relieve the chill that was forming inside him. Pulling a blue-and-white ceramic bowl towards her, Dolly took a spoonful of sugar and held it over his cup.

"How many?"

"Two. Please."

While he watched, she ladled two heaping measures of sugar into his coffee, then stirred it, as you would for a child.

"Drink up, dear," she instructed. "Don't burn your tongue."

Obediently, he raised the cup to his lips and took a sip. The strength of the brew restored him; he could feel the caffeine acting on his tired brain, firing up those neurons, sending out signals to his body to wake up — act — get moving. He assumed Dolly, too, would pour herself a cup but instead she topped up her drink: a little more vodka, another dollop of tomato juice. Settling back in her chair, she reached a hand towards him and laid it on top of his.

"Skippy, dear, I don't know why I started telling you all these things, I really don't. I guess I just wanted you to be careful, you know? When it comes to Doris."

"Be careful? What should I be careful about?"

"Doris is my daughter and I love her. But I don't understand her, I never have. She's got a kind of toughness in her. And you seem like a nice person. So just be a little careful, okay? That's all I'm saying."

He finished his coffee in silence and when he was done Dolly took the cup and rinsed it in the sink. Then, gathering up the silver cigarette case, the box of matches and the rest of her drink, she led the way to the staircase. "I'll show you to her room but I can't promise you'll be able to wake her up. That girl could sleep through the last trumpet."

He followed her upstairs, keeping his eyes fixed on the way her robe swayed back and forth as she moved. At the top of the stairs, she stopped and indicated the door on the right.

"That's Doris' room. Good luck. And that —" she pointed to the one across the hall, "is mine. Just in case."

Just in case what? But he smiled and thanked her and she disappeared into her own room, pausing just before she closed the door to peer out at him and — he couldn't be sure but he thought she winked at him.

21.

The Hallowe'en session with the man in the mask put an end to Doris' modelling career and her relationship with J.P. She turned to him for comfort and he stroked her and patted her on the head like a small child and let her cry for a very long time. She hadn't cried since Candi died and when she finally stopped she was exhausted and lay on the couch while he sat next to her, holding her hand.

And then, when he was sure she was finished and there were no more tears, he explained that sometimes in this business there were things she might be asked to do like that, things that she might not be happy about, but they paid well. And if she was a good girl and did them and didn't complain and smiled at the camera like the wonderful actress he knew she was, she would make a great deal of money for both of them.

Doris sat up and stared at him. "You knew," she said and he shrugged.

"Well, yes," he admitted. "I gave the okay."

"You knew what was going to happen to me. You let it happen."

J.P. reached for her hand but she pulled it away. "Doris, you are my — how shall I put it? My property. No one is going to lay a hand on you without my permission."

"Get out."

He tried to put his arm around her and she stood up and backed away from him.

"Doris, don't be silly. You're behaving like a child. What did you think? You could go on posing in those little nightgowns for ever? You're not a new face anymore, you need a new market. There's very big money out there, Doris. You should be grateful."

She said nothing; she was afraid if she spoke she would cry. She wanted to throw herself at him, hit him, punish him. Instead, she walked over to the apartment door and held it open.

"Please leave," she said. "I don't ever want to see you again."

He stood up and for a minute she thought he was going to argue with her. Slap her, even, as he had done years before with Candi. But he didn't. With a shrug, he picked up his coat and gloves from the chair by the door and gave her a small, disdainful smile.

"You don't want to work? Fine. I certainly can't make you. I was doing you a favour, Doris, that's all. You don't think there are other pretty young girls out there who'd like to make such easy money? Doris, there are hundreds in this city. Thousands."

He turned to go and stopped at the door to adjust his tie in the mirror, as always. His back to her, he continued, "You were a nice girl, once upon a time, Doris. Sweet, innocent, there was something very appealing about you. But it's gone now." Satisfied with his appearance, he turned back to her and smiled. "You're nothing special now, Doris. I would have given you another six months in this business, a year, maybe. I felt sorry for you, that's all. I was just being kind."

When he left, she locked the door behind him and listened to his footsteps disappear down the hallway. He wouldn't be back.

She didn't work after that for almost two months. She didn't do anything. Every afternoon she woke up around two and made herself coffee and a piece of toast and took it back to bed where she could eat and listen to the radio. Sometimes she'd go all day without getting dressed, without going outside even once. The phone rang now and then, but she never picked it up. She'd made no close friends after Candi had died; J.P. had discouraged it.

And then there was the afternoon when she woke up and realized there was nothing in the apartment to eat and no money to pay the rent. And so she got dressed and did her hair and her makeup and it took her a very long time because everything did, these days, she moved very slowly. And when she was finally ready, she took a last look in the mirror in her bedroom and imagined she could see Candi standing just behind her, looking unhappy about what she was going to do.

"It's all right," she reassured the dead girl. "I know what I'm doing. I'll be okay."

And then she left the apartment and made her way down to the street and walked the few short blocks to the cocktail lounge she'd heard of, the one where men went to pick up girls. A man in a tailored sports jacket and a bright red tie approached her and made nervous conversation about the weather. His nervousness relaxed her, it gave her a feeling of being in control, and she smiled and stroked the sleeve of his jacket and asked about his work. After he'd had a second drink and a cigarette, he managed to bring himself to ask if she had a place nearby, and she linked her arm through his and they left. It was so easy; she'd never realized how simple it would be, an elementary business transaction, that's all. She had enough sense to make sure he paid her first and he didn't even haggle over the price — he seemed to think she was worth it. Should she have asked more, she wondered? But all she wanted was money for food and something towards the rent. Once she'd made enough to cover that, she wouldn't do it again. She wasn't about to become a full-time hooker.

Afterwards, as he was struggling into his clothes, the man asked her name and if he could call her again, "Next time I'm in town, eh? I mean, would it be okay, do you think?"

So she wrote her phone number down on the back of an envelope and as she handed it to him, he took her hand in his and held it for a moment. Did he want something else, she wondered? Did he think he hadn't gotten his money's worth?

All he did, though, was study her face for a few seconds and when he released her hand, he said, "Thank you." There was something sad in the way he said it and it occurred to her that although he was married, he had very likely had only a little more experience in bed than she had. She felt sorry for him but this was new to her, too, and she had no idea what to say to put him at his ease.

"Well, so long," she said and he nodded and turned around and fumbled with the lock and she had to unlock the door for him, to let him out.

When he was gone she ran herself a hot bath and sat in the tub till the water turned cold.

You had to be careful not to look like you were working when you made the rounds of the pick-up places. A woman on her own was always a target for the hotel dicks and you had to look respectable, wear nice, but not flashy, clothes, check your watch now and then like you were waiting for a friend. Doris always wore a simple, discreet black sheath with a strand of pearls, elegant but approachable. And she was careful, too, not to appear too friendly at first. It could be an undercover cop, you never knew.

Once she'd satisfied herself that the guy was an ordinary john, she'd do her best to hustle him out of the place and back to her apartment as soon as possible. She didn't want to attract attention.

The bartenders always knew; they had a nose for it. But they didn't care. She was just a girl out there earning a living, just like them. And she was an attractive addition to the scene, they were happy to have her there, a pretty girl like her. Some of them bought her drinks now and then — Shirley Temples, she wasn't about to put their jobs in jeopardy by trying to drink underage — and told her jokes when things were a little slow. The guy behind the bar at the St. James' was from the Bay, like her, and he had funny expressions that she remembered from living up north. "Smart like bull, strong like streetcar," that was one of them. Another time he leaned across the bar and winked at her and said, "Hey, Doris, what's the definition of an expert?"

"What?" she asked, getting ready to smile.

"Any sonofabitch from Toronto with a set of slides."

They both grinned; after all this time she didn't really consider herself a southerner. She was happy to have a laugh on the big city slickers.

And that was her life, for a little over a year. Three or four nights a week, just often enough to pay the rent, she would get dressed up and go down to one of a half-dozen nearby hotels. A nice-looking girl, sitting in the cocktail lounge, waiting for a friend. Stood up, maybe. She'd glance at her watch, now and then, and eventually a middle-aged salesman or a Shriner in a party mood would sidle over beside her and say something like, "Looks like your friend isn't going to show." Which would be her cue to smile a little ruefully, tell him he was probably right, and say, Well, yes, thanks, she would have another drink. Just a Coke, if you don't mind. I wouldn't want to drink and do anything silly. And the Shriner would grin and say, "Hell, no, we don't want that." There were variations on the theme, but that was pretty much how it went.

And, sooner or later, the john would suggest going back to her place or up to his hotel room and she'd get a little coy and reply that that could probably be arranged. What, exactly, did he have in mind? It was important to make sure they were in no doubt about what was going on here. Some of these out-of-towners could be unbelievably naive. She was willing to pretend she was madly in love with them once she'd been paid but she wasn't going to get herself picked up by some fellow who thought this was some kind of "date", and he'd just gotten amazingly lucky.

They tended to get a little sappy, once the actual act was finished, wanting to show her pictures of their children or grandchildren. Travelling salesmen were the worst, they were on the road so much and were usually awfully lonely. Sometimes the hardest part of the night was getting them to leave afterwards. She even had some marriage proposals, in spite of the fact that ninety-nine per cent of them were already married.

It was too good to last. Toronto went through one of its periodic moral upheavals and letters to the editor appeared in the paper about the "loose women" frequenting otherwise respectable establishments. There were appeals to the mayor and the chief of police to stop the "slide to Sodom and Gomorrah," and finally the vice squad stepped up its activities. One hotel barman after another let her know the cops were casing the place and she'd better find somewhere else to hang out. She tried streetwalking and got picked up her very first night out, ending up in a jail cell with three other girls and a character of uncertain gender. When they finally let her out the next morning, after a brief court appearance in which the charges against her were stayed because of her age, she went home, took a bath and dialed the number of an escort service. Her life as an independent working girl was over; now her appointments were arranged over the phone and she met her clients in hotel rooms, not in bars or on the street.

It was through the escort agency that she met the Pill Man, the doctor the girls all went to whenever they got an infection. Or worse. Doris was putting on weight and he gave her a prescription for diet pills and they worked: her appetite disappeared and she had much more energy during the day. But now she was finding it harder than ever to get to sleep and so she went back to see him and this time he prescribed stronger sleeping pills and some others which she was to take whenever she was depressed. She liked him and he was funny with her, he made jokes and kidded her as he wrote out the prescription.

"Now don't take these all at once," he would tell her and on the way out he would give her a quick, friendly pat on the bottom and call out, "Next! Come on, girl, I don't have all day."

He wasn't quite so jovial the time she went to see him because her period was late. Two months late, in fact, and she'd been throwing up in the mornings and feeling sick most of the day. She hadn't been able to work in almost a week. He gave her an internal exam and when she was dressed he called her into his office.

"Sit down," he told her, and when she did, feeling like a child who has been misbehaving, he leaned back in his chair and frowned.

"You're pregnant," he said, in the flat, impartial tones of someone who has delivered bad news hundreds of times before. "Twelve weeks, by my reckoning. Maybe thirteen. Why didn't you come to see me sooner?"

"I didn't know." She began to cry and was ashamed of herself, blubbering like a baby, right there in his office.

Her tears served only to irritate him. "Oh, for Christ's sake, it's not the end of the world."

But she couldn't reply and after a moment he shoved a box of Kleenex across the desk towards her and told her to take one.

While she wiped her eyes and blew her nose, he scribbled something down on a piece of paper, then handed it to her.

"Here's who you need to see," he said. "He's reliable, a little expensive but you don't want some back street butcher. Phone this number, leave your name and number and he'll call you back. And whatever you do, don't mention my name. All right? You did not hear about this from me."

Doris stared at the name and the address on the piece of paper, then looked up at the doctor. "But, I thought —"

"Yes?" He was pressed for time; he had a waiting room full of patients.

"I thought that you, well, you know —"

The doctor pushed back his chair and stood up, indicating that the appointment was over. "You thought wrong," was all he said and held the door open for her. "Next!"

The address the doctor had given her was in Rosedale, a large old house on a genteel street, set back on a quarter-acre of lawn. A thousand dollars, the man on the phone had said — in cash. She was to bring sanitary napkins and a change of underwear and someone to wait for her in the outer room and take her home when it was over. There would be no anaesthesia; there was no time for it. She had to be in and out of the building in under half an hour. If there were problems, afterwards, if she bled for a long time or got an infection, she was to go see her own doctor. And she was not to say anything, ever, about what had happened.

One of the girls from the agency came with her. Her name was Sheila and she was a Bay girl, too; she'd worked in a bawdy house up north until she got pregnant and came to Toronto to get rid of it. And stayed.

"You meet a better class of guy here," she told Doris. "Back home they were all sailors and hardly none of them ever spoke English. And they smelled. This is better."

She patted Doris' arm and told her not to worry, it wasn't so bad, it'd be over before she knew it. Doris tried to smile and tightened her grip on her handbag, to take her mind off her stomach. Her purse held a fortune in hundred dollar bills — ten of them, five of which amounted to her life's savings, so far, and the rest were a loan from the agency. They'd take it back, with interest, out of her earnings, but it was a godsend and she was grateful.

"They do this all the time," Sheila said. They were heading north in the back of a taxi and Doris was looking out of the window, telling herself not to think about anything, just to remember that by this time tomorrow it would be all over and she wouldn't be feeling as if she was going to be sick every other minute.

"It's a business expense, is what. All part of running the business. That's why you don't want to be doing this kind of thing alone, Doris. Imagine, if you didn't have the agency looking after you? I mean, then where would you be?"

Doris turned to look at her. "Where would I be?"

"Well, you know." And then, unable to come up with anything specific, Sheila just said, "Well, I guess you'd be in a fix, that's what."

Sheila waited in the outer office, pretending to read a magazine and listening for sounds from the other room. When Doris finally came out, moving very slowly, the colour drained from her face, Sheila dropped the magazine and started towards her, then stopped.

"Doris, are you okay?"

Doris nodded and leaned against the wall, to steady herself. The doctor, who had followed her out, told Sheila, "She'll be fine. Just see she gets home okay and let her rest for a while. Tell her to douche once a week and if she bleeds for more than ten days, she should go see her doctor." He was talking about her as if she wasn't there, as if she wasn't even a person, really, just this body he'd scraped out, nobody important. He opened the door and the two women left, Sheila's arm around her as they made their way slowly down the wide steps of the verandah, to the taxi waiting on the quiet street below.

"It's okay," Sheila whispered, giving Doris a shy but comforting squeeze. "You'll feel lots better tomorrow. It'll be all right."

She held on to Doris with one hand and opened the car door with the other. Doris lowered herself into the back seat and slumped against the far door. Just before the driver pulled away from the curb, she turned and looked behind her at the beautiful stone house, protected by a well-tended hedge and surrounded by a profusion of lilac trees, their pink and purple fragrance permeating the air. She turned to Sheila and whispered through lips which were swollen from where she'd bitten them, trying not to scream: "You said it wouldn't hurt."

"I know. I'm sorry." She, too, was whispering; they didn't want the driver to overhear. "It wouldn't of helped, if you'd of known, would it? It wouldn't of made it any better."

Doris shook her head. No. It wouldn't have.

It was Sheila who found her the night she took the pills. Doris had missed an appointment and the agency was concerned, her phone was off the hook and they couldn't get through. Judy, who ran the place, called Sheila and told her to get over to Doris', pronto. Sheila let herself in with the key Doris had given her and called 9-1-1. Then she called Judy and told her. And then, like Doris had done with Candi years ago, she sat and held her friend's hand until the ambulance came.

The following afternoon she arrived at the beginning of visiting hours and found Doris hooked up to an I.V., looking like death warmed over.

"Boy oh boy oh boy. You sure gave me one hell of a scare, I'll tell you. Why'd you do it, Doris? Did you mean to? Was it an accident?"

Doris tried to smile and patted the bed next to her. Her throat hurt too much to talk; they'd put a tube down inside her stomach to pump it all out. She picked up the notepad and pencil the nurse had left by her bed and scribbled a few words.

"Here," she whispered, handing the pad to Sheila.

"It was no accident," she had printed, "and I'll do it again."

When Sheila read that, she frowned and shook her head.

"Oh, no you won't. I talked to the doctor on the phone this morning and he says they're keeping you here for a while. Gonna knock some sense into that head of yours, Doris."

More scribbling. "Do they think I'm crazy?"

"No, sweetie, of course they don't. They're gonna help you, Doris, help you figure out why you wanted to do such a terrible thing. Why did you, anyway?"

Doris shrugged and wrote something on the notepad. "It seemed like a good idea at the time."

And so for six weeks Doris stayed in the hospital, playing cards when she was bored, which was much of the time, as this was a place for sick people and she wasn't sick, not really, only depressed and unable to come up with any good reason why she shouldn't be. For much of the day she would sit on the hard, narrow bed that the nurse had made up in the morning (coming in at six-fifteen, "Rise and shine" in that nursery voice, as if everyone in her care was an infant, senile or hard of hearing) and she would stare out the window, over the rooftops to the green branches of the trees in the park, which she saw without seeing, without caring much if she ever saw them again. She had walked through that park many times when she first came to this city, sat on its hard wooden benches and watched the old ladies who fed the pigeons and the self-important nannies who strode briskly down the paths, pushing large English baby carriages before them. It felt like home, sitting there, because people in parks generally behave much the same way everywhere — old men read newspapers, young couples neck, small children chase each other and play hide and seek among the trees.

It had been a very long time since she had any desire to sit on a bench and watch other people.

She wonders, sitting here in this sterile room, what else her life might have been. Who she might have become if she hadn't met J.P., or if Candi had lived, or if she'd never run away from home in the first place. She might have been married by now. Most of her old friends from school are married — Lindy Folgram married a dentist. And she's heard that Bobby Matthews married a local girl, a teacher, and lives in a house out in the country. He has ten acres of land and keeps chickens and geese and horses.

She has had a letter from her mother — the hospital demanded a name and address of next of kin and she told them about Dolly, although she hasn't heard from her mother in ten years, apart from the occasional Christmas card. Now it seems a doctor has written her mother and told her that Doris is in hospital and is depressed.

Which is strange, because she doesn't think she is depressed at all. Bored, perhaps, and tired of making appointments with old men, tired of drinking too much and taking too many pills. When she thinks of going on and on like this, for the rest of her life — well, death seems like a reasonable alternative. But she's not depressed.

Dolly's letter is full of remorse and self-pity. She's alone now, Ted died of cancer last year. She would have written Doris but she didn't know where she was. Nobody hears from her anymore, not even Lindy Folgram, who wasn't Folgram anymore now that she was married — some Jewish name, Dolly couldn't remember. It was awful, the last six months before Ted died, he was in terrible pain and he needed her there all the time, she couldn't go out, couldn't do anything. She had to take time off work to look after him but Mr. Pullen was retired now and her new boss wasn't very understanding, he told her if she didn't come back to work soon he'd have to lay her off. Lay her off, Doris, after all this time! Twenty-five years she'd worked in that place, putting up with Grant Pullen always grabbing her and trying to see down her blouse, and now they were looking for a reason to get rid of her. They still were, she wrote, even now that Ted was gone and she'd come back to work. They wanted to hire somebody younger, is what. They wanted to promote that new typist in the other office. And if they lay her off, what will she do? Ted left her with nothing, he never had any money, how will she live? And now this doctor says Doris is in hospital, she has tried to kill herself, is that Dolly's fault? Is the doctor suggesting that Dolly is to blame for what her daughter has done? Her daughter left home years ago, refused to have anything to do with her family, and now it's supposed to be Dolly's fault that there's something the matter with her head.

And on and on. Doris stares at the words on the page and wonders about the woman who wrote them. It's been so long since she saw her mother, it's as if a stranger was making claims on her. As for Ted — she can scarcely remember what he looked like. She used to think she would like nothing better than to hear he was dead; now, it doesn't seem to matter.

At the end of the letter, her mother writes, "Come home, Doris. I'm sure whatever's wrong with you could be fixed if you were here. And I don't like being on my own in this place. It's scary, being alone after all this time."

When the afternoon nurse comes in with her juice and medication, she sees the letter lying on the bed where Doris left it.

"Oh, a letter, Doris? Is it from somebody nice?"

Doris says nothing and the nurse picks it up and slips it back into its envelope, and tucks it away in the night table drawer.

Twice a day she takes the elevator down to the second floor to the large, airy room where they hold "group". Eight or nine other women, in various stages of undress, gather here to talk about themselves and each other; attendance, for those who are here due to "emotional problems", is mandatory. A nun who dresses in street clothes, but is still a nun, leads the sessions and directs each of them, in turn, to spill their guts. Its easier for some of the women than others; Doris stays silent most of the time, giving away nothing. She would tell them about a dream she's been having, almost every night, but she thinks she can work out what it means. She doesn't need their help.

She is walking down the street towards her grandmother's house and a man is walking beside her. It's her father, in his army uniform, grinning and making jokes, but it doesn't look like her father. The way he talks, the things he talks about, remind her of J.P. — or maybe it's somebody else altogether. At first they are walking together but after a while she realizes he is following her and she begins to walk more quickly and he follows her, step after step. She reaches her grandmother's house and goes inside and locks the door, leaving this man, this stranger out on the steps and she feels safe. It's all right, Grandma, she says, he can't get in. But then she sees one of the windows is open and he is reaching through, with great long arms and thick, hairy hands, like a gorilla. She slams the window down, pinning his arms between the window and the ledge, and then she takes an axe and cuts off his hands, at the wrists. And then she cuts the hands themselves into small, square pieces, little cubes of flesh. Like croutons, she thinks. Exactly like croutons.

The nun asks her why she thinks she is here, and Doris replies that it's obvious. Because she tried to kill herself. But why? the nun wants to know. What was her relationship with her father? How does she feel about her mother? What is she afraid of? Doris tells them she never knew her father and says nothing about Ted. If the nun knows the truth about her, what she does for a living, she keeps it to herself and Doris wonders if she is supposed to be grateful for that. She isn't; she could care less what these women think of her — these housewives, secretaries, teachers. They lead soft, protected lives with husbands and children to take care of them. What do they know about anything?

The nun talks about making choices, about admitting responsibility. Doris interprets that to mean it is her fault, Ted getting into bed with her, the man in the gorilla mask, the decision to kill her unborn baby. (None of which she has talked about; there are some things you can never talk about, with anyone.)

"God forgives everything," the nun says. "He sees into the human heart and understands all. Because He was human, too, in

Jesus Christ. There is nothing you cannot tell Him that He doesn't already know and nothing that cannot be forgiven. But, once forgiven, He expects you to try harder, to learn how not to repeat your mistakes."

The concept of forgiveness is foreign to Doris. She will never forgive Ted or her mother or J.P. And she does not expect God, if He exists, to forgive her; if she was God, she certainly wouldn't.

Her own saviour arrives in an unlikely form: a short, arrogant thug from her home town. A pimp, a gambler, a small-town con man. A hooligan with a heart not of gold, but of iron and steel, forged from the pit mines of the dense northern bush. His name is Arty Peach and Sheila has brought him, thinking he might amuse Doris, and the two of them sit with her at the long, low table where she glues small ceramic tiles together in a show of co-opera-tion. ("I'm afraid you're not trying," the nun has told her earlier that day. "You're withdrawing and not being part of things. You won't get better if you don't make an effort, Doris." And so she's come to this part of the ward where they teach women to weave potholders and make little, three-legged stands for teapots, and she feels like she's back in kindergarten.)

Smoking's not allowed in this room but this Arty fellow smokes anyway, is reprimanded by the ward nurse and tosses the cigarette into a wastebasket, which is, mercifully, empty of paper.

The following afternoon he is back on his own, bearing gifts, flowers and a cheap box of chocolates, the kind you buy in drugstores the day after Easter, and he sits on the end of her bed and tells her off-colour jokes, one after the other, scarcely drawing a breath between them. The jokes make her laugh but he doesn't crack a smile; it's almost as if he doesn't see the humour in them, although he has a natural ability for telling them. He wants to know when she's getting out and when she admits she could be out tomorrow if she wanted, he is puzzled.

"So why stay?"

"I'm not ready to leave."

He considers this but says nothing. When she goes to group that afternoon, the nun asks her about Arty, and it's obvious she doesn't approve. He's just a friend, Doris says. A friend of a friend, actually. Be careful, says the nun. You don't want to trust just anyone.

On the third day he's back with a present for her, a toy he bought in a joke shop on Yonge Street. It's a plastic model of the Pope and when you pull a string the Pope raises his arms in benediction and his robe goes up as well. He's naked underneath and anatomically correct. It's a silly, ridiculous toy, but it makes Doris laugh and that seems to satisfy Arty. She tells him to be sure not to let the nurses see it, they'll be shocked, and he tells her a joke about a nurse and a St. Bernard and she finds herself liking this tough, funny little man.

They sit out in the waiting room where they can smoke, and the room is empty except for a very overweight girl with lank, greasy hair who does not take her eyes from the TV when they come in. He says it's funny how they're both from the Bay and he never saw her around.

"I left years ago. When I was thirteen."

"Ran away from home."

She nods and for a few moments they smoke in companionable silence. The overweight girl is watching a quiz show and the host asks, "Who won the American Triple Crown in 1948?"

Arty says, "Citation," and Doris asks him if he watches a lot of TV.

"Naw. I just like to play the horses."

They watch in silence for a few more minutes and then Arty asks her about her hair, if she ever wears it up.

"I used to."

"You should. It'd suit you."

"And what do you know about women's hairstyles?"

"Not much. But I know what I like."

He's like a character out of a movie, she thinks. Bogey or Cagney or Edward G. Robinson. He speaks in a kind of tough-guy shorthand, picked up from the gangster films he grew up on. Her mother would have liked him. She would have played Bacall to his Bogey, Maureen O'Hara to his John Wayne.

He picks up a paper and leafs through it, casually. Without looking up, he asks, "You get out to Woodbine, much?"

"The race track? I was there once, a couple of years ago."

"Fella gave me a tip on the three o'clock tomorrow afternoon. Wanna come?"

"I can't. I'm in here, aren't I?"

"Then maybe you'd better check out."

The following day, at one o'clock, Doris stands by her bed, dressed in street clothes for the first time in over a month, her small, vinyl overnight bag packed, her hair back combed into a bouffant. The nun is upset that she's leaving, she says Doris isn't ready, she hasn't come to terms with her spiritual nature. Doris replies that she's not sure she has a spiritual nature and the nun says, Oh, no, dear, we all have a spiritual nature, it's just a question of finding it. In the end, though, she takes Doris' hand and tells her she'll pray for her and not to be afraid to call if she ever feels she needs a person to talk to. Then she leaves, a tidy, compact woman, troubled in her heart as always by the one that got away, the errant lamb that has yet to be rescued.

The clock over the door ticks past the hour; at one-oh-three the sharp click of the metal taps on the soles of Arty's boots is heard outside her door. He appears, resplendent in a powder-blue blazer and a bolo tie, and she sees that, in heels, she is a good four inches taller than he is.

He reaches for her bag and offers her his arm.

"Ready?"

Doris takes his arm and finds reassurance in the solid flesh beneath the sports coat.

"Ready," she says and turns to wave good-bye to the women in the rest of the ward.

"Take care of yourself," one of the women calls out and another adds, "Yeah, Doris. Don't forget to write."

Outside, on the sidewalk, she waits while Arty hails a cab and turns to look up at the building behind her. Her room was on the fourth floor but you can't pick it out from here. Rows of windows fastened shut, protecting the women from giving into any sudden, unfortunate impulses. She feels a brief, unexpected shudder run down her spine and experiences a momentary panic, a sense of loss, like when she took the pills and suddenly understood just what she had done, before slipping into unconsciousness.

Settled in the back seat of the cab, Arty offers her a cigarette and lights it.

"Okay?" he says and she nods. It's not true, not yet, anyway, but she thinks that one of these days, it will be.

When Arty first told her he was going back to Cambrian Bay, she was surprised to realize she would miss him. She'd been out of the hospital just over a month and had spent almost all of that time with him, sitting in her apartment, watching TV, going out to the race track in the afternoon, getting dinner afterwards at one of the places downtown. For someone who'd been in the city such a short time, Arty seemed to have a lot of "contacts", nervy, side-glancing hustlers like himself, in too-loud jackets and flashy ties.

"The stuff I do, you meet a lot of people," was the way he put it, although he didn't elaborate upon the nature of the "stuff".

Now he said he had to get back home, there were things he had to get to, plans he'd made. Big plans. He couldn't hang around much longer.

"Do you have to go?" she asked him, trying not to think of this place, trying not to visualize this apartment with just herself in it, nights of not sleeping, taking pills again just to get through the days. "Can't you stay a little longer?"

Arty flicked his lighter open and shut — it was silver, with a large, square turquoise stone set in the front of it — and said, "Maybe you should come with me."

"Back to the Bay? I couldn't. I haven't been home since I left. Not once."

"Do you good, maybe. Get you back on your feet."

She shook her head. "No, I couldn't. I really couldn't go back."

Arty shrugged and picked up the racing form and settled back into the sofa. "Suit yourself," he said. "It's no skin off my nose."

Sheila insisted on coming along to the train station, to see them off. She'd worn her new, broad-brimmed straw hat, for the occasion, and presented a remarkable, if somewhat unorthodox, figure in her teetering high heels, her off-the-shoulder peasant blouse and tight red skirt, clutching a garland of flowers. She pressed the pale blue clusters into Doris' hands and said, "They're forget-me-nots, right? I got them so's you wouldn't forget me. Oh, Doris, I'll sure miss you."

And to Arty's consternation she began to cry, right there in the station for all the world to see.

Doris thanked her for the flowers and gave her friend a hug. "It's okay, Sheila, you'll come visit. Maybe you'll move back one of these days, too."

Sheila shook her head, mournfully. "I don't think so. There's nothing there for me no more. I don't think I'll be going back."

"Well," said Doris, determined to be cheerful, although she, too, felt a little weepy, right at the moment, "we'll write, anyhow, eh? We'll be pen pals."

Sheila nodded and Arty grabbed Doris by the arm. "Come on," he said, pulling her in the direction of the train, "we gotta go. Dry up, Sheila, get a hold of yourself."

The women had one final embrace and Sheila asked if her mascara was running.

"A little," Doris admitted, "but it's okay. You look fine."

"I'm a mess and I gotta meet a fella in a half hour. Anyways, you guys have a great trip, eh? Say 'hi' to everybody for me."

Just as the train shuddered into motion, Sheila shouted something to Doris, who was leaning out of the window and waving.

"What?" Doris called. "What did you say?"

But it was too noisy and too late and with a roar of its engines the train pulled away from the station and Sheila was left, hanging on to her hat with one hand and waving frantically with the other.

22.

Doris' bedroom. He was about to enter Doris' bedroom, her most private place, and she was in there right now, asleep. Dreaming, maybe. Perhaps even dreaming of him. He thought that if he could keep this moment for ever, standing just outside her door, guarding her room while she lay sleeping, never waking up, he would like to do that. The sentry at the door, he thought to himself. The guardian angel.

Dolly had said she was a heavy sleeper but even so he turned the handle stealthily, opened the door slowly, not wanting to wake her, almost afraid to see her there, so still, so vulnerable. Heavy curtains were pulled shut across the window so the room, in spite of the morning sun, was pitch dark. He shut the door and carefully felt his way over to the bed which he could just make out was small, the bed of a child, tucked into the corner of the room. He trod on something soft and stooped to pick up a large stuffed animal: a rabbit, it felt like, or maybe a bear. Carrying the toy, he moved forward again until he felt the wooden frame of the bed against his shins; he was close enough now to hear her breathing, softly, with just an occasional gentle snore. Carefully, he lowered himself until he was perched on a small space beside her on the bed and placed the stuffed toy at the far end, against the wall.

Doris was sleeping on her side, one arm curled under her pillow, the other resting above the blankets. That arm was bare and Skippy wanted to reach out and stroke it with the tips of his fingers, but he held back, not wanting to wake her up. Not just yet. It was too dark to tell what she was wearing or if she was wearing anything, but he pictured her in the white, filmy dress she had worn in his dream. Something loose and flowing, he thought, sprinkled with flowers. He caught the scent of her perfume, still strong as though she had dabbed some behind her ears before going to bed. And something else, a smell of soap, or toothpaste.

She was like a girl out of one of those shampoo ads on TV and she smelled as you knew they did — fresh and pure, like summer. For some reason, just then, the young girl with the whip came into his mind and he remembered how he had thought it was Doris, had been desperate to get into that upstairs room and save her. But it wasn't Doris, it was Ruby, and he thought that maybe there were hundreds of girls like that, thousands, maybe, who were sweet and pure and needed saving. Someone else would have to save Ruby; his quest lead directly to Doris.

Gently, he put a hand on her bare shoulder. Her skin was smooth and cool to the touch, like the porcelain figurine of the dancing lady his mother had kept on her dresser when he was young. Skippy used to sneak into her room when he was little and run his fingers over the dancer's body, her arms and legs and her long, lithe torso. He wasn't allowed to pick her up, he wasn't supposed to touch her, but he craved the feeling of her cool limbs in his grubby little hands. Whatever happened to the dancing lady, he wondered as he stroked Doris' arm and watched her breathe in and out, the blankets moving gently up and down as she slept? Had he broken the figure in some childhood accident now blotted out and forgotten? Or had his mother tired of her and packed her away in a box in the attic with his childhood toys and his Captain America comics? Art Deco, his mother called her, picked up on impulse years before when she was a young working girl just out of school. The only nice thing I ever bought myself, she told Skippy once, and he'd been filled with a longing to buy her lots of nice things and to scatter them all over the house.

Now he ran his fingers up and down Doris' arm and whispered her name. She stirred in her sleep and he bent his head close to hers and said, "Doris, it's me. Wake up, Doris. I need to talk to you."

She opened her eyes and looked up at him. "Arty? What are you doing here?" And then her eyes closed and she was asleep again.

Well, of course she would think it was Arty. She would never expect Skippy to be here in her bedroom, uninvited. He refused to be upset by this, it was only natural. Once she woke up, really woke up, that is, she would see it was him and not Arty and she would be happy to see him, he knew it.

Taking care not to disturb her, he stood up and went over to the window, pushing back the curtains to let a little light into the room. Now he could see that this room was in stark contrast to the rest of the house, its walls painted a plain, untinted white, the floor covered in a dark linoleum with an oval scatter rugjustbythebed. Exceptfortheheavydarkcurtainsandthenylons and bra thrown over the back of a chair, there was no indication of the kind of person who slept here, no sense of who she was or what she liked to do. There were no photographs on the dresser, no books or magazines beside the bed, not even the mystery novels he knew she liked to read. Besides the bed, the only other furniture was a small dressing table covered with some flouncy material and a matching chair that looked too small, the property of a child, as was the bed. Perhaps they had belonged to Doris when she was a girl; if so, he wondered why there were no pictures of her as a child. The stuffed toy looked out of place — he wondered if it was a recent acquisition, something she'd won at the fair. Or something someone had won for her.

He walked back to the bed and knelt down beside her, delighting in the perfect features of her face, revealed now in the light through the window. She wore no makeup, and she looked, if possible, more beautiful than ever. He thought she suited this pale creamy look, her dark eyebrows contrasting with her hair and eyelashes, which were so light they disappeared altogether without makeup. There was a poem he'd learned in high school, what was it? The Lady of Shalott, that was it, floating downstream with pale hands folded on her chest — that's how Doris appeared now. The beautiful, peaceful Lady of Shalott, virginal heroine of Tennyson's poem.

Skippy leaned over and kissed her, softly, on the lips, and tasted the mint of her toothpaste along with something else, face cream, perhaps. He loved kissing Doris. She'd told him once that she didn't particularly like kissing, she'd laughed and said she wasn't very good at it. But he knew that wasn't true; there was something so perfectly passive about the way she held her lips slightly open when he pressed his against them, the way a child would. Some women used their lips as a challenge, a sort of weapon to draw a man in even further. But there was nothing sexual about Doris' kisses — their very lack of cunning made them almost painfully intimate. She didn't kiss so much as let herself be kissed, a small, sacrificial token which gave almost excruciating pleasure.

He kissed her again, then carefully pulled the blanket down and kissed her on the neck and on the shoulder that was nearest him and then, very gently, he put his lips against the soft, silky material that covered her breasts. Here she was warm and he kept his face there and felt her heart beat, felt her chest rise and fall with her breathing.

"I love you," he whispered and then said it again, more loudly, "Doris, I love you."

He stroked her face, her hair and the hollow of her neck and felt the delicate bones of her upper chest. His hand moved further, to touch the top of her nightgown, and then, carefully, he slipped it under the silk and felt the smooth fullness of her breast. Slowly, with his free hand, he pulled back the top of her nightgown until the breast was revealed and placed his mouth over the nipple. Beautiful, he thought. Beautiful, perfect Doris, his Doris, asleep with his lips on her breast. His breast, a breast that belonged to him. He was more aroused now than he had ever been in his life — in bed with Benny's wife Margaret, conjuring up images of the shiny brown body of Mardou Fox, these moments were nothing to the excitement he felt at this moment with his head bent over Doris' breast.

He felt her move under him and then a hand touched his hair.

"Arty. When did you get here? Why didn't you tell me —"

He raised his head and she stared at him, bewildered, seeming not to know who he was. Then, "Skippy? Is that you?"

He smiled, his hand still cupping her breast. "Doris. I came to see you —"

Doris pushed his hand away, roughly, grabbed the blanket and pulled it over her, then sat up in bed. She was wide awake now and she didn't look happy.

"What the hell are you doing here?" she demanded. "Are you crazy? How the hell did you get in here, anyway?"

Skippy didn't know how to respond. This wasn't what he had expected, she seemed so angry, in fact, she seemed furious and it took him a minute to adjust. He stood up and stepped back from the bed, stumbling against the chair and almost knocking it over. Reaching for it, he lost his balance and ended up sprawled on the floor beside her, his bad leg twisted beneath him.

"Answer me, for Chrissakes," she said. "What do you think you're doing, breaking into my room, feeling me up like that? I tell you, Skippy, you answer me this minute or I swear I'll call the cops. No, I'll call Arty, that's what. He'll be here in two seconds flat and you'll be in deep shit, you know that? Really deep shit."

"I didn't break in. She, your mother — she let me in."

"My mother? What the hell did she do that for?"

"I told her I had to see you. I said it was urgent."

Doris was silent for a moment, watching him. He felt she was sizing him up, trying to decide if he was safe or if she should go ahead and kick him out.

"Oh, for God's sake, get up off the floor," she said, finally. "You look ridiculous."

Using the chair for support, Skippy got to his feet and said, "I'm sorry, Doris, I didn't mean to upset you. I came in to talk to you and

I guess I just got carried away."

"I'll say you did. They should carry you away, that's what I think."

Now she sounded almost humorous, almost like her usual self. Skippy was relieved; he didn't know this other, angry Doris who swore and spat out words at him like they were poison darts, aimed straight at his heart.

"What time is it?" she asked and Skippy looked around for a clock. There was one on the night table by her bed, its hands and numbers glowing in the dark.

"A quarter to nine," he told her and she looked shocked.

"In the morning? A quarter to nine in the morning? Do you have any idea how early that is for me? I didn't get to bed till after five. I'll have bags under my eyes all day long."

"I'm sorry," he said again, thinking he should say something but not wanting to set her off again.

She groaned and slumped back against the pillow. "Oh, shit, Skippy. Sit down. Don't stand there hanging over me like that. You're making me nervous."

Immediately, he obeyed and settled himself at the end of the bed, nudging the stuffed toy to one side.

"I guess you don't have a cigarette." It was a statement, not a question; she knew he didn't smoke.

"I could go get you one," he offered but she shook her head.

"Forget it," she said, "I'm trying to quit anyway."

She stared at him and sighed. "How long have you been here?"

"About half an hour."

"Half an hour? You were creeping around in the dark in my room for half an hour before I woke up? What are you, Skippy, some kind of pervert?"

"No, no. I was downstairs. Talking to your mother."

"My mother?" Doris sounded more alarmed than ever. "What were you talking to her about? What did she say about me?"

"Nothing, Doris. Nothing at all." He tried to reassure her. "She was telling me about herself, that's all."

"Oh, I'll bet she was. Dolly McGillvray's favourite topic is Dolly McGillvray. Did she tell you how she was practically a baby when she had me? Did she tell you how I wrecked her life?"

"I thought she was kind of lonely, actually."

"Don't waste your time worrying about her. She has plenty of company, believe me."

Suddenly she threw back the covers and made her way over to the dressing table. Opening a drawer at the side, she rummaged around for a minute, coming up empty-handed. "God, I could use a cigarette."

"Do you want me to go get one from your mother?"

"Where is she?"

"In her room. She went back to bed, I guess."

"And she didn't invite you to join her? Gee, she must be slipping. Getting old I guess."

"I think she worries about you."

"I'd say it's a little late for that." Climbing back into bed, she pulled the covers over her and settled back against the pillows. "All right, Skippy, why don't you tell me what you're doing here? What's so urgent that you have to wake me up in the middle of the night and practically give me a heart attack?"

There was something he wanted to ask. It wasn't what he'd come for but now he had to know. "Are you in love with Arty Peach?"

"What?"

"When you woke up, you thought I was Arty. Were you hoping it was him? Do you love him?"

Doris laughed, in spite of herself. "So you've come all the way over here just to ask me if I love Arty? Skippy, don't you think this could have waited till tonight?"

"Do you?" He knew he was sounding like a stubborn little boy but he couldn't help it. If she loved Arty, that small-town thug, the guy who might even be her pimp, for all Skippy knew, if that was the case — well, he didn't know what to think. But he had to know.

She sighed and said, "Arty and I have a relationship, I told you that. We sort of take care of each other. The truth is, if it weren't for Arty, I'd probably be dead by now."

"But do you love him?"

"I don't think that's any of your business."

"How can you say that? I love you, Doris. Everything about you is my business."

"Well, Skippy, that's very sweet, but —"

"Do you love him?" He was desperate now, desperate to find out, to hear her say, No, of course she didn't love him, she loved Skippy, didn't he know that?

"Look," and now her voice was losing its tenderness, she was beginning to sound a little fed up, "I don't know what's got into you, coming over here like this, giving me the third degree, but I've had just about enough. I'm tired, I worked last night and I've had about three hours' sleep. I think you'd better go. Okay?"

Skippy stood up and felt in his pants pocket for the photograph. He took it out of the envelope and tossed it in her direction and it fluttered through the air and landed on top of the blanket, right beside her. Doris picked it up.

"What's this?"

Skippy went over to the window and pushed the curtains all the way back, flooding the bedroom with light. He wanted to see her face, he wanted to see the effect the picture would have on her. But if he was expecting her to be upset or surprised or angry, he was disappointed. She studied the photograph and when she looked up at him there was a smile on her face.

"Well?"

"It's you, isn't it?"

"Well, it ain't Annette Funicello," she said.

She was teasing him, trying to make him feel foolish, and this made him angry and more belligerent than he would have been otherwise.

"I asked you if it was you."

"Oh, for God's sake, Skippy. Yes, it's me. You know that."

"Don't you want to know where I got it?" he asked.

"I suppose you got it from Harlan."

"Who?"

"Harlan Wilson," she said. "The old guy who likes to take the pictures. Wasn't it him?"

"Harlan," he repeated. "So you and *Harlan* are on a first-name basis, is that it?"

"Skippy, what's the matter with you? Have you been drinking?"

"Of course," he continued, "you're not going to call him Mister Wilson, are you? It would be a little strange, wouldn't it, calling him *Mister* Wilson when you're lying there with nothing on having your picture taken? You wouldn't say *Mister* Wilson then, would you?"

Doris got out of bed and brushed past him, on her way to the door. He grabbed hold of her arm and she said to him, in a very cold voice, "Let go of me, Skippy. I think this has gone far enough."

"No." He was shaking and he felt sick to his stomach. He hadn't eaten since yesterday, he'd had four hours sleep, maybe five. He felt like he was going to throw up. But his voice, when he spoke, was surprisingly calm: he didn't sound frightened at all. He sounded like a man whose mind was made up.

"I'm not leaving, Doris. I'm staying right here until you explain to me how you could let that old man take pictures of you like that. I want you to tell me."

"Let go of me," she repeated. "I'm not about to talk to you at all while you're treating me like some kind of criminal."

So he did as she said and dropped her arm and she picked up her hairbrush from the dressing table and sat down on the small wicker chair in front of the mirror. While Skippy stood beside the bed, hoping that somehow she would tell him something that made sense, something that would put everything back together again, Doris began to brush her hair with short, angry strokes. She was quiet for a long moment.

"What do you want me to say, Skippy? You want the truth, is that it? You think I lied to you or something, is that what you think?"

Before he could answer, she continued, speaking to his reflection in the glass. "Well, I never lied to you, Skippy. I just never talked about some things is all."

"That's not true. You lied about Minneapolis, you said your mother got you the cigarette case. You went there with Arty, didn't you? It was Arty got you the cigarette case. And the watch. And what about Christmas? You told me you went to Las Vegas with your mother. That was Arty, too, wasn't it?"

"All right, I did lie about some things. I felt bad about standing you up that night, I knew you wouldn't want to know I'd been with Arty. So I lied. And Christmas — well, I was going to tell you but then you gave me that coat and it was just so terrific and so sweet of you, well, I didn't have the heart. I mean, I just felt so bad about taking this expensive present and then leaving on you like that."

"Not bad enough to cancel your trip."

"I couldn't. Even if I'd wanted to, I couldn't. Arty, he'd been planning it for ages, it was sort of a working holiday, I guess. I couldn't cancel on him, it wouldn't have been fair."

"But it was fair to lie to me about it? To make up all that junk about your mother and her boyfriend and all that? You think that was fair?"

She lay the brush down on the table and turned to face him.

"I thought I was protecting your feelings, that's all. And anyway, it's not like we were going to spend Christmas together, were we? I see you once a week, down at the club, right? What I do the rest of the time is my own business."

He walked over to the window and looked down at the street below. The girls had abandoned the shopping cart for a skipping rope and were pretending to be horses — at least, the bigger girl was, the rope tied around her waist as she bucked and neighed and shook her head in the air, while the other girl attempted to pull her into line.

Keeping his eyes fixed on the street, Skippy said, "You were never honest with me, Doris. You never really told me anything."

"I didn't think it mattered. I mean, you never asked me what I did, except for that one time. You must've known, you must've guessed, and I figured — well, I figured it didn't matter to you. I mean, all that stuff you talk about, beatniks and Buddha and all, I just figured that people like you didn't make a big deal about what a person did. And I thought —"

She stopped, and now Skippy turned towards her and urged her to go on, he wanted to hear what she had to say.

"I thought you didn't want sex. I mean, some guys, they aren't interested, you know? I thought you were one of those."

One of those. She thought he was a eunuch. His voice, when he spoke, was flat. "You told me you were a model."

"I was. I did a lot of modeling, when I was in Toronto. And I did pose for Chatelaine that one time, you saw the pictures. But most of the stuff I did, well, it wasn't the kind of thing you'd find in ladies' magazines."

The photograph was lying on the bed, on top of the covers where she had dropped it. Skippy picked it up and studied it.

"You were smiling," he told her. "You looked like you were enjoying it."

"I was enjoying it. For God's sake, it's a helluva lot easier than some of the things I'm paid to do and Harlan is very appreciative." She smiled and somehow that made him angry all over again, that she would think of the old man and smile.

"I bet he is." Skippy didn't try to keep the bitterness out of his voice; his world was falling apart, right here in Doris' bedroom.

"Do you know how much he pays me to pose for him, Skippy? One hundred dollars. Can you believe that? Do you know how hard I have to work to make a hundred dollars?"

"I don't want to know," he said, "I don't want to hear about it. Why can't you do something else, some other kind of work? Why can't you work in an office, like other women, or be a waitress or — something? Why do you have to do this, Doris? Why?" He stopped and turned away, embarrassed that she should see him like this, pleading with her, almost crying. He longed for that cold anger that had given him so much strength just a few minutes ago; it was gone now, he was weak and unhappy and contemptible. He wished he had never come, but more than that, he wished he had never seen Wilson's collection of photographs.

If Doris was aware of his misery, she didn't show it. "Waitressing," she said. "Let me tell you about waitressing. They pay you ten dollars a day and tell you to make it up in tips and how do you get tips? By smiling and wearing your uniform nice and tight and leaning over the table so the guys can see something. And that's not prostitution? Forget it. Being a whore is a lot more honest and it pays better. A lot better."

"But what about me?"

"What about you?" she asked.

"I love you, Doris," he said, hating the way the words came out, weak and feeble sounding, like a sick, unhappy child. "I want to marry you."

Of course, she thought. Of course he would want to marry her, his kind always did, eventually. He had kissed her, he had held her hand, he had bought her presents and she had thought that was it for him, he got his kicks being near her, probably couldn't do anything else. After all, there was that leg of his, maybe the polio had killed off some other parts as well, it wouldn't be the first time. She'd known other guys who couldn't do anything, they paid her to walk around naked, talk dirty. Or just sit there and look gorgeous. It wasn't so unusual. As for the presents he'd given her, the mink coat and the television set, well, she'd earned them, hadn't she? She'd given up her time to be with him, he could certainly come up with the occasional gift.

Not that she hadn't enjoyed it. It had been a pleasant break — she had enjoyed her three hours each Sunday night, sitting in the dim light of the club, listening to music, feeling relaxed. It had been worth it to get away from Arty for a while, telling him she was working, she had a regular customer who met her at the club, telling him the guy was shy so he, Arty, should stay away, she didn't want to scare him off. Just spending time each week with some guy who wanted nothing from her, that was what she liked about it. But she was wrong: he did want something from her, after all.

"I'm sorry, Skippy, but I don't want to get married. I just don't feel like that about you. So forget it."

"It's my leg, isn't it?" he said. It was a low blow and he knew it but at this point he felt he would do just about anything to make her agree to be with him, even if it was only out of pity.

"You make too much of that leg," she told him, echoing his mother. Walking over to the closet, she pulled a dressing gown from a hanger and slipped it on. When she had tied the sash into a bow, she came back to the bed, sat down next to him and took his hand in hers.

"Skippy, let me tell you something," she said. "You think you can make both our lives better by marrying me, don't you? You think that'll change things. It won't. It won't change a single thing except make both of us very unhappy."

"You're wrong, Doris," he began, eager to prove to her that *this* marriage, the marriage he had in mind, would be different.

But she wasn't listening. "You know what marriage is to me? Marriage is just exactly what I've been doing, only worse. You don't get paid and you don't have the right to say no. I can't imagine giving up what I do just to turn around and do it with some guy for nothing. And then when you're old and your looks are gone, he walks out on you, and then where are you? Or maybe he just dies on you and you're like my mother, stuck on welfare and living in some housing project, drinking too much and relying on married boyfriends to buy you presents now and then. Forget it, Skippy, that is definitely not for me."

He opened his mouth to argue with her, to explain that he'd never treat her like that, he'd never drop her for someone younger, someone more beautiful — but she placed a finger on his lips and shushed him.

"You're a good person, Skippy, but let me tell you something: Everybody wants something in this world. Anybody ever tells you they don't want anything, don't believe them. They're lying. The only thing I ever wanted was my freedom. I ran away from home when I was just a kid because of it and I supported myself for years and one of these days I'm going to be free and nobody is going to be able to make me do anything I don't want to do. And if you think I'm going to trade one form of prostitution for another where you don't even get paid and have to iron the guy's shirts as well —" She paused, shook her head and smiled: "Well, then, Skippy Jacques, if you think that, you're crazy."

"But I thought — I wanted —"

"What? Go ahead, tell me. What did you want?" She was smiling now; she'd forgiven him for bursting in on her like this, for waking her up and demanding to know about Arty and Wilson and all that. And he knew, by the very kindness he saw in her face at this moment, that what he was about to propose was doomed.

"I wanted to go away with you."

"Go away? What — for the weekend?"

"No. For a long time. For good, maybe." The next few sentences sounded odd, even to him: "I wanted us to go on the road, to New York. I thought we could buy an old car, or rent one, and drive across the States, just the two of us. We could go see Johnny Carson and listen to music and hang out in Time Square. I've got the money. I've even got clothes for you to wear. They're packed. I brought the suitcases with me."

Doris was staring at him; there was a wary look in her eyes as if she thought he might be just a little bit crazy.

"You're saying you planned a trip," she said and he nodded.

"You worked it out that you and me should go away and you even bought clothes for me and brought them here. And you figured you'd tell me this and I'd get dressed and go away with you. Is that it?"

He nodded again. For a moment she looked as though she couldn't quite believe what she was hearing and then, unexpectedly, she started to laugh. There was nothing malicious about her laughter — she wasn't meaning to be unkind — but it obviously suddenly struck her as very funny and she leaned back against the pillow and laughed for several minutes, while Skippy sat there, sinking more and more deeply into a state of abject misery. Finally, she calmed down and sat up and shook her head, still grinning, and told him she was sorry.

"I really am," she said. "But, well, Skippy, the whole idea — it's just —"

"Funny," he said and she placed a hand on her chest and gave out a huge sigh.

"I'm sorry," she repeated. "But tell me, Skippy, what were you going to do about Arty? I mean, what were you planning to tell him?"

Feeling sulky and more than a little ridiculous, he muttered, "I wasn't planning on telling him anything."

"But I couldn't just up and leave Arty like that. I wouldn't want to. And anyway, he'd never let me go while I was still useful to him. Another few years, he might be glad to get rid of me. Arty always says there are two things the world doesn't need: honest cops and old whores."

"But we could be halfway across Minnesota by tonight, he'd never catch us. I've got it all figured out. We could be in Minneapolis by suppertime, if we left right now —"

"Skippy." There was a finality in her voice and he knew he wasn't going to like what came next.

"You know what I learned a long time ago? I learned that sometimes you have to know when to let go. When to get out of the ring before somebody punches the shit out of you. It's not going to happen, Skippy. Let it go, okay? It's just not going to happen."

He looked so sad, so completely defeated, that Doris knew it was all right to be kind to him. It was over and he knew it.

"Give me a hug," she said. "It's not the end of the world."

He held on to her and buried his face in the warmth of her robe and let himself believe, just for a moment, that this was the way it was. Too soon, she pulled away.

"I don't know about you but I think I need a cup of coffee."

Feeling very bleak, he followed her out the door and down the stairs to the kitchen. While Doris measured out the coffee and water into the percolator, he sat at the table and thought about the suitcases parked in the hallway. He wouldn't be needing them now, or at least, Doris wouldn't. Or the car. Or the Rand McNally road map. The whole road trip had gone up in smoke, just like that. It had disappeared as suddenly as it had three years earlier, when Margaret got pregnant and Benny had dropped everything to marry her. First Benny, then Doris had let him down.

But had they, he wondered? Maybe it was he who'd let himself down. He had spent so many years asking for nothing, accepting whatever came along and accepting just as easily when it was taken away from him. It wasn't Benny and Doris who had betrayed him — he had managed that all on his own. He'd listened to his heart and ignored his stomach. He'd been a fool. When it came right down to it, Skippy Jacques was a poor, pathetic chump who stood on the sidelines of life, waiting for the odd handout and getting splashed with mud as the rest of the world drove by.

Doris sat down at the table across from him and took his hand in hers.

"You're a nice guy, Skippy," she told him, "and I've really enjoyed our evenings together. I want you to know that. You were always a perfect gentleman and in my work you don't meet a lot of guys you can say that about. And actually, I'm glad you came by this morning. I wanted to tell you something and I was going to wait till I saw you tonight but no time like the present, huh?"

Once again, Skippy sensed he wasn't going to like what he heard but it didn't seem that there was much more she could tell him this morning that would make him feel any worse. She wasn't going to go on the road with him — wasn't that enough?

"I'm leaving town," she said.

It took a minute to register and when it did, Skippy felt as if he'd been kicked — hard — in the stomach.

"What do you mean?"

"I'm going to Vancouver. That is, we're going, me and Arty, next month. He's been talking about it for a long time, he says this is a one-horse town and the horse is dead, and he's got all these deals coming up out west —"

"What kind of deals?" His voice came from some far away place that wasn't part of him and the part that was still himself wondered how he was managing to speak at all.

She laughed. "Oh, Arty type deals. He's got these big plans. He always has, he's always working on the big deal, the one that's going to set him up so he's rich and never has to do another one. But you know what I think?"

"What?" he managed to say, although he had no desire to hear anything, ever, about Arty Peach. Not now. Not ever.

Doris leaned forward, confidentially. "I think Arty's never going to be rich and he'll be planning deals until the day he dies."

Skippy waited until he knew he could speak again. "So why are you going with him, then?"

"Does it matter?"

"I need to know."

She considered before speaking, judging what she knew about him, how much he would be able to understand. "He needs me," she said, finally. "He's the first man I ever met who did. You'll probably find that hard to believe, thinking of Arty like that, but I knew it the first time I met him. And I guess I decided that was important."

Doris stood up and went over to the cupboard and took out a couple of cups and saucers. "You know," she said as she carried them back to the table, "I'll probably never have children. I couldn't stand to have a kid and turn out to be the kind of mother I had. I just wouldn't want to take the risk. So I guess you could say that, in a way, Arty's my kid. Some women have cats, I've got Arty."

"What about me?" he asked. "What do I do, now that you're leaving?"

She patted his hand — it was an affectionate pat, the way you'd pat the hand of an old friend. "You'll figure something out, Skippy. You'll work out what to do. For one thing, you've got a club to run, right? You'll be 'way too busy to be worrying about me."

He stood up. "I have to go now," he said, feeling as if he might be going to be sick.

"What about your coffee? Don't you want a cup before you leave?"

He shook his head and made his way through the living room, past the paint-by-number clowns in their bow-ties and bright orange wigs. It occurred to him now, although he hadn't noticed it earlier, that they all had large, unhappy eyes, not just the ones who were supposed to be sad but all of them — wide, melancholy eyes above enormous painted grins. As if they knew they were defeated before they'd even begun.

Doris accompanied him to the door and she stood there, her arms wrapped around her body. "I'll sure be glad to get out of this place," she told him, indicating the paintings on the walls. "These guys give me the creeps."

The suitcases were waiting on the front step where he'd left them.

"What do you want me to do with these?" she asked and when he said he didn't care, she said she'd send them on to his boarding house, in a cab.

They stood on the concrete step in front of the house and the smell of her perfume mixed with the faintly muddy, watery smell of spring.

"It's going to be a nice day," she said and he nodded.

"I don't have a picture of you," he said, wanting to put off saying good-bye, wishing he was still upstairs in her room, his questions still unasked, no final words spoken.

"Yes, you do. It's in your pocket."

He reached into his pants and pulled out Wilson's photograph and stared at it, thinking how strange it was that it had already begun to lose some of its power. A pretty girl on a bed in a short, dark wig. Looking up at the camera as if there was still something good to be found there, some reason to smile, if only because an old man was watching, an old man admiring her body.

"Do you want me to autograph it?" she smiled and he let her take the photo and go back into the house with it, in search of a pen. In a moment she was back and she handed the picture to him with a flourish.

"There you go," she said. "It's all yours."

He flipped it over and read what she had written: In a careful script, the letters rounded, child-like, "To Skippy: Keep climbing. Love, Doris."

"Will I see you tonight?" he asked, knowing the answer.

She shook her head and smiled. "I don't think so." And then, unexpectedly, she leaned forward and kissed him, gently, on the cheek.

"Take care, Skippy," she said. "Be good to yourself."

Outside, the sun was already moving high in the sky and the two little girls were nowhere to be seen. Skippy walked down the sidewalk to the end of the street and stood for a moment with his hands in his pockets, looking back at the house on the corner. He felt empty, the way you do when you've come to the end of something, but there was also a sense within him of having faced the worst that could happen, stood and looked it in the face and not run away. He was alone and he was foolish but he was not afraid.

The wallet with the money in it pressed against his chest. If he caught the next bus downtown, he could transfer to the one that went out to the west end and catch Margaret and Katie before they left. He'd slip the money through her mail slot, with a note. *For Margaret from Skippy. Your friend.* Something like that. And maybe one of these days he'd hitch a ride out to the reserve, see if he could find the place Benny was living now, invite him to come down to the club. He'd ask him, anyway. It couldn't hurt to ask.

Epilogue

Across the Jackknife Bridge and west along the old River Highway, the Ojibway are enclosed in a section of land known as the reserve. Here at the foot of the mountain these people, once the proud caretakers of the spruce and birch forests and the trout-infested waters, live out of sight of the rest of the community. It is a wealthy reserve, as reserves go, but you would never know it by the condition of the homes, each with its requisite clutter of rusted-out vehicles abandoned in the yard and a roof that needs mending or replacing altogether.

In the midst of these houses, a short distance along the dusty road that leads up to the first ledge of the mountain, stands the chapel of St. Francis, recently restored, and behind this chapel, in an unshaded area exposed to the harsh sunlight, Benny Carter is building a garden. For three days now, with the blessings of the parish priest, he has been digging up the soil, uncovering rocks of various shapes and sizes which he sets aside, in order to study them later in more depth. The rocks, of which there are an overabundance in this hostile part of the world, have plagued settlers for four hundred years. Benny, however, welcomes them, for he is building a rock garden, a *karensansui*, according to the philosophy of the *Sakuteiki*, the ancient Japanese book of gardens. Small in scale, in the *kansho* style, it will be a place for contemplation, an attempt to express the universe in a small, dry space. "Seeing the great in the small," as the Chinese have put it.

Having completed the digging for the moment, Benny has been hard at work all morning with a long-handled rake, creating a smooth, flat surface on which to assemble his garden. In many ways this is the most difficult part of the project; there must not be a ripple that is not planned, a bump that has not been carefully thought out. When he has finished this task, he will roll the soil flat and cover it with fabric and six inches of white sand or gravel. And he will build an enclosure for the garden, a woven cedar fence that will serve two purposes: it will keep out the packs of stray dogs that roam the reserve and it will stop the eye and the mind from wandering and facilitate meditation.

As he pulls the rake back and forth across the coarse ground, he visualizes the garden when it is finished: clusters of carefully-chosen rocks placed at strategic intervals across a gravel bed which has been patiently raked to depict the flow of a river, with concentric circles drawn around the rocks themselves, ripples in the stream. A low stone bridge spanning the upper part of the "stream", where visitors to the garden can sit and listen for the sound of the water in the dry rocks and gravel. Balance and harmony, the achievement of equilibrium between the yin and the yang; that is the purpose of the Zen temple garden.

The building of the garden itself is an exercise in Zen meditation and when it is finished it will be watched over by the *kami*, or spirits, who live in the mountain. A holy place, well suited to the purpose.

The sun is high in the sky when Benny lays down his rake and wipes his forehead with the back of his hand. Already the garden is beginning to take shape — he can almost hear the ripples of the pebbles in the stream. It's hard work and will take most of the summer to complete, but he has a lightness in his heart that has not been there for a very long time. The act of beginning this work has released something within him and for that he is grateful.

He has just bent down to pick up his rake when he hears the approach of a car, slowing down as it nears the entrance to the chapel. A door opens and shuts and the car's engine revs up, continuing down the road to the mountain. There is little traffic out here, especially at this time of day, and Benny looks up to see a small, familiar figure coming towards him with an irregular, lop-sided gait. For just a moment he hesitates and then, laying his rake down on the ground, he dusts his hands on his jeans, wipes his forehead once more and walks out to the road to welcome his friend.

Margie Taylor is a former Canadian Broadcasting Corporation-Calgary radio personality, having hosted *Wild Rose Country* and *Morning Stretch*, among other shows. She left the CBC several years ago to devote herself to family and writing. This is her first novel, set in a part of Canada the author knows well, the Thunder Bay area at the head of Lake Superior.